I0637040

MAGNESIUM AND ICE

TYRANTS OF MARS, BOOK ONE

ALEX P. BERG

Magnesium and Ice, Tyrants of Mars #1
Copyright © 2022 by Alex P. Berg
All rights reserved. Published by Batdog Press.

No part of this work may be reproduced or transmitted, in any form or by any
means, except by an authorized retailer or with written permission from the
author. For permission requests, please visit: www.alexpberg.com

This is a work of fiction. Names, characters, places, and incidents portrayed in this
novel are a product of the author's imagination.

Cover Art by: Elias Stern (www.artstation.com/elias_stern)

If you'd like to be notified when the next Tyrants of Mars novel is released, please
sign up for the author's mailing list at: www.alexpberg.com/mailing-list/.

1

MAY 9, 2154

EVERYONE ALIVE REMEMBERS the moment they heard Los Angeles had been nuked. I'd just walked through the front doors of Western Michigan's Bernhard Center, on my way to my nine o'clock signal processing lab, when I spotted a throng of students crowded around the newsfeeds outside DiMaggio's Pizzeria.

Even before I caught a glimpse of the displays, I knew something was wrong. Everyone stood with slack faces, their mouths open. Some spoke in whispers, way too quiet considering there were at least thirty students clustered there. A girl in the back cried on the shoulder of her girlfriend, who herself looked pale and frozen.

I was tall enough to gaze over the crowd, but it took me a moment to process what I was seeing. An anchorwoman inset in the corner of the display talked animatedly while klaxons sounded. Multiple tickers whizzed across the bottom of the screen, but the majority of the display was dominated by dark chaos. Freeways packed to the gills with rideshares, most of them moving at a crawl as people fled between the cars on foot. Emergency vehicles with flashing red lights swam upstream against the panicked masses on the shoulders. A journalist on the scene vomited words into a microphone. An electric whir sounded. People screamed, including the reporter, but it was only a fleet of aircabs, whizzing away along the same path as everyone else.

The live feed cut to a video. Darkness filled the screen, broken only by the distant glow of skyscrapers and the snaking brake lights of commuting vehicles. A clock in the corner read 5:47 PST. Then the screen flashed white. As the glare faded, I saw it in the sky. A mushroom cloud, like the ones I'd seen in history class from the Saharan water wars of the twentieth century.

The guy next to me stared, unblinking, muttering to himself as he did so. "I can't believe they did it. Those bastards..."

My hands ached from the bite of my fingernails cutting into my palms. I forced them to unclench. "Who dropped the bomb?"

The guy shot me a wounded glance. "The Reds, man. Who else?"

As if on cue, an all-caps bulletin streamed across the bottom of the display, reading: *MARTIAN SEPARATISTS TAKE CREDIT FOR EXPLOSION, THREATEN FURTHER VIOLENCE.*

At first I didn't get it. If the Martian separatists wanted to strike a blow at Earth, wouldn't they go for the superpowers first? China, or perhaps India? But as the tickers streamed and I read and watched, the reason dawned on me. Los Angeles, home of the first commercial space organization. The city that designed the first rocket to carry humans to Mars. The city that birthed a new planetary civilization.

And the separatists had nuked it. It was a symbolic gesture. The bloody slash of a knife at Earth's outstretched hand.

I'd never considered myself particularly patriotic. I got goosebumps every time I heard the national anthem, especially at one of my basketball games. I admired our greatest presidents, Washington, Lincoln, and Zheng, same as everyone else, but I'd never been the type to wear a gaudy t-shirt with an enormous bald eagle on the front or drape an American flag outside my dorm window after a World Cup win. Yet as I stood there, watching the carnage on the feeds, a hot bubbling cocktail of emotions rose from the pit of my stomach, overtaking the emptiness in my chest. Resentment. Anger. Rage, even. Maybe I wasn't that much of a patriot, but I'd be damned if I'd let a bunch of frostbitten dust farmers vaporize tens of millions of my fellow countrymen from orbit while I sat around and watched. And in that moment, awash in fire and fury, I made the most momentous decision of my entire life.

My lab forgotten, I marched back to my dorm room, dumped my books onto my desk, replaced them with clothes, and hailed a rideshare on my tablet. It met me outside Bernham Hall on Arcadia Loop and, after I hopped inside, whirred off toward the downtown Kalamazoo vactrain station. I checked my tablet for the nearest United Space Corporation recruitment office, which happened to be in Chicago, so I loaded a ticket on my tablet, and a short vactrain hop followed by another rideshare later, I found myself standing outside a seventy story building at the corner of South Lakeshore and Eighty Third, the letters 'USC' bulging from the facade in burnished gray metal.

After the time change, it was barely after nine o'clock, but apparently I wasn't the only one who'd suffered from sudden onset patriotism. The building's front doors were propped open. People streamed inside, most of them young like me, some with backpacks or shoulder bags, almost all with tight jaws, narrowed eyes, or clenched fists. I joined them as I pushed my way inside to a lobby in the middle of which stood a large man with an even larger voice. He bellowed the same thing over and over as he pointed. "Recruitment office, to your right! Recruitment office, to your right! Recruitment office, *to your right!*"

I followed the sea of humanity, which slowed as we approached the office doors. The guy behind me, a sour looking tom wearing a Chicago Bears baseball cap, wasn't happy about the slowdown. "Jesus Christ. What a cluster. Can't somebody move this shit along?"

The young brunette beside him shrugged. "Give 'em a break. It's not as if USC knew Mars would decide *today* was a great day to declare war."

Despite the guy's complaints, the line did move. Within five minutes, I'd managed to shuffle my way into the recruitment office, a basketball court-sized room filled with kiosks. A line wound serpentine toward the mouth of the workstations, while a much shorter line led straight to a set of ten manned desks in the back.

A middle-aged woman in a crisp navy USC uniform stood at the base of the shorter line. Like the guy outside, she seemed to have been chosen based on her voice's ability to carry. I caught her mid-spiel, but she soon started over from the beginning. "For those of you arriving, this is the United Space Corporation's recruitment office. If you're here to apply to join USC's peacekeeping forces, congratulations, you're in the right place. Otherwise, please exit in an orderly fashion though the door furthest on your left. You may have noticed we have two lines. Those of you with MindNets should be receiving requests from the local wifi. Please accept it and download the application form, then take the fast pass lane to the receptionists in back. Everyone else, please wait your turn in line for the next available kiosk.

"When you arrive at one, you'll be prompted to fill out the same form as the Net-equipped folks. Please answer all questions truthfully and honestly, otherwise you risk expulsion from USC's military as well as fines for all costs incurred during your contracted enlistment period. I'm legally required to encourage you to read all clauses, stipulations, and amendments to the USC naval enlistment contract, located at the end of your application, but due to high volume of applicants today, I also *highly* encourage you to be respectful of your fellow enlistees and to make your decision quickly. The final version can and will be messaged to you later in full disclosure."

I'd never had a MindNet implanted—my parents were solidly middle class—so I got in line for the kiosks and got busy waiting. The Bears fan behind me passed the time coming up with new and creative ways to curse the poor USC saps working the recruitment office for their sloth and incompetence. Normally, I would've played games on my tablet until it was my turn at a kiosk, but the newsfeeds at the sides of the room kept playing coverage from the blast site.

In the full light of day, the destruction transcended words. Where once a thriving metropolis stood, there was nothing but a smoking crater. The reporters onscreen claimed a blast radius in the range of thirty-five kilometers, but the long-range views of the city center weren't even the worst part. The faces of the newly-minted refugees fleeing from what remained of the city were. How many more would die from radiation poisoning before they could get treatment? How many would develop aggressive cancers that killed before they could be properly diagnosed? Christ, how many *kids* would?

Eventually, I reached the front of the queue. A USC employee instructed me to go to station twenty-nine and wait for the person in front of me to finish. That took another five minutes, at which point I was finally able to sit in front of a workstation and complete the application—or at least get it started.

The form opened with the obvious stuff. Name? Ambrose Drake. Gender? Male, cisgender. Height? One point nine eight meters. Weight? A hundred and seven kilos. Education? Some college. But the form kept asking for more and more information. It needed my medical history. It made me take a personality test that graded me on five attributes: openness to experience, conscientiousness, extraversion, agreeableness, and neuroticism. Then the form started asking me truly oddball questions. Can you swim?

Yes, although I didn't know what good that would do on Mars. Have you ever manually operated a rideshare, recreational, or commercial motor vehicle? I'd grown up on a decent plot of land to the south of Jackson, Michigan, so yeah, sure, I'd driven an ATV before. Have you fired a real, live ammunition firearm? It might as well have asked me if I'd grown up in the Confederated States of Siberia. No.

As I worked, a foot tapped impatiently behind me, and I heard the occasional irritated sigh. Thankfully, it wasn't the Bears fan waiting on my kiosk. Still, I knew I'd taken significantly longer than the person in front of me—and then I reached the fine print.

I blinked as a wall of legalese stared me in the face. I scrolled down a little, and the progress bar on the side of the display barely moved. "Holy crap..."

The person behind me had finally had enough. "Could you hurry it the hell up, man? Some of us want to join before the war's over."

Whatever. I scrolled to the bottom of the display as quickly as I could, affixed my digital signature, and hit submit. A thank you screen instructed me to head to the desks in front, so I grabbed my backpack and did just that.

At least I didn't have to wait. A young woman at an empty station waved me forward. "Name?"

"Ambrose Drake."

"One moment, please." She stared at her display, her fingers dancing over the keypad in front of her intermittently. The keys made a soft tap with each of her presses.

Tap.

Tap tap tap.

Tap tap.

"So... what's next?" I asked.

She lifted an eyebrow, only sparing me a fractional glance. "If you could give me a moment, sir..."

"Right."

Tap.

Tap tap.

Tap tap tap tap.

"Is there training that occurs before we ship out? Where do we complete it? California? Florida?"

This time all I got in response was a sharp glance.

Tap tap tap.

Tap.

I tried to wait patiently. Really, I did. But after having spent the last two hours standing in line with only the calamitous droning of the newsfeeds and my buddy the Bears fan's melodious cursing to keep me company, I was starting to get antsy.

"Can you at least tell me how long it'll take before we head off planet?"

That line of questioning finally garnered some attention. *"If."*

"If what?"

"If you're accepted into the corps," she said. "First you have to pass your medical examination. Then you can worry about everything else."

"If I'm accepted...?" I turned to look at the crowd waiting for the kiosks. Many of them were like me, tall, fit, probably genetically altered. But I was eighteen years old. The backup point guard for the Western Michigan University Broncos. I could complete a lane agility drill in ten seconds flat, grab a regulation height rim, and dunk on a pre-height adjusted era rim in my sleep. What the hell did she mean, *if?*

2

MAY 9, 2179

I GAZED out the tinted window of our rideshare, watching the bright white streetlights pass by with predictable frequency. Dusk's wan light had long since faded from the sky, its last pinkish-red vestiges hidden by the Elysian skyscrapers. I glanced up, seeing if I could catch a glimpse of the stars, but the glow of the streetlights playing off the Mylamene pressure layer three stories up made viewing them impossible.

The reflected light of the holodisplay dancing off the interior of the window didn't help matters, either. Forgetting the stars, I turned toward the middle of the rideshare and the squawking holo. It was set to one of the mainstream local newsfeeds, anchored by none other than the impeccably dressed, consummately professional socialite newswoman Gloria Carano. I caught her in the middle of the broadcast, a video inset mirroring her monologue.

"—which so far has led to a stalemate on trade. In apparent retaliation, sources tell us that USC administrators have raised the possibility of instituting a tariff on Martian magnesium exports, however, their official statement is that no such tariffs are currently under consideration. Nonetheless, even a threat of such action could be enough to sway the city council of Olympus, which so far has been the most resolute in their refusal to agree to the new trade policies. The mayors of Elysium, Utopia, Isidis, and Olympus are scheduled to meet again early next week to continue the talks.

"The mayors' hands may be tied, however, as demonstrations continue across all four of Mars's major cities in response to surging inflation rates and unemployment which many are blaming upon restrictive USC policies, most notably their monopolies on municipal services and space flight. Following marches in Elysium last week, demonstrations in Utopia today were estimated to have attracted upwards of five hundred thousand people. While most of the protestors remained peaceful throughout the day, pockets of violence were reported by the joint Utopian USC police force. Seven people have been hospitalized, but thankfully there are no reported casualties so far."

The video inset disappeared, and the holo centered on Gloria Carano. "Finally, we'd like to end our broadcast tonight with a moment of reflection. Twenty-five years ago today, Martian separatists, referred to by many as the so-called Red faction, detonated a nuclear device in the Earth city of Los Angeles. Tens of millions of lives were lost, not only in the immediate aftermath of the bomb itself, but in the near decade long war the attack spawned. Given the current political climate, we here at Mars One wanted to pay tribute, not only to the brave men and women on both sides who lost their lives in the conflict, but to the heroes who helped bring about the lasting peace that has held since. Let us never forget that peace, safety, and security are blessings that are not guaranteed. Only by the strength of our leaders and the compromise of all can we maintain them."

The holo wiped to a montage, that of first responders flooding into the wreckage of Los Angeles, USC rockets flaring and spewing plumes of steam as they blasted off into space, soldiers patrolling alongside hulking armored vehicles. The music was somber and slow, but it grew in intensity and shifted to a more melodic, hopeful tune. The imagery shifted, showing soldiers tossing supplies from the backs of trucks to outstretched eager arms, shaking hands and smiling. A young girl came up to a soldier in full combat attire and offered him a sprig of holly. In the background, the sun rose over the Martian expanse, the color strengthening from pink to butterscotch. People hugged over gravestones, some with heads down, others with tears in their eyes, as again the music took on a more subdued tone.

The holo blinked out of existence, the sound disappearing into the void alongside it. I looked past it at my partner Mwenge, the images still fresh in my mind, superimposed over his rich chocolate skin and crisp uniform.

"Why'd you turn it off?" I asked.

"It's depressing, that's why. Civil unrest. Trade wars. The black stain of nuclear war. I'm going to need mood enhancers after listening to all of that. Besides, we're nearing the hotel."

"Are we?" I consulted my Net and saw we had less than three blocks to go. "I guess you're right."

Bishop glanced at me, faint lines creasing his brow. "Are you doing alright, Drake?"

"It's nothing. It's just the, ah…" I waved toward the space emptied by the holo. "You know. Seeing all that. It takes me back."

"Not in a good way, I imagine."

"Not really, no." I glanced out the window at the polished silver-gray surfaces of the buildings at the street side. "How old were you when the bomb went off, Bishop?" Normally, I called my partner by his last name, but he was lax about formalities when it was just the two of us.

Bishop crossed his long, lean legs, his build a byproduct of his Martian upbringing. "I was six. I still remember when it happened, too. Watching it on the newsfeeds. Honestly, it's one of the first memories I can stick my finger on. Funny how certain things burn their way into your mind forever."

"Traumatic events, especially."

Bishop nodded. "You know, Ambrose, I know you don't particularly like to revisit that portion of your life, but if you ever want to talk about it... Well, I'm a good listener."

"That's always how it goes, isn't it? The younger generations listen while the older ones talk."

"I don't mind. Not in this case, at least. Now, listening to you ramble on about your Masters level swimming accomplishments, on the other hand..." Bishop smiled, flashing his pearly whites.

I chuckled despite myself. "I appreciate the offer. It's just... hard to believe it's been twenty-five years, that's all."

My partner nodded as the rideshare came to a stop outside the Légendaire, which wasn't quite as ostentatious as its name suggested. It was a nice hotel to be sure, perhaps one of Elysium's twenty finest, but not within the top ten, which was fine by me. I'd never craved luxury, and given the Légendaire provided a substantial discount to the department for hosting its galas and graduations there, I'm sure the police bookkeepers were perfectly happy with the level of opulence as well.

I exited the rideshare and headed in, Mwenge at my side. If not for the high ceilings, the mass of officers, spouses, and family members milling about the lobby would've made it feel cramped. I spotted a few familiar faces, as well as a healthy number of starry-eyed new ones, the latter of whom stared at the chandeliers overhead, shifting their weight between the balls of their feet, unsure where to put their hands or how strict to keep their posture.

I waved to a couple people, but I didn't join the throng, instead heading for the ballroom in back.

"Did I look that young when I joined the force?" asked Bishop.

I snorted. "Are you kidding? You still look that young."

"Yeah, well, for you the war might feel like it was a million years ago. For me, it's this. I'm starting to feel like the old man on the block."

"Don't even start with me. So help me god, I'll pull rank on you if I have to. *You're* feeling old. Give me a break."

"Sorry. Wasn't trying to be insensitive." There was a twinkle in Mwenge's eye that said otherwise.

The ballroom was mostly empty when we arrived, though a few eager beavers had started to claim their seats. I headed for a door in the back, but a hand arose from a group of talkers and waved me over. It was a hand I couldn't ignore.

"Detectives Drake. Mwenge. Come join us."

"Police Chief De Loof," I said. "Good to see you, sir."

"You, too, detectives." The Chief, in his late fifties with sharp eyes, an arrow straight nose, and a crop of steel-gray hair that he seemed to be quite proud of, shook our hands. "You know Detectives Nassar and Cho, of course?"

Nubia Nassar and Harold Cho, the department's head detectives in charge of major crimes, nodded and extended their hands in turn.

"Oh, I'm familiar with these two," I said jokingly as I shook their hands. "More familiar than perhaps I should be."

"What Detective Drake is trying to say is he's gotten in trouble with us before," said Nassar. "Good thing for him, his crimes were minor, not *major,* so we let them slide."

"Yeah," said Cho. "Mostly fashion crimes and faux pas, to be honest."

"Don't forget word crimes," I said. "I excel at those, too."

"Yeah... I wouldn't say you *excel,*" said Mwenge.

My partner bobbed to the side as I threw a fake punch at his shoulder, all while the others chuckled at my defeat.

"Well, I hope you're better with words than their associated crimes," said the Chief. "Tonight's graduates are expecting something motivational, something uplifting. You won't disappoint them, I hope."

"I'm not sure why you asked me to give the recruits the graduation speech, sir, but rest assured, I've been working on it for several days. It's as rousing as it's going to get."

The Chief snorted. *"You don't know why I asked you?* Don't be so modest, Drake. Even if your personal experiences weren't inspirational enough, your track record in homicide speaks for itself. Hell, Nassar told me some of the new detective recruits wanted to meet you. They're assembling in back for the ceremony."

"If they want to meet me, someone fed them a line," I said, glancing meaningfully at Bishop.

My partner shrugged. "Wasn't me. You know I wouldn't publicly praise you."

Nubia clapped me on the shoulder. "Come on. We have time before the proceedings. I'll introduce you. Some of them will be joining your department."

She headed toward the door I'd initially made a bee line for. I followed her, along with Cho, Mwenge, and the Chief. As we entered the wide service hallway in back, a group of young men and women chatted in their pressed uniforms. Some of them looked uncomfortable. Hell, it was probably the first time they'd been allowed to wear full regalia.

One of them saw us approaching, and the word spread like a vacuum leak. They lined up against the wall, stood straighter, and saluted.

"At ease, recruits," said the Chief as he walked before them. "We'll try to save the formalities for later. I'm just here to introduce tonight's speaker. Perhaps some of you have heard of him. Senior homicide detective Ambrose Drake."

The young detectives-to-be all saluted and stiffened again. I waved them down. "You can dispense with that. The Chief already told you to be at ease. I'm just here to congratulate you. Not everyone makes it through basic training, and only the best get recommended for detective duty. You should all be proud of yourselves."

Several of the recruits responded with thanks, some forcefully and others at mumble level. One of them, a young woman with dark hair and light brown eyes raised a hand.

"Yes?"

"Sir, if I may ask. You're really *the* Ambrose Drake?"

"Oh, god. Don't tell me Sergeant Maldonado at the training center has been filling your minds with legends and lies? What did she tell you? That I shot the ice off a moth's wings at five hundred meters with a sidearm? That I tracked down a band of murderers using nothing but a shoe print and a chewing gum wrapper?"

"Ah... no, sir. Just told us about your history, is all. Veteran of the Red uprising. Survivor of the Cassini Basin siege. Were you really a POW for six years?"

"More like five and three-quarters. What's your name, young lady?"

"Keller, sir."

"And what division are you going into?"

"Cyber crimes."

I smiled. "A detective after my own heart. Anyone else joining her?"

A few hands.

"Major crimes?"

A few more hands.

"Burglary?"

None.

I lifted an eyebrow. "*Arson?*"

One young man lifted a hand.

"You poor bastard," I said. "Whose coffee did you pee in?"

The young man flushed, but the others chuckled. "Ah, no sir," he said. "I'm actually quite fond of arson. I'm excited about it. It'll be a great stepping stone, I'm sure."

Another young man came running down the hall. He sidled

next to the arson recruit, breathing hard as he came to attention. "Sorry, sir. I ran into unexpected traffic."

"No need for apologies," I said. "You're not late. This is all informal. Now, lastly, but I would argue most importantly, how many of you are joining me in homicide?"

Three hands went up, including that of the newest arrival. I gave the young man a nod. "Your name?"

"Watters, sir. I've heard all about you. Trying my best to follow in your footsteps."

"Welcome aboard, Watters. Unofficially, of course. You're technically not detectives until you cross the stage and shake the Chief's hand. So try not to be late to that portion of the festivities."

"I'll let it slide," said the Chief. "They assign you odd hours in training—which is good, because we work odd hours ourselves. At least you all have a week off to adjust to a more normal schedule before your official start dates. It might be the last vacation you have for a while, so I wouldn't waste it."

I heard a ringing in my head. Normally I would've ignored it given the company, but the call identification listed none other than Captain Cecilia Reyes. I held up a finger toward the boss. "Excuse me, Chief. Net call."

Mwenge approached, indicating he was getting it too. We answered simultaneously, using the silent MindNet chat feature so the recruits wouldn't overhear. "Captain. What's going on? You on your way to the gala?"

I heard Reyes' voice in the middle of my brain. "Unfortunately not, Detective Drake. As a matter of fact, I'm at a crime scene. I need you and Mwenge here on the double—and don't say a word to anybody. This is strictly need to know."

"Pardon me, Captain," said Mwenge, "but we're with the Chief. He'll want to know what's going on, not to mention Drake has his speech tonight."

Reyes swore. "Damn. I'd forgotten about that. Not that it

matters. What I have takes precedence. Tell the Chief I've summoned you. He'll understand. I'll send you the address."

I gave Mwenge a look as Reyes signed off, and he returned it full bore. Reyes wouldn't pull us away from the gala unless something serious were afoot.

"Chief," I said, interrupting a speech he was giving the recruits. "That was the Captain. She needs me and Mwenge right away."

"Now?"

"Yes, sir."

The chief sighed. "Very well. The perils of the job. Detective Nassar? I hope you're up for giving a replacement speech."

The major crimes detective balked. "What? *Me?*"

"Drake can send you his script. What do you say?"

"I'd say his script won't help me a lot if he included extensive passages about his time as a young man in the military."

"It's the best we can do," said the Chief. "Drake?"

"Sending it now, sir." I shot the file off.

Nubia nodded glumly. "Thanks."

The Chief clapped me on the shoulder. "Well, get on with it, Detective. Captain Reyes doesn't like being kept waiting."

3

MAY 9, 2154

I SAT in a stiff chair in the lobby of a doctor's office. My stomach growled. As I glanced at the backpack tucked between my legs, I wished not for the first time that I'd packed food instead of merely clothes. I'd bought a granola bar and a bag of soy crisps from a vending machine, but they'd only dented my hunger. Silly me for assuming USC would take care of me as soon as I'd enlisted, but as the glare-prone young woman who'd made sure my application had been thoroughly tapped told me, I wasn't *officially* part of the USC marine corps yet.

The good news was USC had consolidated operations. When the receptionist told me I'd need to go to medical processing next, I'd assumed I'd be stuck trying to hail a rideshare alongside however many hundreds of other enlistees, but instead she directed me to take the elevator to the forty-third floor. So it was I found myself awaiting a physical.

At least I seemed to have passed the first test, a conclusion I based on the unique group of would-be marines in the office around me. For once in my life, I felt decidedly *average*. I couldn't be sure because everyone was sitting down, but I judged that all of the men in the room were right at two meters tall, give or take a twentieth, and the women were all at least a meter eighty—and not the frail, lanky sort, either. Muscles bulged from underneath shirts, or through leggings for many of the girls.

I wasn't intimidated. I'd been driving into the paint against two and a half meter tall behemoths since I was fourteen. I was used to navigating giants. What I wasn't used to was being around people who were so *uniformly* tall. So uniformly modified.

A guy sat in the chair next to me, an inch shorter than me but ten kilos heavier. A tuft of scraggly hair sprouted from his chin, which I imagine he thought provided his youthful face a more sophisticated, mature look. It didn't.

"Where you from?" I asked him.

He ripped his eyes from the newsfeeds at the far side of the room. "What's that?"

"I said where are you from?"

"Milwaukee. You?"

"Jackson, Michigan. I'm in Kalamazoo, now."

He nodded. "Nice."

His look told me he didn't know the first thing about either Jackson or Kalamazoo. Not that I could blame him. My knowledge of Milwaukee didn't extend much past the statistical achievements of Bucks legends Oscar Robertson and Giannis Antetokounmpo.

I extended a hand. "I'm Ambrose."

"Desmond." We shook. "What brings you here?"

I assumed he meant my personal reasons for wanting to enlist, because given that he'd been staring at the newsfeeds of Los Angeles, the alternative meant he was dumber than a sack of rocks. "I can't honestly say. I sure as hell didn't expect to be here when I woke up this morning. I guess I don't like being pushed around. My dad always taught me to be tough. Give 'em an inch, they'll take a mile, he's always said. Which is a stupid saying, but I hate English units."

"Right, right." Desmond nodded.

"You?"

"Just can't wait to kill some fucking Reds." Desmond smiled, a toothy, awkward grin that set me on edge.

"Drake?"

I turned at the sound. A doctor in a white coat stood at the door in back.

"That's me," I said. "Best of luck."

I stood and headed to the doctor.

He glanced at me. "Ambrose Drake."

I wasn't sure if it was a question, but I answered in the affirmative anyway.

"Great. Come with me. We'll get you checked out."

I followed the man to a small exam room, one with a few cabinets, a single chair, and an exam table. A white plastic shell a little bigger than a helmet was attached to a flexible arm at the head of the table.

"Have a seat, Mr. Drake," said the doctor, waving at the exam table. "I'm Dr. Eroğlu."

"Nice to meet you." The sanitary paper over the table crinkled as I sat.

Dr. Eroğlu reached into a drawer and removed a few electrodes. "I'd like to talk to you about your medical history. While I do that, I'll be measuring your vitals. Is that all right?"

I had similar vital measurements every day after practice. "Sure."

Dr. Eroğlu pasted the freestanding electrodes to my right temple, my chest, and upon the interior of my right elbow pit. "You had prenatal gene editing, correct?"

I nodded. "That's right. Before birth, my parents had my genome processed for chromosomal disorders, autoimmune diseases, cancer predispositions. All the stuff that's covered by insurance."

"Sure, sure." The doctor nodded and settled into a chair opposite me. "But your parents also paid for enhancements, isn't that right?"

"Yes. My dad's a big basketball fan. He always hoped I'd be able to play ball at the college level, which is kind of impossible now without gene editing, so him and my mom scrimped and saved to pay for a number of optional modifications."

I felt a pang of remorse as I told the doctor that. What would my dad think once he found out I'd bailed on my full-ride scholarship to Western Michigan, quit on my degree in Computer Sciences and Electrical Engineering, all so I could join USC's space corps? On some level, I imagined he'd be proud, but on another? Either way, I needed to call my parents. I needed to tell them.

"What modifications did your parents pay for, do you remember?"

I ticked them off on my fingers. "Height. Muscle tone. Fast-twitch fiber density. Bone density. Oh, and intellect. All boosted the twenty-five percent allowable by law, except for height. Point guards don't need to be quite that tall."

The doctor smiled. "Of course."

The way he said it made me think he suspected my parents had travelled to Ecuador to have stronger procedures done illegally.

"But," continued Dr. Eroğlu, "you have no MindNet, correct?"

I shook my head. "No, sir."

The doctor blinked and glanced at my electrodes. "Shame, that. Still, you have excellent vitals. I'm sifting through them now. And everything you've told me about your medical history matches public records. Given all that, I'd say you're an excellent candidate for admission into the USC marine corps. Congratulations, soldier."

I blinked. "Really? Is that it?"

"Almost." The doctor pulled a tablet from his coat and activated it. "Press your thumb here at the bottom to accept and you'll be ready to go."

I hesitated for a fraction of a second as I remembered the interminable stretch of legalese at the bottom of my application form, but god damnit, I was here to join the fight against the Reds, and USC was the only viable way to do that. I reached out and pressed my thumb against the glass.

"Excellent." The doctor pulled the tablet back and returned it to his pocket. "Now, do you have any dental implants I should know about?"

"Nope. My teeth are healthy as can be. Why?"

"Sometimes those can wreck havoc on the mini-fMRI echoes. Now, if you could, please lay down and let me adjust the scanner. It won't take more than a couple minutes. Once it's done, assuming everything checks out, I'll implant your new MindNet."

I blinked. "What? *Now?*"

"No time like the present, Mr. Drake. You can't officially join USC's forces until you receive your Net implant. All in the contract, you understand."

Of course it was. I lay down and Dr. Eroğlu moved the white shell over my head. As he did so, I noticed something attached to the folded robotic arm. Was it a *drill?*

Dr. Eroğlu sensed my hesitation. "There's nothing to worry about, Mr. Drake. You'll be sedated during the procedure. You won't feel a thing. You're familiar with how the Net works, correct?"

"Uh... yeah. But in an academic sense, not a personal one."

"Of course. I'll attach a few more electrodes while I explain the procedure to you, yes?" The doctor started attaching pads to my left side, same as he had to my right. "As I'm sure you're aware, the procedure to install a Net is rather simple. We'll start by using the mini-fMRI to generate a detailed map of your intracranial cavity. Once I've had a chance to run it through some analytics, I'll secure your head and neck and sedate you. While you're under, I'll drill a small hole into your skull—just a millimeter in diameter—after which I'll inject the Net mesh into the cerebrospinal fluid of your subarachnoid space. This is the area immediately over your cerebral cortex. There, over the next twenty-four hours, the Net's mesh will unfold and expand, eventually to the point where it will cover all of your cerebral cortex and even some of your cerebellum. At the same time, the mesh will shrink, giving your brain a gentle hug. As that hug occurs, the Net will begin to record your neural activity, allowing it to sync with your brain, if you will. That process should be complete within forty-eight hours. I'll equip you with an external wireless monitoring device to assist with the transition. After that? There will be a learning curve as your body adapts to the Net's capabilities and as you learn how to interact with the system, but seeing as you're majoring in computer engineering, I imagine you won't have any issues. With that said, do you have any questions?"

I felt like a wimp for asking, but I couldn't help myself. "Is it... going to hurt?"

The doctor smiled. "The procedure? Not at all. You'll be fully anesthetized. As far as post-operative recovery, you might experience a *small* amount of discomfort, but in general, the greatest difference you'll notice is the sense of newness and discovery resulting from the Net's integration into your mind. Now lay back, relax, and stay still. It's time to start the scan."

4

MAY 9, 2179

MWENGE and I stepped from our rideshare. The multipurpose hotel and residential building Captain Reyes had directed us to loomed over us, its sixty-plus stories shrouded as much by darkness as by the Mylamene. When I'd first arrived on Mars twenty-five years ago, I'd been surprised by the omnipresence of skyscrapers. After all, Mars had an abundance of buildable land, if nothing else. Building up didn't seem as cost efficient as building out, but I'd been oblivious to the particular challenges Mars provided that tipped the scales toward denser populations. For one, Martian code mandated each building be a self-contained pressure vessel, with multiple safety barriers at the exterior, hall, and room level, which increased costs dramatically and made it more efficient to build fewer larger buildings than many smaller ones. Given that Martian gravity was a third of Earth's and that the planet wasn't seismically active, structural requirements for tall buildings were a fraction of what they were back home. Besides, increasing urban density also minimized the Mylamene needed to cover streets between buildings and meant fewer kilometers of pipes, electrical conduits, and sewers that needed to be insulated underground.

You could say a lot of negative things about USC, but their

economic sense was unimpeachable. 'Minimize Costs' would've been a more apt company slogan than 'Reach for the Stars.'

Mwenge and I walked inside the building, heading past the check-in desk to the elevators in back. I punched the button and waited.

Mwenge looked toward the lobby. "Nice place."

I followed his gaze, taking note of the faux leather couches, expensive rugs, and polished wooden tables in the lobby. They might've been a polymer composite, but at the very least they *looked* like the real thing. "Not as nice as the Légendaire, but yeah."

The elevator dinged, and we stepped inside. The door closed and I punched the button for the fifty-fourth floor.

"Any guesses on what we'll find up there?" asked Mwenge.

"We're homicide cops, Bishop. I think it's pretty obvious what we'll find."

"I'm just saying," said Mwenge. "When you get summoned to a dump, you always know what to expect, but a nice joint like this? Weird shit happens in nice apartments."

The chime sounded, the doors opened, and we headed into the hallway. The address Reyes had given us led to the far end of the corridor, apartment 5435. There was a keypad with a thumb reader at the side of the door, but I pressed the ringer next to the eye-level display instead.

"Are we sure this is the right place?" said Mwenge after a moment.

"You got the missive, same as me."

"Yeah, but where are the beat cops? The caution tape? Shouldn't there be someone stationed *outside* the door by now?"

"Not if Reyes wanted to keep a lid on whatever happened."

The door opened with a puff as the positive pressure from inside the condo equalized with the hall, another standard safety measure. A uniformed officer stood inside. He nodded to us when he saw us.

"Detectives Drake and Mwenge. I'm officer Jamison. Captain Reyes is waiting for you."

He stood to the side to allow for our passage. I walked past him into the living room of a lavish apartment, one furnished with a quartet of matching upholstered sofa chairs, a pair of bookshelves that I would've bet really *were* made of wood, and a display that covered an entire wall from floor to ceiling. An equally expansive window took the place of the far wall. Nearer to us, a woman in dark blue pants and a lighter blue dress shirt sat on one of the couches. Her hand shook as she sucked on the mouthpiece of her pocket vaper and blew out a stream of white mist from between puckered lips. Her face barely had more color in it than the vapor.

Captain Reyes stood near her, flicking her hand to disperse the aerosolized stimulant. At a meter seventy, she was extremely short for a Martian, but she made up for her stature with a fierce gaze, an iron will, and a wit that could sever a steel tow cable. She wore her ceremonial uniform, same as us, as if she'd stopped en route to the gala.

Our shoes clacked against the polished stone floor. Reyes turned, surveying us with dark, smoky eyes. She nodded and met us past the quartet of couches, where the woman with the pipe could still hear but where we could at least pretend to have a modicum of privacy.

"Drake. Mwenge," she said. "Nice of you to finally make it."

"Blame the rideshare traffic algorithms, not us," I said. "Besides, its only been twenty-two minutes since you called."

"Feels longer than that," said Reyes. "Then again, I've probably soaked up some of that paramedic's pipe effluent by standing near her. I hate that stuff. Gives me the jitters."

"I'm surprised you're letting her vape at all," said Mwenge. "Isn't this a crime scene?"

"That's the only reason I'm letting her do it," said Reyes. "If you'd seen her when I arrived, you'd understand. Hell, you'll understand yourself in a few minutes."

The living room fed into both the kitchen and what appeared to be an office, but down the hall to my right, I noticed a closed door where I expected the bedroom to be. Despite my years on the job, a chill ran through me. "Give us the rundown."

"According to the paramedic, the victim's Net stopped transmitting at about seven," said Reyes. "Brahe Memorial Hospital sent her over to check if it was a glitch or something more serious. No one responded when she arrived, so she called us for support. Officer Jamison who you met at the door was assigned to the case. They sent the data to central and received authorization to enter the premises at approximately seven forty-five. Upon entering, the paramedic made her way to the bedroom where she found the victim."

"Does this victim have a name?" I asked.

"She does," said Reyes. "Shao Wen. I pulled her public records. Forty-seven years of age. An Earth immigrant, originally born in Shenzhen, China. She also happened to be the Chief Administrative Officer of USC's Water Services division."

I whistled. "So that's why you wanted to keep things under wraps?"

"It's part of the reason."

"Did the paramedic recognize the victim?" asked Mwenge. "Is that why she's spooked?"

"Unfortunately not," said Reyes. "There's more to it than that. You should gird yourselves."

I knew what that meant. I swallowed back a lump in my throat. "Alright. Let's see it."

Reyes led the way down the hall. She stopped at the closed door and held out a couple pairs of latex gloves. "After you."

"How kind," I said, though I knew she'd already seen it. I took the gloves and slipped them on before touching the handle.

The door swung inward at my touch. Unlike the living room, the bedroom was carpeted, covered with a thick beige-grey fiber that gave under the weight of my feet.

Little of it was beige-gray anymore. A dark stain spread across the floor. Dark splatters speckled the carpet all the way to the wall. A more distinct deep red trail led to a bed on the far side of the room. My eyes followed the trail, up to the mattress and sheets atop the bed.

The victim lay there, her black flats still on her feet. She was clothed, wearing a crisp pantsuit, navy blue in color where the blood hadn't darkened it. Those spots were few and far between, though. I counted three dark blotches on her legs, all with matching incisions in the cloth. Two in her abdomen. Four on her arms. I wasn't sure about her chest, because the blood there was omnipresent. It soaked everything, to the point where I couldn't identify what color the blouse underneath her jacket had originally been.

I trailed my eyes to the jagged gash across the woman's throat, deep and devilish. A silent, morbid grin. It was only then I took note of the woman's features.

My heart skipped a beat, and I felt the blood drain from my face. I stared at the woman's pale visage as visions of decades past flashed before me.

5

MAY 10, 2154

THE DOCTOR LIED about the Net. *Mild discomfort* would've been the equivalent of a head cold or eye strain from looking at a display for too many hours. What I suffered from could more accurately be described as a severe migraine crossed with a mild concussion. Noises felt amplified by twenty decibels. Moving made me want to vomit. Hell, opening my eyes made me want to vomit, so I kept them closed. Not that it did much good.

Even with my lids clamped firmly shut, images and videos flashed across my vision. Footage of the carnage from Los Angeles, drone shots from high above the blast zone intermixed with clips of reporters, some interviewing victims, other speaking with government officials, others talking simply to hear their own voices or to fill airtime with something other than the constant wail of sirens. Sometimes I heard the associated audio, sometimes not, but when I did, it threw me off guard. The sound wasn't directional. It didn't originate from a point source, but rather seemed to reverberate from inside my own head.

At first I'd thought the images were memories, but though the scenes of destruction seemed familiar, the voices of the anchors were more measured, the faces of the refugees more resigned. A reporter mentioned the devastation in the past tense. *Yesterday's blast. Yesterday's attack.* They were newsfeeds, live ones, and I couldn't control them.

Which wasn't to say they all were. Memories flashed across my vision, too. My father playing ball with me on our driveway, blocking every shot I put up, telling me the trees in the paint wouldn't go any easier on me. Millie Martinez's coy face as she pecked me on the cheek after our first date in middle school. The sky, a neon green in color as a tornado passed within five miles of our home in Jackson. Less distinct memories, too. Fuzzy ones. Stumbling to my feet to use the bathroom. Getting dressed. Catching a rideshare to...somewhere. I couldn't remember. But it wasn't just images that danced like whirling ballerinas before me. Smells and sounds nipped at me, too. The sterile, alcoholic scent of Dr. Eroğlu's antiseptic. The rich, yeasty scent of my mother's homemade sourdough. The random blaring of a shot clock. Who knows if I'd hit the shot in time—the rest of the memory didn't accompany the sound.

I filled my lungs with air, trying to slow my breathing. It seemed to help with the nausea, and it settled the prevalence of the memories. It didn't stop the newsfeeds, though. The images of the flattened center of Los Angeles switched to stock videos of Mars, the barren rust red plains, the uniform butterscotch sky, the cities with their tall skyscrapers webbed at the base with enclosed roads and walkways. Then a new video replaced those, one of an individual dressed in a white pressure suit with a blood red visor that hid his face. He pointed his finger at me—or perhaps her finger, the voice had been distorted into a low-pitched, gravelly rasp—and spoke. I only caught bits and pieces. Something about death and revenge, pain and victory. But I did catch one final ungarbled stretch as the video ended: *You tested the snow leopard's bite. And now you bleed.*

"Hey... are you doing okay?"

The newest voice hadn't come from within my own head. Carefully, I cracked open my eyes, moving slowly for fear of losing whatever I had in my stomach.

I sat on a padded seat in what looked to be a vactrain. Next to me sat a young woman in a form-fitting blue USC uniform. Her long black hair had been pulled into a ponytail that hung lazily over her shoulder, and she stared at me with large, bright amber eyes that had a distinct almond shape to them.

I worked some saliva onto my tongue. I felt like I'd been eating cotton balls. "Um... yeah. I'm okay. I'm not feeling that great—"

"—because you've just had a Net implant. Yeah, I can tell." She gestured to my arm.

I looked down. Like the young lady, I wore a navy blue short-sleeved USC uniform made of compression fabric—Lycrene, or something similar. On my bare arm I spotted a couple of the electrodes Dr. Eroğlu had attached to me, and I wore a smartwatch on my wrist.

"When did you get your Net surgery?" she asked.

Video clips and images still flashed before my vision. I tried to ignore them. "Is today the tenth?"

"That's right."

"Then yesterday afternoon."

She blinked, her pink lips parting in shock. "*Christ alive.* And they let you on a vactrain already?"

I glanced up the train's cabin, past the rows filled with USC recruits in similar uniforms, not entirely sure how I'd gotten to my seat. "It would appear so." I felt a pull as the train bent around a curve, and I had to clamp my jaw in a feeble, psychosomatic attempt at keeping my breakfast in place.

The young woman noticed my discomfort. "Did you at least take any metaprochlorperazine?"

I swallowed back the lump in my throat. "Any meta-pro-what?"

"Metaprochlorperazine. It treats nausea as well as migraines. It's basically prochlorperazine that's been specifically engineering for post-Net surgery recovery. In fact..."

Before I knew what was going on, she'd dipped her hand into a small pocket on the front of my uniform. Her hand brushed my chest. When she pulled it back, she held a pill bottle.

"Well, at least your doctors weren't *completely* negligent." She opened the container. "Here. I've got a water bottle. Take two of these."

I wasn't sure I'd be able to keep anything down, but my train mate seemed to know what she was talking about, and honestly how much worse could the nausea get? Moving slowly, I took the pills, popped them in my mouth, and washed them down with the proffered water.

"Thanks. Now if you don't mind..." I stopped in mid-sentence as a wave of cool relief washed over me. The pressure inside my skull vanished, and instead of nauseated, I suddenly felt hungry. *Very* hungry.

"Holy crap," I said. "That's amazing. It's like night and day. Thank you."

"No problem. I can't believe the doctors let you out of their offices without taking some. Although maybe they did." She glanced at the pill bottle. "Looks like you're supposed to take more every six hours. Who knows when your last dose was. I'm Phoebe Zhao by the way." She extended a hand.

I took it and shook. Her hand felt soft but her grip was firm. "Ambrose Drake. Nice to meet you."

"Sorry I didn't mention the metaprochlorperazine as soon as I took a seat," said Phoebe. "At first I thought you were napping."

"I was trying to. Or at least I think I was. I don't remember getting on the train."

Phoebe shook her head. "That's borderline criminal. I'm pretty sure the AMA recommendation is that you monitor a patient for seventy-two hours after Net injection. Not that it'll kill you. Lots of poke and shoot doctors in backwater countries push people out the door as soon as they've cemented the drill hole, but that doesn't make it right."

An advertisement for blue jeans flashed before me. I tried to blink it away. "I'm guessing you got your Net before the attack, then."

"Oh, yeah," said Phoebe. "Got mine injected when I was fourteen."

My eyebrows crept north. *"Fourteen?"*

"What? The legal age is twelve. The brain doesn't grow almost at all past ten. Net elasticity takes care of the rest."

"Oh. I didn't know that." I glanced out the vactrain's window, watching trees whip past at twelve hundred kilometers an hour through the clear plastic outer shell of the vactube. The commercial for blue jeans ended only to be replaced by one for Chartrelle, the only two-ply toilet paper brand made from one hundred percent new, non-recycled wood pulp. "Any idea where we are?"

"Just east of the Chattahoochee National Forest, about twenty miles west of Chattanooga."

I turned back to face her. "Are you from Tennessee? Or are you just particularly knowledgeable about nature preserves?"

"Neither." She tapped the side of her head.

"Right. The Net."

Phoebe stared at me for a few seconds as a smile grew upon her face. "You don't have the foggiest idea how to use it, do you?"

"No clue. In fact, I keep getting peppered with random memories and vids. If I'm looking at you funny, I swear it's not because I'm cross-eyed. It's because I'm trying to avoid having an ad for life insurance superimposed onto your face."

"Yeah, it's a little touch and go during those first twenty-four to forty-eight hours," said Phoebe. "Your phase initializer is to blame for some of that, but it's in the name of creating neuron-to-Net connections."

"My phase initializer?"

"The thing that looks like a watch? It's feeding your Net massive streams of information, seeing what spurs a reaction and what doesn't and recording the results. Then it feeds that back into the Net. It's an evolving neural net, you know. It has to learn before it can work properly."

I knew perfectly well what a neural net was, not to mention how they worked, but I didn't want to come across as a huge dick. Besides, knowing how they worked in theory and getting one to interface with your own brain was an entirely different story. "Right. But my question is... how do I access the OS? You know. Without being able to touch it and code it."

Phoebe shrugged. "That's one of those 'it happens when it happens' sorts of things."

"And until then, I'm stuck watching an infinite loop of iridium ETF ads and twenty-four hour news coverage?"

"Not necessarily," said Phoebe. "As silly as it sounds, the most common advice new Net recipients are given for making the Net brain integration go faster is to sit back, relax, and think of nothing. Apparently, the hardest part of the initialization period is sorting through the junk signals our brains are constantly generating. Once the neural net cuts through those, it can cycle through your phase initializer data much quicker."

"So you're telling me I should stop talking to you and go back to trying to nap?"

Phoebe smiled and chuckled. It was cute.

"What?"

"It's nothing. I just remembered a piece of advice a friend gave me when I got my Net. About how to clear your mind."

Phoebe didn't elaborate, even though I waited patiently. "Well.

Go on. If it helps me get these newsfeeds out of my eyeballs faster, I'm willing to give it a try."

Phoebe looked at me as if she wasn't sure she should tell me. "It's a little... *unorthodox*."

"Try me."

She glanced over her shoulder, then leaned in and lowered her voice. "Alright. Close your eyes, relax, and try to picture the moment right before you orgasm."

"*What?*"

"Seriously. It's the one time your mind is a hundred percent clear. For those few split seconds, your body is entirely consumed by physical reactions. By uniform pleasure. No mental activity at all."

I lifted an eyebrow. "This is the advice your friend gave you?"

She nodded.

"When you were *fourteen?*"

Phoebe cocked her head. "Oh, don't give me that. Like you didn't know what an orgasm was when you were fourteen."

"Right... And so, you're supposed to do that every time you want to bring up the OS?"

Phoebe recoiled. "What? *God no.* Just the first time, to ease the integration. Once you get it once, it'll be old hat. Like muscle memory for your brain. As easy as reaching out and grabbing it."

"And you're sure I should try this *now?*"

Phoebe rolled her eyes. "Christ, I'm not telling you to pretend to have an *actual* orgasm. It's about finding an equivalent mental state. I'm trying to give you some advice and you have to go and make it weird."

"What? *No.* That's not what I meant at all..." I shook my head. "Never mind. Sorry I mentioned it. Here goes nothing."

I leaned back in my chair, closed my eyes, and tried to put myself in the same *mental state* Phoebe had mentioned. It wasn't easy, partly because the newsfeeds of west coast destruction were back, but also because it had been a while since I'd had a steady girlfriend. My high school sweetheart had gone off to UM, and our relationship hadn't withstood more than two months of separation. While there were plenty of pretty girls at WMU, I hadn't had much time to spend with any of them, what with my first year CSEE classes and trying to prove to my coach that I was more than *backup* point guard material. So when I tried to picture myself with a girl, nearing that moment of ecstasy, my mind gave her the most readily available pretty face it could, one with long black hair and almond eyes and—

"Nope," I said, my eyes snapping open. "It's too weird right now. Maybe later. I appreciate the advice, though. Really, I do."

"Don't sweat it," said Phoebe. "To be honest, activating the OS the first time isn't something you can really control. The various pieces of advice you can get on how to speed up the process are probably BS."

Now she told me, after she'd shared her friend's suggestion. "So I'm assuming we're headed to Florida?"

Phoebe nodded. "That's right. USC's Titusville deployment center. It was either that or Brownsville, Texas, and that one's apparently getting the west coast overflow right now."

"I'll bet," I said as yet another clip from Los Angeles showed up in my vision. "You ever been to space before?"

"Once. My parents took me on a pleasure cruise around the moon. You?"

I shook my head. "Nope. Furthest I've ever been is suborbital flight on a commercial rocket from New York to Shanghai."

Phoebe gave me a glum look. "Speaking of parents, are yours taking your decision to enlist as *well* as mine are?"

"I, ah... don't know."

Phoebe blinked. "What do you mean, you don't know?"

I felt like a heel even mentioning it. "I... haven't told them yet."

Phoebe frowned, affixing me with a glare most people reserved for grifters or assholes who kick dogs. "You need to tell them."

"I know, trust me. It's just that I got caught up in everything yesterday, and before I knew it, I was getting the Net implant, and I barely remember anything from then until this conversation with you." I started patting my pockets. "If I can find my tablet, I'll do it now, hard as it might be."

"No point in looking," said Phoebe. "USC probably confiscated it while you were under. Sent it back to your permanent address along with any other personal effects you had on you when you underwent the procedure. At this point, your parents will get that stuff before they hear from you."

Crap. Now I felt like an even worse son. "I'll figure something out. I'm sure there's a terminal I can use at the Titusville facilities. Or if I can just figure out the Net—"

The in-between space of my mind dinged. The videos in my vision collapsed and fled to the edge of my vision. In the top right-hand corner of my sight I saw a text bubble. *Would you like to send mail?*

I snorted. "Now it works..."

Phoebe smiled, my terrible behavior for the moment forgiven. "Your Net initialized?"

"It's asking me if I want to send a message. I just don't know how to reply in the affirmative."

Phoebe gave me a wink. "Don't worry. You'll get there. Baby steps."

6

MAY 9, 2179

I FELT a strong hand grip my shoulder, followed by Mwenge's voice. "Drake. Are you okay? You look like you've seen a ghost."

I took a step toward the bed, blinking as I gazed at the victim. Dark hair framed her face, though blood matted it, plastering it to her skin. Her almond-shaped eyes stared, unshifting, at a fixed point behind me, the irises a familiar hazel in color. I glanced at her nose, but it was too long, a shade too broad. Her lips had a curl to them I couldn't place, and her eyebrows—

"Detective Drake?" said Reyes. "Are you sure you're alright? Do you know Ms. Wen?"

I forced air into my lungs, the tingling in my face and fingers lessening as the blood returned. I tore my eyes away from the body and faced the others. "No. I don't. I thought I did at first, but her face isn't quite right. It's surprisingly similar to someone I once knew, though. Someone I haven't seen in a *very* long time."

Mwenge's latex glove snapped as he pulled it over his hand. "I can perform the initial inspection if you'd like. There's no shame in sitting one out every now and then."

"No. I'm fine," I said. "It was just the initial shock. Threw me into a bit of a flashback. Captain, have you called CSU?"

She stood by the door, her arms crossed and her gaze hard. "Not yet. I'm trying to keep this as quiet as I can until I have a handle on what happened. I did contact Coroner Pham, though. She should be here any minute."

"You notice anything we should know about?" said Mwenge as he stepped to the side of the bed.

"Yeah. She's dead. Come on, Detective. I want to know what *you* think. We'll exchange notes when you're done."

"Fair enough." Mwenge picked up the woman's arm and rotated it slightly toward him. "Off the bat, I'm counting two stab wounds on her right arm, two on her left, one on her right leg, two on her left, two in the abdomen, and I'd say another two in her chest. All of them appear to be the same size, three to five centimeters in length. If I had to hazard a guess, I'd say the weapon was a chef's knife or something similar. And those wounds are in addition to the gash across her throat, of course."

"Which isn't as clean of an incision as it could be." I probed the end of the gash with a finger. "Which implies to me one of two things. Either the blade wasn't as sharp as it should've been, or the hand that held it wasn't terribly steady."

"That's not surprising," said Mwenge. "Given the number of stab wounds, I'd wager this was a crime of passion. That, or it was made to look like one. Do we know if she was seeing anyone?"

"I'm doing a Net search now," I said. "Public records list her as unmarried. I'm not seeing anything on social media on initial glance. If she was in a relationship, she wasn't vocal about it."

Mwenge touched her hand. "She's wearing a ring, too, but on her right hand. That's quite a gemstone. I'd wager three to four karats. Sapphire, maybe. Hand itself is untouched. Another indication this wasn't a robbery."

I glanced about the room. "Have you spotted a purse anywhere, Captain?"

She shook her head. "Most Net enabled women don't wear them."

I opened the top drawer of the victim's nightstand. Inside, I found a box of tissues, chap stick, a jewelry box, a hair brush, and a personal lubricant. I picked up the latter and held it between two fingers. "Looks like Ms. Wen was sexually active, at least."

"Yes, though not necessarily with someone else," said Reyes.

"Touché." I placed the lubricant back, closed the drawer, and headed back toward the door. I paused, glancing at the blood splatters and the heavy pool that had seeped into the carpet. I knelt and poked the stained fibers. My glove came away wet.

"Come to any conclusions yet, Detective?" asked Reyes.

"Suspicions, I'd say." I stood and wiped my glove on a handkerchief I kept in my pocket.

"Anything you'd care to share?"

I pointed toward the blood splatters. "The victim's throat was cut. As we know, that's a messy business. Given the heavy pool of blood at my feet and the splatter pattern arcing toward the far wall, I'm guessing the deed happened here. Wen's assailant probably hid behind her door. When Wen entered the bedroom, the attacker grabbed her from behind, slit her throat, and held her for a moment as she struggled. Once the bleeding slowed, the killer carried her to her bed and arranged her body for display."

"You think the stab wounds are post-mortem?" asked Mwenge.

"They'd have to be," I said. "Coroner Pham can confirm, but the blood splatters around the room are consistent with a single attack. If the attacker tried to stab Ms. Wen first, not only would the blood pattern be different, but there'd be secondary wounds on Wen's body. She would've tried to defend herself. Even in failure she would've accumulated cuts on her hands, slashes on her clothes, perhaps bruises and contusions on her face. We haven't seen any of that."

Bishop nodded. "Post-mortem defacement of the body would

also suggest a crime of passion. My bet's on a secret boyfriend, or girlfriend depending on which way Wen leaned."

"Let's hope so," said Reyes. "That would make finding the killer a relative breeze."

"You have any different conclusions based on what we've found?" I asked.

The Captain shook her head. "Not yet, though I'm surprised the blood is contained within the bedroom. Despite the carpeting, the killer's shoes should've tracked some to the hallway outside. Perhaps they did. CSU can tell us for sure, but I expected more. To *not* have done so means the killer must've wiped his or her shoes with a towel or rag that we so far haven't found. Along with your proposed staging for the murder, Detective Drake, that suggests to me this was premeditated. That's at odds with the whole 'crime of passion' idea."

"Passion and premeditation aren't exclusive," said Mwenge.

Reyes chewed her lip. "Not always, but passion makes people more reactive, not more analytical. Why don't the two of you check the rest of the apartment? I'm going to call Pham to see how far out she is."

I nodded, and Mwenge and I headed back into the hallway. The paramedic still sat on the couch in the living room, vaping away, so I didn't stop there. Like the Captain, I didn't care for unwanted aerosol contact highs. Instead, I rounded a corner into the kitchen.

Like the rest of the apartment, it was higher in quality than most. The appliances were all enrobed in gleaming aluminum, the counters topped with polished stone. I skirted the central island until I found what I was looking for: a knife block, tucked in-between a blender and the side of the refrigerator. None of the knives were missing, however.

I turned and headed back. Bishop had bypassed the living room as well, instead opting to poke around the study. I found him hunched over a holoprojector set in the middle of a teardrop-shaped desk.

I glanced at the holo, which was stuck on a login screen. "Not making a lot of progress there, are you champ?"

He gave me a sour look. "You want to take a crack at it?"

"I'm good at coding and cryptoanalysis. Guessing passwords? Not so much. Is the operating system on a local server?"

"I checked the desk and didn't find a thing. I'd wager it's a cloud system. The login screen says USC, so I'm guessing they're the host."

I tapped my nose, which elicited an unkind glare from Bishop. I circled the room as he stared at the holo, taking note of the potted plants in each corner situated under special full spectrum grow lights. One of the bushes was a bromelia with a bright red flower jutting from amid a cluster of long, spiny leaves like those of a succulent. A holly bush, ubiquitous in the grow farms of the local maché tea distributors, took up the other corner. Maybe Wen preferred to brew her own.

A feature wall beyond the plants contained a series of three art pieces, all of them apparently crafted by the same impressionist painter. The one in the middle seemed to hover off the wall on one side, however.

I plucked at the bottom corner. The picture swung out, revealing a safe set in the wall behind it. "Bingo."

Bishop sighed. "Go ahead. Tell me about your superior observational skills."

I smiled. "It's an established fact, at this point. No need for me to gloat. Now, gloating about my general preparedness, on the other hand..." I reached into my coat and produced a small compact of dusting powder.

Bishop snorted and shook his head. "I'll get the lights."

I dusted the powder over the safe's keypad and handle before fishing a tablet out of my pocket. When Bishop hit the lights, I turned on the UV flashlight.

"Need me to scan Wen's prints?" asked Mwenge.

"I can pull them off the USC database, but thanks." I tilted my tablet to and fro to get a good scan. "And... yup. We've got several partials, but they look like Wen's. I'm not scanning any bogies. In fact..."

I leaned in, peering at the safe. The crack between the door and the edge of the frame seemed larger than it should've been. On a whim, I pulled on the handle. It swung out, same as the picture had.

"Well, I'll be damned." Mwenge turned the lights back on.

"That it's open isn't the surprising part." I extracted a tablet from the safe. "Who breaks into a safe and leaves the contents behind?"

Mwenge joined me. "Maybe the tablet wasn't the only thing in there."

"Possible." I tried to activate the tablet, but it required a passkey. I wouldn't be able to get into it—not here, anyway.

"Or perhaps nobody broke into the safe at all," said Mwenge. "You didn't see any prints that didn't match Wen's, right?"

"I didn't, but if you're arguing that Wen forgot to close her safe all the way the same night she was savagely murdered, I'd say that's a hell of a coincidence."

I looked up at the sound of the door chime echoing through the apartment. With the mysterious tablet in hand, I walked back to the living room. Coroner Pham was walking in as Officer Jamison closed the front door behind her. She gave us a nod. "Detectives. Looks like you got pulled off the graduation gala. Sucks for you."

Like Reyes, Trinh Pham didn't fit the mold of a typical Martian, not because she was short, but because she was round. Not fat, mind you, though she did carry a few more pounds than most locals. Rather the shape was all in her face. With puffy cheeks, a low-profile nose, and a head that was nearly a perfect sphere, she reminded me of a rodent filling its cheeks with food for the winter —minus the whiskers and tiny ears, of course. The bang-heavy bob cut she kept her black hair in helped her look less rodent-like, but it didn't solve her more pressing roundness issues.

"It sucks less then you think, Trinh," I said. "I'm actually not a fan of public speaking, so the joke's on Nubia Nassar. The chief stuck her with speech duty in my wake. Got any evidence bags?" I lifted the tablet.

"What was that about your general preparedness, again?" said Mwenge.

"Shut it."

Trinh put the case she held in her hand down and cracked it. "Never fear, Coroner Pham is here. I've got you covered." She flicked a bag at me as she closed her case. "I hear the vic is in the bedroom?"

"Down the hallway," I said as I slipped the tablet into the plastic baggie. "We'll follow you."

Pham had that prototypical coroner gene that made her immune to blood, gore, and other external stimuli that would make normal people's stomachs churn. As she entered the bedroom, she gave the Captain a curt nod, headed to the body, and popped open her case. She might as well have been called over to provide carbon dating on a fossil for all the emotion she showed.

Pham pulled a tablet from her case and scanned Wen's fingertips first, followed by a retinal scan of her eyes. She talked as she worked. "So why all the secrecy with this one, if you don't mind my asking, Captain?"

"Mostly I didn't want to make a big fuss the night of the gala," she said. "Also because I fear once word gets back to USC that one of their top administrators is dead, they're not going to be pleasant about it. The media won't be either once they sink their teeth into the story."

Pham pulled a DNA reader from her case and slipped a strip of blot paper into the tip. She pressed it into Wen's neck wound and waited for the blood to seep into the paper. "Between USC and the media, I'd rather deal with USC."

"Lucky for you, you don't have to deal with either," said the Captain.

Pham removed the strip and bagged it. She crossed to the blood pool by the door and took another reading, then did the same at a random splatter near the far wall.

"All consistent?" I asked.

"So far," said Trinh. "Patience is key. We'll get CSU to spot test the whole room. Once I get the vic back to my lab I'll start checking other likely spots. Fingernails, the wounds, the mouth, other orifices."

"Can you confirm cause of death?" asked the Captain.

"I'd hazard laceration of the neck, but again, I'll have to take her to my laboratory to be sure."

The Captain sighed. "I guess it's time to have the mortuary van drive itself over, then. I'm just not looking forward to having the vultures descend on us so soon."

I cleared my throat. "There might be a way to postpone their arrival, if you want, Captain."

"No," she said. "Coroner Pham is right. We're wasting time. We need to move the body for analysis."

"That's not what I meant," I said. "This building's bottom floors are hotel rooms."

Reyes arched an eyebrow my way. "So?"

"So, I can think of at least one way to move a body without bringing extra officers and a full medical team up here."

Reyes frowned at me, but she didn't tell me to take a hike when I told her what I had in mind.

7

MAY 10, 2154

THE VACTRAIN SLOWED as it approached Titusville. From my window I spotted a sparking white expanse abutted by a swath of mid-Atlantic blue, broken only by a thin strip of piled boulders some three or four kilometers off the coast. On it perched a giant gleaming statue, some ninety meters of polished aluminum depicting one of the first commercial rockets to take mankind to space, hovering over the watery graveyard of Cape Canaveral that the seas had reclaimed some sixty or seventy years ago. Its placement made it a monument to mankind's ignorance and stupidity as much as to our ingenuity.

Thankfully, the drugs from my pocket continued to do their job as the vactrain hit its final deceleration. My stomach barely complained, except to remind me it was still hungry. As the train came to a complete stop, I heard the rumble of the exterior seals and the hiss of air being let back into the outer tube. A moment later the doors slid open, and along with the other eighty or so new enlistees in the pod, I stood and disembarked onto the private USC platform outside.

The heat and humidity punched me in the jaw. As I wondered how hot it was, a small indicator flashed at the corner of my vision.

40.1°C, 93% humidity. Even if I hadn't learned to control it yet, my Net had started to listen. The newsfeeds thankfully hadn't returned, but as I headed along the metal railing in the direction of a broad, sprawling complex of USC buildings in the distance, I saw a quick string of text flash before me: *USC Upload Requested – Basic Services Package.* Before I had a chance to try and respond, I saw another two flashes: *Request accepted, Upload complete.* Immediately several three-dimensional bubbles popped into view. One pointing toward my feet read *USC Titusville station 8C,* while another pointing to the track at my right read *USC Titusville station 8D.* The one pointing directly in front of me read *USC New Enlistee Training – Report Immediately.* It blinked repeatedly to get my attention.

The overlays reminded me of the virtual reality combat games I'd played with my buddies growing up. The heads up displays on those games were far more complex than a few sets of bubbles. Then again, my Net was only now initializing. It still felt bizarre that I could see digital overlays without a pair of VR goggles strapped to my face. I kind of missed my haptic feedback gloves, though. They'd make wrangling my Net's OS into submission a lot easier, I wagered.

Still, as impressive as the digital constructs in my field of view were, the tangible ones were the most awe-inspiring. Past the cluster of USC-branded buildings at the bottom of the walkway, past the lawns and training fields and service warehouses behind them, sprawled a massive expanse of interconnected concrete rings. Planted upon at least half the pads stood hundred and fifty meter tall behemoths, the USC Mark VIIs, gleaming white bullets perched atop ten meter wide boosters eager to belch out clouds of steam and let loose with mighty roars as they pierced the vacuum of space. Even from a distance, they made the half-sized commercial continent-jumper I'd taken to Shanghai in high school seem like a pop-gun.

Phoebe walked close by, staring at the distant rockets, same as me. Apparently, whatever space cruise she'd taken hadn't departed from a major spaceport. Either that, or the sight remained impressive even to those who'd seen it before.

Sweat slicked my brow by the time we reached the frontmost USC building, but thankfully my USC jumpsuit wicked moisture away like a dream, even in Florida's oppressive humidity. Nonetheless, I welcomed the cool blast of air that greeted us as we walked into the reception lobby.

A group of four, two men and two women, all dressed in the same USC uniforms as the rest of us, approached our group. An olive-skinned brunette only a couple centimeters shorter than me stepped to the front and spoke, her voice echoing off the lobby's polished cement floors and the shiny metallic trusses above.

"Welcome, everyone, to USC's Titusville stage one training center. I'm ensign Agarwal. Hopefully you're all here as enlistees into USC's marine corps. If not, you'd better hope the doctors who cleared your entry onto the vactrain missed something on your physical, otherwise you might be in for the longest mistake of your life." She flashed a perfect white smile, the kind that indicated she was joking. *Mostly.* "Behind me are ensigns Patterson, Guerrera, and Tanaka. We'll be your liaisons over the next few days as we prepare you for transport to USC's lunar base in the Mare Nubium where you'll begin the second phase of your training. I know you all surely have a number of questions, but we'll be able to address those better in small groups during the training exercises we have scheduled for you over the remainder of the day. Now, if I could see a show of hands. For those of you who've recently received your Nets, are any of you currently *not* receiving text to Net notifications?"

I assumed the bubbles I'd received on the vactrain platform counted, but before I could ask, a popup appeared in my vision. *You are in: Group 3, Guerrera.*

Only one person raised their hand. "Alright, we'll get you taken care of. You can come with me. The rest of you, please report to your assigned group leader. I'll be leading group one, Patterson two, Guerrera three, and Tanaka four."

Phoebe's voice sounded quietly to my left. "What group are you in?"

"Three. You?"

She held up a single finger. "Bummer. Good luck. Don't forget to take your meds."

"If I start feeling like death on a stick again, I'll know what to do. Thanks." I gave her a nod as she headed over to the group forming around Ensign Agarwal. I joined the group around the hispanic girl.

She looked around as I approached, ticking numbers off. "Nineteen, twenty. Good. That's everyone I have on my roster. As Agarwal already mentioned, I'm Ensign Guerrera. According to my logs, about a third of you have recently gotten your Nets. You all should've received doses of metaprochlorperazine. I'm assuming you're all current on your dosages?"

I had half a mind to speak up about the lackluster care I'd received, but I bit my lip. It wasn't her fault my doctor had failed me. At least she was asking.

"Good," she said when no one spoke up. "Now, first task on today's agenda is a fitness test. Before you ask, yes, it's perfectly safe to complete within twenty-four hours of a Net injection, especially because we'll be able to properly monitor your biometrics using your Nets. And don't worry about how you perform. You've all been preselected in part for your athletic abilities. Your results will simply help us place you in the proper role on a squad later on. With that said, we'll begin in the gymnasium, facility 2C if you look on your minimaps. Any questions?"

I had one—how the hell do I access my minimap?—but I didn't want to look like a noob, so I kept my mouth shut. A black girl with legs for days who looked like she could spike a volleyball well into the Florida panhandle raised her hand.

"Yeah," she said. "I've got one. When are we getting lunch?"

Guerrera smirked. "We've found it's best to wait until *after* the physical examination to feed new recruits."

I STOOD in a gym that reminded me of the ones I'd visited during my unofficial recruiting trips to Big Ten schools, except this one was about three times bigger, twenty years newer, and smelled more of a salty sea breeze than sweaty gym rats. Guerrera motioned for us to stop as we reached a set of squat racks.

"First up will be the strength test," she said. "I hope you're all familiar with the standard power lifts. Squat, deadlift, and bench. No olympic lifts, so don't worry about those. We don't need anyone tearing a rotator cuff on their first day. We'll be looking for your max weight on each of the three lifts, with a total of three attempts apiece, but I'd suggest you warm up first. Good lifts will be measured via Net biometrics. If your lift bubble turns green, it's good. Red, it didn't count. We'll also have timed push-up and pull-up drills. Two minutes apiece. Don't wear yourselves out, because this is only the first portion of today's exercise test. For safety, we've assigned each of you a spotter." Guerrera started to read out names.

I glanced at the racks. I still wasn't sure I believed Guerrera's spiel about athletic activity being completely safe following Net surgery, but thanks to the drugs I'd taken in the vactrain, my queasiness at least had vanished. And I *certainly* didn't believe Guerrera's claim that our results in the lifts didn't matter. If they didn't, they wouldn't bother testing us. Luckily for me, I had more than modified genetics going for me. My D-I strength and conditioning training should give me an edge over most everyone else.

"Drake, you're paired with Stanić," called Guerrera.

I turned, wondering if I was supposed to use my Net to identify who that was when a bruiser approached me. He rocked a high top fade in need of some trimming, not to mention one of those weird braided chin beards. He flashed me a toothy smile as he extended a hand.

"You Drake?"

"That's right. Ambrose."

"Maarten."

We shook. His grip felt robotic, crushing metal driven by actuators and surrounded by living flesh. Our eyes were level, but the guy must've outweighed me by forty kilos, none of it wasted.

"*Maarten?*"

"That's right," he said, letting go. "First name's Dutch. Last is Latvian."

"Which one are you from?"

He laughed. "Iowa."

That made sense. Maarten looked he consumed his fair share of corn and milk.

"Everyone ready?" called Guerrera. "Take a station. Squats first. Two minutes for warmups, then we'll get started."

Maarten slapped me on the back, possibly rearranging a vertebrae. "You lift, hoss?"

I cleared my throat. "Yeah. You know... *Some.*"

"Rock on. After you."

My self-confidence held strong until halfway through the first warmup set. By the end of our first three max reps, it had been thoroughly trampled, and things only got worse from there. Everything I could do, Maarten could do better. I put up a respectable two hundred and thirty kilos on the squat only for Maarten to put up three twenty. He smoked my bench by seventy kilos and my deadlift by over a hundred and fifty. Worse was that he held even with me on the push-up challenge and only lost to me on the pull-ups by one, despite his size. It wasn't until Guerrera sent us packing outside to the track for the 5K run that I finally managed to best him decisively.

"Not bad, Drake," said Guerrera as I crossed the start line on the track for the fifth and final time. "Sixteen forty-one."

Sweat rolled off me in sheets. I leaned over, sucking in as much of the humid, Florida air as my lungs could handle. "Could've done better... if not for this heat. And my legs... still burning from earlier."

"If you hate the heat, then you'll love Mars," she said. "Now hoof it to the natatorium. The five hundred meter free is next."

"You're kidding, right?" I glanced over my shoulder at Maarten, who still had about a third of a kilometer to go. My Net feed proved her seriousness, however, as a map to the indoor swimming facility appeared in front of me.

"We're just getting started, Drake. Now move it. I'll deal with your partner."

BY THE END of my half-kilometer swim, I'd convinced myself Guerrera must've been screwing with me for shits and giggles, but as I changed out of my swim trunks and back into my jumpsuit in the men's locker room, I received a Net command to return to the gymnasium. Once there, Guerrera smiled as she handed me a twenty kilo weight jacket and instructed me to perform the push-up and pull-up drills again with a two minute body weight squat drill added on the end for good measure. Then, perhaps out of anger at being forced to babysit us, she forced me and everyone else in our group back outside for another run, this time a 10K—while wearing the weight jacket of course.

As I stumbled back into the locker room, I tried to console myself with the positive results and non-results of the exercise gauntlet, namely that I'd beaten all but three of the other nineteen people in my group during the final run, I hadn't puked, and I'd yet to start bleeding out of my mouth or nose, which I took as a good sign regarding the health of my Net-enmeshed brain. With my jumpsuit stuffed into one of the auto washers outside the showers, I leaned my forehead against the tiles within and turned the cold tap open as far as it would go. The white noise of the shower filled my ears. Somewhere in the background I heard the buzz of the auto washer as it finished its drying cycle, but I didn't move, letting the flowing water wick my body heat away as best it could—which was slower than I wished given the temperature of the Florida groundwater.

I might've stayed there for a half hour if not for the Net notification I received telling me to report to the cafeteria. The promise of food provided newfound motivation and helped me get dressed and out the locker room in record time, though Maarten nearly beat me. Together, we booked it to the nearest mess hall, where I grabbed a tray and Maarten decided to double fist a pair. Perhaps it was the ravenous expanding black hole in the pit of my stomach, but the food didn't even look half bad, at least compared to the fare I was used to at Bernham Hall. I loaded my plate up with scrambled eggs, roasted vegetables, and a couple vat burgers, while Maarten grabbed at least one of everything on offer, including the questionable noodle and tube chicken casserole labelled only as 'King Ranch.'

Neither one of us was willing to waste valuable mouth time on idle chatter when there was food to be eaten, but I did learn a little about my workout buddy between bites. For one thing, he wasn't quite the hay bale-toting, cow-wrestling farmhand I'd assuming him to be. He hailed from downtown Des Moines, the son of a financial services analyst and a political consultant. He'd never even gone apple-picking, much less tilled a field. In fact, his primary hobby outside practicing for amateur strongman competitions was taking part in combat drone derbies. Maarten claimed he was almost good enough to get on the NDDL's midwestern junior training circuit for the three to five kilo drone class, but I got the impression he was exaggerating. I also learned that like me he'd gotten his Net implant the day before, which reminded both of us to take another dose of our meds lest out appetites disappear mid bite.

Guerrera didn't give us much time to digest, though, as she rounded up our group and sent us packing to the site's medical facilities. There, I met a diminutive woman by the name of Dr. French who asked me how I felt following my Net implant. I gave a smart-ass response which I later regretted, mostly because she seemed concerned that I hadn't been properly prepped regarding post-operative care, going so far as to claim she'd contact Dr. Eroğlu to make sure he wasn't cutting corners, but just because I'd been mistreated in Chicago didn't mean I was going to be coddled in return. The afternoon dwindled as Dr. French performed a battery of tests on me: blood tests, urine tests, VO_2 max measurements on a cycle ergometer, CO_2 cycling which the doctor claimed would help them equip me with a pressure suit later on, and an oxygen deficiency test where I lay on an exam table and ended when I finally passed out. After that, I had to wait around for an hour before being given another brain scan via mini-fMRI, the results of which Dr. French assured me were completely normal.

The highlight of the afternoon, however, came in the aftermath, when Dr. French reviewed the data from my wrist-mounted phase initializer. When asked if I'd been able to access my Net's OS of my own volition, I replied in the negative, and she told me that she was going to try and see if my Net had formed enough neural connections for her to map the OS navigation system to my primary motor cortex. I didn't really know what that meant, but she then had me go through visualization exercises where I moved my arm and imagined doing the same thing while accessing my

Net's OS. Within ten minutes of trying, I managed to bring up a menu.

I think I laughed out loud. Dr. French didn't hold it against me.

I checked my Net messages as I left the medical facility—I only barely moved my arm to do so—and found I'd been assigned a room in one of the nearby dormitories. Dinner would be in an hour, and I didn't have anything left on my schedule, so off I went in search of my quarters.

When I opened the door, I found a room barely bigger than a walk-in closet, equipped with a pair of bunks. Only one was occupied. A face looked up from the top one as I entered.

Surprise, surprise—it was Maarten.

"Hey," I said as I lay down in the bunk underneath him.

"Hey."

I took a deep breath, feeling the dull ache of my muscles and a tingling feeling of exhaustion in my chest. Maarten didn't say anything else, and I didn't press him. He'd probably been napping, which my experience from two-a-day basketball camps told me was a great idea, but I couldn't. Not today.

I was a computer geek with access to a brand new OS implanted directly into my head. Of course I was going to play with it.

As Phoebe had promised, the graphical interface I'd learned to access thanks to Dr. French's efforts was pretty similar to the ones on modern commercials touch-based systems. I didn't seem to have access to many applications—call services, messaging, newsfeeds, weather, and the like—but there were a few intriguing ones, notably one called 'bioadjustments.' I'd have to try that later. In the meantime, I found a terminal and opened it to a text interface.

That's when I realized I hadn't trained my brain how to write text via Net. Hoping the system was intuitive, I thought of the words I wished to input, and sure enough, they showed up, though slowly at first. Once I'd made the mental leap, I was able to dig one step further, down to the Net's kernel to see how the magic happened.

That's where my level of understanding hit a brick wall. I'd learned basic computer architecture in high school and was learning more at WMU, but we'd never ventured into something as complex as a Net. It was so fluid and dynamic, with process instructions dictated by complex webs of signals defined by the system's neural net.

I blinked and closed the terminal. I'd parse through it some day. Maybe.

In the meantime, I snapped open the newsfeed app and took a gander at the stories. The first three ones autoplayed in minimized form, without audio, but it was the one at the very top of the queue that caught my eye, mostly because of the inset still photo.

I zoomed it to full view. An anchorwoman sat behind a desk, the still behind her portraying a familiar image, that of a masked individual in a white pressure suit and a blood red visor. The ticker at the bottom gave the time of the clip as early this morning, just after eight. I activated the sound.

"The top story this morning continues to be the nuclear devastation of downtown Los Angeles. Top security officials from the People's Republic of China, the Republic of India, and our own National Security Administration immediately released statements suspecting Martian separatists of the attack, reports that have since been corroborated by United Space Corporation intelligence monitoring communications out of Martian settlements, but as of seven thirty-five eastern time this morning, we have official confirmation of Martian culpability coming in the form of a video posted directly to the Martian intranets by the Martian rebellion leader known only as the Snow Leopard. We advise our viewers to watch with caution, as the following video may be disturbing to some."

The inset expanded and started to play. Bits of the clip felt familiar, snippets that had smuggled their way into my subconscious as I'd sat there on the vactrain, unable to keep them out of my eyes.

The masked, suit-clad individual spoke, the voice modulated to sound like a ransom call. "Citizens of Earth. Of the United States of America. To those who have fled the smoking remains of Los Angeles. Mars feels your rage. We feel your suffering. We feel your pain, your sorrow, your fear. We know it well, because we suffer through it every day, every hour, every second. We feel that crippling fear when we look into the butterscotch sky and see the contrails of transports hurtling toward our cities. We feel it when we see the hulking fusion powered beasts rumbling across our plains on tires as black as the souls of those inside. We feel the fear when we see the muzzles of your rifles leveled at our eyes, and see the cold gaze of the men and women who wield them. The fear oozes from our veins when you cut us, sublimates into the ether with our blood, vaporized like the bodies of your loved ones who recently rose into your soup-thick skies.

"So, yes. We know well your pain and fear. And we know you are angry, without understanding that you have been served precisely what you sought to dish. But there will be no victory. No glory, no retribution for the dead. Only more who will die, more who will suffer the same fate and more who will feel the same pain we share—should you choose to walk the path before you."

The individual shot a finger at the camera. "Know the deaths you have experienced are on your hands. *You* tested us. You tested Mars. You poked us, not thinking we would bite back. You tested the Snow Leopard. *And now you bleed.*"

I closed the newsfeed app, a chill rippling down my spine. Was that who we were up against? A lone man in a subterranean room with a pressure suit, a camera, and an arsenal of nuclear weapons at his beck and call? A man who'd murdered thirty million and still believed he stood on the side of right?

"You still up, Maarten?" I asked.

He didn't respond, though I thought I heard a creak from the bed above.

I tried again. "Maarten?"

The bed shifted. "Huh?"

"Sorry. Didn't wake you, did I?"

"Uh... No."

"You get your Net fully initialized?" I asked.

"Yeah. Yeah, I did." The bed kept creaking.

"Watch any of the newsfeeds?"

"Ah... Watching some vids now, hoss."

I waited a moment, but Maarten didn't say anything else. His bed simply creaked and swayed above me. I couldn't blame him. What was there to say in the wake of genocide?

The bed wobbled a bit and creaked some more, and I heard a soft moan. On second thought, maybe I didn't want to know what sort of vids Maarten was watching. Ignorance was relative bliss, bed creaks and soft breathy groans notwithstanding. I could've told Maarten that anything we accessed was almost certainly being monitored by USC, but I didn't want to interrupt him. Besides, the monitoring was undoubtedly automated. Certainly, no living person would be interested in monitoring what Maarten seemed to be up to.

Besides, I had more pressing concerns. Ignoring the sounds above me, I pulled up my Net's messaging program. It had video, audio, and text capabilities, but I took the easy way out and selected text.

With a sigh, I started writing. *Dear Mom and Dad...*

8

MAY 9, 2179

AS IT TURNED OUT, moving a body into a laundry cart wasn't much different than moving one onto a gurney, at least a relatively fresh body that hadn't yet stiffened through rigor mortis. I still felt icky doing the moving though. Perhaps there was something about using a gurney that gave the operation a more distinguished feel, but despite the fact that I was a police officer of almost nineteen years working under the direct command of my captain, I still couldn't help but feel like I was breaking the law, or at the very least some unwritten code.

"You know," I said to Mwenge as we wheeled the laundry cart into the building's service elevator, "I still don't totally understand the Captain's desire for secrecy. Wen's a top level USC official, I get that. But the story's going to come out sooner or later."

"Well, for one thing *later* means she can tackle the media in the morning after a good night's sleep," said Mwenge. "For another, it means she doesn't run the risk of interfering with the Chief's graduation ceremony any further."

"The *Chief's* ceremony?" I punched in the ground floor. "You know he's not the one graduating, right?"

"No, but he's the one the Captain has to worry about keeping happy. You know the man better than I do, but I get the impression he actually *likes* the pomp and circumstance. His face fell when you told him the Captain had summoned us."

I stretched my eyebrows. "Maybe you're right."

The elevator dinged as it reached the bottom floor. We wheeled it through the hotel's back hallways, casual as can be, before exiting through a side door. The coroner's van the Captain had hailed waited there for us. After making sure there weren't any curious bystanders nearby, Mwenge and I opened the van's back hatch, collapsed the gurney that was inside, and loaded the hamper beside it. Despite my line of work, it wasn't often I moved bodies. When I did, I was always happy to be doing so in Martian gravity. I wasn't sure how Earth paramedics did it with any degree of grace.

As we closed up the back, Captain Reyes and Coroner Pham appeared at the side door. Trinh gave us a nod and hopped into one of the van's front seats, but the Captain paused beside us. "So what's your plan of attack, Detectives?"

"Well, first we need to get the building's security feeds," I said. "What we do afterwards is going to depend heavily on those. Are you having CSU sweep the apartment tonight?"

"It's getting late," said Reyes. "I was thinking I might postpone that until morning."

"Are you putting a detail on the apartment?"

"That's actually part of the reason I asked about your plans," said Reyes. "Officer Jamison's shift was over an hour ago. As long as you two are going to be on the premises, I figured I'd let him go until his replacement arrives."

"The building's security office should be on site," said Mwenge. "Can't imagine why it wouldn't be."

"So you're fine with that?" said the Captain. "I wouldn't be surprised if it's an hour before I can secure an overnight detail here given the graduation ceremony."

"It'll be fine," I said. "It'll probably take us that long to sift through the security feeds. Let us know who you're sending and we'll meet and brief them before we call it a night."

"Much appreciated, Detectives." Reyes gave us a nod before getting in the van. It purred to life and took off, vanishing out the back of the ill-lit alleyway.

Mwenge and I headed back inside and found our way to the check-in desk. The receptionist there already knew us, having introduced ourselves earlier when we'd asked her to show us the laundry room. This time, the young lady's expression was decidedly less curious and more concerned when we asked if the building had a safety officer on site. She showed us the way to the security office, a small room tucked behind the hotel's kitchens on the third floor. There we found a man in a black shirt and slacks playing on a tablet as we arrived.

He startled as we knocked on the door frame. "Excuse me. I'm Officer Drake and this is Officer Mwenge. We're with the EPD." Normally I would've showed him my badge, but the uniform I wore for the graduation ceremony was proof enough of my status. "Mind if we ask you a few questions?"

The security officer put the tablet to sleep and shoved it in a back pocket, as if doing so would exonerate him from having slacked off on the job. "EPD? What's going on? Someone call in a disturbance?"

"I'm not at liberty to say at the moment." I pointed to a rack of servers humming at the back of the small room. "Any chance you store your security data on those?"

"Some of it," said the officer. "We keep all the feeds from our cameras for six months on our local banks. We store it indefinitely in the cloud. Why?"

"I'm going to need to see some of the feeds from the past day or two."

"Sure. By all means." The officer stood and waved us in. "I've got a display I can pull the feeds up on, or you can connect via Net if you like. Although..."

The room was warm thanks to the servers, and it was only going to get warmer with the three of us packed into it. I wondered if taking my formal jacket off would be bad form. "Although, what?"

The security officer looked nervous, like a boy about to cop to breaking his father's tablet. "Well... Look, I'm sorry to have to ask this, but don't you need a warrant to access our feeds?"

Lucky for us, justices didn't attend the police graduation alongside the officers. Captain Reyes had acquired what we needed while Mwenge and I moved Wen into the laundry hamper. "I'll transfer it to you. You've got a Net?"

"No, actually. Here to the display is fine. Network is CTC Security."

I sent the file over. The officer logged in and checked the document on the display. He sure as hell didn't read it though, as he nodded after glancing at it for five seconds. "Alright then. What feeds do you need? I'll pull them up for you."

"Actually, we're going to have to ask you to step out while we look them over ourselves," said Mwenge.

The officer blinked. "You're serious?"

"We already told you we weren't at liberty to discuss the matter," I said. "We'll cue you into our investigation if and when we can."

The officer's cheeks reddened, but he had the good sense not to argue. "I'll be in the lobby if you need me, I guess."

He left, leaving Mwenge and me alone in the room. I shut the door. Mwenge stared at the lone chair in front of the display.

"Roshambo you for it," I said.

"You take it," he said. "You're the one with the old knees and the lingering problems from a childhood spent in high gravity."

"Call me old one more time and you'll be the next one getting shoved into a laundry hamper."

Despite my complaint, I took the seat. The building's security ran on a familiar software platform. I flicked through the available cameras: multiple exteriors, shots of the lobby, conference rooms, laundry, kitchens, ground floor restaurants, as well as the elevators and a pair of cameras in each residential hallway of the building's sixty-two stories. I pulled up the feed for the camera on the fifty-fourth floor that pointed in the direction of Wen's apartment and located the time management controls. I pumped the speed up to thirty-two times and ran the feed in reverse. A few people came and went, but none to Wen's apartment. Then Wen herself arrived. I paused the feed and checked the time. Six thirty-five.

I resumed the feed, watching as the hours ticked back through the day. At just after eight in the morning, Wen's door opened, and out she walked, wearing the same outfit we'd seen her in.

I paused the feed again and looked at Mwenge. "Well, that's surprising."

Bishop blinked, his brow furrowing. "Run it back from present time again, at sixteen x instead of thirty-two. Maybe we missed something."

I did as he suggested. Again, we saw Wen arrive at her apartment at just after six-thirty. Neighbors came and left from their apartments, but nobody touched Wen's door until she left early in the morning. I paused the feed again.

"Well," said Bishop. "I suppose it's possible Wen's killer hid in her apartment overnight."

"Possible, but not remotely likely. You can cycle through more of the older feeds on your Net. And run anyone who exited the fifty-fourth floor elevators through facial recognition. Maybe we'll get lucky and come across someone with a prior conviction."

"You don't think we will, though."

I minimized the security video software. "Nope."

Bishop frowned. "You going to do your super spy computer voodoo thing?"

I gave him an unamused look. "It's simple police work. It wouldn't hurt you to look over my shoulder every now and then."

"No time like the present."

"Less now, more then. Check the video feeds."

Bishop leaned against the desk and adopted the distant look of a man diving into his Net. Meanwhile, I tapped my way through several layers of the security computer's OS until I found my way to the log files. If someone had tampered with the security feeds as I suspected, either by pausing the cameras at opportune times or by splicing looped video into the feed, there should be a record of the changes.

Upon finding the right log, I opened it and ran through the last day's worth of changes. Unfortunately, all I saw were standard uploads and deletions of six month old files from the local servers to the cloud.

Perhaps whoever had hacked the security system actually knew what they were doing and had hidden their tracks. I pulled up the file history for the log itself and compared that to the data it contained, but the log hadn't been modified except when the uploads and deletions had occurred.

I chewed on my lip. Perhaps I was wrong about the security feeds having been hacked. Then again, perhaps I was still underestimating the ability of the hacker.

I closed the logs and tried to recover the most recent trash files. A list of feeds came up, most of them showing as unsalvageable, likely because parts had already been overwritten with more recent video, but I wasn't concerned with them. What I searched for was anything else that had been deleted in the past day.

I didn't spot it right away. It was disguised as a video file, but the file size was too small and the moment it was trashed didn't match the predicted schedule of the feed deletions. I tried recovering it but failed. Less than ten precent of it was left. There was no way for me to determine what the file had been, but I couldn't help but suspect it was a shell a hacker had placed over the logs while they did their dirty work. The only problem with shells was that they didn't disappear into thin air when the work was done.

I minimized the system utilities and turned to my partner. "Find anything?"

Bishop's eyes remained glazed. "Not so far. I haven't gotten any matches on ex-cons. I've found a number of non-residents, but they were with tenants at the time. None appear to have gone near Wen's apartment, or left the company they were in." He turned to me and blinked. "Hey! You've found something."

"A suspicion only. The system might've been hacked."

"No. That." Bishop pointed to the display.

I glanced at it. The security feeds had maximized. Currently, four feeds ran simultaneously, including one of the hallway camera pointed toward Wen's door. Someone in an oversized coat with a fur-trimmed hood walked towards Wen's apartment. They stopped and knocked on the door with a gloved hand.

"What the hell...? I didn't locate this. What's the time stamp?"

"I think you have to zoom to that feed to see it," said Mwenge.

I clicked on it, and the sole video filled the display. My eyes widened as I read the clock. "Holy crap! This isn't a recording. *It's live!*"

The individual in the feed glanced down the hall, but a glare shot off their face. They pulled a tablet from their pocket, held it to the thumbprint reader, and the door popped open. They headed in.

Bishop glanced at me, mouth agape. I hesitated for a moment before darting out of my chair and heading for the elevators at a dead sprint.

9

MAY 11, 2154

I WOKE up to the intermittent buzzing of an alarm clock. I cracked my eyes and swept them across my darkened quarters, looking for the source. It only took me a couple seconds to realize that like every other notification I'd received since arriving at the USC training facility, this one too was only in my head.

The alarm stopped as soon as I glanced at my internal clock, the time reading 0600. Above me, I heard Maarten stirring. A message from USC titled Schedule popped up, so I opened it.

I rather wished I hadn't. Testing began at 0630 sharp and kept going until 1200, followed by more tests with Dr. French until 1530. The day ended with a bang, literally, as I was instructed to report to the gun range at 1600. The entry for 1730 simply said 'Training Exercise TBD,' which I found a little odd. Thus far, USC's training and testing regimen had been as structured as could be.

A notice on my sidebar also indicated I had an unread message. I opened it as I sat up and yawned.

Ambrose,

While I appreciate the thoughtful message you sent us last night, you could've at least talked to us before heading off to Chicago to enlist. I can understand where you're coming from. The news out of Los Angeles hit your mother and me hard, too. I think we're all scared and confused at the moment. But I don't think you've fully grasped the magnitude of your choice, son. You had a full-ride scholarship to a good school, studying in a program that should've gotten you a foot in the door at a decent tech firm. Now all that's gone, as you will be. I mean, honestly, son. Seven years? That's a long enlistment contract, and it's not as if you can pop home for a weekend between deployments. If you ever make it home at all...

I'm sorry, son. I'm trying not to be worried, but I am. Moreover, I'm struggling to understand your choice. It's not the one I would've made in your shoes.

Love,
Dad

P.S. You should facecall your mom before you deploy. She's pretty upset. You owe her that, at least.

The bed rattled, I heard a thump, and then bright light filled my field of view. I blinked, shading my eyes with a hand.

Maarten stood by the door, his hand hovering at the switch. "You coming, Ambrose? They ain't gonna hold our trays for us."

I glanced at my clock again to make sure I had the time right. I'd wake my dad, but my mom might be up—assuming she'd slept at all. "Go on. I'll meet up. I've got to take care of something first."

I STUMBLED out of the exam room, my stomach rumbling and my brain feeling as if someone had battered and deep fried it. Not even the end of fall semester gauntlet where I'd suffered through three midterms in one afternoon had produced the same effect. Maybe I'd have performed better if I'd eaten a better breakfast, but after I'd finished getting cried and yelled at by my mom, I barely had time to grab an egg sandwich as I ran out of the mess hall in the direction of the academic facilities.

Luckily, my fleet feet paid dividends once again, as I arrived at the testing center a bare thirty seconds shy of six-thirty. The proctor, a middle-aged, overweight bureaucrat with a thick gray mustache, had snarled at me as I snuck in and found an empty chair, but it could've been worse. Three people showed up after he closed the door.

The first test showed up automatically in my Net as time began, making me grateful I'd stayed up late writing the letter to my parents. I might've lost a little sleep, but at least the exercise had given me a handle on Net navigation and text generation. It also helped that the first few tests were on subjects I felt pretty good about: physics, mathematics, computer science, and to a lesser extent, chemistry. Of course, even as I answered the questions and looked in my applications folder for a good scientific calculator— the online features of my Net had been disabled the moment the test started—I couldn't help but wonder why I was being tested on the subjects in question. After being shuffled into the meat factory at the Chicago USC doctor's lobby, I'd assumed the only traits USC cared about were physical.

My luck didn't last forever. After the mathematic and scientific portions of the exams were done, I was thrust into an equally extensive set of tests on military history, political theory, public policy, planetary science, and even a test specifically on military tactics in everything from full to zero g. I'm pretty sure I bombed the lot of them.

But that wasn't all. Before Proctor 'I Can't Believe I've Wasted My Life This Way' let us leave, we had to complete two final tests, one about the role of USC in transport, trade, communications, and peacekeeping between Earth, Mars, and Luna, and another filled with brutal situational what-if questions meant to test decision making, stuff like 'Your squad mate is trapped underneath your overturned rover. Two more are bleeding out while you take fire from insurgents. Your weapon's magazines are at one third capacity. An enemy rover is within sprinting distance, but you're the only member of your squad healthy enough to make it. What do you do?'

I think I answered all of those questions incorrectly, too, but seeing as they were fill in the blank, not multiple choice, it was more about the degree of wrongness with which I responded.

After a much heartier meal than the sandwich I'd filched on my way to the academic facility, I found myself back in the lobby of the campus medical facilities. Thankfully, Dr. French called me to her office within minutes.

"Have a seat, Mr. Drake," she said, pointing to a sofa chair opposite a cart lined with medical devices. "You're feeling better today, I hope?"

"Much better than yesterday afternoon," I said. "A hell of a lot better than yesterday morning."

"Glad to hear it." She took a seat. "You'll be glad to know I spoke to Dr. Eroğlu regarding your post-operative care. I can't confirm whether or not your treatment was an isolated incident, but I think I was able to successfully impart to him the need for better communication between him and his patients regarding medication and symptoms. Speaking of which, are you still taking your metaprochlorperazine?"

I nodded, wanting to be miffed at my my handling but knowing Dr. French had been the most helpful of any of the USC folks I'd interacted with thus far. "That's right."

"Good. Keep taking the pills through tonight. And your Net initialization? Any further issues there? Are you starting to get a handle on interaction and navigation?"

"I think so. I can access all the apps, use communication and messaging capabilities. I tried to dig into the OS's source code, but I got a little lost."

She lifted an eyebrow. "You're familiar with the Net's neural architecture?"

"Not really, but I was a computer and electrical engineering student before I enlisted. I'm a bit of a coding nerd. That and basketball were my time sinks."

"Interesting," she said with a disinterested face. "Now, if you don't mind, I'd like to conduct a few tests regarding the efficacy of your Net. All of these are designed to make sure your Net is fully integrated with the various portions of your brain—that the Net's learned to correlate the actions of your neurons with expected responses. Some of these tests will provide us with data, making sure your Net is receiving the proper signals. Others will create some measure of voluntary or involuntary feedback."

"*Involuntary feedback?*"

"Like when a doctor strikes your knee with a plexor, creating a jerk of the lower leg. Now, if you could place your forehead here. This is an occular synthesizer. It'll test your Net's visual synthesis in your occipital lobe. Just look straight ahead and keep your eyes open."

The station looked like a pair of VR goggles attached to a stand. I leaned forward and pushed my forehead against the front. The screen within was black as night. "Like this?"

"Perfect."

The screen pulsed, brightening and darkening in quick succession. Then it began to cycle through colors, full screen at first before turning into a rainbow road. Dots appeared among the colors, small concentric circles that grew and spread. They dotted the landscape like a slow rain, gathering in strength into a furious downpour. Colorful lines shot across the expanse, spinning and swirling, leaving echo trails behind them. All I needed to turn the experience into a good time was a few cannabis pills.

"You can pull back now," said Doctor French. "All the data I'm receiving looks good. Visual systems appear fully functional."

I pulled back, struck with a sudden thought. "Hold on... Was that light show projected on the screen or in my own vision?"

The doctor smiled. "The fact that you couldn't tell is proof the system is working. To save time, I'm going to conduct the next test while I prepare you for the third and final one."

She grabbed a couple of boxes from the cart. She opened the first one, producing a pair of mesh gloves. "Here. Put these on while I attach a few electrodes." She opened the second box and produced a stack of ten or so of the white sticky-backed wireless tabs. "Now focus, Mr. Drake, and answer a simple question. Am I speaking in Mandarin?"

"Excuse me?"

She popped an electrode on my forearm. "It's a simple question. Am I speaking in Mandarin?"

I put the first of the gloves on. "No..."

"Excellent. What about now?"

"Still no."

She nodded, adding an electrode to my temple. "And now. What language am I speaking?"

"Sounds like English to me."

Dr. French smiled again, and I realized I'd answered a question I hadn't asked yet. "Wait. The Net has auto-translation?"

French nodded. "I was speaking in Mandarin at first, then in Spanish. The fact that you didn't notice means the system is fully functional and suggests your Net has integrated with your temporal lobe. If you don't mind, let me attach a power source to these haptic gloves."

She hooked a wire to the wrist of each of my mesh gloves. "So what's the third test? To test another portion of my brain? The frontal lobe?"

"We already tested that," said Dr. French. "The frontal lobe controls movement, among other things. We received all the data we need to confirm integration in that sector during your physical exams yesterday. It's usually the first lobe to fully integrate with the Net. We simply need to make sure your parietal lobe is functioning as expected."

"That's what the gloves are for?"

She nodded. "Please close your eyes and relax."

I did as she asked. "So is the parietal lobe in charge of touC-CHHAAAHHH!" I jerked back as shooting pains lanced up my fingers, through my arms, and into the sockets of my shoulders. The wired connectors for my gloves snapped off as my chair skidded backward. "What the hell? Jesus Christ!"

"My apologies," said French. "I hate having to run that test, but it's imperative you don't know what to expect. But to answer your question, yes. The parietal lobe controls touch and pain, as you've clearly surmised. The good news is, once again, your Net appears to have fully integrated. Congratulations, Mr. Drake. You're officially the proud owner of a fully functional, fully initialized MindNet."

"Uh... thanks. I guess." It was hard to show proper appreciation when your fingers felt like you'd stuck them in electrical outlets.

"Don't forget your final doses of medication. Now move along. You've more testing to complete before the day is done."

———

ENSIGN GUERRERA MET me at the entrance to the firing range. "Drake. You'll be in lane seven. Your application says you've never shot a firearm?"

"I mean, in video games, sure. But seeing as the second amendment was repealed almost a hundred years ago, no, I haven't ever fired a real gun."

"I don't need your sass," said Guerrera. "I'm required to ask. You'll find a Browning Hi-Power V3 and a M6A Carbine at your station. Your targets will automatically refresh when you finish your cartridge. Two each for the pistol and the assault rifle, the former at three and ten meters, the latter at twenty and forty. If you're unsure on operational procedures, consult the instructional manuals via Net. And do not screw around with the M6A. It's got a hell of lot more kick than whatever haptic crap you've dicked around with in VR. I highly recommend you take advantage of your Net's biometric sensors to correctly locate your shoulder pocket prior to firing. And I shouldn't have to say this, but again, I'm required by USC to do so, so here goes: if anyone should manage to enter your line of fire for any reason while you're in your firing booth, *do not fire on them*. Do not fire on yourself. If you do, USC will not pay your medical expenses, and you will be subject to immediate discharge. Are we clear?"

"Bullets come out the end with the hole. Don't shoot myself. Got it."

Guerrera gave me a nod and I got moving. It was only after I arrived in my lane and put on my hearing protection that I realized the idiocy of scheduling target practice after a medical procedure that zapped my fingertips into a state of numb shock, but I did the best I could under the circumstances—which wasn't great, to be honest. I did fine with the handgun at three meters, landing all my shots within the red or gold central portions of the target. Ten meters wasn't much harder, but despite my extensive video game experience, my form went to shit the moment I picked up the M6A. True to Guerrera's word, the rifle kicked like an angry chicken, and though I'd managed to squeeze off one shot at a time with the Browning despite my tingling fingertips, the trigger on the

M6A was infinitely more temperamental. By the time I finished with the forty meter target, I was fairly sure I wouldn't be assigned to any sniper teams.

As I left my lane, I found Guerrera standing near the exit to the range. Maarten stood with her, as well as the muscular, leggy black girl who'd complained about not having lunch the day before.

Guerrera waved me into the group. "Drake. I'm going to go check on a few others. Everyone stay here, got it?"

Maarten popped me in the shoulder as Guerrera left. "Ambrose. How'd you score, hoss?"

"Great. That target'll think twice before it spouts off about my mother again, let me tell you."

The tall dark-skinned girl snorted and shook her head, but Maarten bellowed out a laugh. "Good one, hoss."

"Why do you keep calling me that? You're easily the biggest guy here."

He peered at me quizzically. "It's just my thing, I guess. I call everyone hoss. Right, hoss?" He elbowed our fellow enlistee.

She stared at him with unfiltered disdain. "Don't ever do that again."

I stuck out my hand. "I'm Ambrose, by the way. Clearly you've met Maarten."

"I've been exposed to him. I'm hoping he's not contagious." She shook my mitt. "Janeece Johnson."

As much as Maarten had sapped my self-confidence in my strength, Janeece had done the same on the track. "You came in first in yesterday's five K, didn't you?"

She nodded. "In our group, at least. Don't feel bad. I was all-SEC track last year."

"Yeah?" said Maarten. "What happened this year?"

"The season's not over until June, smart-ass."

Guerrera came back empty handed. "Well, apparently I've got a few folks in my charge who couldn't hit the broad side of a barn with a water balloon. That's all right. I needed to split you into a few groups anyway. We'll meet the ones who are already done for the next test."

I checked my schedule. We'd reached the nebulous last entry. "Has the final exercise been assigned yet?"

"It's been assigned," said Guerrera. "Come with me."

She started walking, and we followed, or at least Maarten and I did. Janeece kept pace with Guerrera in the front.

"Excuse me, Ensign," she said. "Maybe I'm out of line, but at what point are we going to be treated like soldiers and not like pieces of meat wired together by spinal tissue, neurons, and wifi connected brain mesh?"

The ensign gave Janeece a sideways glance. "Pardon?"

"We all enlisted. We all want to fight. We all want to feel like we're going to make a difference. But so far, nobody's talked to us. No one's explained a damn thing about what the next few days or weeks or months have in store for us. We've just been herded from point to point, getting poked and prodded and tested. That's not why any of us are here."

"Cool your thrusters, private," said Guerrera. "You've been here for less than thirty-six hours. If you'll recall, this is phase one of your training. Can't start phase two until we know where to place you. Don't worry. You're almost done. You're all shipping for Luna in the morning."

I blinked. That hadn't been on the schedule. "Seriously?"

Guerrera glanced back. "Bright and early. Launch window starts at oh-six-fifteen. Got to move you out to make room for the next batch."

She paused at the lobby, motioning for a group of three enlistees to join us. They followed us out the front of the firing range, across the lawn to the first floor of the academic building, and down a long hallway. Guerrera opened a door at the end. "We're still working on setting up the final test. Please wait here. Shouldn't be long."

She motioned us into a room empty of chairs before closing the door behind us. Two of the recruits who'd followed us drifted off toward the far corner, chatting in hushed voices, leaving their third wheel, a guy with short dark hair and a stubble beard, behind.

"Your friends ditch you?" I asked.

"Who? Them?" He tilted his head toward the chatting pair. "I don't even know their names. They finished target practice right before I did."

"Yeah?" said Maarten. "How'd you do, hoss?"

"Don't mind Maarten. He calls everyone that. I'm Ambrose. That's Janeece."

"I'm Ranbir Gupta," he said, nodding. "And I did pretty good... *hoss*. Not that I had any worries. I'm an expert marksman."

"You are?" I scoffed. "Where'd you grow up, Bolivia?"

"Not exactly. I cut my teeth on the front lines of Ranastar Five fighting the Hoard."

Janeece rolled her eyes. "Oh, brother. Here we go..."

"Hey, Andromeda Siege might be a game," said Ranbir. "But it helped me out. And it's not like USC doesn't use combat sims. Supposedly that's all you do on the voyage to Mars."

"Says who?" said Janeece.

"My older brother, Neeraj. He's deployed on Elysium right now. Always said I'd follow in his footsteps. I hate it when he's right."

"Yeah, nobody cares about your brother," said Maarten. "The important thing to focus on is the fact that you play a game that sucks hairy donkey nuts."

Ranbir sneered. "Don't tell me you're a Call to Action fan? Or let me guess? Apocalypse: Blood Feud?"

Maarten smiled. "I'm a Death Rites man myself."

That spawned a ten minute discussion about the respective

merits of shooting simulated aliens versus genetically modified humanoids and the potential impact thereof on actual marksmanship. A consensus wasn't reached, but we did successfully drive Janeece away in search of less asinine conversation.

Eventually, I tired of it. I flexed my fingers as I checked my internal clock, wondering what the next activity would be. Some sort of martial art? I wasn't sure I relished the idea of hand to hand combat, especially if Maarten was in the same group as me. I rather doubted that would be it, though. Despite pushing us to our limits and employing questionable speed with regards to post-operative assignments, USC seemed keen on keeping us alive and healthy. No point in having us join the ranks of the injured before we deployed, after all. So what then? Mind games? Pilot simulations? Psychological experiments?

Maarten and Ranbir argued. Janice sighed as she stared out the windows toward the lawns. The other two introverts continued to chitter away, having given up standing in lieu of pressing their butts to the floor.

I checked my clock again. Almost twenty minutes since we'd entered the room.

I crossed to the door and tested the handle. It gave.

Guerrera stood on the other side. She glanced up as I opened the door. "Ah. Private Drake. Nineteen minutes, thirty-six seconds. Not a bad time."

"Pardon me? Not a bad time for what? When's the next test?"

"Believe it or not, that was the last test. Congratulations. You beat everyone else." She leaned into the room. "Alright, everyone. Test's over. Report to the cafeteria in five. You'll receive your pre-launch briefing tonight at nineteen-hundred. I'd suggest you don't stay up late. You don't want to miss your flight."

10

MAY 9, 2179

I PUNCHED the button for the fifty-fourth floor as Bishop jumped into the elevator beside me, eying the live feed from the hallway outside Wen's apartment via Net.

"I've got eyes on the hall," I said. "Any chance you can run the feed through facial recognition? I want to know who's in Wen's room."

"Already on it," said Bishop. "I'm not having any luck, though. I've located feeds of the suspect on the street, passing through the lobby, and in the elevator, but I can't get a view of the face from any of them. Looks like whoever's up there is wearing a reflective visor and a glare enhancer."

Glare enhancers were a fancy term for bright flashlights. "I don't get it. Why the hell would someone hack the computer system and hide their tracks only to waltz right back into Wen's apartment after the fact?"

"Hard to say. Criminals are stupid."

"Whoever hacked the computers isn't, trust me." I checked my sidearm reflexively. "Not to mention whoever killed Wen staged her body and cleaned up after themselves. Now they're coming back to the scene of the crime? This doesn't smell right."

"It doesn't have to. Soon enough we'll have a witness to—"

The elevator jerked to a stop. A red light at the top of the panel flashed, and a low, wailing siren started to sound.

"Is that the fire alarm?" I logged remotely back into the security computers. "Son of a... *Someone* tripped it on the fifty-fourth floor. How'd they know we were coming?"

"I'm not sure they tripped it, per se," said Mwenge. "I haven't seen anyone approach the handle in the hall. Either they did it remotely, or someone set an actual fire."

I glanced at the elevator panel. We were stuck between floors forty and forty-one. I pushed the door open button but the elevator didn't respond. "Damnit. I'm calling for backup."

A familiar voice responded as the call went through. "Detective Drake. What can I do for you?"

"Macey. Detective Mwenge and I are trapped in an elevator in a residential unit on Goddard Street. We're in pursuit of a suspect who we believe tripped the fire alarm. To our knowledge, suspect is on the fifty-fourth floor, wearing jeans, a white jacket with fur trim, and a reflective mask."

"Sending backup to your location now, Detective. ETA two and a half minutes."

"Thanks. And Macey, if you could—"

The elevator shuddered again. Another light flashed at the top of cab, this one blue, and a separate, higher pitched siren started to wail.

"Holy crap," said Mwenge. "That's the pressure loss alarm."

I flicked through the alerts on the security feed. "Fifty-fourth floor. Wen's apartment. Hallway seems to be secure. Christ, what the *hell* is going on up there?"

REYES FROWNED as she surveyed the mess in Wen's apartment. Shards of glass littered the living room floor. The couches and table had shifted a good two meters toward the windows, one of which was now covered by a sheet of clear, hard plastic secured in place by Vacuseal bonding agent. Knives, pot and pans, linens, and dishtowels in the kitchen had been pulled to the floor by the same explosive pressure loss that had shifted the furniture. Black scorch marks singed the floor, walls and ceiling of the office, the desk turned into a steaming, unrecognizable mass. Despite the cleanup crews' efforts, dark, soot-stained water still slicked the floors.

"You know," said Reyes. "I knew I'd be back here. I didn't think I'd be back *this evening*." She glared at Mwenge and me as if the fire-bombing of the apartment was somehow our fault.

"Trust me, Captain," I said. "We're not pleased with the turn of events, either."

"I should hope not. You do realize we wanted to keep this murder quiet, don't you?"

"Captain," said Bishop. "I know this isn't what you want to hear, but this could've been worse. The individual who broke into Ms. Wen's apartment was clearly armed and dangerous. If Officer Jamison or his backup had been in the condo when they arrived, they could've been injured or killed. As it is, only the apartment suffered damage."

Captain Reyes took a deep breath and let it out slowly. "I know, Detective. I'm frustrated with the situation in general, is all. But it's hard to spin this as a win, for you, Drake, or me. While I know the two of you were doing your job reviewing the security feeds, the media will wonder why you hadn't been assigned to Wen's quarters. And who knows what excuse I'll give them as to why I didn't report Wen's death immediately."

I glanced toward the front door, where caution tape had been strung to create a barrier. It was more for the residents of the floor than anyone else. Our security detail at the elevators wasn't letting media representatives up, but they clogged the lobby nonetheless, waiting to swarm anyone who looked like they might have clout within the department. The blast and subsequent pressure loss from Wen's room had brought them to the building like moths to a flame.

"You can throw us under the vactrain if you want," I said. "I don't mind being reviled by the general public as long as it doesn't come with a cut in pay or a demotion."

"Just him, though," said Mwenge with a smile. "I've worked hard to build the adoration I've got."

Reyes shook her head. "I'll give them a version of the truth. You were both following orders. You won't get any flak from anyone if I can avoid it. Which isn't to say I won't skirt the journalists downstairs for as long as I can. At least the couches in this place aren't destroyed. I could nap on them if push comes to shove."

"Excuse me. Captain?" Detective Fields approached from down the hall. He was a wormy sort of man, with bad posture and an unhealthy pallor to his skin, but underneath the awkward exterior lay a sharp mind and a watchful pair of eyes. His black hair stuck to his forehead from the lingering heat in the bedroom, and soot covered his fingers.

"When are you going to learn to wear gloves, Fields?" I told him.

He frowned and sniffed. "In arson, we refer to gloves as swimming pools for your hands. I'll suffer the CSU team's ire over sweaty palms any day, Drake."

The Captain gave him a nod. "What do you have for us, Detective?"

"Not a ton," said Fields, "but that's the nature of the crime, as you well know. Fire and evidence aren't exactly best friends. What I can tell you is the fire in the bedroom burned hot and fast, and it expanded through the space rapidly. It was well on its way to destroying the mattress, carpet, and whatever evidence the two of those contained when the sprinklers activated. What I can also tell you is the fire in the office behaved the same way—as in it expanded in an almost identical manner to the one in the bedroom. That tells me the explosive wasn't home brewed. My guess based on the ferocity of the initial burst is the incendiary devices were military grade. I've found a few scraps so far that seem to validate that theory, but it'll take some lab work to be sure."

"And the charge that took out the window?" asked Reyes.

"Not really my area of expertise," said Fields. "Besides, that one didn't leave so much as a mark on the floor. I'd guess a compact directional charge. Could've been breached by high-velocity gunfire, too. You hear anything on the security feeds?"

"One sound, muffled amid the alarms," I said. "But it was there. The directional charge is the most likely explanation, I think. Those are common military gear, too."

"Anything else, Detective Fields?" asked Reyes.

"Not at the moment."

Reyes nodded, and he headed back toward the bedroom. The Captain eyed the panel that had been affixed over the broken window. "Run me through the events one more time, Detectives, including what you gathered from surveillance."

"I first spotted them on the display in the security room, ma'am," said Mwenge. "Drake and I rushed to the elevators. He kept an eye on the live feed while I tracked the intruder through building security using the elevator, lobby, and street cams. We still haven't been able to get a facial scan off the feeds. At the time we suspected use of a visor and glare enhancer. It wasn't until later that we realized the suspect was wearing a full pressure suit."

"And the suspect didn't leave Wen's apartment upon entering?"

"No, ma'am," I said.

"You mentioned you suspected the security system had been

hacked," said Reyes. "Is there any chance you missed the suspect's exit as a result of that?"

I shook my head. "The digital trail I found indicated the system had possibly been hacked, but it wasn't being tampered with any longer. I've double checked since. No further strange activity. What we saw on the feeds happened."

Reyes nodded toward the window. "Which leaves us with this."

"After looking at the feeds again, Drake and I believe the suspect could've been hiding a parachute under their coat. It was pretty bulky, after all."

"Do we have security feeds from the exterior of the building?" asked Reyes.

"Not this high up," I said. "No reason to have feeds above the Mylamene pressure layer, and they're all pointing down."

"No need until today, anyway," said Reyes. "So we can't track where the suspect might've landed?"

"I've put in a request with the department," said Mwenge. "They're going to see if our fire-bomber shows up on any public cameras in the wake of the blast. I think we'll have a better shot of tracking them along their journey in, though. I've put in a request for that feed analysis, too."

Reyes shook her head. "Christ. This is nuts. Are we really to believe someone broke in here, firebombed the remaining evidence, then parachuted out a window to safety?"

"It's plausible," I said. "Not as simple as on Earth, but the lower gravity here helps mitigate the lower drag on the chute, at least to a degree."

Bishop looked at me like I was crazy.

"We had ops during my time in the corps where we had to consider parachuting to safety from high altitude. What can I say? Information stays with me."

"So what's your intuition telling you?" asked Reyes. "Was this our killer? An associate? A rival? An unrelated party?"

I chewed the inside of my lip. "I'd be shocked if this were our killer. For one thing, the inherent stupidity of returning to the scene of the crime is at odds with the rest of the killer's modus operandi. Second, as I mentioned, the handling of the security systems was entirely different. The killer seems to have hacked the system to hide their entrance entirely, while the second intruder used a cruder, if equally effective, disguise. While I'll acknowledge it's possible the arsonist was hired by the killer to hide his or her tracks... well, I don't buy it. Honestly, I don't know what to make of this."

"Mwenge?"

My partner shrugged. "Sometimes my intuition comes through when Drake's doesn't. Not today."

Reyes sighed. "Very well. It's late. This place is a disaster. Both of you head home. We'll dive into this with the full force of the department behind us tomorrow."

"You going to be okay managing the vultures downstairs on your own?" I asked.

"I'll live," said Reyes. "Now scram, before I change my mind and sacrifice you to those jackals instead."

———

I CLOSED the door to my apartment before going to work on the buttons of my jacket. The department operated on the idea that the more buttons there were, the more formal the coat. I half worked my fingers to nubs, but eventually I shrugged out of the thing and hung it in my closet. I'd have to return it to its garment bag eventually, along with the slacks I wore, but I should have both cleaned and pressed first. Chances were I'd acquired a hint of

Wen's blood somewhere on the ensemble, even if I didn't know where.

I slipped off my shoes and headed toward the kitchen. I'd eaten before leaving for the graduation ceremony, but that had been around six. Now the clock read five after midnight. I didn't raid the fridge for a snack, though. Hunger wasn't the primary sensation I suffered from. Instead, I sifted through my liquor cabinet until I found a half-empty bottle of Callaghan and Sons bourbon. I didn't drink it often because of the cost—charred oaken barrels came at a premium on Mars, after all—but I felt tonight warranted a few drams. I poured two fingers of the caramel-colored liquid into a lowball glass and brought it with me to the couch.

I flicked the holodisplay in the corner on as I took a sip of the whiskey, turning the feed to the same channel I'd been watching in the rideshare earlier. As expected, the fifty-fourth story explosion on Goddard Street dominated the coverage. A reporter stood outside the building, blathering about possible causes of the explosion and the fire that preceded it. A long range shot taken from the upper stories of a nearby building showed the exterior of Wen's apartment, including the panel that had been affixed over the broken window. The reporter switched gears, describing the police response before cutting to the Captain's speech, which she'd apparently given moments ago.

She stood at the base of the elevators, a mass of humanity pressed in close around her. Reyes might as well have been giving a lecture to school children for all the nerves she showed. She answered only the questions she wanted to, giving minimal details on Wen's murder and the resulting torching of her quarters. Most notably, she neglected to tell the media the apartment had been breached a *second* time after the murder. She let everyone assume the second intrusion had been the only one. What a clever old fox.

I flicked the holo off and drained the last of my bourbon. I kept the glass in my lap, trailing a finger across the rim. Something gnawed at me. Not the Captain's speech. She'd kept her word, making no mention of Mwenge or me at all. Not Wen's murder, either, at least not the act itself. I'd seen grislier in my time. The way in which the murder had been concealed did irk me, though. Most murderers weren't skilled in hacking security systems, and they certainly weren't friends with fixers who had access to military grade explosives and concealed parachutes. But even that wasn't what dug at me.

It was Wen herself. She wasn't Phoebe. Her features, as similar as they were, didn't match. But they were close enough to have thrown me for a loop around Mars momentarily. And to have chanced upon such a woman on the eve of the twenty-fifth anniversary of the Red's attack on Earth, the day before I met Phoebe?

I shook my head as I set my glass down upon the coffee table. For once the source of my disquiet wasn't the detective's curse—the unwillingness to believe that any event, no matter how random, was a coincidence. Rather, it was the fact that Ms. Wen's murder had taken me back in time, transported me to another era.

An era I didn't particularly care to revisit.

MAY 12, 2154

WE LAUNCHED AT 0620, a few minutes later than planned due to high wind shear in the upper atmosphere. I'd lain there strapped into my bed, my legs tingling out of anticipation as much as fear. I knew the statistics. Launches were as safe as airplane flights, safer than rideshares, but logic and statistics didn't have any effect on my emotional response. My Net didn't either. I had no idea if it could.

The tingling intensified as I heard the roar of the engines and felt the acceleration push me into my bed. It wasn't too bad at first, as if a twenty kilo weight plate had been set on my chest. It grew as we increased in speed, peaking a minute and a half into the flight at three gs, or so my ship systems app indicated. I couldn't remember exactly how I'd felt during my trip to Shanghai—I think the USC rocket packed more of a punch—but the total force still paled to what I'd experienced on roller coasters at Cedar Point. Maybe that was why high-g centrifuge exercises hadn't been a part of our stage one training.

I was also surprised at how quickly the g forces evaporated. Booster separation occurred at two minutes and thirty seconds into launch, and though the ship's engines kept burning, piling speed onto our vessel, the g's melted away as soon as the booster stopped kicking us in the ass. Not only did the weight plates vanish, but so too did the pull of my own body. At the five minute mark, we received the all clear.

I unclipped and pushed myself out of my bunk—the top one, this time. Maarten had been assigned the one beneath me thanks to his greater mass. The micro gravity would've brought me to the floor eventually, but I pushed off the ceiling to speed the process up, thankful for the anti-nausea pills I'd taken prior to takeoff. Maarten had already unclipped from his bunk, too, floating toward the porthole in the side of our room, as were the other two guys who'd been assigned to the cabin: Ranbir and a tom I hadn't met until this morning, a broad-shouldered sunshine and surf type by the name of Chevy.

I joined them, bumping into Maarten from behind and pressing him further against the porthole. He grumbled and I muttered an apology, but we were both too consumed with the view to care. The Earth hung there amid a midnight backdrop, a floating blue marble swirled with white, misshapen not by gravity but by the sun's uneven illumination. Faint patches of brown shone through, muddied by the skies and shiftless clouds, without nearly as much green as expected.

I couldn't tear my eyes from it. I'd pored over dozens of photos and vids, gazed upon Earth through VR sims of actual launches, not just over the past two days, but growing up as a child, gazing to the stars and dreaming of adventure, but even the most realistic imitations couldn't compare to the real thing. I wasn't sure why. Perhaps the lack of gravity added a certain something to the experience, or perhaps my mind simply knew this time it was real, and that made all the difference.

I floated there, watching the Earth over Maarten's shoulder. Not a man from our cabin said a word. It was more than the grandeur of the sight that kept us silent, I think. Seeing the Earth hovering in space, feeling the loss of gravity slosh the breakfast in my stomach, hearing the roar of the engines and knowing there was absolutely nothing on the other side of the porthole, it didn't merely solidify the reality of our space flight. It solidified the reality of our commitment. In all likelihood, I wouldn't see the Earth again until the end of my deployment. I wouldn't feel cool, spongy grass underfoot, wouldn't taste a brisk spring breeze tinged with rain, wouldn't hear a bird's trill or marvel at a painted sunset for seven years. *God, what had I done?*

A crackle brought me out of my reverie, followed shortly by a voice on the PA system. "Attention. This is Captain Soto speaking. All recruits report immediately to the ship's assembly corridor for an important announcement."

I spun in mid air, planting my feet against the small of Maarten's back. He grunted as I pushed off. "Last one there's a rotten egg."

I flew toward the cabin door, which blinked open upon my approach. I hadn't gotten much of a chance to explore the Mark VII as I'd boarded and strapped into my bed in the wee hours of the morning, but I'd pored over the ship's blueprints the night before. The assembly corridor was in the middle of the vessel, an open cylindrical space that stretched from the storage compartments all the way to the observation deck at the ship's nose. In zero g or the microgravity of slow acceleration, it was the best way to traverse the ship's many levels.

I also couldn't exactly miss it. As I shot from my room, I nearly flew right into the middle of the corridor. Only thanks to my quick reflexes did I managed to grab onto a railing at the edge and swing myself back around to the thin walkway that surrounded it. At least I wasn't the only recruit to make a fool of myself in the microgravity. Maarten slammed into the railing with a clang as he and Ranbir fought to make it through our cabin door second, and at least three recruits from other cabins on my level squirted clean across the corridor after failing to find grips on their side.

On the levels above me, more young men and women struggled slowing themselves, all as a diminutive hispanic woman in a navy jumpsuit, one striped with white across the shoulders, floated down from the top. She intercepted one of the free-floating recruits, using her momentum to spin the young man toward the side, then kicked off him and rebounded off the corridor wall back into a slow decent, all with a practiced fluidity.

I heard her voice through the ship's speakers. "All right, every-one, get a grip. I know most of you've never experienced zero gravity before, but that doesn't mean you have to turn into flying rhinos the minute your stomachs lurch. USC picks you for your size, among other things, but that doesn't mean they want to use you as human missiles."

She turned in space as she descended through the corridor, taking measure of everyone assembled. "As you've undoubtedly surmised, I'm Captain Abigail Soto. Welcome to my ship, a Mark VII, serial number AGH859. I like to call her the *Sunbittern*, because I'm an amateur ornithologist and because—again—I'm the captain and I make the rules. But just because I'm the ship's captain doesn't mean I'm *your* captain. You're in the marines, now. You'll learn the difference. Which brings me to the first important point of this assembly—squad assignments. You'll be receiving those via Net."

On cue, I saw a popup with a new message. I opened it to check where I'd be assigned, all while Soto kept talking.

"Open the messages. Check your assignment. Afterwards, I'd encourage you to use your Net's search function to seek out the remaining members of your squad. You won't have any official duties together until we reach Luna in three days, but it would still behoove you to learn one another's names before you dive headfirst into training together. And no, I did not misspeak. It *will* take three days to reach Luna, not because the *Sunbittern* is an outdated piece of shit, but because USC doesn't rate expediting your voyage to Luna as worth the extra fuel. So sit back and relax. We'll be orbiting Earth for the next twenty-four hours until we receive a refuel from a methalox booster, then it'll be a slow cruise to Luna for the following forty-eight."

I received a message as Soto talked, the notification listing it as from M. Stanić. I opened it. *Hey hoss. What's your squad?*

Soto slowly descended past my level, talking about what we'd find on Luna once we landed. I typed back, trying to focus on the speech and Maarten's text at the same time and failing. *Zeta squad, Company C, 35th Battalion. You?*

I think we're all 35th Battalion, hoss, but yeah. Company C. Zeta Squad. How tight is that? Then a moment later. *Hey, Ranbir is with us, too. Just our luck, am I right?*

I couldn't tell if he was joking or not. After their fight over immersive gaming, Maarten seemed to have genuinely lost some respect for the guy.

I tried to refocus on Soto as she flew back up the corridor, having rebounded off the bottom level. "—which means for the next seventy-two hours you all find yourselves in possession of the most valuable commodity there is: free time. We have plenty of distractions to keep you busy—VR games, books, movies, exercise facilities—but I suggest you use your time wisely, by which I mean adapting to your new surroundings. Part of that is physical. By the time you launch for Mars, movement in zero g should come as second nature. Might as well start practicing now. As soon as I dismiss you, my fellow officers will set up the central corridor for microgravity dodgeball. Don't get me wrong. It's fun as hell, but it's also an exercise. Play to win, and it just might save your life down the line. Also, and I repeat, spend the time to get to know your fellow recruits. They're as much your surroundings as this ship, or Luna, or Mars. Hell, more so. They'll be around you when everything you ever knew is long gone, or at least you'd better hope they are. The alternative means you're on your own, in which case you'll soon be dead.

"On that cheerful note, let me leave you with a few final rules. Rule number one. No fighting, no exceptions. I mean it. Save your rage for the Reds, because if you don't, you'll wish you'd never set foot in a USC recruitment office. Learning how to sleep in a two cubic meter box will be the least of your worries when USC fines your family for every dime they're worth. As of two or three days ago, you're what the USC brass considers a *sunk cost,* but they'll sure as hell try to recoup that asset however necessary. Second rule. Keep it in your pants, regardless of what *it* is. I don't have time for that crap on my ship, and in case you're wondering how we'll know..."

A new message popped up in my vision. *Surprise. We'll know!*

"Finally, rule number three. Obey all additional directives from myself and First Officer Grossman. That's it. Enjoy yourselves, and good luck. Dismissed."

I STOOD in line at the bottom of the central corridor, gazing past the nets at the dodgeball game going on above me. Balls whipped back and forth, most of them without the same zip they had on Earth, probably due to the awkwardness of their casters more than anything gravity specific. Occasionally, one would bounce off the nets near my face, losing its momentum in the collision, but I wasn't particularly focused on the balls. I kept gazing into the levels above me, searching for a familiar face.

Phoebe Zhao. She'd been on the Zeta Squad list alongside me, Maarten, Ranbir, Janeece, and a number of other names I didn't recognize. I'd assumed our squads would've been picked from within our Titusville stage one training groups, but that wasn't the case. Certainly, I hadn't expected to find Phoebe's name on the list. I'd assumed she'd already left, rushed through the training faster than I had due to her Net familiarity. Either way, I'd be happy to have one more friendly face among my squad, especially one that was easier on the eyes than Maarten's.

"Next group. Move it along."

I blinked as the young woman near the front of the line waved me and a couple other folks forward. She wore the same USC jumpsuit as the rest of us, but she must not be a recruit, otherwise I couldn't imagine she would've volunteered for managing those in line.

She put out a hand as the first of us reached her. "That's it. You're all next. Familiar with dodgeball?"

I squinted at her. "Are you suggesting some people aren't?"

"I've gotta ask." She pointed toward the action. "Regular rules. Catch a ball, the thrower's out. Get hit, you're out. You can deflect attacks with a ball in hand. Mid court is marked with red flags around the perimeter of the corridor. Cross over, you're also out. We're using a continuous feed system for play. Keeps the game moving and gives everyone a chance. When you see someone leave through the side exits, hop on through. Got it?"

We all nodded.

"Good." The line manager pointed up. "There's one now. Go on in."

The first of our group hopped in and launched herself into the fray. I watched as she promptly got nailed on the crown of her head by a rival baller camping near the red flags. She cursed as she latched onto the netting and made her way toward the exits slits at the third level.

The guy in front of me had paid attention. When he launched he twisted his body, ready to grab a ball thrown by the camper. Unfortunately, that left him open to attack from another enemy diving across the corridor above. He took a ball to the gut as he drifted into the flags at mid court.

I'd put together a plan by the time the line manager waved me forward. I glanced at the jackals waiting for me above, but I didn't dive into the fray, nor did I jump toward my own team's remaining players who clung from the nets above, deflecting missiles with balls clutched in claw-like hands. Instead, I hovered near the bottom of the corridor, resting my feet against a railing underneath the nets.

The players on the other team jeered me, but that only proved my strategy was sound. They couldn't reliably hit me from so far away, not without exposing themselves to being caught. My problem was I needed a ball, and there weren't any near me at the base of the corridor.

A group of the other teams's players began to converge, which I took as a sure sign of conspiracy. I launched myself at an angle across the corridor, drawing fire from the camper by the flags.

Lucky for me, he didn't know I had the best hands on the WMU varsity basketball squad. I caught his throw with ease, spun in midair, and rebounded off another railing. Before the group who'd coalesced knew what was going on, I'd pelted one of them in the back with my newly requisitioned dart. That's when my fellow teammates on the walls decided it was worth going all out. A quartet of balls sailed toward the other team in unison.

It was a massacre. We would've taken all five of them if not for the fact the two furthest in back used their teammates as shields.

I grinned and chuckled to myself until I realized I was heading straight for mid court with nothing to slow me down. Thankfully, one of my teammates decided I was worth saving. He launched himself off the nets and caught me, carrying me into the barriers on the other side a few paces shy of the flags.

"Careful," he said as he disentangled.

I nodded, my eyes already on the trio of fresh meat coming through the opposing end of the corridor.

It didn't take as long to adapt to the zero gravity as I would've thought. I already knew how to control my body, how to place myself to take advantage of other people's position on a court. I simply had to adapt to the fact that I couldn't change trajectory in mid air. Once I realized zero gravity athletics was more of a physics problem than a game, more pool than dodgeball, I became a threat.

I spun. I landed and launched. I caught. I threw. I chucked balls to my teammates before taking out enemies with meticulously-timed chest passes. The other team's entrance became a turnstile, their players forced to take cover at the nets and sacrifice their new meat to the slaughter. My teammates cheered when I engineered another mass exodus, taking out four of five players in a little over ten seconds.

I felt unstoppable, a zero gravity god. I clutched a ball, clinging to a net like a gibbon as a new wave flowed into the court. I flung myself across the corridor, cocked back my arm as I took aim at...

"Phoebe?"

A full speed ball took me square in the face.

"SORRY AGAIN ABOUT YOUR NOSE," said Phoebe.

I held a cold pack over my nasal bone, waving her off with my free hand. "It's not your fault. You didn't even throw the ball. Besides, that's what the game's all about."

We sat on one of the bottom bunks in her cabin, the rest of her roommates having left to explore or play games or relish in the mess hall's unlimited refill policy on lemonade and iced tea. My nose radiated heat despite the ice, but I was sure nothing was broken. Worst case scenario, I'd look like I'd tipped back one too many drinks and sat out in the cold for the next day or two.

"I was watching you while I waited in line," said Phoebe. "You looked really good. I don't suppose you play dodgeball on a regular basis?"

I laughed. "No. Basketball. It has a similar skillset, though."

Phoebe smiled. "In some ways. I can't imagine a two-and-a-half meter tall center would do well somersaulting in zero g."

I tried to imagine our team's resident ball-swatter, Demarcus, doing flips while being pelted with red rubber balls. I couldn't help but laugh. "Yeah, you're right about that. You did pretty well yourself after I went out, though. You've got a nice whip to your arm. Softball?"

Phoebe shook her head. "Tennis. Played a little badminton, too."

"Badminton?"

She scowled playfully. "It's a real sport, gourd-face."

"I'm just messing with you." I pulled the compress off my face, letting the cold seep into my fingers. "It's cool we ended up assigned to the same squad, though. What are the odds?"

Phoebe lifted one of her already arched eyebrows. "We're on a ship with a capacity of two hundred. Given Captain Soto's speech, I have to assume we're assigned to this ship for a reason. Two hundred. Ten to a squad. So a five percent chance."

I tried not to smirk. "You're a math nerd, too. Don't worry, I'm a CSEE major."

Phoebe snorted. "Yeah. I divided two hundred by ten. I'm a real mathematics whiz."

"Don't lie. What were you studying before you enlisted?"

"Architecture."

"So you're *kind of* a math nerd."

"Not as much as you, apparently." She followed that up with another smile.

I heard the puff of the door and turned to find Maarten and Ranbir standing in the gap.

"There you are." Maarten curled his lip. "What the hell happened to your face?"

"I tried to get a whiff of space. Don't try it. Spontaneous decompression hurts like a mother."

Ranbir chuckled, but Maarten looked like he didn't get it. What he certainly got was the look of Phoebe. He smiled and extended a hand. "Hi, there. Maarten Stanić. You are?"

"Phoebe Zhao. You're on Zeta squad too, right?"

"Yeah. Been Ambrose's roommate since day one." Maarten gave me a sly smile. "Been making the rounds, hoss?"

"Phoebe and I met on the vactrain in," I said. "She's partially responsible for my nose."

"Please," she said. "If I was responsible, you wouldn't be able to breathe right now."

Maarten laughed, shaking the bunks in the room. "Hey, I like her. Anyone who takes pleasure in kicking your ass is all right with me."

Phoebe smiled, and I couldn't help but do the same. Not because I liked being the butt of the joke. More because I was starting to find Phoebe's smiles were infectious.

12

MAY 10, 2179

I SPOTTED Mwenge by the doors to the morgue, swimming in bright white artificial light, so I quickly finished the Net chat I'd been engaged in on my way there. *Sounds good. I'll see you tonight.*

Bishop smiled as I approached. "Tell me one of those is for me."

"One maché tea for the local," I said, handing him a cup. "One coffee for the stuck-in-his-ways Earther. Though I don't know why *I'm* the one grabbing the morning drinks. Whatever happened to seniority perks?"

"Oh, you mean those little things like job security, more generous vacation accrual, and better pay?" Bishop's smile widened.

"As if I ever take vacations."

"And whose fault is that?" Bishop sipped his tea and sighed. "Ah. That hits the spot."

I shook my head. "I'll never understand the maché addiction. It's fine, don't get me wrong. I just don't know why it's a thing."

"Umm... because it's good? Why do you drink coffee?"

"To keep me awake, mostly. Drinking something that grows on

trees makes me feel like less of an addict than popping caffeine pills."

Mwenge took another drink. "Seriously. Take a vacation. After we wrap this case up, of course. And after you find yourself a family. People enjoy vacations more once they have one of those."

"Your daughter's... what? Three? Young enough that she won't remember her old man after I choke him to death in a totally justified fit of rage." I nodded to the door. "Get moving."

We headed into the morgue, a sterile, metallic space with all the warmth of a midnight stargazing session in the Elysium Planitia—metaphorically of course. The actual temperature of the morgue hovered around eight degrees Celsius, with the cadaver vaults kept lower. Despite the persistent stereotype of Martians as frostbitten icicle huggers, I found the opposite to be true. Most of them craved warmth, being keenly aware of the excruciating pain and swift death bitter cold could bring.

Coroner Pham was an exception. She stood over an exam table in nothing more than a light sweater, swiping through the air in methodical strikes, a scalpel in hand. Wen lay on the table before her, a white sheet covering her to the neck.

"Good morning, Detectives," she said as we approached, her eyes distant and focused.

If I hadn't seen her go through the same motions before I might've thought she were crazy. Either that, or playing Net games on the job. "Morning, Trinh. Mind putting the scalpel down while you traverse your 3D models of the vic? One person with a severed jugular is enough, I think."

"*What?*" Her eyes focused on her hand. "Oh. Sorry. I forget I'm holding it sometimes."

"I can imagine the headlines now," said Mwenge. "Coroner accidentally disfigures fellow officer after forgetting to set scalpel down during briefing. Captain Reyes would be pissed."

"Don't mind him," I said. "He's hopped up on maché. What have you got for us?"

Pham eyed Mwenge with contempt as she set the scalpel down on a side table full of similarly wicked tools. "Good if perhaps unsurprising news, mostly. Ms. Wen died from blood loss resulting from her lacerated throat. The stab wounds covering her body appear to have been inflicted after the initial laceration, though only shortly thereafter. As far as bruising, I didn't see any that indicated to me Ms. Wen fought against her attacker. If you'd like, I can show you the—"

I put a hand to Pham's arm as she started to lift the white sheet, memories of Phoebe flashing through my mind. "We've got good imaginations. Your analysis will be enough."

"Not a problem." Pham replaced the sheet and proceeded to walk us through the murder as she'd pieced it together. Mostly, she drew a picture similar to the one I'd already presented, where the killer had hidden, sliced Wen's throat from behind, and staged her on the bed afterwards. Pham provided much more detail on the angle of attack and thrust pressure on the stab wounds, however.

Mwenge took another sip of his tea and nodded to the exam table. "So if we're in agreement the stab wounds happened post mortem and the victim was staged in her bed, are we thinking serial killer?"

"Serial literally refers to a *series* of actions," said Pham. "So unless the murderer strikes again with a similar MO, no, we're definitely *not* dealing with a serial killer. And while I'd normally say the multiple stab wounds suggest the killer is disturbed, I'm not so sure in this case."

"Why do you say that?" I asked.

"It's the placement of the wounds," said Pham. "They're methodical. Two to three incisions in each limb, with only the torso exhibiting more. That tells me the killer didn't inflict them in a bloodlust or a rage. They were placed there with intent—which perhaps suggests the murderer has a psychological makeup more akin to that of a serial killer, it's true. Or it could be whoever committed the crime wants us to think that."

"If they were smart enough to wipe the security computers of their presence, I wouldn't put misdirection past them," I said. "What about DNA? I'm assuming you've gotten the CSU samples by now."

"Theirs, and my own," said Pham. "And here's where I have better news for you. I got three hits. Wen's, obviously. A single unknown hair, golden brown in color. DNA indicates it belongs to a caucasian male. And finally, a third sample from inside the victim."

"*Inside?*" said Mwenge.

"You're a big boy, Detective. Don't make me spell it out for you. That particular sample comes with even better news, because it matches an existing DNA profile from USC's database. The semen belongs to one Victor Kuznyetsov, a senior space weapons engineer working at the United Space Corporation's research laboratory near the spaceport. I already took the liberty of looking him up."

"Anything we should know about him?"

"He's married. Not to Ms. Wen."

I snorted. "Of course not. I'm assuming you have his work address?"

My Net messages pinged. "There you go."

"Thanks, Trinh," said Mwenge. "Honestly, what did detectives do before the advent of modern forensic science?"

"Walked around, asked a lot of questions, and probably engaged in more than their fair share of illegal beatings." I nodded toward the door. "Come on. Time to catch a killer."

AS MWENGE and I stepped from our rideshare at the curb of USC's space research complex, I got a joint call from the department, which I promptly answered. "Dean. How are you doing this morning?"

Dean worked in technical services. When he'd first joined the department a decade ago we'd bonded over our love of computer architecture and all things digital. Sometimes I envied him. His job involved a lot more hours spent in front of a display and fewer spent staring at dead people. Then again, my position was the more impactful of the two.

His warm baritone sounded in my head. "Doing well, Detectives. Got a moment?"

Mwenge closed the door on the rideshare and the vehicle took off. "Sure. What's new?"

"I completed Detective Mwenge's request from last night using public security cameras," said Dean. "I was able to track the masked individual who broke into Wen's apartment to a subway station. From there, I followed her to the twenty-second street exit all the way back to a mixed use market residential building on Figueroa. I skimmed through the available security feeds on that building for the past week, but I didn't see anyone of her height or build exit at any point. Of course, the building doesn't have complete exterior coverage. It's possible she knew that and used it to her advantage."

"I'm sorry," said Mwenge. "She? *Her?*"

"It's an educated guess," said Dean. "I never got a look at the intruder's face due to the mask and glare enhancer, but I ran some numbers. Given height and build, minus the added bulk of the pressure suit, jacket, and parachute, my models spit out an eighty-two percent chance of the individual being a Martian female. I could run some gait analysis if you'd like."

"When you have a chance," I said. "What about checking security cameras further from that building looking for possible matches?"

"I'll get on it," said Dean. "Might take a bit, though. With an expanding radius and an indefinite scan period, my program will start chewing through computer power like gum."

"I know. Keep us updated, Dean."

He clicked off, and Mwenge and I headed into the research building. It was far more opulent than it needed to be, with a flight-used Mark VI fairing, Mark IV spaceship, and Mark III booster on display in the cavernous entryway. The booster in particular drew my attention due to its massive size, yet I knew from personal experience the booster on which I'd travelled to Mars dwarfed it, to say nothing of the ones in operation today. Perhaps there was something about seeing it on its side rather than stretching toward the stars that made it seem more gargantuan.

Bishop and I headed toward the elevators but stopped short of them, pausing at an automated kiosk. I pushed the help button and a holodisplay flicked to life. A pleasant, blue-eyed blond woman looked at me from amidst the hovering images and flashed me a smile. "Hello, and welcome to USC's Huygens Space Flight Research Center. My name is Emily. How may I help you?"

The woman on screen was almost certainly computer generated—why would anyone employ full time staff to man a help desk, after all?—but she looked and sounded as convincing as real flesh and blood. "Hi, Emily. I'm Detective Ambrose Drake with the EPD. We're looking for a senior USC weapons scientist by the name of Victor Kuznyetsov. Could you direct us to his lab or his office, wherever he might be?"

"Could you please confirm your identity on the touchpad below, Detective?"

I pressed my thumb into the reader. It blinked green.

"Thank you." Emily adopted a look of mild dismay. "I'm sorry, Detective but my records indicate Dr. Kuznyetsov didn't report to work this morning. Net data indicates he's not on campus at the moment."

"I see. And where does your Net data indicate he is, then?"

Emily smiled again. "I'm sorry, Detective, but divulging that information would constitute a breach of privacy under section seven, subsection three of the Martian regulatory practices compact. I'm sure you understand."

I glanced at Mwenge. "Bishop. Call Kuznyetsov's wife. Play dumb, but see if she's got a bead on him. Emily, one more thing if you could? Did Kuznyetsov report to work yesterday?"

"Yes, Detective, he did."

"And could you tell me when he left?"

"My records indicate he left the building at roughly five fifteen, Detective."

Plenty of time for him to visit Wen's apartment before her murder. "Thanks, Emily. That'll be all."

I turned to Mwenge and waited for him to finish his call. It didn't take long. He turned to me with a crook in his eyebrow. "For the record, Mrs. Kuznyetsov is now concerned about the where-abouts of her husband."

"Who she thought was at work?"

Mwenge nodded. "Precisely."

"Well, I think that's enough." I made a Net call to the Captain, including Mwenge on the line.

"Reyes," she said. "What can I do for you, Detective?"

"I need to put in a formal Net trace request for one Victor Kuznyetsov."

"Legal justification?"

"His DNA was found inside Wen's body. And he's not at work or at home."

I was on audio, not a facecall, but I could perfectly picture Reyes' satisfied smirk. "I'll fast track it with the justices. And I'll send backup so no one gets away this time."

THE APARTMENT DOOR BLEW INWARD. Mwenge and I surged inside amidst a half-dozen armed SWAT officers. Their cries rang inside the quarters. "Get down! Get down!"

The raid was over by the time I reached the living room. Officers darted into the apartment's branching hallways, rifles sweeping every corner, but the prize had already been found. Two of the SWAT team knelt before me, pressing a sandy-haired, bearded man into the floor as they cinched his wrists together behind his back. He gurgled as his cheeks pressed against the floor, his face easily recognizable from the USC database even in its squished state.

It was Victor Kuznyetsov—and I think he might've pissed his pants.

13

MAY 15, 2154

THE VOYAGE to Luna passed largely without incident. I spent much of the rest of the first day chatting with Ranbir—turned out he was a computer nut just like me, and had been as geeked to get his Net as I was—though I admit I tried to carve out as much alone time with Phoebe as I could. There was something incredibly relaxing about being in her presence. It could've been her soft smile or bright eyes, but I'd met plenty of girls who had those things in spades and drove me up the walls regardless. Rather, it was her personality. She seemed to utterly lack a flair for the dramatic, which made for a terrible actress but a great friend. On top of that, she shared most of my comedic inclinations—namely that sarcasm and dry wit topped slapstick and one-liners any day.

Together, along with Ranbir and Maarten, we explored the ship, though there wasn't much to see. For all the Captain's bluster, most of the entertainment options were Net enabled ones, with the exception of the electromagnetic workout equipment in the lower levels, which drew Maarten's attention immediately. We did spend a fair amount of time on the observation deck, gazing upon the clouded majesty of our home planet. I think Phoebe, Ranbir, and I would've wasted most of the afternoon there if not for the fact that securing window time was a blood sport. As the day waned, we went in search of the remaining members of our squad. We found three of them, Janeece included, though the tall track star seemed less than enthused to find out she'd be stuck with Maarten for the long haul.

She couldn't have found us any more inane than the rest of the folks aboard the *Sunbittern,* though, because on the second day she joined us on the dodgeball court in what turned out to be a show-case of epic dominance. Our team of five ended up getting kicked by the moderators after a half-hour without any outs. Maarten took credit for our superior performance, but the rest of us knew who the real brains behind our victory was, and surprisingly enough, it wasn't me. For all her experience playing singles tennis and badminton, Phoebe had flown around the court, shouting instruc-tions and strategies that helped us out of more than one jam.

It wasn't until the third day that anything pierced our bubble of isolation. As I'd been lazing on my bunk, sifting through the app directory on my Net, Ranbir had busted into our cabin, asking if we'd seen the latest newsfeed. Apparently, the Snow Leopard had released another video. I'd watched it, even though I didn't particularly want to. I was already committed to the fight, and to be quite honest, the rebellion leader's blood red visor and deep, modulated voice gave me the creeps—as it was intended to, I was sure. He—or she—didn't have much to add. The speech was more fire and brimstone stuff, threats of violence couched amid appeals to justice and humanity, but it was the following reports from Earth that were more disturbing. Apparently, government officials couldn't figure out how the Leopard and his separatist partisans had managed to nuke Los Angeles in the first place. Missile defense systems hadn't picked up a thing on the morning of the attack, meaning the Reds had either developed a superior level of stealth technology for their missiles or they'd managed to spread their influence to Earth, indoctrinating Americans and Chinese and Indians into their terrorist cells.

The nervous buzz didn't last, though, replaced instead by a nervous titter as we approached Luna. The moon grew in our field of view, from thirty-five arc minutes of sky in our geosynchronous orbit to a full degree, then two, then five. I couldn't have been the only one who didn't sleep well the last night of the trip, anxious over our arrival even though I shouldn't have been. We still had time for breakfast the morning of the landing before being ordered back into our bunks for our deceleration burn. As I lay there, staring at the ceiling of our cabin, hearing the rumble of the ship's engines as they kicked back into gear, it rankled me that I couldn't stand at our porthole and watch. The g's incurred during our descent to Luna paled to those we'd felt during takeoff from Earth. I could've easily stood there, taking it all in, but regulations were regulations. At least I had access to an external camera feed via Net.

If not for the cessation of the engines' muted roars, I might not have even known we'd landed. The weight of our descent evaporated, and in its place lingered a faint pull, the gravitational embrace of a small child. I couldn't say I welcomed it. After three days in zero gravity, I'd started to adapt to having to launch myself like a pinball, and now I'd have to adapt once again, learning how to hop like a kangaroo.

Not that our superiors gave us any time to learn. Net commands appeared in my field of view, and the ship's speakers flared to life, instructing us to file out, follow the signs to the ship's exits, and make our way to our assigned assembly areas. A minimap appeared, with an assembly room 3F highlighted. I followed the herd of enlistees to the bottom of the *Sunbittern's* personnel levels, out the airlock, and traversed the remaining thirty meters to the ground along a fireman's pole, though in the moon's lower gravity, I probably could've jumped the distance and been fine. I kept my eyes peeled as I descended through the vertical airlock tube, then as I walked through the halls toward 3F, hoping for a sight of the moon's rocky expanse, but not a single window presented itself. Steel ensconced me. I might as well have been two kilometers underground in a rhodium mine for all I knew, except nobody would've bothered insulating the tunnels of a rhodium mine with cellulose foam so thoroughly.

The herd thinned as I followed my map. Maarten was at my side, then Ranbir, too. The hall spit me into 3F, where Janeece had already arrived, as had someone else I hadn't met. Not one of the enlistees, that was certain. The man who stood at the front of the room was probably in his forties, with short brown hair, a few too many creases in his forehead, even more around his mouth and nose, and a pinched scowl that said he didn't care how many more he added to his collection.

My Net continued to blink at me, pointing me toward a spot at the front right of the room. I kept walking until an obtrusive *STOP* appeared. I looked around, wondering if I'd done it right, noticing that everyone else seemed to be struggling with the same system. Maarten stood behind me to my left, Ranbir even with me. More joined us, forming two lines. Lacking further instruction, I stood at attention, watching as Phoebe entered and took her place at the far end of my row.

As our tenth and final squad mate entered and took her place, the man at the front of the room scanned us and gave a curt nod. "Zeta Squad, Company C," he said without a trace of emotion. "Congratulations on surviving stage one of training and making it to Luna. My name is Sergeant Tyler. Did you all have a good trip? Enjoy the views of Earth, make some lasting friendships, and all that bullshit?"

Nobody said anything, though we did look to each other for help.

"I expect an answer, recruits."

We responded with a mixed chorus of "Yes, sirs" and "Yes, Sergeants."

Tyler's scowl deepened. "The correct response is yes, Drill Sergeant."

A few folks muttered it back, but Maarten figured it out right away, barking forth with a full bore, "Yes, Drill Sergeant!"

Tyler surprised me by holding up a hand. "Slow down there, recruit. Before going any further, let's straighten out a few facts. First, let's see a show of hands. How many of you have served before? Nobody? Didn't think so. And yet when you first laid eyes on me, you made a snap judgement, a judgement that solidified when I told you I'm your drill sergeant and I expect you to address me as such. You're expecting the worst, based on god knows what. Movies, books, video games, the stories your cousin Siddharth told you from when he served in the coast guard. Hell if I know. Well, forget all that. It's bullshit. Stories told to get a rise out of ignorant schmucks. Guess what? I'm not a caricature. Sure, I like to curse. I am crude, and a bit of an asshole. Maybe more than a bit. But I'm not a stereotype. I'm a human being, a real live individual. Believe it or not, I don't like to yell, or to be yelled at. The former gives me a sore throat, and the latter a headache. So when I ask for your affirmation, recruits, I expect you to respond in a firm, commanding voice. No more, no less. Am I clear?"

We all responded, more or less in unison. "Yes, Drill Sergeant."

He nodded and started to pace, a slow, deliberate gait that spoke to his familiarity with the gravity. "Good. Now, before I get to know you, it's important you learn a little about me. My first name is Lake. I was born in Battle Lake, Minnesota. My father took me ice fishing on lakes when I was a boy. Everything about my fucking life revolved around lakes until I joined the space corps twenty-one years ago. Make a joke about lakes and I will ride your ass so hard you'd wish your Mark VII had blown up on the pad back in Titusville, sending your body flying into a lake only for it to be eaten by a catfish. That's not a threat, merely a statement of fact.

"The second thing you should know about me is it's my job to get you through the second stage of your training. It's my job to prepare you for combat. Let me repeat that. It's my *job*. So if it seems to you that I'm being cruel, unfair, rude, or mean to you in any way, know it's nothing personal. It's not because I care about you in any way, shape, or form. Trust me, I *don't* care. Let me repeat that again, too. *I don't care about you.* Now, maybe you think that's an unnecessarily harsh thing to say, but it's a self-preservation technique. I train a lot of recruits, and after you leave, I'll never see you again. Beyond that, statistically speaking, thirty-five percent of you will die before you reach the end of your enlistment contract. Even more will be incapacitated in some way. And you're the lucky batch. Your numbers will be even higher. So it's in my own best interests not to care about you. But I do care about myself. I care about my job, and my reputation, and so I'm going to do the best damn job getting you ready for the shitstorm that awaits you as I can. Not that it'll matter.

"And *why* won't it matter? Because I usually get ten weeks to wean you pups into dogs of war. Not this time. To my great displeasure, I've been informed by my superiors that due to recent events which I'm sure you're all aware of, USC is *particularly motivated* to get you to Mars post haste. Which means your normal ten week program has been condensed into just *four weeks.*" Tyler snarled in what I think was supposed to be a smile. "Personally, I'm hoping your casualty rate doesn't creep past fifty, but only time will tell."

As the sergeant spoke, a void grew in the pit of my stomach. I'd known, at least academically, what I was getting into when I enlisted, but *fifty percent casualties?* He was joking, right? Or was he using casualties in the literal sense, including wounded and fatalities? Either way, it was enough to make my blood run cold.

Sergeant Tyler stopped pacing in the center of the room. "Now on that cheerful note, let's get down to brass tacks. Look around you. This is your squad. There are ten of you. There will not always be ten of you. If you lose members but retain your ability to function as a squad, you will do so. Should your squad lose enough members that your functionality is compromised, you'll be reassigned. For obvious reasons, you want to keep your squad at ten, the foremost being that if it isn't, someone is dead. Probably you. And the fewer people remain in your squad, the lower your chances of survival become. So your squad mate might be the biggest asshole you've ever met, but it's still in your own personal best interest to keep that son of a bitch alive. Am I understood?"

"Yes, Drill Sergeant."

"Good. You may be wondering why you've been assigned to Zeta Squad. It sure as shit isn't because I requested you. Computer algorithms put you here. As far as the servers in Titusville are concerned, you ten lucky schmucks collectively give your squad the best chance of survival, given the constraints of assigning another nineteen squads from the same pool, of course. If that makes it sound as if you bring different skills to the table, then congratulations. You're not dumb as a rock. Johnson? Sun? Mandel?"

Janeece and two of the other recruits, a tall asiatic boy and a lithe blonde girl, spoke up. "Yes, Drill Sergeant?"

"You all scored highly on track events. You're on the scout team. Franks? Stanić? Halabi?"

Maarten, along with two other young men I'd met on the *Sunbittern,* the brown haired, brown-eyed Franks, who hailed from rural Indiana, and Halabi, a broad-shouldered guy of Egyptian descent, responded. "Yes, Drill Sergeant?"

"Keep pounding the weights, boys. You're on heavy munitions. Gupta?"

Ranbir nodded. "Yes, Drill Sergeant?"

"You're the squad's tech expert." Gupta started to raise a hand. Tyler glared him down. "No questions. Maybe you're not an expert yet, but you will be. Same goes for the rest of you. Nakamoto?"

The recruit behind me, a relatively short Japanese girl with a pixie cut, spoke. "Yes, Drill Sergeant?"

"You're the field medic. That leaves—"

"Sir?" Nakamoto's voice squeaked. "I'm sorry, but I'm not a doctor. I'm not even—"

"What did I say about questions? Your packet says you were pre-med at Columbia. Is that incorrect? No? Then you're the field medic. Get used to it. Now, Drake?"

I straightened. "Yes, Drill Sergeant?"

"You scored highly on leadership, but not high enough. You're the squad's comms expert, and the deputy squad leader. Which leaves the last one. Zhao?"

Phoebe responded. "Yes, Drill Sergeant?"

"Congratulations. You made squad leader. Don't let it go to your head. The computers make mistakes sometimes. In the meantime, enjoy the hatred of your fellow squad mates."

Phoebe's face fell as Sergeant Tyler about-faced and headed toward a locker at the back of the room.

"Now that you have your assignments, let me introduce you to the final two members of your squad. All of you outrank them. You're smarter than they are. You're more adaptable, and yet you'd be absolute dog shit without them." Tyler opened the locker, grabbed a couple items, and turned. "Without further ado... the Suit, and the gun."

Sergeant Tyler set the white pressure suit on a desk to his side and held up the rifle, a compact gunmetal grey contraption with a barrel that couldn't have been longer than my forearm. "This is the Browning Defensive Automatic Suppressor, otherwise known as the Badass. Yes, it lives up to its nickname." He ejected the rifle's cartridge, worked the action, sighted the weapon along his shoulder before lowering it and slamming the cartridge back into place, talking the whole time. "Automatic and semi-automatic modes. Gas operated. Magazine fed with five-five-six forty-five millimeter cartridges. Net integrated laser sights. Yes, it can fire in vacuum. Yes, it can fire in finger-freezing cold. Yes, it will function in a dust storm so thick you can't tell your ass from your face, though I wouldn't recommend you fire in those conditions. If you're good enough, you can hit a speck of ice on a Red dust farmer's ass at five hundred meters. You're not that good, and you never will be, but it can be done. Learn it. Love it. Take it to bed with you. The Badass will save your life more times than you can count, even with your Net helping you keep track."

He set the gun on the desk and picked up the suit. "However, the Badass is a flighty bitch compared to this. Simply put, the Suit is your best friend. Look at it." He shook it out and ran a hand across the pristine white fabric broken up by hundreds of arcing black lines. "It may not look like much. It's not pretentious. It doesn't have a fancy nickname. It's just the Suit, but trust me, it'll be there for you when nothing else is. When a bullet tries to separate your spleen from your small intestine, the Suit's interwoven fibers will be there to transfer the force of the blow across your abdomen. When a vacuum tries to peel your flesh from your bones, the Suit's active compression bands will keep it in place. When you're stuck on the dark side of Luna or traversing the Martian poles, the Suit's five-ply insulation and resistive heating loops will keep you from freezing into a marinesicle. But the real innovation, your brothers from another mother that do the dirty work of keeping you alive, are back here."

Tyler flipped the Suit over and pointed to a rectangular pack built into the Suit's back. "Here, under the battery compartment, resides the heart and soul of the Suit: the Bacteria Buddy. Think you're tough? You can't hold a butane torch to these sons of bitches. Genetically engineered to survive near absolute zero, the bacteria in your Buddy breathe in when you breathe out. These little bastards love CO_2 even more than they love fucking, and trust me, getting it on is what they live for. Literally. Under the full spectrum light of the LEDs in the pack, they're constantly growing, multiplying, and croaking. When you're not around, they hibernate. When you're there, they feast. When you work up a sweat, it's orgy time."

Tyler dumped the Suit back on the desk. "Luckily for you, your Bacteria Buddy is also armored. It can take anything short of a twelve millimeter round and keep pooping out O_2. But don't take it or anything your Suit can do for granted. The Suit *can* catastrophically decompress. If it does, you die. It can't stop high velocity shrapnel or armor piercing rounds. You get hit by those, chances are you die. And if you fail to charge the battery on your back before it drops to zero? Guess what? You die. Do I make myself clear?"

Crystal, I thought, though like everyone else, I responded with a simple, "Yes, Drill Sergeant."

"Excellent," said Sergeant Tyler. "Now check your internal maps and report to the armory for Suit sizing as well as gun disassembly and reassembly training. Go on, move it. Christ knows we have little enough time as it is."

14

MAY 10, 2179

MWENGE OPENED the door to the interrogation room, and I followed him in. Victor Kuznyetsov sat at the bare metal table in the center of the room, sweating bullets despite the cool air. His eyes stretched wide as we took seats in front of him, his mouth slightly open, his breathing heavier than it should've been. He'd been sitting in the chair for the last half hour, yet he sounded as if he'd just finished a ten K.

I clasped my hands in my lap and took a good look at the man. He had casually wavy sandy-brown hair, the sort that might curl on a humid Earth day but never does on Mars. His beard was neatly trimmed, light enough in color to hide the smattering of gray it contained. His USC profile put him at forty-six years of age, just three years my senior, though he seemed older. Maybe it was the scent of fear that aged him.

"Well...?" he said after a moment. "Isn't anyone going to say anything? Surely I'm here for a reason. You must have questions, right? I mean... Please. Tell me something."

He didn't seem like the type who'd be hard to break. "Victor Kuznyetsov."

It wasn't a question, but Victor responded as if it were. "Yes.

That's me."

"Tell us about Shao Wen."

Victor swallowed hard. "Yes. Shao Wen. She's a... coworker of mine."

"A *coworker?*" I said.

"Yes, technically," said Victor. "I don't see her that often, mind you, what with me in space weapons research and her in water services, but we run into each other on rare occasion."

"And your relationship is purely *professional?*" asked Mwenge.

Victor wiped some sweat from his brow, his eyes as wide as ever. "Ah... What's this about, if you don't mind my asking?"

"Are you aware Ms. Wen's apartment was the target of a fire-bombing last night?" I asked.

Victor worked his mouth a few times before words finally spilled out. "Okay, look. I was at her apartment because I'd heard on the newsfeeds this morning about the explosion. I mean I was at her second apartment, the place where you found me. I've never been to her real apartment, but I know where it is. And the news-feeds didn't have any information on her, just the explosion. So I didn't know what was going on. I tried to call her but it didn't go through. What was I supposed to do? After all I was—"

I leaned forward and held out a hand. "Slow down. I need you to focus on *my* questions. Now, in a calm, coherent manner, tell us about your relationship with Ms. Wen."

Victor hung his head and pressed a hand to his forehead. "Is this going to leave this room?"

"We're not lawyers, Mr. Kuznyetsov," said Mwenge. "Whether or not this conversation becomes a matter of public record depends on whether or not you were a party to anything incriminating. Answer the question."

He sighed. "Shao and I were having an affair. Is that what you wanted to know?"

"It's what we already knew," I said.

Victor brightened. "So she told you about it? Well, why are you asking me? Look, whatever she's involved in that led to someone *blowing up her apartment,* I swear to you, I know nothing about it."

"She didn't tell us," I said. "Shao Wen is dead, Victor. We isolated your DNA via a cervical swab."

Victor leaned back in his chair, his face frozen. *"Oh my God.* Are you serious? She died in the explosion?"

"When was the last time you saw her?" asked Mwenge.

Kuznyetsov blinked. "Ah... three nights ago, at the apartment where you found me. We met there to, ah... you know. Look, you're not going to tell my wife and children about the affair, are you?"

I lifted a brow. "Mr. Kuznyetsov, *clearly* you value your relationship with your family highly, but perhaps the more pressing matter for you is the fact that your mistress has been murdered."

That pulled Victor out of his shock. "Hold on. You're not suggesting I *killed Shao* are you?"

"You were having an affair with her that you apparently wanted to keep quiet," said Mwenge. "Her apartment just exploded and you work in... what research field exactly? Space weaponry? That's a euphemism for missiles, right?"

Victor's face fell. *"What?* No no no. I swear to you, I had nothing to do with this. Look, Shao and I were having an affair, yes, but that's all it was. We met at a USC fundraiser about nine months ago. My wife had chosen not to come with me because... Well, because we'd already started to have marital troubles at that time. I met Wen. We talked. We drank. One thing led to another. We kept in touch after that. We'd see each other once a week, maybe a little less, for dinner, drinks, and the rest. There wasn't much to our relationship, if I'm being honest. It was mostly physical."

"The apartment where we found you," I said. "You said that's Wen's place."

"Yes. That's right."

"Why would you meet there rather than at her condo? Why did she have a second apartment at all? She wasn't married."

"I don't know," said Victor. "Married or not, I guess I always assumed there was someone else in her life. Someone she wanted to hide me from. Perhaps she was embarrassed to be seen with a married man. I couldn't say."

I drummed my fingers against my leg. "So why were you at her place this morning?"

"I told you, because I was concerned. I couldn't get ahold of her. After hearing about the explosion, I hoped that... I hoped..." He didn't have the strength to finish the thought.

"Mr. Kuznyetsov, it's in your best interest to be completely open and honest with us," said Bishop. "If there's anything you can share with us that can corroborate your story, now would be the time."

Victor shook his head. "I swear to you, I had *nothing* to do with this. Pull my Net logs. You'll see I haven't been anywhere near Shao's primary apartment. Not just recently. *Ever.* I don't know why anyone would want to bomb her place, but I swear to God, it wasn't me. I wouldn't even know how to prime an explosive. I work on targeting lasers, for God's sake!"

I glanced at Mwenge. He responded with a small shrug. "Alright, Mr. Kuznyetsov. Someone will be here shortly to process you. We'll be in touch if we have any more questions."

Victor looked baffled that he wasn't being immediately set free, but I didn't pay him much mind as I left the interrogation room.

Bishop closed the door behind us. "So. What do you think?"

I cocked an eyebrow at him. "Do you have to ask? I mean, do you really think *that guy* slit his girlfriend's throat and stabbed her a dozen times?"

"Some people have split personalities."

"We'll pull his Net records, like he suggested," I said. "I don't think he'll show up at Wen's apartment, though."

"That doesn't exonerate him," said Mwenge. "He could've paid someone to do the deed for him. Someone more *professional*."

"I suppose it's possible. But the guy seemed far more concerned his wife would find out about his infidelity than the fact his mistress had been murdered."

"It's a good cover."

I frowned. "Do you actually believe he's our guy, or are you playing devil's advocate?"

"More of the latter than the former," said Mwenge. "Still, we should take DNA samples from under his fingernails and run his closet under a blacklight. It also wouldn't hurt to pull his financial records alongside his Net logs. Just to make sure he hasn't paid any large sums to mysterious individuals on the dark web."

"Or to *two* individuals," I said. "Though I'm not sure why anyone would hire one person to commit a murder and another to burn away the evidence. Seems inefficient."

"Seems plain weird, if you ask me," said Mwenge. "But it happened nonetheless. Well, not necessarily that someone paid two different people to do it. More that the events occurred independently."

"Or so we assume," I said. "That reminds me. We should pull Wen's financials alongside Kuznyetsov's. As the Chief Administrative Officer of a major USC division, she probably could've afforded a spare apartment for trysts without any financial pain, but I find it odd she had a spare apartment at all. What was she trying to hide from Victor?"

"Another lover?" said Mwenge.

"Not one she was sexually active with on a regular basis, according to Trinh. But it wouldn't have had to be a person. Could've been other assets. Information. Don't forget the safe at Wen's apartment."

"With the tablet you still need to crack."

"I'll get on it as soon as we run out of suspects to catch. You remember Dean's call?"

Mwenge nodded. "I'll hail a rideshare."

I RAN the video of the masked assailant exiting the market building on Figueroa through my mind and compared it to the building in front of me. They matched.

"Looks like this is the place," I said to Mwenge. "I'm taking bets on what we'll find inside, if you're game."

Bishop rubbed his chin, which he kept smooth as a babe's. "I'm torn between a sex trafficking ring and an interplanetary law firm subsidiary that stonewalls us from the get go. What's the payout on each?"

"Much better on the sex trafficking ring. This doesn't look like the neighborhood." I gestured toward the building. "After you."

We headed inside and found an indoor market, more or less as Dean had indicated. Stalls lined each wall, with a row of tables and chairs taking up the center aisle. Delectable smells filled the air, from seared tilapia to roasted garlic, cilantro, cumin, sage, and bacon fat, all whirled together into a nearly indistinguishable aroma begging to be tasted. Oil sizzled and fat popped. People called out orders, and the rumble of conversation echoed through the space.

"I guess we were both wrong," I said.

"You never know," said Mwenge. "There could be lawyers hiding in the food court."

I approached the closest stall, which thankfully didn't have a line. I paused at the order kiosk and tried to get one of the line cook's attention. "Excuse me?"

Eventually one of the griddle monkeys looked up. "Kiosk is right there. We'll call out your order when it's ready."

I produced the shiny badge I kept in my pocket. "EPD. I've got some questions."

The cook snorted as he came to the counter, but it wasn't as if customers were piling up behind me. "Yeah?"

I put my badge away and pulled out my tablet. A holo burst to life from the projector built into the back. "This masked individual was caught on public feeds leaving the premises yesterday evening. Were you working here at the time?"

The cook didn't even bother looking at the timestamp. "If we're open, I'm here."

"Recognize the individual in the video?"

"Of course not. How would I know who that is?"

"I mean do you recall seeing them in the food court."

The cook shrugged. "People in pressure suits come through here all the time. We get a lot of maintenance and construction workers. Some don't even take their helmets off to eat, just flip up their visors."

I glanced toward the rafters. "You have internal security?"

"Sure. You'll have to talk to management for access, though."

"I'm happy to take a contact if you have one."

The cook provided one before huffing back to his post. I made a call while Mwenge wandered around, checking out the eateries. I had to navigate a few menus before I got hold of a real individual, but when I did they were more than willing to cooperate. They didn't hassle me for a warrant, simply asked for a digital signature to prove my status with the department. As soon as they sent me the access code, I was able to hone in on the security feed from the night before. Sure enough, I found our mysterious interloper traversing the floor and tracked her to an elevator in the service corridor behind the fast service restaurants. The residential floors above the market didn't seem to have hallway cameras, but there was one in the elevator itself. I zipped through the feed and zoomed in on the panel to see where the masked woman had entered.

I grunted. Bishop was close enough that he heard me. "Find anything?"

"Nothing I like. Come with me."

We headed through the back hallway to the service elevator. When it arrived, I walked in and punched the lower-most button.

Bishop cocked an eyebrow toward me. "She came in through the basement?"

"Nothing gets past you."

He grunted, suddenly on the same page I was.

The elevator dinged and spit us into an overcrowded storage facility. The room was old, with rough-hewn rock walls hidden behind a layer of Mylamene. Racks held shrink-wrapped packages of sesame seed buns, dry noodles, bottles of soy, five liter jugs of oil, and crates full of condiment packs. I made my way around the exterior, past a pair of heavy metal doors that were cold to the touch—freezer cold, not midnight in a Martian winter cold.

I paused at another door, this one older and more beat up than the freezer's. There was a spot for a padlock up high, but no one had secured it—or someone had unsecured it.

I grabbed the heavy handle and cranked it. The latch system creaked, and the door groaned as I pulled it inward.

A dark corridor stretched out in front of me. I swore.

So did Bishop. "Son of a bitch."

I initiated a group call with Mwenge to Captain Reyes. She answered right away. "Detective Drake. Speak of the devil."

"Captain, Mwenge and I are the last known location of the fire-bomber. We have a problem."

Reyes' voice sounded hot in my mind. "No shit we have a problem, Detective. Get your asses over here. *Now.*"

I grimaced. If Reyes was furious *before* she found out our suspect had accessed an unsecured entrance to Elysium's ancient underground tunnel system, I couldn't imagine what *she'd* come across.

15

MAY 16, 2154

MY INTERNAL ALARM woke me at whatever passed for 0600 hours on USC's Luna base. My hands twitched as I blinked away a dream, one in which I detached the barrel of my Badass, removed the slip ring and the hand guard, oiled the ring, cleaned the barrel, and reattached the hand guard before sliding the barrel back into the upper receiver, over and over and over again. Of course, it wasn't so much a dream as déjà vu. The cynical part of me wondered if my Net had been programmed to replay the experience in my subconscious as I'd slept, but I'd spent enough nights after marathon VR gaming sessions twitching in response to endless gameplay loops to know how my mind functioned in response to repetitive stimuli.

I heard Maarten creak in the bunk below me, and I checked my schedule. It instructed me to report immediately to the training facility's natatorium for morning exercise, so ignoring the faint rumbling in my belly, I slipped into my swim trunks, threw my jumpsuit over the top, and hopped to it—literally. As I'd quickly realized, a skipping gait was the most effective mode of transportation in the moon's one-sixth g, even if it did make me look like a giddy buffoon. At least everyone else used it, too, even the irritable, heavy lidded recruits wiping sleep from their eyes who I passed on my way to the pool.

Or rather, *pools*. Given the base designer's disdain for placing observation windows in the hallways, I'd started to think the entire USC base was nothing more than small rooms connected by a web of tunnels, but the natatorium was *huge*. As long as a football pitch and twice as wide, it contained a two by two square of fifty meter pools subdivided by bulkheads into twenty-five meter ones, all under a gaping arched roof lined with red and blue backstroke flags. I made my way to pool 3B, as per my Net instructions. I was supposed to swim twenty-five hundred meters of whichever stroke I desired, which I was fairly sure was a warmup to a real swimmer but seemed like a hell of a lot to me.

As I also discovered, swimming in low gravity wasn't particularly easier than swimming on Earth. By the thousand meter mark, I was sucking wind, and by the two thousand meter mark, I started to wonder how long it would take a USC official to question why the pallid corpse in lane six had stopped thrashing its arms. I gasped as I finally pulled myself to the deck after my last lap, feeling like a drowned rat. I crouched on one knee, filling my lungs with air as I willed away the burning sensation in my quads, all the while reminding myself to send a message to my former coaches urging them to add swim workouts to their arsenal. My former teammates would hate me for it.

A splash a few lanes to my right drew my attention. I turned to see Phoebe emerge from the pool like a mermaid from a lagoon, springing to her feet as if the swim had been nothing more than a light jog. She pulled the swim cap from her head and shook out her hair, letting it cascade down her back in a waterfall of glistening black. Her one-piece suit bared her legs and back and left little to the imagination everywhere else, hugging her body in a vice grip, showcasing her lean muscular arms, the swell of her breasts, and the toned curve of her bottom.

She turned her head to the side, squeezing the water from her hair, and spotted me. Apparently, my ogling didn't register as creepy, because she gave me a subtle wave. I waved back, which made her smile, but she didn't dawdle on the deck, instead heading toward the changing rooms. I didn't take it as a personal slight. We still had weights to worry about before our first scheduled activity at 0730, and I was highly motivated to make time for breakfast in there somewhere.

I SLIPPED into a chair right as my clock hit the half-hour mark, pleased that I'd managed to make up the time I'd lost figuring out how to tune the gym's electromagnetically-resistive squat rack en route to and from the mess hall. At least I'd beaten Maarten—not on the strength of my lifts, mind you. Only at eating my eggs, soy bacon, and hash faster.

The big guy slid into the seat behind me, huffing slightly from trying to catch me. He sent me a message. *Trying to make me look bad, hoss?*

Oh, I'm doing more than trying, I shot back, though truth be told, Maarten and I were the last ones into our seats. We'd both have to try a little harder to make anyone look bad.

A caramel-skinned instructor at the front of the room looked up, scanning her charcoal eyes across the seats. "Ah. Looks like you're all here. And on time, no less. Either Sergeant Tyler lucked out or he's already beaten his unique motivational wisdom into you. Knowing him, I think I know which."

The woman stood and clasped her hands lightly behind her back. She started to pace the aisle. "Welcome, then, to your first class of the day. I'm Dr. Chakrabati. Not corporal or sergeant or lieutenant. Just doctor. I'm a USC employee, but a civil one. As I'm sure Sergeant Tyler explained to you—or perhaps he didn't, given your condensed schedule—physical education, weapons training, and squad exercises are only part of your training regimen here at USC Luna. The biggest part, certainly, but not the only one. Learning how not to die *is* crucial, and in Sergeant Tyler you have a capable teacher of that particular skill, but at the same time, as soldiers it's critical you know what you're fighting for and why fighting for it is a virtue in and of itself. That's where I come in."

A display winked to life behind her, displaying a presentation title. *Mars: History, Geopolitics, and Economics.* Dr. Chakrabati waved at the screen with a hand as she paced. "As you can see, this particular class will be focused on providing you a focused history of Mars, from the landing of the first commercial human-bearing spacecrafts in 2028 to the founding global Martian charter signed in the city of Utopia in 2076 all the way to the emergence of the Red wave beginning around year 2147—and know that I don't use the term Red as an insult. As I hope you'll learn, there's a clear distinction between a separatist Red and a Martian. I'll help explain to you the role of government on Mars, the dichotomy between prominent city-states and the largely unconnected colonies in the Martian wastes. We'll discuss planet-wide development projects, from the earliest and most basic—the electromagnetic shield placed by early scientists at Mars's L1 Lagrangian point—to the more recent, including USC's roving CO_2 sublimation stations at the poles and the failed scientific core convection experiments that ultimately handed the Reds the H-bomb."

Dr. Chakrabati rounded on us, gazing into our midsts. "Before we begin, however, let me pose you a simple but important question. All of you are presumably here because you're enraged by the Red's act of war, by the mass genocide of your fellow man. But the Reds aren't insane. They act with purpose. So what *was* the purpose of their attack? What do they seek to gain because of it?"

One of our scout team raised his hand. Dr. Chakrabati pointed at him. "Yes? Sun?"

"To make us afraid?"

"That's a means of achieving their greater purpose. Which is...?"

"Independence?" offered Phoebe, raising her hand.

"Correct," said Chakrabati. "And as Americans, all of you, you've been ingrained with a great love for independence. Your history is one of breaking free from an oppressive foreign government. So what makes the actions of Red separatists distinct from those of the American founding fathers?"

"George Washington and Thomas Jefferson didn't nuke anyone, for one thing," said Maarten.

Dr. Chakrabati nodded. "The mass murder is a new wrinkle, yes. British colonial forces were the first to initiate violence against the nascent American colonials during the Boston Massacre of 1770, whereas Reds began their war of independence against us with the terrorist bombings of Isidis government buildings in 2151. So that's a fair point. But what I was after is that the American forefathers, the heroes of the revolution, sought a noble goal. Freedom of government. The Reds claim the same goal, with one obvious distinction. Mars is not the America of 1776. Mars is a cold, arid, desolate wasteland, habitable only through the blood, sweat, and dollars of generations of earthborn scientists, engineers, and visionaries. When the Reds propose independence, they do not hawk an ideal. They preach a communist takeover of all industry on Mars, a system to which they have no claim, simply because they cannot live without it. Their ideal of independence rests upon a foundation of theft, and *that* is the difference. When the Snow Leopard speaks about a free Mars, what he seeks is to pull the ladder up behind him, to close Mars off from those who dream of a new life simply because *his* ancestors were the first to arrive. The Red movement is one of selfishness and isolation, fueled by the smash and grab mentality of petty thugs. Never forget that."

Chakrabati's face hardened. "The only difference is, most thugs don't have nuclear weapons." She turned toward the display and advanced the presentation to the next page. "But let's not waste any more time with inevitabilities. You're aware of the threat. So let's learn what created it..."

AFTER DR. CHAKRABATI'S sobering pep-talk, our squad met back up with Sergeant Tyler, who expounded upon yesterday's lecture on all the various ways Mars could kill us. Whereas yesterday he provided an overview, today he delved into the luscious details. Frostbite. Hypothermia. Hypercapnia, otherwise known as carbon dioxide poisoning. Uncontrolled decompression. Hypoxia. He even described in gut-wrenching detail the effects of ebullism. As I was already well aware from high school physics, water boils at lower temperatures at lower pressure. As Sergeant Tyler described it, ebullism was when all of your bodily fluids boiled as a result of said low pressures, turning your body into a meat skin that held the internal pressure of those boiling fluids. As if it wasn't immediately obvious, Tyler also made sure to point out that, yes, ebullism would kill us.

That led to an hours long exercise where I donned and doffed my Suit at least three dozen times while a rotating cadre of squad mates monitored my procedure and took notes on how I could improve my times and minimize the risk of catching my Suit on my fingernails, nose, or dick. Under the command of Sergeant Tyler, I, of course, returned the favor. At the end of the exercise, I would've bet every dollar I had in my credit union back home that Tyler was a hundred percent certain we'd all die within the week, but he shuffled us along regardless so we could run through the same endless loop of Badass disassembly and reassembly steps we'd already done yesterday. Eventually he released us to attend specialized classes based on the squad specializations we'd each been assigned. Mine was on MindNet communications, which sounded appealing but just introduced me to the various voice, text, and video comm options available to us via Net. As I left the classroom, I held out hope future sessions would be more technical in nature.

Regardless, I was exhausted by the time I reached the chow hall. I loaded up my plate with as many sources of protein and vegetables as I could find and set out into the hall in search of a seat. Having been separated from my squad, I found myself in the odd position of not having Maarten pushing me towards the nearest table so he could fill his maw and have time for seconds. I was about to use my Net's location features when I spotted a familiar face.

I set my tray down on the table as I sat. "Hi, Phoebe."

She looked up from her food as I joined her, swallowing whatever was in her mouth. Lasagna, if her plate was any indication. "Hey, Ambrose."

Her plate didn't have more than a few bites left. "You almost done?"

She shot my a shy glance. "I wasn't about to leave, if that's what you were getting at. Believe it or not, I've only been here a couple minutes. Guess I was hungry."

"Yeah, I'm still trying to replenish the calories I burned during this morning's swim." I dug into what looked like a tube chicken marsala. "Speaking of which, you totally sandbagged me."

Phoebe's eyes narrowed. "How so?"

"You said you played tennis and badminton. You were definitely on a swim team growing up, too."

She shrugged. "They're all country club sports. Why? Don't tell me you thought the morning workout was *tough?*"

"Me? Nah. I sprawled across the deck after my swim like a squirrel in the summer heat because I needed a good stretch." That drew a smile from Phoebe's lips. I popped a piece of broccoli into my mouth. "So what was your best event?"

"The eight hundred."

I blew a raspberry. "Of course."

"What's that supposed to mean?"

"It explains how you're half fish. Plus you've got the body proportions to be a distance swimmer. Slimmer shoulders. Long legs. And, ah..."

I got another glare. "Yes?"

As much as I'd lovingly bathed her with my eyes as she'd left the pool, I wasn't sure I should admit to it. "You just seem the type, that's all. Persistent."

She rolled her eyes. "Right."

I sensed a smidge of hostility, so I changed the subject. "How was your squad leader training?"

She groaned and shook her head. "Don't ask."

"About as good as my communications class, then."

That drew her interest back. "You didn't like it?"

"I could've learned more playing around with my Net's system utilities for fifteen minutes. Heck, I *did* the first night I learned how to access them—thanks in part to you, I might add."

She brushed off the compliment. "You would've figured it out."

"I know. I still appreciate your help. So what didn't you like about your class?"

She averted her gaze again. "I don't know. It was fine, I guess..."

I gave her a moment, plowing through my meal while she gazed at the nearest table. "It's okay. You don't have to tell me. But I'm willing to listen if you'd like to talk about it."

She gazed into my eyes, and I melted a little. She seemed to chew on my words before taking a deliberate breath. "You said you played basketball, right? That you were a point guard?"

"That's right."

"You clearly did well on the leadership tests. Sergeant Tyler said so."

"Where are you going with this, Phoebe?"

She looked down at her now empty plate. "I'm struggling to understand why I was selected as squad leader. I told you, I never played any team sports. I was never on my school's leadership council, or took part in the young politicians groups. So why me?"

I chuckled. "You clearly didn't notice yourself during zero g dodgeball."

"What?"

I caught a hint of hurt in her voice, so I cut the humor. "Sorry. I'm not trying to minimize your feelings. But when we played dodgeball on the *Sunbittern,* I saw someone people naturally gravitated toward. Maarten, Ranbir, Janeece? They paid more attention to you than to me by the end of the match, and—I mean this in the nicest possible way—it wasn't because of your throwing arm. You have a natural magnetism. Could be that's the most important part of being a leader, at least in combat. Plus, you're compassionate. Look at how you treated me on the train. That's got to count for something in a combat scenario, to have a leader you can look up to and trust. Just give yourself a chance is all I'm saying."

Phoebe's pursed lips grew into a smile. She reached out and squeezed my hand. "Thanks, Ambrose. I appreciate that."

"No problem." I chuckled. "Besides, you'd better do a good job, because if I get promoted to squad leader, I want it to be because I smoked you, not by default."

She swung at me with an open hand, but I darted out of the way before she could hit me. "Jerk."

"A jerk with a silver tongue?"

She picked up her tray and stood. "More like a full of shit jerk."

I could tell she was playing. "A cute full of shit jerk?"

She started toward the tray return, but paused to shoot me a backward glance. "Maybe a little."

I watched her walk away, my eyes drinking her in. Despite her admission to being a distance swimmer, I could see why she hadn't pursed the sport long term. She simply wasn't streamlined enough, a fact which didn't bother me in the least.

16

MAY 10, 2179

MWENGE and I sat down in the conference room outside the Captain's office. Dean closed the door behind us, and someone activated the tint feature on the exterior windows.

Reyes stood by the holodisplay in the corner. It flickered to life beside her, showing a navigation screen. "Have you seen this yet?"

"Have we seen what yet, Captain?" I asked.

She snorted. "I guess it's good you're not wasting time watching newsfeeds on the job. I'd tell you to sit down but you already are. Ready?"

"For the unknown? Never. But go ahead."

The holo flicked over to an image of a windowless room, one with a white sheet draped across the back wall. An individual stood in the center of the display, one wearing a white pressure suit and a visor with an eerie blood-red tint.

My mouth fell open, and I felt a twitch in my cheek. "It can't be..."

The Snow Leopard spoke in the same low-pitched, modulated rasp I remembered so well from twenty-five years ago. "My fellow Martians. I stand at the lip of a precipice. Perhaps you don't see it, but the chasm looms large. It yawns before us all, growing larger every day. It manifests as surging unemployment. Rising inflation. The looming specter of trade wars with Earth. Government corruption. Police overreach. The iron grip of heartless USC trillionaires living in their private cities, separated from us by tens of millions of kilometers of frozen vacuum, but separated even more so by a lack of understanding of our culture, our ways, our needs and hopes and dreams.

"Look around you. Do you see the chasm now? I do. I'm quite familiar with it. For thirty years, my feet have dangled over the edge, as have yours. For years the precipice shrank, but no more. The actions of our governments, our bloated institutions, and most importantly of USC widen the chasm by the minute. That, my friends, is why I have returned. In many ways I never left. Mars is my home, same as yours, but I wish more for her than to be raped by avaricious conquistadors from afar. So I implore you, my brothers and sisters. Be ready. The moment will soon come when you are called upon to aid in the fight. To free Mars.

"But to the rest of you. The sycophants, the co-conspirators, the government oppressors, the corrupt elite. Know we are coming for you. Yours will be the first to be evicted from our frozen home, cast into the eternal abyss. Perhaps you do not believe me. Perhaps you think the years have softened the Snow Leopard's bite. I assure they have not, but you need not take my word. I offer you evidence."

I blinked in confusion as the video switched to one of Wen's apartment. It swiveled around her bedroom, sweeping across the bloodied carpets and splattered walls, before coming to rest on her savaged corpse. The Snow Leopard spoke as the camera zoomed on her head and neck, the slice through her neck as eerie in the three-dimensional display as it had been in real life. "This is Shao Wen. A corrupt USC administrator who profited off the backs of Mars's hopeful youth, exploiting Mars's bounty and taking it as her own. Her avarice was spectacular, but not abnormal. She is but one of many, and many will fall alongside her. *Soon.*"

The holo flicked back to the Snow Leopard. He leaned toward the camera, and his modulated voice deepened. "Stay ready, my friends. The time for action approaches."

The holo vanished, turned off by Captain Reyes in all likelihood. She looked at me, her face frozen into a scowl. "Are you okay, Detective?"

My heart beat heavily in my chest. My head swirled with half-thoughts, all of them clouded by more immediate emotions. "That... can't be. The video. Where...?"

"It's all over the web," said Reyes. "Was uploaded about an hour ago. That's why I was surprised you and Detective Mwenge hadn't heard about it."

"Where did it come from?"

"That's a good question." Dean quit hiding, emerging from his spot by the door. "I've spent the better part of the last hour trying to track it, *trying* being the operative word. Whoever uploaded this thing knew what they were doing. As far as I can tell, they bounced it off at least two dozen servers on their way to the file sharing system they ultimately dumped it into. It's been copied thousands of times since, but as far as the original source? I traced it to a public library terminal in Hellas Basin's New Chennai settlement. Captain Reyes has already contacted local PD. They're on their way to confiscate the computer system, but if you ask me, it's a wild goose chase. A good hacker could've uploaded the file anywhere along the dozens of servers it pinged off on its way to the dump. Even if we isolate which server it was, that won't tell us where the drop actually occurred. Chances are someone uploaded it to an unsecured server via tablet without anyone being the wiser. If it were me, I'd have put that tablet in an incinerator hours ago."

"All of which means it'll be virtually impossible to figure out who's responsible for the video, at least through digital signatures," said Reyes. "But that's not my primary concern at the moment. The *content* of the video is far more worrisome. We'll get to the implications of Wen's death being included in the feed, but first things first. You served in the corps during the uprising, Detective Drake. I didn't, but I kept track of the political situation at the time. I paid close attention to the Snow Leopard's videos, same as you. I have my suspicions, but I want your opinion. Is the individual in that video the Snow Leopard?"

"You mean is it the same Snow Leopard from during the uprising?"

"Yes."

I took a deep breath to still my nerves. "Honestly? I don't know. As you're well aware, the Snow Leopard was never caught. Individuals were killed and arrested, any number of which *could've* been the Snow Leopard, but there was never enough evidence to prove beyond a shadow of a doubt any of them had been behind his operation. If you're simply looking for my opinion... I'd say it's possible. I haven't seen any of those videos in a very long time—I rather wish I'd hadn't seen *that* one, to be honest—but from what I remember of his size, height, manner of speech? Yeah, it could've been him. Not that it's hard to impersonate someone who never shows their face or uses their real voice."

Mwenge hadn't said a word. He lifted a hand gingerly. "Excuse me, Captain? I'm not the expert either of you are so perhaps my opinion doesn't mean as much, but does it really matter whether this is the same Snow Leopard or not? Whoever is responsible for this video clearly has similar goals in mind and is willing to use similar methods. If that's the case... Well, it's concerning either way, Captain."

"It is, Detective," said Reyes. "And in the grand sense, you're right. It doesn't matter. What does is what the public makes of it. If they *believe* this is the same Snow Leopard. If they're frustrated enough, desperate enough, scared enough to be moved by his rhetoric, they'll follow him, impostor or not. But if push comes to shove, I'd rather be dealing with a copycat than the real deal."

I shot a finger at the silent holoprojector, still trying to wrap my head around what I'd seen. "Can we take a moment to talk about the second half of that video? The part where he shows a feed taken in the immediate wake of Shao Wen's death?"

Captain Reyes sighed. "Trust me, Detective, this case was already a public relations disaster following the firebombing last night. Now it's a full-fledged nightmare. I'd led the media to believe the arson and explosives had been the whole of it, but the cat's out of the bag now. Again, it'll be my responsibility to handle them. Yours is to solve the murder. And priority number one is determining who took that video."

"You mean uncovering who the Snow Leopard is," said Mwenge.

I shook my head. "Not necessarily. The Snow Leopard, whoever he might be, almost certainly didn't commit Wen's murder. The bigger question is whether he's responsible. Either he ordered a subordinate to do it, hired a mercenary to do the job, or possibly, wasn't involved in her death at all."

"Explain," said Captain Reyes.

I ran a hand through my hair. My blood pressure had finally started to equalize. "This is guesswork, so take it as such, but its odd to me the first Snow Leopard video that's surfaced since the end of the uprising includes snuff footage. Think about it. We haven't seen hide nor hair of this guy in almost two decades and here he is, murdering a USC official? Why?"

"Are you suggesting this is a set up?" said Reyes.

"No," I said, shaking my head. "Just that it might be opportunistic. What if someone has compromising information on Wen? The sort of thing the Snow Leopard alluded to. Deep corruption. Someone doesn't like it, so they eliminate her, but instead of letting the murder stand, they offer the compromising information on the dark web for a price. The Snow Leopard finds it. Pays a premium for a feed of the deed. It could be he simply surveyed the current political climate, saw an opening, and took a shot."

"Just so we're clear then, Detective," said Reyes. "It's your professional opinion that the Snow Leopard—the individual we saw in the video—was not directly responsible for Shao Wen's murder?"

An image of the blood red visor flashed in my mind. "I can virtually guarantee it."

Reyes nodded. "Good."

"*Good?*" said Mwenge. "Am I missing something?"

"It's good because it would mean we're not directly dealing with the individual who single-handedly led Mars into interplanetary war two and a half decades ago," said Reyes. "But more importantly, it's good because it keeps the two of you on the case."

I blinked. "I'm sorry, Captain. Did we do something wrong?"

"Not at all, Detective. However, about five minutes before you arrived I received a call from USC's counterterrorism task force. They're taking ownership of the case, at least to the extent they can. We can't go after the Snow Leopard. That's not our job, and it's almost certainly a task that extends out of our jurisdiction. But we do have a duty to bring Shao Wen's killer to justice. As long as it's not the Snow Leopard, or whoever we saw in that video, I figure we're good to proceed."

I balked at the mention of a counterterrorism task force, but I suppose it made sense. If any version of the Snow Leopard really was on the loose... I almost didn't want to finish the thought. "Good to hear, Captain. However, on that note, Mwenge and I have news regarding last night's firebomber."

"I hope it's something good, Detective. I've about had enough bad tidings for one morning."

I cleared my throat. "In that case, I'll let Mwenge tell you."

17

MAY 21, 2154

THE NEXT FEW days passed in a blur of classes, weapon drills, Suit usage prep, firing range practice, squad trust building exercises, virtual reality combat sims, and good old fashioned sweat-inducing cardiovascular exercise. Our weight and calisthenic routines varied, but the swimming remained a staple of our diet. In fact, it got worse. Every day, the powers that be added an additional hundred meters to our pool workouts. I figured it would have to stop at some point, from a time standpoint if nothing else, but I assumed Sergeant Tyler would simply pivot by forcing us to swim a harder stroke or by strapping a weight belt around our midsections. My muscles screamed at me every morning when I woke up, more so than I would've expected given that I'd already engaged in a rigorous strength and conditioning program in college and that we'd shifted to a low gravity environment, but I couldn't argue with the pain of microtears re-knitting themselves in my legs. Whatever we were doing was working.

Our activities took a less mind-numbing turn when Sergeant Tyler informed us we were ready for obstacle training in a 'benign simulated environment,' which basically meant we'd be fully suited, with our masks and Bacteria Buddies in place but still performing exercises indoors, where should the shit hit the fan and some moron vented his helmet accidentally, we wouldn't die before we were supposed to. As Tyler told us time and time again, we *would* die, but it would be a tragedy for his resume and reputation if we were to do so before we left his charge.

The actual obstacle training turned out to be enjoyable. Tyler split us into two teams, one led by Phoebe and the other by me, before cutting us loose with little explanation into the giant warehouse that served as the course home. The obstacles themselves were self-explanatory, from barbed wire crawls that didn't feature barbed wire—wouldn't want to ruin the expensive Suits—to monkey bars, cargo net climbs, and wall jumps, though the latter were massive to account for the moon's low gravity. The course ended with us carrying a massive, fifteen hundred kilo, three meter long sandbag up, over, and through a variety of hills, ditches, walls, and tunnels. That part wasn't so fun, even in the low gravity, though I was pleased at the end to learn my team of Ranbir, Janeece, Halabi, Nakamoto, and myself beat Phoebe's squad by a clean twelve seconds.

Having been pleased with our performance, or at least confident none of us were going to shred our Suits on a sharp corner or jab a rock through a faceplate, Sergeant Tyler escalated the exercise the following day. He ordered us to suit up and meet him at test airlock 3G. When we arrived, we found him in his own Suit, standing inside the lock holding a Badass. A stack of ten of them rested against the wall to his right.

"Fall in, recruits." He held up the rifle. "Tell me. What do I hold in my hand?"

"A Badass, Drill Sergeant," we all replied.

"Wrong," he said. "What I hold in my hands is a *simulation* Badass, made to look and feel exactly like the real thing in all respects but one. You can't kill someone with it, at least not by firing it. I suppose if you were determined enough you could bash someone's skull to pulp with the butt, but I'm hoping even you idiots aren't dumb enough to try that. See this?" He tapped the rifle's magazine. "There are no bullets here. This is a compressed CO_2 cartridge, the cycling of which will accurately simulate the recoil on a real Badass." He flipped the rifle, pointing it toward us. "And even if there were cartridges in the magazine, you still wouldn't be able to fire it. The muzzles of these practice rifles have been sealed, filled with steel and capped with a high lumen LED to simulate the muzzle flash of a real discharge. Nonetheless, you will treat these practice rifles with the same caution, care, and respect that you would a real Badass."

He stepped to the side, setting the rifle alongside the others as he jerked a thumb at the airlock. "What we have behind me is a live environment, active training scenario, a series of secure corridors and rooms designed to simulate what you might walk into when tracking down a Red threat in a subterranean Martian environment. It is in vacuum. It is cold. It is dark. You will respect these threats if you value your life. Nonetheless, there are no real enemies, only holograms. You will not die. You will not be shot." He grinned. "Though I can't guarantee you won't feel as if you were. To make this exercise as realistic as possible, your Nets will be tied into the sim. That means that should a simulated enemy hit you with a simulated bullet, you will feel as if you've been hit by the real thing. Don't worry, though. These Red bastards are only firing simulated nine millimeter rounds. With your Suit's impact resistant weave, a direct shot to the chest shouldn't even slow your breathing. Now grab a replica Badass, lock your visors into place, and fall into two columns. Squad leader and deputy leaders at the helm. I'll be leading you through the exercise this first time."

We grabbed our rifles, secured our face masks, and fell in behind Tyler. The airlock doors opened, and we marched through. I heard the clank of them closing behind us, followed by the whoosh of air being evacuated from the chamber.

Tyler's voice sounded in the middle of my brain. "Net communications only from now on. Make sure your voice, text, and video apps are set to squad only settings. No distractions." The lights went out. "Activate Badass and helmet lights."

I activated both of them via Net, pulling the squad vitals app open into one corner of my vision while minimizing the chat app to the other. Standing there in the dark, even knowing I was about to walk into a simulation, I felt my heart beat harder in my chest and saw the resulting boost in my heart rate and blood pressure on the vitals screen. I rearranged the grip on my Badass, took a deep breath to slow my nerves, and glanced at my side toward Phoebe. In the darkness, her visor appeared black and indifferent.

"On my lead," said Tyler. "Zhao. You'll lead your four along the left side of the engagement area. Drake. Do the same with the four behind you but to the right. I'll instruct you as we go. Ready?" The doors opened silently in front of us. "Move out."

I crept forward, following Sergeant Tyler along the right side of a dark, dirty passageway, scanning my Badass across the corridor in front of me looking for threats. Between the light of my rifle, helmet, and those of everyone behind me, the hallway was awash in concentrated beams, flowing back and forth like spotlights at a choreographed show. My Suit clung to my body, the active compression lines hugging my flesh, but apart from the silence around me and the faintest of chills, I couldn't have told we'd entered a vacuum. My heart continued to hammer, and I felt a bead of sweat form at my temple before being wicked away by the Suit's humidity controls.

We reached an intersection without incident. "Activate infrared sensors," said Tyler. "We're close. Zhao, take your team left. Drake, yours right. Remember, our enemies are armed and dangerous. Stay in cover. Shoot to kill." He waved us forward.

I crept around a corner into a room with a ceiling of carved rock. A newsfeed flickered across a section of wall that had been polished smooth, flashing images of the devastation of LA alongside a still image of the Snow Leopard. Couches pointed toward the display, ratty, threadbare things that belonged in a college student's basement. Food wrappers, tufts of synthetic down, and ammunition shells littered the floor. Rifles and handguns lay piled atop steel crates. Two black holes yawned in the far wall on either side of the display, hiding dark secrets in their midsts.

My visor illuminated a figure in red, seated, muddled by the cloth and padding of the couch. They started to rise at our entrance, alerted by our lights. I saw the flash of a blood red visor as they started to turn.

If it was a hologram, it was a damn good one.

"Open fire!" yelled Tyler.

I cut loose with a short burst. The Badass tapped into my shoulder three times in quick succession, the muzzle flashing in the darkness. Around me, my squad mates' rifles did the same, but in the vacuum, I couldn't hear a thing.

The Red went down, his body jerking under a hail of bullets. I glanced back toward the hallway, wondering if Tyler had followed us in and how Phoebe was faring on her side when the lights flickered to life above me.

"Take cover!" shouted Tyler.

I didn't think, merely did as I was told, diving to the floor behind one of the moth-eaten couches. Maarten slammed into me, knocking me in the shoulder with part of his rifle. I felt a thump in my chest, then saw cushions flying through the air above me, trailing puffs of synthetic down. Ranbir and Hao Sun dove behind a metal crate while Sergeant Tyler poked the muzzle of his rifle over the couch opposite us, firing away. Nakamoto, caught in the open, dove for Tyler's couch but tripped on air. She fell to the ground, clutching her leg. Her scream carried through the Net chat.

"Damnit, open fire!" cried Tyler. "Engage! Engage!"

I whipped my visor toward the previously darkened hallways, spotting heat signatures deep within the corridors. I sent Maarten a frantic message. *Take right. Now!*

I popped my rifle over the edge of the couch and opened fire. The butt worked my shoulder, pounding away at me at five times the speed of my hammering heart. My teeth shook as I fired, Nakamoto's pained cries cutting through me like a knife.

Enemies poured from the hallways, three, four, five, all going down under our onslaught. Sergeant Tyler waved us forward, screaming at Gupta and Sun to cover Nakamoto. I lurched forward, my legs refusing to work properly as I took cover at the corner of the hall. Tyler provided suppressive fire then shouted me forth. Whether by the force of his yelling or a lopsided fight or flight reaction, I dove in when he told me. My mind screamed at me not to, despite the logical safety of the simulation. The lights flickered and cut out again, but I used my IR visor to pinpoint more enemies, shooting at them regardless of what obstacles might be in my way.

With Maarten at my side, we pushed around another corner into a second darkened room, diving behind a stack of supply crates. Heat signatures stirred across the black-as-night expanse. I poked my rifle out to fire, but stopped with my finger on the trigger as I saw the names of Phoebe and my fellow squad mates superimposed upon the outlines.

The lights flared back to life as Phoebe's team poured into the room from the other side. Sergeant Tyler walked past us, followed by Ranbir and Sun helping Nakamoto hobble along on one leg.

I checked my Net clock. A minute and a half had elapsed. *A minute and a half.*

Tyler scanned the room, nodding. "Decent work. Drake. Only one casualty on your side. Zhao. I kept an eye on your feed as you went through your side of the course. No injuries. You were slow on the trigger—all of you—and your decision making was sluggish. Not great, but I've seen worse first runs."

Maarten and I joined the rest of the squad in the center of the room. Sergeant Tyler gave Nakamoto a nod. "How do you feel?"

"Like hell," she said. "My leg feels like it's broken."

"It'll go away as soon as we exit the simulation," said Tyler. "Speaking of which—you may have extinguished the Red threat, but the simulation isn't over. Now we get to run it in reverse."

Someone on the Net chat groaned. "Seriously?"

"It gets better," said Tyler. "Think Nakamoto has it bad? As it turns out, the enemy lured you into a trap. Let's see how you really perform under pressure."

The lights cut out again, and I felt two massive explosions of pain, one in my right shoulder and another in my left leg, above the knee. My squad mates cried out and hit the floor around me, their vitals spiking same as mine.

Tyler's scream rattled around my head. "Get up! Up! To the extraction point! Fire! Fire!"

It was the worst four minutes of my life.

I SAT in a sofa chair in one of the base's rec rooms. Maarten sat in the chair opposite me, while Phoebe and Janeece sat on either side.

Maarten knuckled his thigh, working his fingers deep into the tissue. "That was some bullshit."

Janeece finished sipping her low-alcohol beer—the one amenity we'd been provided after our simulated brush with death. "Finally we agree on something."

"I mean, was that even legal?" said Maarten. "Not the training exercise. We've got to practice combat scenarios, I get that, but the bit where every single one of us went down with multiple gunshot wounds at the *exact same time*. That wasn't a simulation. It wasn't even plausible. That was straight up Net manipulation to cause us pain and suffering."

Phoebe sniffed as she put her empty beer glass on the table at her side. "I'm guessing you didn't read the fine print of our enlistment contract."

Maarten snorted. "Are you kidding? That thing was like a hundred pages long. Don't tell me you did?"

"Not at the time I signed, no," said Phoebe. "But I've pored over it since. You wouldn't imagine the rights we forked over when we put our prints to the page. USC has full control over our Net architecture for the entire seven years of our contract. They control the information in and out, and they have a fair amount of leeway with subliminal Net activated processes, too. I mean, everything they're doing so far seems to be in our best interests, but... there's certainly a potential for abuse."

"Subliminal Net activated processes?" I said.

"Yeah," said Phoebe. "You know. Like with the nightly muscular activation? It's meant to combat the effects of low gravity. There's only so much exercise can do to fight it."

I wanted to slap myself. "Christ. So that's why my muscles have been so sore each morning?"

Phoebe nodded. "USC's been zapping them nightly. I learned about it in my leadership course." She recoiled under the combined force of our glares. "Hey. Don't give me that. I didn't know we were going to get fake shot today, if that's what you're thinking."

I shook my head. "I don't get it, though. Why simulate the experience of being shot at all?"

Maarten looked at me with furrowed brows. "Uh... cause we might get shot, hoss."

"That's not what I mean," I said, leaning forward in my chair. "If the Net can simulate pain, it can block it as well. If USC wanted, they could make it so we'd never feel we got shot in the first place—in a real, live fire environment, that is."

"Seems like that could be dangerous," said Janeece. "Pain is useful. It tells you when you've got a problem. Take that away and you could die on your feet without ever knowing something was wrong."

"You could still deliver the information without the actual pain," I said. "That's why we have the vitals app."

"You're thinking about this wrong," said Phoebe. "USC tests us under pain because they can't guarantee they'll be able to prevent it in a combat scenario. As complex as it is, the Net functions under an OS like any other computer. There are glitches. Lapses in wireless communication. Not to mention it can be hacked. I mean, that's why you're taking those cyber communications courses, isn't it?"

I blinked. We'd broached the subject of cyber attacks in my class, but for some reason I'd never fully realized the possibility of a directed Net attack. Given what Phoebe had mentioned about subliminal Net activated processes...

"Hold on," I said. "Can you kill someone via Net? I mean, could you use a Net to force someone to stop breathing or to stop their heart?"

Phoebe shook her head. "Thankfully, no. Even if someone could bypass the Net's root failsafes that make it turn off when it suspects vital systems are compromised, the Net can only access the outer portions of the brain, the cerebrum and to a lesser extent the cerebellum. The body's involuntary functions are controlled by the brain stem and limbic system, so I don't think you have to worry about Net-inflicted heart attacks. Same goes for the hypothalamus. That's why the Net can't be used to mitigate thirst, hunger, fatigue, to mess with your body temperature, or to modify hormone production. Although it would be nice if it could do that last part. Would make birth control easier and periods a lot more pleasant."

"Amen, girl," said Janeece with a tip of her glass.

Maarten scowled at the turn in the conversation. Normally I would've wanted no part of it either—except that I was pretty sure Phoebe winked at me as she mentioned the last part about her birth control. Suddenly, my aching shoulder and leg felt a lot better, and it had nothing to do with the solitary beer I'd drunk.

18

MAY 10, 2179

I LEANED back in my chair, the bustle of our thirty-second floor office moving around me as if in slow motion. I kept replaying the Snow Leopard's video in my mind—not via Net but involuntarily, a result of the obsessive, over-analytical portions of my brain.

I couldn't believe it. The Martian uprising had ended almost nineteen years ago. Nineteen years had passed since USC forces had raided the Red camp I'd been held in and released me. Nineteen years since the Snow Leopard had shown his face—or not, given his opaque helmet. I'd kept a watchful eye on the darker portions of the cyberscape in the interim, prowled in chatrooms and sniffed around the edges of conspiratorial gathering spaces, not for my job but out of curiosity, self-preservation, and need. I served as a homicide detective now. Captain Reyes was my superior, but it was the people of Mars to whom I bent a knee. I served a higher calling: to ensure the continued progress of a peaceful, prosperous, and safe Mars. Catching killers was one part of that, but murderers could be responsible for handfuls of deaths. Generals and reactionaries could murder millions. So I'd kept sniffing, knowing that USC believed the Snow Leopard had never been caught. In those nineteen years, I'd kept my eyes peeled, because I had no other choice.

Yet suddenly, here he was. It didn't make any sense. If the Snow Leopard's forces had been planning something, there would've been signs. Signals. Digital traces. Murmurs. Hints of activity. Maybe not signs I would've noticed, but others would've. The people's whose jobs it was to keep track of that sort of thing, and right or not, legal or extralegal, I kept track of the people who did the watching. The Snow Leopard simply hadn't resurfaced —until now.

It couldn't be the same organization that stood behind him. The Reds had fallen apart in the wake of USC's final push at the end of the war, crumbling into a misfit group of rebels and spies that rarely stepped out of the shadows. They still existed, but they didn't have the resources or interest to reveal themselves to the world, so far as I knew. So who'd resurrected the Leopard? Was their goal as simple as the one the Leopard had stated in the video, or was it a front? Misdirection intended to cover an ulterior purpose? And, most importantly to me and my fellow officers, what did Wen's murder have to do with it all?

"Ambrose?"

I looked up. Bishop had snuck up on me, assuming it was possible to sneak up on a person by walking up to them and standing smack dab in their field of view. Dean stood at his elbow, a cup of steaming liquid between his fingers.

Bishop held out a cup for me. "Dean and I figured we'd replenish our reserves. Need a perk?"

"Sure. Thanks." I accepted the cup and took a sip. It was a good brew, genetically engineered to thrive in the underground farms of Mars. There were still those naturalists who preferred heirloom species to modern variants, citing undetectable health concerns to mask their superstitions. They were the same folks who pined for the days when chickens were packed into cages, covered in their own filth, force fed corn slathered in pesticides before being slaughtered, plucked, and mechanically separated, because somehow that was *safer* than growing chicken protein with a fixed fat content in a vat. Me, I'd take a good cup of flavor-tailored coffee and a vat burger over the alternative any day.

"So," said Dean. "Hell of a morning, huh?"

"That doesn't even come close to covering it." I set my coffee down on my desk.

"On the bright side, the Captain took the news about the fire-bomber well," said Mwenge.

"Hard to make a shit sandwich any worse," I said. "Besides, it's not a dead end. We can comb through the city's public security feeds from the hours before the suspect entered the tunnels. It'll take a ton of computer power, but we might get lucky and find something." I glanced at Dean as I said the last part.

"Right," he said. "I'll put in a request for processor time. Should get moved to the front of the queue. Probably would've been fast-tracked even before that video hit the web."

"You really don't think there's any chance of tracking the upload?" said Bishop. "Even if it did lead us to nothing more than a burner tablet, that would give us one more avenue to pursue."

"I'll try, Detective, but I'm not promising anything," said Dean. "If the combined might of USC wasn't able to identify the Snow Leopard through a decade plus of warfare or in the twenty years since, I don't think one computer jockey is going to turn the tide."

"Don't sell yourself short, Dean," I said. "You're no slouch. You're almost as good in the digital realm as I am."

"Maybe not *as* good, but certainly more diligent. Speaking of which, I have a few things for you."

I lifted an eyebrow. "Seriously? I thought you spent the last hour tracking the Snow Leopard video."

Dean smiled. "As I said. *Diligent.* The first item probably won't be that useful to you. I skimmed the access history off Ms. Wen's door lock. Looks like the person who murdered her broke into her apartment the same way the firebomber did—using a wireless cracker off a tablet. Single entry. Timestamp was five thirty-five. An hour and change before Ms. Wen's Net stopped transmitting."

"Is there any way to track the tablet through the cracker app used?" asked Mwenge.

Dean shook his head. "Swing and a miss."

"You said there was something else?" I asked.

"Shao Wen's financials," said Dean. "I've got them available. They're... *expansive,* to say the least. Looks like Ms. Wen was loaded and had her fingers in a lot of different pies, including some that look less reputable than others."

"How so?" I asked.

"Well, I noticed Ms. Wen was receiving large, regular dividends from a company by the name of Red Summit Financial. I tried to gather data on them, and while they do have an online presence, it's a thin as can be. A landing page lists their address and a call number and that's it. No testimonials, no about this company page, no lists of partners, references. Nothing. That made me suspicious, so I plugged Red Summit Financial into our database to see if we had anything on them, and sure enough, I got a hit. Turns out they've been investigated previously by the fraud division."

"Who was the lead on the case?" I asked.

"Detective Zaira Arroz."

"You talk to her yet?"

Dean shot a finger my way. "That's your job, not mine."

I glanced at Mwenge. "Ready?"

"I could use some lunch, but I won't perish." He drained his cup and tossed it in the recycling bin next to my desk. "Lead the way."

Together, Mwenge and I headed to the elevators. Dean left us, taking the stairs down to his office on the twenty-ninth, while Bishop and I zipped up to the fraud offices on the thirty-fifth. I used the department's floor map to guide me, weaving my way through desks on the way to Detective Arroz's.

I found her sitting at her station, navigating spreadsheets on her holodisplay. Zaira Arroz had skin the color of milk chocolate and frizzy black hair that cupped her head. I knew I'd met her before, but I couldn't for the life of me remember when. Probably a training exercise or an intramural weekend volleyball tournament or something.

"Excuse me?" I said. "Detective Arroz?"

She looked up and blanked the holo. "Hi, there. Detective... Drake. And Mwenge. From homicide, correct?"

Her voice hitched in the manner of someone quickly confirming an identity via Net. I didn't hold it against her. A lot of people worked at the station. "That's right. We were hoping you might be able to help us out."

"How's that?"

"The victim in the case we're investigating. She's been getting distributions from an entity by the name of Red Summit Financial. We understand you've investigated them previously?"

Zaira's eyebrows lifted. "Red Summit. I haven't heard that name in a while. You mind if I bring up the case file?"

"By all means."

The holo burst back to life. Zaira's eyes focused on the images, flipping through menus before a case document filled the projection.

Zaira nodded to herself as she scrolled through it. "Yes, that's right. It's coming back to me now. The case first came into the department through the property crimes division. A business owner came to us claiming members he believed belonged to the Silicon Road gang had approached him demanding protection money. He refused. Roughly a week later his storefront was vandalized and his property stolen. The gang returned, and made the same offer. The store owner told them he'd pay, but instead he came to us."

"What does this have to do with Red Summit Financial?" asked Mwenge.

"They're the institution he was directed to pay up to," said Arroz. "Property crimes investigated the vandalism case, but the gang didn't strike again, so they left the case unsolved. That's when they passed it off to me with instructions to investigate Red Summit."

"And what did you find?" I asked.

"Not enough," said Zaira. "I mean, it's a front, obviously. That much is clear from running an online search and glancing at the business's listed address. But I wasn't able to prove a connection between the attack on the store owner's property and the company."

"So that was the end of it?" asked Mwenge.

"More or less," said Zaira. "We didn't have enough evidence to prosecute. Heck, we didn't even have enough evidence to get a warrant to pull their bank statements. All I had to go on was their tax records, and yeah, those were shady as hell if you ask me. So I forwarded them to revenue services and told them to take a look, but as far as I know the request's been held up in audit limbo for the past year. Maybe they don't have enough evidence to prosecute Red Summit Financial, either."

I grunted. "Well, that was less useful than I was hoping."

Zaira shrugged. "Sorry, Detective. I'd be happy to forward you the case file if it might help."

"Sure. Thanks for your time, Detective Arroz."

I headed with Mwenge back to the elevators. "Well... One more piece to a larger puzzle, I guess. Too bad it's not an edge piece. Those ones are always more useful."

Mwenge blindsided me. "Do you know Detective Kellerman?"

I blinked. "Who?"

Mwenge looked distracted. "Kellerman, in narcotics. He works on Silicon Road gang cases all the time. I seem to recall him telling me he had an informant in the gang once."

"Name doesn't ring a bell," I said, "but I assume the property crime detectives involved in the store front vandalism must've checked with organized crime and narcotics to see if they had any leads."

"I'm sure they did, but informants are limited resources. You don't waste them on vandalism cases. Murder, on the other hand..."

"You seem to know Kellerman. Want to handle it?"

"Sure. But order me some lunch. I'm starving."

I SAT AT MY DESK, rewinding through footage from the nearest public security cameras to Red Summit Financial's office building, a skinny single tenant structure with a single entrance, as far as I could tell. Holos were easier on the eyes than solid displays, but I nonetheless felt a bit of tension building in my temples.

I checked the time. Almost six. No wonder. I'd been at it for hours—and without anything to hang my hat on after the effort, either. I'd tripped over a few false positives, to be sure. A member of sanitation services had approached the door, as well as a religious proselytizer, a bum who'd spent half an evening on the doorstep, and one briefcase-toting individual who'd knocked on the door, waited, and ultimately left. I'd run his face through a scan and gotten nothing, but I'd tabbed it for safekeeping. However, nobody—not one person—had actually entered or exited the building, and I was approaching a week's worth of feeds surveyed.

I told myself I'd give it another fifteen minutes before I called it quits, but just as I made the promise, I struck gold. At dusk six days past, someone zipped across the street in reverse and disappeared through the door. I paused the holo, reset the speed, and ran it forward this time. The tom exited the building, at a normal pace this time. A young man, skinny with short hair. He looked around before heading off down the street. I snapped an image of his face and sent it to the database for scanning. He walked out of the field of view, so I switched to another camera angle as I waited for the results to come back.

As he walked, another someone popped out of the shadow of a building and started off after him. I hadn't spotted it in the first zoomed in feed, but the action was too deliberate to miss, not to mention too coincidental with the exit of someone from Red Summit Financial. I paused the video and zoomed on the new individual, but the image quality wasn't good enough. I flipped the feeds around looking for one that would give me a closer shot. It took me a moment, but I found a shot of the tail as he was still in waiting, one with a good view of his face.

I paused, my eyes frozen on the image before me. I think I spoke in a whisper. *"What the hell...?"*

"Ambrose."

I wiped the paused image with a mental flick as Mwenge approached. He gave me a nod. "How's the feed trawling going?"

I forced my face into a calm mask. "It's as thrilling as ever." A popup showed in my holo's menus. The facial scan had returned. I opened it and forced a smile.

"What have you got?" asked Mwenge.

"Good news, that's what." I put the scan up on half the holo. Then I selected the feed of Red Summit's exterior and rewound it to the moment of the suspect's exit, being careful not to include any of the angles that showed the presence of his tail.

"We've got a hit." I pointed to the scan. "Mark Paul Boothe. As you can see from the scan, he's a known Silicon Road gang associate. And here he is exiting Red Summit Financial six days ago."

Mwenge clapped me on the shoulder. "Nice. We were starting to run low on suspects."

"Well, I wouldn't call him a suspect. More of a person of interest, at this point. Speaking of which, any word from the informant?"

Mwenge shook his head. "That's the problem with folks who aren't Net connected. It's easy for them to avoid your communications. We'll just have to wait and see when he responds. Back to Boothe, though. You want to try and rouse him?"

I glanced at the clock. "Sorry, pal. I'm running late as it is. Tomorrow morning?"

Mwenge snorted. *"You're* running late? For what? Do you have a racketball court reservation you didn't tell me about?"

I killed my holo and stood, frowning as I pulled my jacket off the back of my chair. "Not all of us have happy families to go back to every night, Bishop. Doesn't mean we sit around waiting for death to take us. I'll see you tomorrow. Give me a call if you hear anything that can't wait."

19

JUNE 1, 2154

THEY SAY PRACTICE MAKES PERFECT, but after a couple weeks of training, I'd started to think all it did was reduce the magnitude of the shitshow. Despite our hours spent in the active training environments, our squad's performance never seemed to rise above adequate, mostly because Sergeant Tyler kept finding new and creative ways to screw with us. Thankfully, he never again ambushed us with partisans who materialized out of thin air with guns in hand, but he did expose us to any number of other deadly scenarios. In one scout mission, our environment underwent a rapid decompression. In another, simulated civilians pulled arms on us as soon as we turned our backs. Tyler even went so far as to randomly deactivate various of our Net and Suit functions, from nerfing our infrared visor overlays to garbling our chat systems. That last one resulted in a sixty percent casualty rate for our squad in what Tyler gently referred to as a 'ham blasting.' An entire day of non-verbal communications training followed.

The jacking of our comms systems led me to put more of my preciously limited free time digging into how exactly our Net sent and received wireless signals. At least my communications course had finally picked up, showing us which apps and systems utilities to use to detect and hopefully deflect malicious incoming signals. Unfortunately, the class stopped short of delving into the code for said utilities, hence my creative late night spelunking efforts. As I figured it, if Reds launched a cyber attack at us in the field, they wouldn't bother playing by the rules.

Eventually, we graduated to a point where Sergeant Tyler felt comfortable releasing us outside the evacuated testing chambers and into the cold, unforgiving arms of Luna itself. Not that our activities changed much once freed from the base's pressurized embrace. We still took part in squad exercises, obstacle races, and simulated raids in chambers drilled into the moon rocks underneath our feet, but at least the surface activities had the added bonus of finally providing us a view of Earth.

About two and a half weeks after our first arrival, Sergeant Tyler assembled us in one of the base's transport hangars. He stood in front of a beast of a vehicle, twice my height with honeycomb lattice non-pneumatic tires as big as my outstretched arms.

"Everyone? Meet the Marauder. Five thousand kilos when empty. Remote operated mounted guns. Armor plated, with a seven gigawatt hour battery and a twelve hundred kilometer range, even in loose regolith. Active shielding technology to keep your asses cool under a barrage of directed energy fire. If the Suit is your first line of defense against dying a horrible death on Mars, then the Marauder is your second. Now, some of you may already be familiar with this beast—" Tyler nodded in the general direction of Maarten and Halabi, who'd received driving lessons as part of their heavy munitions courses. "—but for the rest of you, you're finally going to experience the majesty of this fine stallion for yourselves. Suits on, grab your replica Badasses, and mount up. Today you're testing your skills in the field."

We changed into our Suits, boarded the Marauder through the ramp at the back, and took our seats along the benches on either side of its belly. Maarten and Halabi took the helm, though they didn't have to do anything at first. After we'd finished boarding, the garage cycled, the doors split open, and the Marauder rolled away toward our destination, its engine purring with quiet restraint. Sergeant Tyler had stayed behind, but he joined us via a display at the front of the vehicle.

"I hope you've been paying attention, recruits," he said, "because in today's exercise you'll need everything you've learned to come out on top. That's because, for once, you won't be going up against holograms. You'll be tackling none other than Company C's own Epsilon squad."

That sent a murmur through the cabin.

"That's right," continued Tyler. "We're about to see how you adapt to an unscripted encounter, to an opponent who can think for themselves. Right now your Marauder is taking you past the edge of the Mare Nubium into the shot to hell regions beyond. This is a surface exercise, but visibility will be limited once you hit the craters. Once you arrive at your designated drop off, you're to disembark and find the enemy by any method at your disposal. They'll have been dropped off within fifteen kilometers from your location, but where exactly is privileged information. The rules for engagement are simple. You may use your replica Badasses, which once again have been tied to your Nets for gunshot wound simulation, though for the purposes of this exercise, once you've been neutralized by the opponent, your Net will stop torturing you and you'll be marked as a non-combatant. The rest is up to you. Treat Epsilon squad as an enemy and exterminate them. Good luck, and don't fuck this up."

Tyler ended the communication, leaving us to figure out how exactly we were supposed to locate and neutralize Epsilon squad without knowing where to find them. After putting our heads together, Phoebe and I came up with a two-pronged plan of attack that seemed as good as any. Our scout team members, each of them with another squad mate for backup, would head out from our landing site on the ridge between the Delandres and Walther craters, one pair each to the south, east, and northwest. Phoebe would hang back with Ranbir to explore the immediate area, while I'd stay in the Marauder with Maarten trying to coax the vehicle's sensors into catching a hint of Epsilon team's chatter. I didn't have a lot of confidence in my chances, mostly because we checked the Marauder's comm logs on our way to the Walther ridge and found nothing but signals originating at the home base, suggesting Tyler and Epsilon squad's drill sergeant had other plans in mind for the exercise, but Phoebe talked me up, telling me if anyone could sniff out of their Marauder's radar arrays it was me. She also batted her eyelashes at me, so how could I say no?

Our Marauder parked, the back gate dropped, and everyone except for me and Maarten hopped out. For what it was worth, I don't think Maarten appreciated being left behind.

After a few minutes of drumming his fingers on the control in front of him, casting me impatient glances through his visor, I heard his voice through Net chat. "Give it to me straight, hoss. Is this actually going to get us anywhere?"

I checked the app to make sure he was on a private channel, not the squad one. "I haven't struck gold yet, but it's worth a shot. If I can catch any of Epsilon squad's communications, we can triangulate their location and ambush them."

"Kind of a big if."

"Admittedly, I'm not having any luck, yet. Whoever's in control of the Marauder seems to have locked us out. Apparently, they want us to find the other team the old fashioned way."

"So, let's move out, then," said Maarten.

I heard some chatter in my ear, the scout teams checking in on the squad channel. "Can't. Phoebe gave us orders."

Maarten blew a raspberry. "You'd do anything she asked you to."

"She's our squad leader. We're in an active combat scenario. You're damned right I would."

He lifted an eyebrow. "That's not what I meant, and you know it."

I double checked the channel privacy again as I tried to finagle my way into the Marauder's locked systems. "So I like her. What of it? Not like you don't have your eyes on a squad mate."

He snorted, through the action didn't sound right coming through my Net. "Me?"

"I've seen the way you look at Janeece."

"*Janeece?* She hates me, if you haven't noticed."

I cocked my head. "Doesn't mean you feel the same way about her, big fella."

Phoebe cut in on the general channel. "Ambrose? Any luck?"

"Negative," I said. "The Marauder's giving me the cold shoulder. I'm still trying to crack my way in, but I'm not hopeful."

"Keep at it," said Phoebe. "We need an advantage, because right now—hold on. What happened to Sun and Franks?"

I glanced at the vitals app. Only eight names were listed. "What the...? Sun? Franks? Do you copy?"

Nobody responded.

"Damnit," said Phoebe. "All teams, converge on Sun and Franks' last registered location. Beware enemy fire." Phoebe switched to a private channel. "Ambrose. What the hell happened?"

"I have no idea. I haven't been able to locate any of their signals yet."

"Maarten," said Phoebe. "Get the Marauder to Sun and Franks' last known whereabouts. We might need cover."

"No can do," said Maarten, punching the controls. "We're locked out, same as with the comms. Looks like this baby was programmed to drop us here, and that's it."

"Shit," said Phoebe. "Then move out. Ranbir and I are on our way."

Maarten and I grabbed our Badasses and hopped out the back, joining Phoebe and Ranbir as they approached in a loping gait from the south. "Talk to me, Ambrose," said Phoebe. "Sun and Franks didn't jump off the face of Luna."

"Epsilon team must've spotted them and jacked their transmissions," I said. "We've played around with signal blockers in my comms course, but they must've made contact first. I might be able to do something if I have an idea of their whereabouts, but right now I'm running blind."

Phoebe motioned for us to slow as we neared the crest of a ridge. "Careful. Sun and Franks were about a click north of here according to my Net logs. Use your IR scans."

We slowed our skipping to a measured crawl, spotting Janeece and Halabi approaching from the west as we reached open space.

"Rock formations at two and ten o'clock," said Phoebe. "Anyone see—"

Ranbir cried out as I saw the muzzle flash. Maarten slammed into me, shoving me into a shallow crater with a meaty arm. Phoebe dove behind us as Ranbir fell, a cloud of regolith floating into the vacuum around us. Via Net, we heard Janeece and Halabi's cries and watched their vitals spike, taken down by simulated Badass fire.

"Damnit! Stay down!" said Phoebe. "Johnson? Halabi?"

Their vitals fluctuated on my squad app before flatlining, replaced with a simple *OUT*. "Never mind them. Epsilon took them down."

Ranbir groaned, squirming in the moon dust. "God damn it! I'm getting really tired of getting fake fucking shot!"

"Anyone see where the muzzle flashes came from?" said Phoebe.

"Two from the north, to the right of a rock formation before the end of the ridge," said Maarten. "I think I saw more from the northwest."

"Shit." Phoebe pounded her fist into the regolith. "We need a plan. Maybe Mandel and Nakamoto can sweep around them."

"Seconded," I said, peering over the edge of the microcrater, "but don't give the order yet."

"Why not?"

"Because I think I finally got a trace on one of their Net signals."

"Doesn't do us a whole hell of a lot of good now, hoss," said Maarten. "We sorta figured out where they are."

"I beg to differ." I clicked through the subroutines I'd set up in preparation for just such an event and started to upload the program I'd developed a few nights before. I grinned as it slipped through the standard USC blocking software on one of Epsilon team's crew like a hot knife through butter.

"Ambrose...?" said Phoebe.

I cackled, the sound echoing through my helmet as I opened a terminal with access to the Epsilon squad leader's Suit control. "So, guys?" I said. "Believe it or not, we just won this encounter. The question is simply how quickly we want to end it."

———

I DIDN'T DO anything particularly cruel. The worm I'd injected into Epsilon squad's Net's couldn't affect any of their thoughts or biointeractions—the neural networks controlling those were so far above my understanding of coding I was surprised USC's best were able to even administer pain as effectively as they could—but I was able to crack the Suit's fairly simple architecture.

I merely disabled every Epsilon member's visor enabled optics —IR, UV, you name it. I even jacked up their tint settings so not a man or woman would be able to see more than a meter in front of their faces. And with their GPS locations in hand via their Nets, it was a matter of minutes before we rounded them all up. Epsilon's squad leader, Mike Murdock, even surrendered after he understood how thoroughly his squad had been hosed.

Sergeant Tyler called me into his office upon returning to base. I wasn't entirely sure what to expect when I walked in, and I left as confused as I'd entered. By the letter of his speech, he'd dressed me down, telling me my actions went against established USC combat protocols, but he'd done so with a smirk on his face and a glint in his eye the whole time. He told me to leave and reconsider my actions, but upon finding me, Phoebe informed me he'd assigned every member of our squad two whole drink tickets and given us the rest of the afternoon off.

So it was that I found myself back in my room at a reasonable hour, with a full belly, the barest hint of a buzz, and nothing to do —or almost nothing.

Phoebe lay in my bunk beside me, staring at the ceiling as we chatted. She'd wanted to learn all about my hacking efforts during dinner. That led to discussions on our Suit's cyber defenses, Net defenses in general, and what got me into computers. Before we knew it, we were the last ones in the mess hall, so we'd retired to my room. By the time we got there, the conversation had drifted to more amusing topics—mostly the look on Tyler's face as he'd tried to discipline me.

"Really, I should've recorded it," I said. "It was halfway between a smile and a scowl, and his eyebrow kept drifting up in curiosity. I'm not even sure if he knew he was doing it."

Phoebe laughed and turned onto her side to look at me. "I'm surprised he didn't take the opportunity to lecture you about new ways you could've died. Like if your worm had backfired and caused your visor to explode."

I smiled. "I think he was tempted."

We both chuckled. As the laughter died down, Phoebe put her

hand on my chest. "You know, I'm not sure I ever got a chance to thank you. No way we would've come out of that encounter *alive* without your counterattack of questionable means."

My heart accelerated in response to her touch. I hoped she hadn't noticed. "We're a squad. All for one and one for all, or something like that, right?"

She smiled. "Yeah. Although it's hard to see the big picture sometimes when you're hogging all the glory."

"I can't tell if you're joking, but if you're about to start doubting yourself as a squad leader again, I'm going to nip that in the bud. You did great, you've been getting better each and every week, and after thinking it over, I really don't want the job. So there."

"How chivalrous of you." She leaned forward and kissed me. I stiffened out of shock, momentarily overwhelmed by the warmth of her lips, the taste of the strawberry tart she'd had for dessert, and the faint scent of chlorine and apple shampoo in her hair.

She pulled back. "Sorry. Maybe I shouldn't have."

"Are you kidding? Why'd you stop?"

I wrapped an arm around her and pulled her in. Her lips met mine again. I breathed in the scent of her, feeling her body press against my side.

Whatever sense of hesitation there'd been in either of us evaporated, wicked away like droplets of sweat in the Suit. I sought her lips hungrily. She kissed me back eagerly, her breath hot on my neck. I gripped her hips and felt her rock in my grip. Her hand roamed over my chest, tracing the edge of my pectorals, then down over my abdominals, and lower still.

I was hard as a Martian icicle, but I pushed her back. I panted, my heart hammering. "Hold on. You sure we should be doing this?"

Phoebe glanced toward the door. "Relax. I'm the squad leader. I know where everyone is. Maarten went to the gym for a late night lift. He won't be bothering us."

"That's not what I meant. Isn't this... you know? Against the rules?"

"Against Captain Soto's rules, maybe, but not any others. I've read the USC military code of conduct in leadership class. Trust me, it's fine."

"And you're sure you want this?"

Phoebe's hand slid over my crotch. She found me and started to stroke me. "This answer your question?"

I moaned, but I sure as hell didn't stop her, although my jump-suit tried. Even with all the practice we'd had, those suckers were hard to take off in a hurry.

20

I CLOSED the door to my apartment behind me, stripped off my jacket, and hung it in the coat closet. I'd taken my left shoe off and started to work on the right when I heard the sound of footsteps behind me.

I spun, ripping the pistol from my side and leveling it down the hallway toward the noise.

A slender, olive-skinned woman in a knee-length black coat and high heels stood there. Her hair hung to her ribs in a rich brown cascade. Her eyes were dark pools, accented by smoky eyeshadow, and her lips shone from a nude gloss. She lifted her hands in response to being drawn upon.

Her voice was like fingers trailing along silk. "Come, now. You wouldn't shoot a woman, would you?"

Air escaped my lungs in a sigh. I returned my gun to my holster, trying to will the adrenaline out of my suddenly stressed system. "Jesus Christ, Sophia. Don't do that. You almost gave me a heart attack."

"Do what?" she said, taking a step toward me. "You gave me the passcode to your apartment. If I'm not allowed to use it, what good is it?"

"You know that's not what I mean," I said, slipping out of my second shoe. "Don't scare me like that. Sneaking into my apartment without letting me know. Popping out of the shadows when I have my back turned. What are you doing here, anyway? I thought we were meeting for dinner."

"That was the plan," said Sophia, taking another step toward me. "But I decided I'd rather eat in. If nothing else, it'll be easier than finding another discreet restaurant off the beaten path. Also, I didn't want to wait."

"Wait for what?"

"You." Sophia reached to her waist, undid a button, and shrugged out of her coat. It fell to the floor with a soft crumple, leaving her, and *only her* standing in my hallway.

She undulated toward me, naked except for the heels that clicked against the floor with each of her steps. I couldn't tear my eyes off her. Her long, graceful legs. Her narrow waist. The pert breasts that Martian gravity had barely touched in her thirty-eight years.

She wrapped her arms around my neck and pressed her nakedness against me. I lay my hands against her hips, feeling her toned flesh under my fingers as my body responded to her touch.

She leaned in and kissed me, her breath hot, her scent intoxicating.

She left me in a daze as she pulled back. "Well, when you put it that way. I guess dinner can wait."

I LEANED INTO THE PILLOW, my arm tucked behind my head as I stared at the ceiling. I took a deep breath and let it out slowly. Sophia's arm rose and fell with my breath, draped as it was over my chest. Her head rested on my shoulder, her hair tickling my neck when she shifted.

I glanced her way, but with her head tucked into the crook of my neck, I couldn't get a good look. Her breath was slow and steady, warming me where it met my bare flesh. She hadn't said anything in a while, but that wasn't uncommon for us after sex. Sometimes we lay in bed for fifteen minutes, thirty, an hour afterwards, often without saying a thing. Sometimes we'd doze off, other times we'd lay in wakeful silence, simply enjoying each other's warmth, the sensation of our bodies intertwined, the comforting feel of each other's heartbeats. We'd never specifically addressed our needs post intimacy, but like the act itself, we'd found a routine that satisfied us both.

As I peered at her out of the corner of my eyes, I delved inside her mind. It wasn't an intrusion of privacy. We did it willingly. There were sections of our minds we could share during our intimate moments, the portions that conveyed joy, desire, arousal, and pleasure. Learning to access someone else's Net was an imprecise science, though. Like the act of sex itself, it was more trial and error, slowly learning what sensations meant what and how to separate your own emotions from your partner's. Over time, I'd found it led to more intense pleasure and more intimate encounters.

Sometimes, more than emotions seeped through, though. I'd catch tidbits of thoughts. Memories. Net logs. Anything, really. I think it was a side effect of the Net's unique neural architecture— systems that had evolved in separate minds couldn't meld seamlessly. Today I caught a passing glimpse of a vactrain station, the smell of ginger cookies, and some lingering lines of code. What were they? *They shouldn't be there...*

I jerked and blinked. Sophia's arm stirred. Her fingers trailed through the tuft of hair at my chest. She pulled her head back just enough to speak. "Still awake?"

"Uh... yeah. Figured you were, too. You hadn't started twitching yet."

"Speaking of twitching..." Her hair slid over my shoulder as she adjusted position. "Something on your mind?"

"You know me. There's always something on my mind."

"Work?"

"When isn't it?"

We lay there for a few long moments. "You can talk to me about it if you like."

I took another deep breath. "I'm not sure I should."

Sophia propped herself up on a forearm and brushed the hair out of her face. "Uh-oh. That can't be good."

"Trust me, it isn't."

"I meant for me. The only time you've refused to talk to me about work was when you were investigating my father's right hand man."

"We'd just met at that point," I said. "The murder investigation into your father's crony Arcenio is the reason we crossed paths, if you'll recall. You'll forgive me if I was still cautious about you at the time."

Sophia smiled. "Implying you're not cautious about me now?"

"You're Sophia Demetriou. The kingpin's daughter. I walk on eggshells in your presence."

"Because of who my father is, or because of who I am?" Sophia's smile adopted a devilish quality.

"Can't it be both?"

Sophia settled back into my shoulder crook. She tried to wrap her fingers around my chest hair, but it wasn't near long enough. "So this work thing isn't about my father, then?"

"Depends. Is your father working with the Silicon Road gang?"

"I've told you before, I'm not involved in my father's business dealings. I've no desire to follow in his footsteps, only to live large off his ill-gotten gains."

"Which makes you no more of a criminal than any of the business class, I suppose."

"Exactly."

I slid back into quiet contemplation as Sophia played with my chest hair, but apparently tonight wasn't a night she was willing to sit for an hour in silence. "Is this about that woman whose apartment was torched? The USC Administrator?"

I sat up and frowned. "How do you know about that?"

"Sweetie, it's all over the feeds. It's all anyone can talk about, especially since that video was released. The Snow Leopard's, I mean, with her murder in it." Sophia ran her hand along my arm. "Look, I know you have some sort of history with that man. I don't know what exactly, because you refuse to tell me. It might not be a part of your life you wish to revisit, your internment. I get that. But you can talk to me. Honestly."

I settled back into my pillow. "I know I can talk to you."

A long moment passed. "But you're not going to."

I didn't respond.

Sophia sighed. "You know, Ambrose, I love mysterious men, but there's a limit to my patience. If you're not going to let me into your public life, at least let me into your mind."

"The latter is easier said than done. And the former? You realize the bind that would put my department in, right? If Captain Reyes found out about us? Not that anything we're doing is illegal, but the optics aren't great."

"Someone is going to find out sooner or later, Ambrose," said Sophia. "We should think about how we want to address that eventuality before it arrives."

"I don't know. Maybe it won't ever become a problem."

Sophia's brow furrowed. "No, I'm pretty sure it will. And if you're not careful, it could cost you your job or our relationship. Maybe both."

"That's not what I meant. With this Snow Leopard business cropping back up, the trade wars, the general sense of civil unrest? I've been thinking about quitting the force and looking for a safer occupation. You know, like a vacuum arc welder or a landmine repairman."

Sophia snorted, but a bit of the smile returned to her lips. "As if you could ever quit your job."

"You never know. I might surprise you. Regardless, we've got more immediate concerns than the state of our clandestine relationship or the growing threat of a second Martian rebellion."

"Being?"

I sat up and peeled the sheet off me. "What we're going to cook for dinner. I think I have fixings for chicken marsala. What do you say? Still willing to be my dinner date?"

I GAVE Sophia a kiss at the door. "Sure you don't want to spend the night?"

"Oh, I'd love to," she said with a smile. "But what would the people in your life think if they found me here?"

"They'd probably wonder who you were and be secretly glad I'm not the curmudgeon they think I am. Also, *people in my life* is probably overstating things. There's you and coworkers. That's about it."

Sophia gave me another kiss. "Aww. That's so sweet of you to be willing to pass me off as a faceless nobody to your partner and boss. But the fact of the matter is I probably shouldn't spend the night for my sake, either. I'm not sure how father would react if he found out about our relationship."

"You're thirty-eight. I think you're old enough to make decisions for yourself."

"You've clearly never had a daughter." Sophia cracked the door. "Talk to you soon. Thanks again for dinner. And the other stuff."

"Anytime."

Sophia exited. The door closed behind her, the air systems whirring as the room's positive pressure was restored. With a full belly—the chicken marsala had really hit the spot—I walked back to my couch and turned on the holo. I didn't put it on the news-feeds. I'd had enough of that for one day. Instead I picked up where I'd left off on a scripted series, one about a disgruntled stock-trader turned hit-man for hire. The show was kitschy and the writing was mediocre at best, but I got a kick out of dissecting the show's numerous logical errors and fallacies, and I often laughed at the lengths the protagonist went to protect his identity. In reality, the schmuck would've been caught within twenty-four hours of his first hit.

This time, I didn't laugh at all through the two episodes I watched. I barely followed the story, if I was being honest with myself. Thoughts of Wen's murder kept distracting me. Why had her death been appropriated by Martian separatist forces? What had Wen been involved in that could've catapulted her into a renewed push for Martian independence? And who had tried to hide her murder via fire bombs and explosives?

As puzzling as those questions were, the one I couldn't shake was why someone would tail the Silicon Road gangbanger from the Red Summit Financial offices. And not just someone. *Him,* of all people.

I checked my clock. Eleven PM. A good time to retire, but rest was the furthest thing from my mind at the moment. I doubt I could've willed myself to sleep without drugs, and I had no inten-tion of using any.

I checked my messages, knowing full well I would've gotten an alert if any had arrived. Still, better safe than sorry. With the itch satisfied, I headed to my room and changed into street clothes. Before leaving, I knelt next to my bed stand and pushed on the panel on the lefthand side. It slid up at my touch. Reaching in, I pulled out both things inside—an unmarked tablet and a Net transponder.

I activated the latter and double-checked my geopositional data. Satisfied that the transponder was working, I went into my Net settings and turned the wireless functionality off.

You weren't supposed to be able to do that. Disable active Net systems, yes. Disconnect from the grid entirely, no. But I'd learned my fair share of tricks in the forty-three years I'd spent between Earth and Mars. Even with the offline portions of my Net still active, I felt naked, but turning the system off with a backup transponder was the only way I could leave my apartment and appear not to have done so. Some tasks were better left off the official record.

I snagged a flashlight from a drawer in the kitchen, placed it in my pocket opposite the tablet, grabbed a coat from the closet, and headed out.

21

JUNE 11, 2154

THERE WAS NO GRADUATION. No ceremony where we were handed slips of embossed paper adorned with gold stamps. Sergeant Tyler simply assembled us one night and informed us we'd be shipping out to Mars the following morning on a USC Mark X, this one dubbed the *Osprey*. If he felt any emotion in our new assignment, he hid it masterfully, except possibly by omission. For once, he didn't mention that he expected us to all die. He merely wished us good luck and commanded us to get a good night's sleep before launch.

Boarding took longer than it did leaving Earth, but that's because the Mark X contained two and a half times the carrying capacity of the Mark VII that had carried us into space, all without adding the requisite engine power to get that many soldiers and pieces of equipment out of Earth's gravity well. The Mark X was primarily used for Luna to Phobos runs, though the lumbering ship could get off Mars with a full tank of fuel and no cargo.

When the Mark X's engines roared to life underneath me, my body stiffened, same as it had leaving Earth, but the response was instinctual more than anything. The gravitational forces experienced were a fraction of the ones we'd felt in our first liftoff, and within a minute we were free of Luna and accelerating toward Mars at a uniform two-hundredths of a g. The Captain informed us the engines would continue to burn at a slow, solid clip for nine straight days, at which point we'd perform the standard skew flip turnover and decelerate for another nine days before our pre-Mars pitstop at Phobos.

Despite the increased size of the Mark X, the layouts of the *Osprey* and the *Sunbittern* were nearly identical, with the majority of the additional ship space turned over to crew quarters and non-pressurized storage. The only real improvement from a crew stand-point was to the ship's gymnasium, which featured a wider assort-ment of electromagnetically-resistive squat racks, bench presses, and pull up harnesses, not to mention an array of water-filled tubes equipped with flow pumps and breathing masks. Apparently, USC really valued the cardiovascular benefits of swimming, and self-contained tubes were the only way to get said exercise in micro-gravity.

Our company's major, a stern faced woman by the name of Marjory Watson, ensured that not a second of potential swim time went to waste, rotating our schedules so the ship's two dozen tubes were in constant use, and though the ship didn't have the same practice spaces and equipment USC's Luna base did, that didn't prevent Major Watson from filling the rest of our schedules with as many activities as possible. Some of them were useful, if boring. I spent a good three to four hours a day taking digital courses on everything from Martian political history to squad tactics. The courses I took on cryptography and cyber defense were the high-light of my curriculum, though I perpetually stayed ahead of the coursework with the side projects I coded in the evenings.

VR combat sims were regular elements of our schedules, too, as were mundane janitorial and maintenance tasks that were assigned to us on a rotating basis, but despite the Major's best efforts, she simply couldn't fill every gap with a productive exercise—which

was good, because Phoebe and I found a *different* sort of productive exercise to take part in, sometimes multiple times a day. It
wasn't always easy—the ships bunks were designed to hold a single
body, and the microgravity made it so we'd drift around unpre-
dictably during the most frantic portions of our sexual escapades—
but at least Phoebe's position as squad leader made it so she had
access to everyone's schedules, meaning we could time our efforts
when we knew our bunk mates wouldn't be in their cabins.

At least we weren't the only ones. At some point during the
first week on the *Osprey*, Halabi and Nakamoto starting seeing
each other, Sun began spending a fair amount of time with a tall
blonde girl from Epsilon squad, and much to the surprise of everyone, Maarten and Janeece began to simultaneously disappear for
extended periods of time. Maarten claimed he was busy maintaining his muscle mass in the gym, and Janeece remained as
publicly contemptuous of the big fellow as ever, but we all had our
suspicions.

It was within this sex-crazed atmosphere that Major Watkins
called us into her quarters a week into our voyage. Though she had
a cabin to herself, it wasn't any more ostentatious than what the
rest of us received. There was a cot along one side and a floor
mounted swivel chair across from a display on the far wall. Even
her porthole was the same size as everyone else's.

Phoebe and I entered the room, the door sliding shut behind us
as we ever so slowly drifted into standing positions against the
floor. "You asked to see us, Major?"

Major Watkins turned in her chair, gripping the side to keep
from sliding out. She wore her sandy-blonde hair to about chin
length, the sharp edge of the bob cut giving her a more severe look
than her rounded cheeks and button nose otherwise could, but
she'd perfected her cold blue-eyed stare into a lethal weapon.

"Privates Zhao and Drake, Zeta squad." She stated it as a fact,
not a greeting. Her eyes softened for a moment, becoming distant,

possibly as she referenced her Net. "I've been reviewing your logs and those of your squad. As far as I can tell, you're making the most of your exercise allotments, completing your coursework, and performing satisfactorily on the graded portions. Are there any matters of importance you wish to raise while we're here?"

Phoebe replied diplomatically. "Nothing I can think of, ma'am."

"So you know, I'm meeting with all the leads and deputy leads from my squads," said Watkins. "Making sure everything is proceeding as smoothly as possible. That no *interpersonal problems* are developing. Do you feel there are any I should know about?"

Uh-oh, I thought. *We're boned.*

"Problems?" said Phoebe. "No, ma'am. We're all getting along as well as could be hoped. No disagreements or altercations to report."

"That's good to hear," said Watkins. "And I hope it stays that way, because a relationship such as yours could be detrimental should it sour."

Phoebe and I shared a glance.

"Yes, I'm aware you two are seeing each other," said Watkins. "Before you gather a defense, let me state clearly that I don't particularly care. Everyone aboard this ship is an adult. I don't care who sticks which body part into who, as long as it's consensual. And your situation isn't particularly unique. Try putting five hundred eighteen to twenty-two year olds in *any* enclosed space for more than six hours and see what happens. The only difference is the two of you happen to be your squad's leaders, which could make things tricky going forward. As long as you're aware that your responsibility is to USC first, me second, your squad mates third, and each other a distant fourth, then we won't have any problems. Am I understood?"

"Yes, Major," said Phoebe.

Watkins turned her cold eyes on me. "Drake?"

"Understood, Major."

"Good," said Watkins, nodding. "Now, while I have you here, let me discuss a few points. First off, I see that you faced off against Epsilon squad in one of your training exercises on Luna. Hopefully, you took the opportunity to introduce yourselves, because together, you'll be forming a platoon on Mars. Your lieutenant will be assigned once you arrive, but it won't be one of you, or a member of Epsilon squad. That honor is earned, given to someone who understands the purpose of our mission on Mars.

"Which brings me to my second point. I notice from your records that your squad, along with most of the other squads in my command, took classes on Luna under the instruction of Dr. Chakrabati. While I have great personal respect for the doctor, I've made it known to my superiors that her particular views on the Martian rebellion and your role in stopping it are not conducive to preparing you for your mission on the red planet. Tell me. Dr. Chakrabati gave you a spiel about how ending the Red threat is a noble cause, justified by the illegal and immoral actions of the Reds and their leader, the trumped up fear artist who calls himself the Snow Leopard? Am I right?"

Phoebe and I both responded with, "Yes, Major."

"Well, forget that crap right now," said Watkins. "You may believe our actions on Mars are justified, and to be honest, I'd agree with you. But your role, my role, and the role of the men and women around you is *not* to stop the Red uprising. It's *not* to gain revenge for the murders and destruction of Los Angeles, and it's *not* to subject the people of Mars to our Earthborn flavor of justice. Any idea what our mission is, soldiers?"

Phoebe and I glanced at each other. I couldn't think of a good answer, so I didn't offer one.

"Our *mission*," said Watkins, her eyes steely, "is to protect USC assets. Fusion plants. Air recyclers. Water extraction services. Spaceports. Vactrains. Cities, both on Earth and on Mars.

All of these are assets. Mars *itself* is an asset, and our mission is to protect that asset from competing interests, Reds among them. So whatever your personal motivations for joining this fight, remember our ultimate goal, and couch your behavior accordingly. Am I understood? Good. Dismissed."

I SHOULDN'T HAVE BEEN SURPRISED to find that Major Watkins was as cold, detached, and pragmatic as Sergeant Tyler, but it nonetheless struck a chord within me that every one of my USC superiors, with the exception of the civilian Dr. Chakrabati, seemed intent on divesting me from the notion that I'd signed up to fight radicalism, terrorism, and injustice and instead signed over seven years of my life in pointless, likely fatal service to a hulking, multi-planetary organization.

Not that I could blame Sergeant Tyler and Major Watkins for their views. They'd been in service to USC long before the start of the Martian uprising in 2151. They'd seen the Reds grow from a fringe movement to a serious threat. They'd experienced the terrorist bombings in Isidis. To them, the nuclear devastation of Los Angeles was an escalation of an existing conflict, the logical conclusion of a war as much about fear as action.

But it bothered me that I'd let their views start to color my own. I wasn't cynical by nature. I'd joined the space corps to fight the Reds, to protect my nation, my family, my friends. I'd joined out of a sense of patriotism that I hadn't known lurked inside me. I'd wanted to do it—*needed* to—and yet, after a month and a half of training, exercises, drills, and courses, I couldn't help but feel as if I'd given up on my admittedly farfetched dream of playing in the NBA for nothing more than a job with long hours and a higher than acceptable risk of injury and death.

If not for Phoebe's constant and enthusiastic companionship, I might've sunk into a funk. Certainly, the constant Net-enabled combat simulations we enacted as a squad didn't help. Whereas the ones we'd taken part in on Luna had seemed instructive, the ones we enacted aboard the *Osprey* became progressively harsher, pitting us against impossible situations in which we inevitably suffered complete losses either at the hands of the Reds or Mars itself.

I closed the simulation app and sighed, staring at the ceiling above my bunk. "Well, that was some bullshit, don't you think?"

Maarten responded from his bunk underneath me. "They're all bullshit, if you ask me. I don't care what anyone else says, those sims can't compare to the real thing. No smells. No sense of motion or gun recoil. It's a waste."

"I meant the situation we got placed in was bullshit. How the hell was our squad supposed to survive a three-pronged assault by Reds in an urban environment where we didn't even have maps or reconnaissance going in?"

"Oh. That," said Maarten. "Well, I guess they're trying to toughen us up. Fuck us every which way but sideways now and hope it sticks when the dick is real, I guess."

I snorted. "You have such a way with words."

"Hey, guys. Come check this out."

I leaned over the edge of my bunk to find Ranbir at the window. I pushed off, joining him as I drifted slowly toward the floor. I would've asked him what he meant, but the scene spoke for itself.

Mars hovered in view, a rusty red globe made imperfect by its own shadow. A cluster of dirty white shone at one of the poles, only slightly marred by wisps of white clouds immeasurably fainter and weaker than even their highest atmosphere counterparts on Earth. A point of light shone from the crescent of the planet that lurked in shadow, but only one. One of the planet's major cities, I assumed. Olympus, probably, given its solitary nature.

I'd spent the morning in my usual routine—exercise, eating, VR drills. I couldn't remember the last time I'd stopped to gaze out the porthole. Now I kicked myself for not making it a regular occurrence. "Damn. How the hell does a freezing cold deathtrap look so beautiful?"

"Don't joke about that," said Maarten from behind me, "otherwise USC might leave you there at the end of the war."

I snorted. "Yeah. Me. I'd make a joke about that happening when hell freezes over, but... you know." I gestured at Mars.

Ranbir chuckled. "Ship's systems say we've got less than four hours until docking on Phobos. Be a shame to spend the last of it with our heads stuck in our Nets." He cocked an eyebrow.

I shook my head. "I'll see what Phoebe has to say."

I sent her a message telling her to look out the window. She responded with one word. *Wow.* Given her response, I broached the next subject: ignoring our remaining coursework and enjoying the view until the Captain told us to strap into our bunks. To my surprise, she agreed, though she told me she'd stay in her room with Nakamoto and Janeece. In that regard, at least, we'd follow the protocols.

Her decision gave me time to joke and laugh with the guys. Given our busy schedules and my burgeoning relationship with Phoebe, I'd barely spent any alone time with Maarten and Ranbir over the past couple weeks. We joked and shot the shit, sharing increasingly ridiculous stories of the obstacles we'd overcome and the conquests we'd make upon arriving on Mars. Maarten went so far as to claim he'd single-handedly conquer the Martian wastes armed only with a dull spoon, wearing nothing but a pair of tight white underwear, all while he hyperventilated into a paper bag. Neither Ranbir or I could top that, so we made do with coming up with creative nicknames for Maarten's alter ego. The Frostbitten Avenger was my favorite, but Ranbir preferred Captain Dumbass.

Mars continued to grow in our window, its rocky outcroppings growing starker, the shadows cast by its mountains and canyons growing darker. When the ship's intercom crackled to life with forty-five minutes to Phobos interception, I figured it would be to give us information regarding docking procedure, but instead the Captain's voice barked out a sharp, simple order.

"All personnel change immediately into pressure suits. Repeat, pressure suits on. This is not a drill."

I glanced at Ranbir and Maarten as a Net message conveying the same information appeared in my field of view. *"Pressure suits? How janky is the Phobos docking station?"*

And then the ship's sirens went off.

22

MAY 11, 2179

MY FLASHLIGHT CUT a bright swath through the darkened tunnel, its ovoid projection bobbing across the floor as I walked. The walls to my sides were of rough hewn rock, though I'd passed areas in which the walls had been shrink-wrapped with Mylamene or sprayed with expanding foam. The measures differed based on the permeability of the rock. In those spots where the air couldn't escape, no membrane was necessary. I still preferred the sections of tunnel with membranes, though. They made me feel less on the brink of death. Never mind that the tunnels had survived for over a century without issue or that should there be a pressure loss in one part of the tunnel it would race through the entire subterranean system in seconds, killing me regardless of whether there was a plastic layer over the rocks at my sides, but fear wasn't logic based.

My breath left my lips in a mist. While the occasional service pipe or electrical conduit travelled alongside the walls of the underground tunnels, they weren't heated, nor had they ever been. Even in Elysium's prepubescent days, the tunnels had been designed for function, not comfort. If they could get you from point A to point B without freezing or asphyxiating, they'd served their purpose. Like the cold, their perpetual musty smell was merely a feature.

I paused at an intersection, revisiting the path I'd taken in my mind. I'd walked the route countless times, enough that I didn't have to reference the saved map in my Net for directions, but even should that get corrupted or lost, I wasn't totally dependent on memory. A small notch in the rock at the corner of the intersection told me I was close.

I kept walking, wondering what the chances were that I'd run into the mysterious fire-bomber Mwenge and I had tracked to one of the underground tunnel system's entrances. Extremely low, I wagered. I'd used a different hatch to gain entrance, for one thing—I hadn't even been aware of the one she'd used until we tracked her to it. Also because there were hundreds of kilometers of tunnels in the aggregate. The combined length was unknown, partly because of the many layers. I glanced at the dusting of regolith that covered the floors. I rarely even spotted tracks, though the faint circulation in the tunnels did mar footprints over time. I supposed if I hadn't run into anyone in the decade I'd been snooping around underground Elysium, I'd probably be safe for another night.

A decade, I thought. *Hard to believe it's been that long. How mysterious do you like your men, exactly, Sophia?*

I caught a glint in my flashlight's beam and approached it. A series of pipes ran up the wall, sprouting from the ground before disappearing into the rock above. They ran from an ancient abandoned dwelling a layer below to the aboveground portions of the early Elysian settlement that replaced it—or at least they had. They'd been capped ages ago.

A hose clamp kept the biggest pipe hooked into place at the wall. I reached up and unscrewed the tightening screw, slipped the clamp off, and set it on the ground. I grasped the top of the unsecured pipe and gave it a good shove to the side. It slipped right out. I upended it, and an unmarked tablet slid into my hands.

I turned it on, flicked through a few menus, and found the message that had been left there. My eyebrows rose as I read. *Welp. That wasn't what I'd hoped to find.*

I slipped my own tablet out of my pocket and held it up to the one I'd found in the pipe. My tablet chimed as the data I'd preloaded onto it successfully transferred. I double-checked to make sure it was there before returning the tablet to its pipe and fixing it back into place. Then I turned around and headed back the way I'd came.

23

JUNE 29, 2154

I BLINKED, staring at the red light that flashed above our cabin door, the sound of the ship's sirens blaring in my ears. "What the hell?"

Maarten shoved me. "Move it, hoss! Pressure suits!"

I stumbled into action, unfrozen by Maarten's push. I ripped the Suit from a compartment built into the bottom of my bunk and unfurled it, stepping into the legs with an ease acquired through hundreds and hundreds of practices. Crouch and pull on the thigh pockets, arms through the sleeves, activate the compression lines to cinch the Suit tight to the chest. I pulled my helmet from the locker on the wall, tossing Ranbir and Maarten each of theirs as I secured mine into place. Suit systems looked nominal, but I took a deep breath regardless to make sure the bacteria in my Buddy hadn't somehow fallen asleep.

I activated my Net chat. "Phoebe. Talk to me. What the hell's going on?"

"Working on it," she said.

The intercom flared to life with the Captain's voice cutting above the sirens. "All personnel secure yourselves in your bunks.

Prepare for possible impact. Repeat, *secure yourselves for possible impact.* This is not a drill."

"*Impact?*" said Ranbir.

I hopped into my cot, pulling the retractible straps across my legs and chest before activating the tightening mechanism. A cold sweat beaded my brow. My lungs felt empty, but my heart ignored them and hammered away.

"Phoebe," I said again. "Talk to me."

She didn't respond immediately, but I spotted her vitals. Slightly spiked, otherwise normal. It didn't keep me from worrying.

Eventually Phoebe responded on the squad channel. "Everyone suited and strapped?"

We all responded in the affirmative, one by one.

"Good. Here's the situation. Ship's systems detected a surface to space missile taking off from somewhere in the Hellas Basin. The ship's automatic defenses are going to try to disable it."

"It's headed our way?" said Ranbir.

"It appears to be, yes," said Phoebe.

Mandel spoke up. "What are we supposed to do? Lie here and hope for the best?"

Phoebe's voice was cold when she responded. "Yes."

Several people responded simultaneously in anger and shock.

"There's nothing we can do," said Phoebe. "The missile is accelerating at 20 gs. We can't get out its way even if we wanted. If the ship's computers determine we're the target, they'll fire the flak cannons, chaff guns, and flares. If they make contact, we should be okay. We'll know in about two minutes."

Everyone on the channel fell into silence. The siren blared, its wailing klaxon setting my teeth on edge. I switched my Net chat to a private channel. "Phoebe?"

"Yes?" she said.

I didn't know what to say. Part of me wanted to tell her I loved her, but I wasn't sure if I did. Neither of us had ever broached the subject. We'd been too busy enjoying each other's company and bodies to put more than a cursory thought into the future. But strapped there, unable to do a thing, morbid thoughts flashed through my head. If nothing else, I wished I could be strapped in beside her, wished I could feel the warmth of her shoulder pressed against mine and hear the beat of her heart.

"Ambrose?"

I blinked. "We're going to be ok, Phoebe. Just wanted to tell you that."

I felt stupid saying it, but if insincerity laced my words, Phoebe didn't acknowledge it. "Yeah. We'll be fine."

Her chat cut out. I stared at the metal bulkhead above me, a knot of anxiety and terror forming in my chest as a million emotions washed through me. I forced my lungs into regular action, trying to still my racing heart and banish the tingling in my fingertips. I wanted to run and scream and dive for cover, but my straps held me in place. As morbid as it might seem, I was probably as safe there as anywhere on the ship. There wasn't anywhere to hide, no reinforced tank where we could cram ourselves in the event of an explosion. My life was entirely out of my hands, placed in the care of a computer armed with a laser targeting system and chaff cannons packed with metallized glass fibers.

I glanced at my clock. Seconds ticked away, each of them feeling like minutes, hours. For the first thirty seconds, I raged and fretted, my heart threatening to stop before the missile ever arrived. For the second thirty, I silently made my goodbyes, penned a two sentence note to my parents telling them I loved them and was sorry, knowing the message would never make it out, the ship's computers too overloaded to send personal communications to Earth on a collimated beam. By the second minute, I simply waited to die. None of the sims had prepared me for this fatalistic reality, all of them making me think my training and target practice and team exercises would somehow give me a fighting chance, yet here

I was. Immobilized, waiting to be shot. Sergeant Tyler knew it all along, tried to tell us, yet we'd thought ourselves the exceptions when really we were just meat in a tube.

At the t-minus forty-five second mark, I heard Maarten's voice cut over the blare of the siren. "Ambrose? Ranbir? You there?"

I swallowed and nodded, knowing he couldn't see my head. "Yea, bud. What's up?" Ranbir chimed in too, his voice undulating with worry even via Net.

"I just wanted to tell you—you know, given this might be our last few moments alive and whatnot—that, Ambrose? You'll never be as strong as me, hoss, no matter how hard you lift. And Ranbir? Andromeda Siege still sucks. Death Rites forever."

I laughed despite myself.

"Fuck you, Maarten," said Ranbir, but his voice sounded stronger, lighter, more playful. There might've even been a bit of a chuckle to it.

I thought about asking Maarten about him and Janeece, but the ship rattled, the flak cannons cracked, and the moment was over. Icy dread gripped my heart as I glanced at the clock. Nineteen seconds until impact. Eighteen. Seventeen.

A whistling roar filled my ears, burying the siren with the strength of its howl. My body lurched to the side, thrown against my restraints by an invisible force. I screamed, an unintelligible mixture of rage, fear, and curses as my head was yanked to the side.

Then I saw it. A hole the size of a fist in the side of the hull, a handspan away from the porthole, now flared with hairline cracks.

Within seconds, the roar died, replaced by utter silence despite the insistent red flashing of the cabin's warning alarm. Something drifted lazily across the cabin, an aerosolized red mist, followed by a snaking trail that undulated in the vacuum. It was then I noticed the vitals on my Net.

"Ranbir? RANBIR!" I fumbled at my straps, unhooking them only after a couple failed attempts.

Maarten beat me to our squad mate. "Aw, shit, hoss. *Shit, shit, shit.*"

Blood soaked Ranbir's cot, floating in globules from a ragged gash that travelled from above his hip to near his pectoral. Torn meat pushed out of his Suit, forced out from within. Cracked white ribs punched through, pointing toward Ranbir's shoulder at an unnatural angle.

My stomach churned, and I forced my eyes toward the interior bulkhead. A bloodied impact spot bowed outward, but it didn't seem to have punched into the ship's interior.

Phoebe's voice surprised me in the silence. "Ambrose? What the hell happened? Ranbir's vitals..."

"He got hit," I said. "Shrapnel or something from the explosion. Christ, Phoebe, it's bad."

Ranbir's arm moved. His eyes fluttered through his visor, and I saw his lips part, but he didn't say anything.

"He's not responding to chat," said Phoebe. "Ambrose. Tap into his Suit controls. Tighten the compression lines. If he's got an open wound, you need to cover it and apply pressure. You've lost atmosphere."

"No shit," I said, scrambling in the bunk compartment for a spare blanket as I logged into Ranbir's Suit controls.

"A makeshift bandage isn't going to cut it, Phoebe," said Maarten. "He needs medical attention, now. Ambrose, help me with his straps. We need to get him to the med bay."

I realized Maarten was right, abandoning the blanket in favor of unstrapping him.

Phoebe's voice rang in my mind. "Guys. You can't leave your cabin."

"Yeah?" said Maarten, tossing aside Ranbir's straps and pulling him from his bunk. "Try and stop us."

"It's not me trying to stop you, moron. Your room's on lockdown. Ship systems indicate the missile was successfully disabled, but we still got hit with several dozen pieces of debris. Luckily, the ship's interior wasn't breached, but that means it's still under pressure."

Maarten carried Ranbir to the door, slamming against it with his shoulder. "Are you fucking kidding me? *Ranbir's dying!* He needs a doctor!"

"I'm on my way," said Phoebe. "We'll get a portable airlock in place over your door as soon as we can, but you're not the only ones who were hit. Looks like twenty-three cabins lost containment. Some of them have multiple injured."

"Well, *fucking hurry.*" Maarten turned to me. "The blanket, hoss."

"Right." I fumbled it back out, wrapping it around Ranbir's wound tightly. He twitched and I saw his face contort in a grimace before going slack. "Ranbir? Buddy? If you can hear me, now would be a good time to acknowledge it."

Maarten kept pounding on the door. "Ambrose, his vitals..."

I glanced at them. "I know, okay? What else do you want me to do, Maarten?"

Maarten lay Ranbir against the floor, turning his full attention to pounding on the door. It was weird seeing him slam his fist against the metal and not hearing a sound.

I turned to Ranbir. His eyes had closed. I grabbed his hand and squeezed it, sifting through his Suit controls as I did so, trying so see if I could boost oxygen or reroute more power to the compression lines or *something,* but I quickly realized there was nothing I could do. I was as powerless as I'd been waiting for the missile.

I'd thought the two minutes I'd spent waiting to die in my bunk were the longest of my life, but I was wrong. The minutes I spent waiting for Ranbir to die were an eternity longer.

Eventually, someone opened the door. Maarten and I passed through, waiting as the flexible plastic airlock cycled. Sound flooded back to my ears. A flurry of hands grabbed Ranbir, pulling him through, diving toward the *Osprey's* medical bay, but I already knew it was too late. Ranbir's vitals hadn't budged in over a minute.

Chaos surrounded me in Ranbir's wake. Soldiers clutched battered and bloodied friends as they carried them down the central corridor, all while teams with portable airlocks fought past them in reverse. Squad leaders shouted orders, soldiers hugged one another or stared at each other in dull shock, all while the ship's alarm continued its death knell.

I didn't know where to go, so I picked a section of hallway, sat against the wall, and for the first time since enlisting, I cried.

24

MAY 11, 2179

I WOKE up at six despite my long night. I sat up, rubbing the sleep from my eyes as I yawned. Sometimes I wished I wasn't such a slave to my habits. I hadn't been when I was young, but decades of routine had molded me. I blamed my time in the military for it. Even though I hadn't spent nearly as long there as I now had in police work, the lessons learned had bored into me like a flesh-eating worm.

I slipped into my swimsuit, threw a shirt over it, and headed to the kitchen, where I sauteed a quick egg, apple, plantain, onion, and soy bacon hash and washed it down with coffee. I was in my building's basement by six fifteen and in the water, swimming laps, within a minute of that. In many ways, my apartment complex wasn't anything special, but it was rent controlled and had its own gymnasium, which for me had made all the difference.

I couldn't say I liked swimming, exactly, yet I did it every morning, day after day without fail. USC had been right in that regard. It was the best exercise to maintain muscle mass in low gravity, and it did so while building aerobic endurance and maintaining cardiac health. The biggest downside was the time commitment, because despite my years of experience, I couldn't describe myself as fast. If anything, I was a grinder. I got in the pool and ground out my three thousand meters, twenty-five at a time. Some people found it boring, the same ones who listened to audiobooks or watched Net videos while they swam, but I'd learned to enjoy the solitude of the endeavor. It gave me a chance to think and reflect. I'd solved more cases than I could count while in the pool, neurons making unbidden connections in my brain as I brought my arms over my head and down, one after another. Somedays, the revelations my physical exertions brought me amazed me.

Today was not one of those days. I kept mulling the Snow Leopard's video as I churned my arms and kicked my legs, but nothing productive came of it. Quite the opposite, in fact. A sense of fear wallowed inside me, not at anything specific the Snow Leopard had said but what his speech portended. Strife. Conflict. *War*. Given the geopolitical climate, Mars was ripe to be whipped into a frothy fervor, and just enough time had passed for the planet's youth to have forgotten the consequences of the last uprising. In an ideal world, older, cooler, more experienced heads would prevail.

No world was ideal, though.

I tried to banish thoughts of the Snow Leopard from my mind, focusing instead on the Silicon Road gang, Red Summit Financial, and Shao Wen. That didn't work either. When I pictured Wen, I couldn't help but also see Phoebe. Perhaps it was because I was swimming. I'd always associated Phoebe with the pool. I'd never forget the moment I'd first gawked at her as she'd lifted herself from the water's edge, her slight curves laid bare by her skintight suit. The smile she'd flashed me twenty-five years ago. Some small part of me still yearned for her.

And then I pictured Wen's mauled corpse superimposed over Phoebe's frame, and the smidge of nostalgic love I'd felt was displaced by decades-old pain.

BISHOP WAS ALREADY at his desk when I arrived at work. "You're here early. You realize they don't give out promotions based on hours spent at the office."

Bishop looked up from his holo and nodded. "I couldn't sleep. Might as well try and be productive."

I snorted as I slumped into my chair. "I hear that."

Bishop clicked his holo off. "Watch any of the feeds on your way in?"

"Would you believe I've been afraid to? Why? Don't tell me the Snow Leopard put out another video."

"Nothing like that," said Bishop. "But there was a demonstration outside Wen's apartment last night. A decent crowd. Maybe two hundred or so. A mixed bag, according to the officers who were there to keep the peace. Some conspiracy theorists, some Mars First activists, some random nobodies. Facial scans of the crowd didn't pick up anyone who'd been flagged in the criminal database. And peace was kept. No casualties of any kind. Mostly they spent the night shouting about corruption and lies and casting us as USC stooges."

"Aren't we, though?"

"Just because the police department is a joint venture between the city and USC doesn't make us beholden to them," said Bishop. "We're beholden to the law."

Gosh, Mwenge could be naive sometimes. "So they've dispersed?"

"Mostly. There are about twenty left, last I heard."

I shrugged. "Could be worse."

"Speaking of," said Bishop. "I do have worse news. At least potentially worse, though it doesn't have anything to do with the demonstration."

"I'm a big boy. Hit me with it."

"Detective Kellerman's mole in the Silicon Road gang hasn't responded, and we haven't picked him up on any public cameras."

"Someone green-lighted a scan for him?"

It was Bishop's turn to shrug. "I want to talk to him. The Captain approved it. Why not?"

"So what's your concern? That Silicon Road found out about him and offed him? Why now? You think the informant was somehow connected to Wen's murder?"

"I have no idea," said Bishop. "Kellerman simply told me his guy usually gets back to him within twelve hours. He hasn't been found dead in an alley somewhere, so I guess that's good news. Not great, given how some of these gangs operate. But I do have one genuinely good piece of news to share."

"I could use some right about now after a barrage like that."

Bishop waved me over as he reactivated his holo. I joined him at his desk as he brought up what looked like a security feed of a seedy nightclub. The sign over the front glowed with pink and silver letters, its colorful glow lighting the darkened street underneath. "Platinum Ecstasy? What the hell is this place?"

"A scummy sex club in the Moto district. This is a public exterior feed from this morning, about five A.M. Hold on a sec." Bishop sped the feed up. A couple toms exited the building, then Bishop paused it as someone approached the front doors. "Here we go." He zoomed in on the face.

I leaned in to get a better look. "Is that the guy I caught exiting Red Summit Financial in the feed yesterday?"

"Mark Paul Boothe. Computers give it a ninety-eight percent chance of a match."

I clapped Mwenge on the shoulder. "Nice work. Maybe someone there knows where we can find him."

"Even better," said Bishop. "The public cameras haven't caught him leaving. He's still there."

"And here you've been wasting my time with talks of demonstrations. What are you waiting for? Let's roll."

THE INTERIOR OF PLATINUM ECSTASY was like the exterior sign on psychedelics. Pink and silver lights shone from behind the bar, the stage, and from under each table and booth, never in direct view but enough to cast the place in a metallic bubblegum glow. A rotating holoprojector covered the naked, gyrating bodies of the girls on stage with a swirling paisley pattern of the same hues as the glowing lights. Pink on pink, silver on silver, with just enough of the seating area left in shadow for the more identity conscious clientele. The whole place smelled of sweat, vape juice, and cheap vodka.

Mwenge and I stood near the front of the club, scanning the tables for our suspect. We weren't there long before a pair of women approached us. Both were tall and slender with jet black hair. One had pale skin and asiatic features while the other was darker skinned with the look of someone of Indian descent. Both had enormous fake breasts and wore nothing more than a c-string, one in pink and the other platinum.

"Hi, there," said the one in pink. "You boys up early, or did you stay up *really* late?"

"The former." I reached into my coat and flashed the ladies my badge.

"Oh." The dollar signs disappeared from their eyes, and their posture relaxed. "What do you need?"

Mwenge pulled out his tablet. He flicked it to a picture of Boothe. "Seen this guy?"

"Maybe," said the one in the platinum. "What's in it for us?"

"You mean other than the heartwarming satisfaction of knowing you provided a valuable public service?" I said. "Depends on what we find on this stiff. Weapons. Drugs. Contraband of any kind. I can't imagine he might've purchased any of those items here, but we'd have to open an investigation nonetheless. That would mean closing the doors for a few days. As much as the loss of that business would hurt, the further loss of clients when word gets around the cops have eyes on you would twist the knife a little more, I bet."

The one in the pink snorted and looked away. "You guys are assholes. Always are."

I nodded to the girl with the platinum hiding her reproductive parts. "What's it going to be?"

She sighed and shot a thumb over her shoulder. "He's in one of the back rooms. I don't know which."

"See. That wasn't so hard."

I nodded to Mwenge and we headed into the darkened posterior of the club. I didn't know my way around, but I'd been to enough seedy shitholes like this one to know the lay of the land. I found the unmarked doors and started barging in, thankful the joint didn't have locks installed. Clearly, the management was more concerned about employee safety than customer privacy.

The first room I busted into was empty of everything but champagne bottles and a sticky sweet post-coitus smell. The second had a couple in it, two women by the looks of things, and while the petting was getting hot and heavy, the client remained mostly clothed. They told me to get lost. Neither half of the couple in the third room was clothed. The gentleman getting his equipment waxed there told me to get lost, too, but in a much louder voice and with about two dozen f-bombs thrown in to make sure he got his point across.

I had my hand on the handle of a fourth door when I heard a creak from down the hall. A man leaned out of the room, cinching his belt as he did so.

I recognized his squirrelly-looking face. "Mark Paul Boothe. Hold—"

He took off before I could finish. I darted after him, leaning into my start to get maximum acceleration. It had taken me years to get a handle on running in Martian gravity—if I ever returned to Earth, I'd probably fall on my face going out for a jog—but now I was as effective as any local. Boothe skidded around a corner, planting his foot against the wall to reorient himself, and I followed, Mwenge hot on my heels. Boothe slammed through an exit door into the bright of Martian morning, the collision slowing him by a fraction of a second and reducing the gap between us to a body length.

The door hadn't even bounced off the exterior wall when I reached it. I planted my foot on the lip beneath me and launched myself horizontally. I flew through the air, arms outstretched. I only managed to get a few fingertips on his shoelaces, but it was enough. Boothe tumbled and fell, rolling across the pavement in the alley before he thumped into the wall opposite him.

The nice thing about having a partner is you don't have to do everything yourself. Mwenge had stayed on his feet behind me. With a hopping gait, he sailed onto Boothe's back, pulled the man's arms tight, and slapped his wrists into cuffs before he could turn his head to look at him.

I stood, dusted the regolith from my pants, and walked over to Mwenge, who had Boothe straddled underneath him. "Good thing he put his pants back on. Your wife might've gotten jealous, otherwise."

"I'm always happy when the perp is wearing pants," said Bishop. "Nice dive, by the way."

I blew on my knuckles. "Still got it."

"Excuse me," said Boothe, his voice muffled by the pavement squishing half his face. "How about you get the hell off me? I've got my rights, you know."

"Sure you've got rights, Boothe," I said. "You just relinquished them when you decided to evade arrest."

"Evade arrest? What are you talking about?"

"He means you running," said Mwenge. "We're cops, but you'd already figured that out, hadn't you? Or are you going to spin me a yarn about how you always go for brisk runs right after paying the Platinum Ecstasy girls to polish your bishop."

"And after someone official-looking calls you by name," I added.

"Get off me," repeated Boothe. "I've done nothing wrong."

"I rather doubt that." I knelt down and rifled through the man's pockets. I found a tablet in one. In the other I found a plastic bag full of dozens of other plastic baggies, each of which contained a gram or two of a fine red powder.

I dangled the bag in front of Boothe's face. "You dealing dust, Boothe? Don't tell me you partition your own stash into such convenient portions."

"That's not mine. You planted it on me. Police corruption!"

Pedestrians walked along the nearest street, but they either didn't care or were too far away to hear. "That's not going to work, small fry. Even if it were true, nobody would believe a little shit like you."

Boothe craned his neck and spat at me. The spittle travelled a whole hands-length before splattering against the pavement a half-meter from my shoe.

Before I could properly respond to the man, I got a call from Dean. "Yeah?"

"Hey, Detective. Got a minute?"

"Little busy," I said.

"Hey, no problem. Just wanted to let you know I've got some financials back on Red Summit. Let me know when you have a chance. I'll give you the rundown."

"We're headed back to the precinct as we speak," I said. "Mind

sending a vehicle my way? Mwenge and I have a suspect we'd
prefer to keep restrained."

"You got it, Detective. One cruiser on the way."

"Thanks." I cut the link and waved to Mwenge. "Come on,
partner. Let's get this cretin on his feet."

25

JULY 1, 2154

WE STAYED at the Phobos USC base for a day, though I'm not exactly sure why. The *Osprey* was in need of repairs, to be sure—not only had the debris punctured two dozen holes in its hull, but it had also taken out two of the engines and damaged the ship's liquid oxygen tank—but our descent to Mars had always been planned via the smaller Mark VIIs anyway.

I suspect the delay was to allow for USC intelligence to determine if additional missile strikes were an imminent threat. Apparently, Red surface to space launches against USC vessels were rare but not unheard of, which made me wonder why we hadn't bothered to train in response to them given we'd performed VR sims of virtually every other combat scenario under the sun. The cynical part of me decided it was because the exercises would've been pointless. What would we have done, laid in a simulated cot and waited to die? The even more cynical part of me decided USC *had* trained for strikes, but only the computer systems had completed the training. The ships were worth a hell of a lot more than the lives of those of us aboard them, I bet.

Regardless, no Red videos surfaced in the wake of the attack. The Snow Leopard didn't take credit for the launch, or make additional threats, veiled or otherwise. Why would he? The attack on Los Angeles had already served the purpose he desired. The deaths of five hundred more a month and a half later wouldn't even have moved the proverbial needle.

The attack did instill in me a newfound sense of righteous rage, which if nothing else proved the monotony of training hadn't fully dulled me to the motive behind my enlistment. My anger wasn't limited to the Reds, though, as the doctors and my superior officers on Phobos refused to let me say a final goodbye to Ranbir. Protocols, they said. His body had already been flash frozen and sealed for delivery back to his family on Earth. Never mind that he wouldn't leave until the *Osprey* had been repaired.

Phoebe told me to let it go, but she hadn't been his roommate for the past six weeks. She hadn't held his hand and watched his eyes flutter in fear and pain as he died.

I tried to distract myself with views of Mars from the Phobos base, but the seas of red no longer looked rusty. They reminded me of blood.

OUR MARK VII brought us to the Utopian spaceport on the first of July. As I'd learned in my courses, all the major city-states on Mars followed the Gregorian calendar, same as the rest of us. Given that Mars's orbital period was six hundred and eighty-seven Earth days, that meant months rarely lined up with their Earth-born hemispherical counterparts, but since the seasonally-adjusted temperatures on Mars alternated between ass-freezing cold and 'really, you should be dead by now' cold, I didn't see how it mattered. Besides, most Martians were city-dwellers, who rarely if ever experienced life outside their climate controlled bubbles, and had been born into the system. They didn't associate seasons with the date, seeing it merely as a record-keeping exercise.

We'd been instructed by Major Watkins to wear our Suits during the entirety of the descent from Phobos, supposedly to facilitate transfer from the spaceport to the city, though I suspected they feared another attack. None came, luckily.

Upon touchdown, we exited through the ship's airlocks, this time walking onto movable platforms exposed to the sky as opposed to the flexible, pressurized tubes we'd found on Luna. The sun shone low over the horizon, the morning sky a pinkish red tinged with blue near the sun, virtually the polar opposite of a dawn on Earth. A light breeze blew, enough to flutter a windsock at the top of the docking platform, but not enough for me to sense it. Desolate fields of red dust stretched as far as the eye could see in all directions, with the exception being toward Utopia.

I gazed toward it as I took an elevator down from the boarding doors and hopped along the path toward the airlocks at the end of the spaceport. Skyscrapers pierced the sky, towering above the surrounding flat expanses, stretching higher than the best efforts of architects on Earth, thanks not to better engineering but more forgiving gravity. They clustered at the city center, but they extended in a diminished density even to the outer edges. Between them, avenues glistened in the rising light of the sun, the polymer fabrics stretched above the streets making them look like rivers of molten plastic.

I passed through one of the massive airlocks and followed my Net instructions into the back of one of the large troop transports waiting for us. Major Watkin's commands indicated we'd be delivered to USC's Utopia West base, where we'd deposit our gear and assemble for introduction to our platoon leaders. I managed to snag a bench seat next to Maarten before our truck filled and lurched into motion.

Most of the other soldiers were removing their helmets, so I did, too, tucking it between my legs for safekeeping. I took a deep breath, but the Utopian air tasted the same as that from the Luna base and the *Osprey*—sterile, cold, and scrubbed.

Traffic increased the further we drove, mostly foot although rideshares clogged the streets as well. Despite the fact that our transports were computer-controlled, most pedestrians gave us a wide berth, some of them eyeing us with sharp glances and poorly hidden scowls. Most of them wore pants and heavy jackets, but a notable minority wore pressure suits similar to ours, calling into question the safety of the flexible polymer-weave atmosphere barriers stretched above us—not to mention the sanity of those who chose not to wear them. USC had labelled Mars's major cities combat zones in the wake of the Los Angeles bombing, after all. Then again, given the threadbare nature of many of the coats and the number of sunken cheeks I spotted among the civilians, maybe their lack of pressure suits wasn't a matter of choice.

Upon arriving at Utopia West, I travelled with Maarten to our quarters—why mess with a pairing that worked, I guess—dropped off everything but my Badass, and followed my minimap to the highlighted assembly location, a garage filled with Marauders, troop transports, and other utility vehicles. Maarten and I came to attention behind a few more of our cohorts. Phoebe was there. I gave her a friendly nod, which she returned, but as the rest of our squad filed in, I couldn't help but notice the gaping, Ranbir-shaped hole among us.

The members of Epsilon squad took position beside us. As the last of their numbers arrived, one of the doors on the Marauder before us opened, spitting out a tall, lanky man with a crisp buzzcut the same color as a Martian dirt pile. He couldn't have been more than a few years older than me—maybe twenty-five, tops—but he had an air of superiority about him that I could smell from twenty paces. He sneered at us, chewing his lip as he did so.

"Well, well. The latest batch of fresh meat from Luna. Heard

you guys took a bit of a dick punch from the Reds on your way in."
He glanced at our squad. "Lost a brother in arms, did you?"

"His name was Ranbir Gupta," I said tersely, glancing at the
single bar on his suit.

"His name could've been Barf Fartsnoggle for all I care," said
the man. "Soldiers come and go. Some on their own two feet, some
in a body bag. Rarely by choice either way. Better for you to leave
those you've lost in the past. You won't be able to remember all
their names before long anyway."

He stepped forward. "I'm Lieutenant Bryce Henson, by the
way. You can call me Henson, or Loot, whatever fires your booster.
Major Watkins assigned me to lead your platoon for the time
being. That makes me the lucky bastard who gets to try and mold
your spoon-fed Luna asses into something resembling a useful military unit. It also means I'm the dope who has to go along with you
on the monotonous, boring shit I'd assumed I'd advanced beyond a
couple years back. You can imagine I'm thrilled. Squad leaders?
Step forward."

Phoebe and Mike Murdock of Epsilon squad did as asked.

"It may be early in the day, but that doesn't mean we don't
have a laundry list of suck set out for us already. Too many crap
sandwiches and never enough mouths to eat them, that's pretty
much the USC motto. First task of the day is a fun one. Patrol duty.
It's exactly what it sounds like. On the bright side, you'll be able to
get your feet dusty in Utopia without ever leaving a Marauder,
assuming you're lucky. So mount up. One squad to a beast. Zeta
squad? Seeing as you've got that extra chair, I'll be riding with
you."

───────────

MAARTEN AND HALABI sat in the driver's seats, monitoring
the Marauder's systems as we rumbled along on the Utopian roads.

Phoebe and Janeece sat across from me. Henson had sandwiched himself between them, purely by accident, I imagined. His helmet was tucked between his feet, his Badass resting butt on the floor with the muzzle across his thigh.

"This next area's called the Lowell Market District," he said pointing out one of the side windows. "It's a little dicier than some of the areas we've already passed through. A few rideshares got bombed within the past week, and there's been a flurry of pro-Red graffiti and propaganda popping up. Command's had us increase patrols as a result."

"Do you have a lot of violent outbreaks in the city?" asked Phoebe. "I'd been under the impression the worst of it was in the smaller settlements."

"That's mostly true," said Henson, "and Utopia is probably the safest of the metropolises. We've got our heaviest presence here. That doesn't mean there's not a lot of Red sentiment among the locals. It usually manifests as small disturbances. Shootings. Looting. Arson. That's why we patrol. Keeps that shit under control."

I'd kept my eyes mostly on the windows as we'd travelled. At first Utopia hadn't distinguished itself from any other major city I'd visited, polymer weave-enclosures and regularly spaced pressure doors on the streets notwithstanding, but the further we'd travelled from the USC base, differences reared their unfamiliar heads. Foot traffic and rideshare traffic had thinned, and the streets features some telltales signs of neglect—fewer trees at the sidewalks, litter in the gutters, fewer flashy signs in storefronts. The buildings looked like they'd all been extruded from the same machine, though, each of them constructed out of the same silvery-gray metal and fitted with tinted windows that looked like they could withstand a sudden exposure to Martian pressure.

Our Marauder jostled as it hit a pothole. "You mostly use your Net for navigation?"

Henson shot me a crooked eyebrow, annoyed that I'd interrupted his conversation with the girls. "What do you mean?"

I nodded toward the windows. "These streets all look the same to me, and the buildings are near replicas of each other, even down to the materials. That's not steel, is it?"

"An aluminum magnesium alloy, actually," said Henson. "USC built a lot of these buildings in public-private partnerships with the city, which is why they're all cookie cutters. And everyone wants to keep costs down. Steel's a lot rarer here than on Earth, hence the alloy walls." The lieutenant sorted. "Yeah. We've got a shit ton of magnesium and ice, and not a whole hell of a lot of anything else."

Janeece frowned. "There's not even much ice."

"I didn't say water ice," said Henson. "You been to the poles yet? You ain't never seen that much dry ice, and there's more of it all the time, despite USC's global warming efforts. The equator might be getting hotter, but the poles are getting colder. USC's got its roving fusion melters working overtime counteracting the extra freezing going on. Supposedly we'll hit an inflection point soon and the stuff will start sublimating on its own—hopefully before the arrival of Swift-Tuttle—but don't ask me why. I'm no climate scientist."

We'd learned about Swift-Tuttle not only in our Luna courses but in grade school. Once dubbed by astronomers as the single most dangerous object known to humanity, the comet Swift-Tuttle, responsible for the yearly Perseid meteor shower, had in the early 2100's become the subject of a massive political campaign launched by then USC CEO Gerrold Lanneskog. While the comet was predicted to pass a comfortable 0.153 AU away from the earth in 2126, its probability of impact increased over time, a fact which Lanneskog used as a cudgel to coerce numerous governments into helping him finance the most ambitious solar engineering project in the history of mankind.

So it was that in early June of 2126, USC launched two dozen spacecraft to intercept Swift-Tuttle. The fact that they all landed on the comet was impressive enough. That they were able to attach the auxiliary boosters and ion thrusters they carried as cargo and successfully nudge Swift-Tuttle into a gravitational slingshot around Earth was all the more impressive. The single maneuver could've been used to shoot the comet into the sun, but Lanneskog had bigger plans, which is why he merely rearranged the comet's orbit in anticipation of the second slingshot two years ago in 2152. Another would occur in 2170, then one in 2177, before the comet would ultimately arrive in orbit around Mars in late 2180. Supposedly, it would help with tidal heating and temperature management, but the real draw was the estimated five petakilos of water ice and ammonia it carried that could be used to refill Mars's oceans and thicken the atmosphere. Supposedly, anyway. Recent chatter suggested there was a lot more water ice and a lot less ammonia than previously thought.

Janeece regarded Henson with the same look she usually reserved for Maarten. "You've been to the poles?"

"The south pole, to be specific," said Henson. "The really cold one. Pray that you don't ever get assigned down there, taking potshots at Reds who are hoping to disable the roving melters. God, that was a shit assignment. Let me tell you about—"

A blast like that of a Mark VII's engines sounded roughly three centimeters behind my head, and I suddenly found myself flying.

26

MAY 11, 2179

DEAN WAS WAITING by our desks when we arrived back at the station. "Dean," I said as I placed the evidence bag with Boothe's tablet and dust on my workspace. "You stalking us?"

"A little. I tracked your return via GPS." He put his hands up when I glared at him. "Hey, don't give me that. Captain Reyes made this case the department's number one priority, in case you weren't aware. Whatever you need, I'm supposed to get on it, lickety-split."

"I could use a fresh mug of maché," said Mwenge.

"Let me rephrase that. Any *technical service* you need, I'll attack it."

"So you said you had some news on Red Summit's financials?"

Dean nodded. "I talked to a nice lady over at revenue services who explained the delay on bringing charges against them. Basically, they have evidence of money laundering, but not enough to make it a slam dunk case. They were waiting for either more evidence to surface or for another, larger shoe to drop before they'd be willing to make their move."

"And Wen's murder is the big shoe?"

"When you put it that way, it sounds silly, but yes. They sent us their full case file on the company. Said they're willing to file charges today, if we want, but they can wait as long as necessary. They don't want to step on any toes. Conspiracy to commit murder trumps fraud any day, obviously."

"Well, we can't prove the former yet, simply a connection between Red Summit and Shao Wen," I said. "Unless you've found something in the records, that is."

"I'm fast, but not that fast," said Dean. "There's a good hundred shell companies funneling money in and out of Red Summit. I've sent the files your way. You can look at them when you get a chance. I'll do the same if I have a free moment. I did notice one interesting thing from the case file right off the bat, though."

"Being?" said Mwenge.

"The owner of Red Summit Financial is a woman by the name of Maldonada Vincenzio. If the name Vincenzio sounds familiar, it should. She's the aunt of Giancarlo Vincenzio, leader of the Silicon Road gang."

"All roads lead to Rome," I said. "Thanks Dean."

"No problem. What are you guys up to next?"

"We've got a suspect to question," said Bishop. "Want to come?"

"Me? I told you how busy I am, right? Besides, I only squeeze information out of systems, not people."

"Suit yourself," I said. "But interrogations are the most fun part of the job."

———

I PULLED up a chair opposite Boothe in the interrogation room. Mwenge took a seat beside me. Boothe's arms were crossed, and his face had adopted an aura of distracted indifference. He looked as if he might have been staring out a car window while stuck in heavy traffic. Apparently, the ride from the Platinum Ecstasy club had given him time to concoct a strategy.

"Mark Paul Boothe," I said.

He stared at me, lips unmoving, but eventually the silence coerced him into action. "Yeah?"

"Let's talk about Red Summit Financial."

"*Who?*"

I'd anticipated this. I flicked a holo on in the interrogation room's corner. It showed a pre-selected clip, the one of Boothe exiting the Red Summit offices a week ago. "This is you, right?"

Boothe glanced at the holo. "Looks like me."

"And that office you're coming out of? That's Red Summit Financial."

Boothe shrugged. "If you say so."

"That feed is from last week. You want to tell us what you were doing there?"

"Checking on my pension."

"That's good," said Mwenge. "Not laugh worthy, but good."

"The name Shao Wen ring a bell?" I asked.

Boothe shook his head. "Should it?"

"I'm guessing you don't watch a lot of news, Mr. Boothe. She was murdered yesterday. Her story's been all over the feeds."

"I don't watch holos. That stuff rots your brain."

This time Mwenge did laugh. "That's rich coming from a guy who deals dust."

"I don't deal anything. I'm telling you, that wasn't mine. The slut at Platinum Ecstasy must've planted it on me."

"I thought you said *we* did that, Boothe."

Boothe frowned and looked away. "Whatever."

"To be honest, I'm not that concerned about the dust," I said. "I'm not concerned with a small time dope slinger like *you* either. But I am concerned about Shao Wen, Boothe. And you're going to tell me about her."

MPB met my eyes again. "I'm telling you, I have no idea who that is."

"Red Summit Financial was paying her."

"So? I'm telling you, they've got a good retirement plan. Lots of high quality investment options."

I slammed a hand on the table. "Cut the bullshit, dickwad. You better give me something, otherwise I'm going to throw every god-damned book I can find at you. We've got you on possession with intent to supply, public endangerment, resisting arrest, and racially-aggravated assault of a police officer."

"Racially-aggravated...? What the fuck are you talking about? I didn't attack him." He shot a finger at Mwenge.

"I'm talking about me, dipshit. I'm an Earther. That qualifies as a minority on Mars. You spit at me. Believe it or not, that qualifies as assault. I've got it on my Net feed, in case you forgot about it. All told we can put you away for almost fifty years, and I've got a long memory and friends on the parole board."

Boothe quieted. His brow furrowed as he stared at me. "You're shitting me."

"Do I look like I'm shitting you? Tell me about Shao Wen."

Boothe took a deep breath and let it out slowly. "Look, man. I don't know anything about any Shao Wen. I'm not holding out on you, I swear."

"Then talk to me about Red Summit Financial."

"They're a front, okay?"

"We know that. Why were you there?"

Suddenly Boothe couldn't meet my eyes. He didn't respond either.

"Fifty years, Boothe," I said. "No parole. By the time you get out, you'll be chasing after the girls at Platinum Ecstasy on an elec-tric scooter."

Still nothing.

"What's the problem, Boothe?" I said. "You don't seem the

type to have a wife and kids. Nobody at home to support. Silicon Road isn't going to be paying you to keep your mouth shut, I guarantee it. So what is it? You scared they'll come after you if you talk? I'm not asking you to testify. I can even put you on a vactrain to Olympus if you want. Set you up with a new identity. I just need info. A little information in exchange for fifty years of your life."

Boothe sighed. "The Red Summit building? It's a *literal* front. It's where I pick up my dust."

"So if we raid it, we'll find more dope there?"

"If you know where to look."

"What about the investment side of things? The money laundering. The fraud."

"I don't know about any of that. I sling dust, man."

"Who's cooking the books?"

"I've never seen an accountant there, if that's what you're asking. Seriously, it's a drop off. Nothing more. If anyone's committing financial crimes through Red Summit, it's news to me."

I rubbed my chin. "What about Shao Wen?"

Boothe threw up his hands. "Come on man. I told you. I don't know who that is!"

"Red Summit, which your gang owns, was paying her regular distributions, and now she's dead."

"If Silicon Road was paying her, then I'm assuming she was providing a service they needed. They wouldn't have any reason to kill her then, would they?"

Maybe Boothe wasn't quite as dumb as he looked. "Why was Silicon Road paying Shao Wen?"

"Are you dense? *I don't know who that is.*"

"You've got fifty years on the line here, Boothe. *Fifty years.* Don't play dumb with me."

"Alright. You got me," said Boothe. "I've heard the name. Once. Yesterday. I was dropping off my earnings at my boss's place. He had the feeds on to coverage of that woman's death. He seemed pissed. Told me to get the hell out. That's it."

"Why was he pissed?"

"I don't know! You think he bothered to explain it to me?"

"You're not buying a lot of time off your sentence, Boothe. *Give me something.*"

The guy was starting to get angry. He leaned forward, his cheeks flushed. "I *am* giving you something. I'm giving you *everything.* You think I'm privy to the inner workings of the gang? *I'm a dust monkey.* All I learn is what I pick up on my own, with my two eyes and ears."

"And what have you picked up?"

Boothe leaned back in his chairs and rolled his eyes. "Christ, man. I don't know... Business is good. The gang's been expanding. Seems like every month they're bringing in more guys."

"More drug pushers?"

"Drug pushers. Muscle. Girls for the clubs. Roughnecks, too. Guys from Earth and Hellas Basin. Don't bother asking me about them. I'll see them once and never again, not like the others. You want to know more, go harass someone higher up the food chain."

I drummed my fingers on the table. "Yeah. Maybe I'd better do that."

27

JULY 1, 2154

I SOARED, my stomach lurching as the blast filled my ears. I slammed my head into a hard surface. Spots danced in my vision as the Marauder spun around me. I fell into Henson, feeling the muzzle of his weapon jab me in the kidneys, but the Marauder didn't stop turning. I slammed into Janeece, then someone's knee—maybe Sun's—before falling hard to the Marauder's ceiling, which was below me somehow. My head swam, my ears rang, and I tasted blood. Next to me, Mandel clutched her arm and groaned in pain. Nakamoto wobbled as she tried to rise to her knees. She stumbled and crashed into the wall, spraying vomit across the inverted padding of the bench seats.

Somewhere, underneath the incessant ringing in my hears, I heard Maarten's cry. "Shit! IED. We're taking fire!"

I wasn't sure what he was talking about, but as the ringing receded I started to make it out. Distant cracks. Pinging noises. Gunfire ricocheting off the Marauder's hard shell.

I glanced toward the back of the truck. The ramp hung half open, bent by the force of the explosion that had hit us. I also felt something. A faint breeze, growing stronger.

"Pressure gauges are dropping!" called Halabi. "Something must've punctured the polymer weave barrier."

"Helmets on!" shouted Henson. "Now, damn it!"

I fumbled on the ground, finding my mask splattered with blood and flecks of Nakamoto's vomit. I snapped it into place as the roar of the breeze intensified before picking up my Badass—or someone else's, I couldn't be sure.

"Stanić. Halabi," said Henson via Net. "Systems check."

"Batteries and comms still functional," replied Maarten. "Hull breached, obviously. Guns are pinned underneath us. Can't move them."

"External cams?"

"Some are functional. Others are covered in debris. Transferring control to Nets now."

"Anyone have eyes on the shooters?"

"Coming from the building to our right," said Halabi. "Second story window, underneath the weave."

"Can you get the ramp open?"

"I'll try," said Maarten.

The back door screeched, faintly over the rush of escaping air, but it did pry open another meter or so.

Henson moved to the back of the vehicle and poked his head out before pulling it back in. "Second story confirmed. I saw muzzle flashes. Probably a single shooter. We can't hit them from down here. We'll have to bust in. Room's vented, but the building's not. Scouts, on me. Badasses hot. Someone get the jaws."

"The what?" said Phoebe.

"The jaws, damnit!" said Henson. "To break the pressure seal on the outer door. They're underneath the bench seat."

"What about civilians in the building?" asked Janeece.

"They'll be fine. Each room is a self-contained pressure vessel. The jaws, now!"

Phoebe looped her Badass over her shoulder, stood, and

opened the compartments, which were now above us. I rose to my feet to help her—and almost fell. My left leg was numb. I looked down at it, surprised to find the fabric of my suit sliced and stained red around the thigh.

"What the hell?" I couldn't believe my eyes. My leg throbbed a little, but it was more of a dull ache than a shooting pain. Was my Net filtering my pain response, or was I in shock?

"Ambrose? Crap!" Phoebe pulled the heavy hydraulic jaws from the compartment. "What happened to your leg?"

"Beats the hell out of me." I tried stamping some feeling into my foot. "I think it's okay. Just a flesh wound."

Mandel grimaced as she pushed herself against the wall. "Well, I'm not. I think my arm's broken."

Janeece and Sun had already taken positions at the end of the marauder. Their muzzles flashed as they returned fire, but I couldn't hear them over the lingering ringing in my ears.

"Nakamoto. Stay here with Mandel," said Phoebe. "Stanić. Halabi. Provide covering fire. Ambrose? Can you help me with the jaws?"

I nodded as Henson shouted at us. "Move, damn it. We ain't got all day!"

Maarten and Halabi squeezed past us, squatting behind Janeece and Henson at the edge of the Marauder. Phoebe followed them, and I hobbled after her.

"Ready?" asked Henson.

"Ready," Phoebe and I both replied.

"Scouts, primary covering fire. Munitions, heavy secondary fire. Go, go!"

Phoebe hopped out of the truck and I sprinted after her, my leg wobbling but holding firm. Two flares of orange burst to life above us, one inside the open second story window, the other erupting outside on the sill. I imagined bullets screaming down toward us, but none made contact, or at least I didn't feel any bites. Phoebe skidded to a stop, back against the lee of the building, jaws in hand. I took position on the opposite side of the doorway.

Phoebe lifted the jaws. "You ever use these before?"

I eyed the contraption. "No, but they look straightforward. Jam the beak between the door seals and activate."

Phoebe nodded, holding out one end for me to grab on to. "On three?"

She counted, and on three, we jammed. The tip of the jaws slid in without a hitch, the rubber seals on the pressure doors fluttering. Phoebe flipped the switch on the backside of the contraption, and it lurched to life. Gears whirred, the scissor arms spread, and the metal doors started to buckle.

"Stanić coming in, make way," said Henson. "Halabi, Johnson, more covering fire!"

Air rushed past me in a whoosh as the doors gave up and slammed sideways into their pockets. Maarten rounded the edge of the Marauder and darted toward us, Badass at the ready. "I'm taking point," he said. "Cover my ass."

"We got your six, buddy," I said as he flew into the gap. I rounded the corner behind him, Phoebe taking the rear. Once inside, we located the stairs. Maarten bounded up them, stopping at the landings before popping around them in a tight spin, sweeping his rifle across the next stretch of corridor. I followed him, my leg starting to feel leaden and squishy between the toes as I mounted the steps.

"Just accessed the building plans," said Henson. "That second story unit looks like apartment two-sixty. Franks and Johnson are coming to back you up."

We surged forward into an empty hallway. The door to the room in question loomed at the far end, shrouded in partial darkness.

"Maarten," said Phoebe. "Set det charges at the hinges, then retreat to me and Ambrose at mid-hall. Lieutenant, do you copy?"

"Rodger that," he said. "Give me the countdown. Use heavy secondary fire as soon as that door's open. I'll provide grenade cover through the window as the charges go off."

Maarten ran to the door, slapping a couple sticky charges on the edges of the door while Phoebe and I covered him with our rifles.

He sprinted back. "All set."

"Coming up behind you." Janeece and Franks joined us, taking positions on the other side of the corridor.

"Count us down, Maarten."

"Three. Two. *One.*"

The door exploded, flying off the frame and spinning in mid air before skidding to a stop a meter before us. We fired our grenades. Fire engulfed the room. Shrapnel flew. Bits of concrete, metal, and who knows what else pelted me, even from our position three doors down.

"Move, move!" called Phoebe.

Maarten rushed forward, as did Janeece and Franks. I followed as best I could, though my leg had started to feel like a club. Smoke and dusk choked the room as I poked the nose of my rifle inside. I waited, crouching at the frame as the particulates settled.

The scene that unfolded wasn't the bloodbath I'd expected. A tripod-mounted machine gun lay on the floor, its barrel twisted fifteen degrees and its receiver scorched. Bits of electronics littered the floor: a cracked display, a shattered lens, a chip board, some melted wires, and burnt casings. There wasn't any shredded furniture. No bloodied bodies, torn apart by gunfire and explosives, though there was a wall mounted display on the far side of the room. Cracks shot across its face, and it seemed to be stuck in an endless loop, that of the Snow Leopard in his nondescript hideout. His blood red visor tipped to the side and his finger flicked toward the camera and back in a herking motion.

"Are you shitting me?" said Maarten. "It was all remote controlled? *Fuck...*"

My leg's protest intensified, and if I was being honest with myself, I'd started to feel lightheaded. Nonetheless, I crossed to the display and fiddled with the side mounted controls. With a couple taps, I managed to turn on the closed captions.

Welcome to Mars, said the Snow Leopard. *Welcome to Mars. Welcome to Mars. Welcome to Mars.*

I turned as Henson waltzed into the room. *"Son of a bitch.* Another remote cell. They blew up our god-damned Marauder and all we took out was a gun, a camera, and an uplink." He shook his head. "Well, on the bright side nobody's seriously hurt. Epsilon squad's been rerouted. They should be here in a moment."

I leaned against the wall, feeling incredibly tired. My injured leg twitched, and even my good one felt weak.

Phoebe stepped toward me. "Ambrose? Your blood pressure is cratering. Are you feeling okay?"

"I'm fine," I said, but my response felt slurred. Sluggish. "I'm just a little woozy. Maybe if I sit down..."

My back slid across the wall, and my last memory was that of Phoebe and Maarten diving toward me.

28

MAY 11, 2179

MWENGE CLOSED the door to the interrogation room behind him. "So... Want to come with me to talk to the gang unit about Silicon Road boss Giancarlo Vincenzio?"

"I'd be more interested in talking to Vincenzio himself than talking to the gang unit *about* him," I said. "You mind taking this one?"

Bishop snorted. "So you can put your feet up and fan yourself?"

"As if. Someone needs to sift through the Red Summit financial file revenue services sent over. As willing as Dean is, he's more of a code cruncher than a numbers guy."

Bishop shrugged. "Fair enough. I'd rather talk. You'd rather read a spreadsheet about bank fraud. I guess that's what division of labor is all about." He stepped to the elevators and punched the button on the panel. "See you when I see you."

I headed to my desk. As I sat down I glanced at the evidence bag with the dust and Boothe's tablet. After taking it from him, I hadn't bothered to check it. Not that I was interested in the names of a bunch of dust-heads needing a fix, but Booth would have contacts to folks within Silicon Road as well.

I pulled the tablet from the bag and tried to activate it only to be turned away by the login security.

I snorted, then stopped, momentarily frozen. I wanted to smash my head into a wall. I yanked on the top drawer of my desk and pulled out the evidence bag containing the tablet from Shao Wen's safe. Somehow I'd forgotten to start a crack on it. Mwenge had even reminded me. I should've called Dean right there and then and had him get started on the process. He wasn't the cryptography expert I was, but I could've walked him through it. Now Mwenge was going to lambast me for my forgetfulness, a byproduct of my *advanced age,* I'm sure he would joke. Captain Reyes was the one I worried about though. She'd offer fewer jokes and more legitimate reprimands.

With the tablets in hand, I hopped from my seat, walked to the stairs, and hoofed my way down to technical services. Dean was in the office when I arrived, surrounded by an array of six holodisplays. His eyes flicked between the topmost ones while his hands danced over a split keypad. He was one of the few people I knew who could multitask using tactile inputs and a Net at the same time. Banks of servers hummed at his back, radiating heat into the small room, and the wide countertop to his side was filled with a variety of docking ports and wireless pads.

"Hey Dean," I said as I pulled up a seat next to him on the counter. I activated a holo as I set the tablets into appropriate docks.

"How's it going, Detective?" He glanced at the tablets. "Got some encryption in need of bypassing?"

I nodded. "One tablet I just pulled off a Silicon Road dust dealer and another from Shao Wen's apartment that I distinctly *did not forget about* over the last day and a half, if you catch my drift."

Dean smiled. "I hear you loud and clear, Detective. If you want, you could always throw me under the vactrain. Say you handed it to me to let me take a crack at it while you had more important things to do. I flailed about, trying to fight my way in before eventually crawling to you and begging for help."

"Well, even though the part about me having more pressing matters to attend to is true, I'm not sure anyone would believe the part where you flail about unsuccessfully at *anything*. Besides, I can't have you being run over by a vactrain. Who would pull the files I need and run through oodles of security feeds for me?"

"I've always tried to make myself indispensable. Harder to get fired, that way." Dean smiled. "But you're better at forcing your way through digital barriers than I am. Always have been. Everyone knows that."

I pulled up the two tablets on the holo and activated a script I'd built for this sort of thing, a targeted approached that used a prese-lected library of likely login terms combined with others deter-mined by scrapes of the owners' public data libraries, social media, and general web searches. "I haven't *always* been better than you at cryptography. You of all people should know computer skills aren't an innate talent, Dean. I have more experience than you, that's all."

"Fair enough," he said. "But it's targeted experience. That makes all the difference you know. I hate that myth that the more hours you spend on a task the better you get. Only productive, focused hours count. That's why I'm jealous of you. You got thrown into the fire so young. I mean, you joined USC at what? Eighteen? How long was it before they assigned you to counter-intelligence?"

"Not long. A few months. I showed promise in cracking, according to my superiors. But you shouldn't be jealous. That func-tional experience came at a cost, Dean. The uprising was no picnic."

Dean's face fell. "Oh... yeah. I didn't mean it that way. I know it wasn't. I just—"

"I know what you meant. No hard feelings."

The script ran through its paces. Preset logins flashed red. Public data queries flashed red.

Dean turned back to his array of holos. "Well, it may not have been easy, but if nothing else, your time in USC intelligence wasn't wasted."

"I learned from the best, that's for sure, Dean."

Social media and web search login strings flashed red, too. I sighed. I'd figured Wen's tablet would be a no go, but I'd remained hopeful Boothe would've used a simple to guess password. No matter. I'd get in. It would just take more time.

I pushed back from my seat. "Dean, I'm going to leave these tablets here. I've got a brute force crack running. I'll check in periodically to see if I need to tweak the parameters, but if something goes wrong and I don't get a Net alert about it for some reason, you'll let me know?"

Dean nodded. "You bet, Detective."

"Thanks."

I left and headed back to my desk. Once there, I got to work on what I'd told Mwenge I'd tackle: the Red Summit financial report.

I regretted my decision as soon as I opened the file. Dean had mentioned a hundred shell companies doing business with Red Summit, but there were an order of magnitude more. Not all shells, to be certain. I imagined most of the companies who'd crossed paths with Red Summit were legitimate. In fact, a database search of the list of companies returned about a hundred and twenty with claims filed against them either by revenue services, through our fraud division, or with the better business association over improper practices. Maybe that was where Dean had gotten his number.

What I needed was a financial statement from Red Summit to Wen detailing her investments and which companies had earned the profits she'd been sent as dividends, but since it was all a front, I doubted I'd ever find that. The next best thing was to guess which companies might've had interactions with Wen and considered which of those might've had a motive to kill her, so I ran my revised list back through the police database, this time searching for companies whose employees or associates had been investigated for criminal activity, not simply those who'd had complaints filed against them. That returned a list of a little over twenty companies. Now we were getting somewhere.

I scanned the shortlist, but none of the names jumped out at me. Whethers Metallurgical Supply. AAA Construction. Michel and Sons Real Estate. Consolidated Entertainment Group, which took the prize for most nondescript name of the bunch, and a host of others.

I sighed. Once upon a time, money laundering operations consisted of a point source of income and a single front. A drug operation laundering money through a car wash, or a prostitution ring operating in the back of a nail salon, back when prostitution was illegal. Now, operations were much more complicated. More businesses. More connections. More misdirection. It made me glad to be in homicide and not fraud, though as the evidence showed, I couldn't escape tangled financial webs completely.

On a whim, I ran the remaining businesses through a third search, this time checking the business owners against the police database. Three came back as hits. My eyes widened as I latched onto the name in the middle. "Son of a *bitch...*"

I leaned back in my chair and blew air from between my lips. As I sat there, I saw Bishop approaching.

He took a seat on the edge of my desk. "Damn, Ambrose. You look like hell."

"It's shaping up to be one of those days."

"Well, time to turn that frown upside down, partner. The gang division was both friendly and accommodating. While they don't think we have enough to move on Vincenzio yet, we're getting closer by the minute. I put in a warrant request with Captain

Reyes, and I'm sure we'll have authorization to move on Red Summit by the end of the day. Assuming the place is a drug front like Boothe said, we should gather enough to slap cuffs on him and start getting some answers... Drake, you even listening?"

"What?" I looked up. "Yeah. Red Summit. Vincenzio. Drugs. Got it."

"What's wrong? You seem out of it."

"I've been looking through the financial documents Dean sent over."

"So?"

"I isolated a few companies that might be up to no good, then narrowed it down some more. Found one by the name of AAA Construction that has done business with Red Summit." I flicked a finger toward the holo. "Know who owns it?"

Bishop glanced at the hovering display. "Well, shit. You think *he's* involved in this?"

"We've investigated his guys for murder before."

"So we have." Bishop's jaw tightened. "But I'm not sure what we can really do about this. We can trace a direct line from Silicon Road to Wen. It's an indirect one beyond that. All this proves is he's working with Silicon Road to some degree."

I chewed on my lip. "How long until the warrant for the Red Summit Financial office comes through?"

Bishop shrugged. "I don't know. An hour or two, depending on judicial backlog."

I nodded. "Good. Just enough time for a quick lunch."

———

WE STOOD in the lobby of the Hotel Macron, outside a restaurant by the name of Kalofagás, its name engraved into the glass in a lowercase sans-serif font.

"You sure you want to do this?" said Mwenge.

"We're here to talk," I said. "What could go wrong?"

Mwenge looked unsure. Maybe he thought we should've notified Captain Reyes first. "We're not even sure they'll be here."

"Public cameras caught them walking into the lobby thirty minutes ago. It's twelve thirty. Where else would they be?"

Mwenge sighed. "Alright. I'll follow your lead."

I headed into the restaurant. The hostess tried to tell me I needed a reservation, but I silenced her with a quick flash of my badge and an assurance that I simply needed to talk to someone. She didn't ask who. Unless she was dumb, she already knew. The guy was a regular.

I headed into the dining space, weaving my way between white cloth-covered tables surrounded with padded, canary yellow chairs, underneath a high ceiling of beige marble streaked with dark grey, and made a beeline for a particular table in the back.

I found it occupied by a quartet of men. Two I didn't recognize. One, I barely spared a glance toward, a thick bruiser who was pushing fifty but could've cracked walnuts with his fists. Staring at him would've only made my jaw ache from the lingering animosity. Instead I focused on the elderly man at the far side of the table, one with dark grey hair, a bulbous nose, and more wrinkles in his forehead than a newborn puppy.

He saw me coming and lifted a single, hoary eyebrow.

His associates quieted at the sight of me and Mwenge. I came to a stop at the side of the table, neglecting to show my badge. "Excuse me. Kosta Demetriou? Could we have a moment of your time?"

29

JULY 4, 2154

WHEN NEXT I opened my eyes, it was to a sea of white. White walls, white ceilings, white sheets, decorated with banks of softly beeping displays and chromed instruments. An IV ran into the vein on the back of my right hand. On a counter to my left, a potted violet iris sagged remorsefully, in need of water or sun or both.

I tried to swallow and mostly failed. My tongue felt as if it had been left out to dry in a warming pan and the back of my throat might've been sandblasted. I looked for water but failed to find any. I also failed to find a call button for a nurse, so I tried to ignore my discomfort by wallowing in my Net.

According to my calendar, I'd somehow travelled forward in time three days. I checked my messages and found a number of unread ones, mostly instructions for squad drills and patrols, but there were a couple from Maarten and Phoebe, too. Phoebe's read heartfelt and warm, telling me she knew I'd be fine and that she'd visit me as soon as I was up and about, whereas Maarten closed his note with a hearty pat on his own back for being the only one of our cabin who hadn't yet eaten a piece of shrapnel at high velocity, a feat of skill he attributed to his bulging muscles and adonis-like jaw.

I'd barely opened my newsfeed app when the doctor came in to talk to me. I'd expected to be informed I'd passed out from acute blood loss, which the lovely doctor did confirm, but to hear her tell it, I was lucky not to have lost my leg. Apparently, a metallic shard had twirled its way deep into my thigh during the IED blast and nicked my femoral artery. Though my Net hadn't taken control of the wheel to mitigate my pain loss, my Suit had sprung into action, tightening the active compression bands around the wound to slow the bleeding. That's what had caused my leg to go numb and what had allowed me to stay on my feet as long as I had. Of course, it couldn't stop the bleeding entirely, so ultimately I'd succumbed and fallen unconscious. Good thing, too, because it would've sucked for me if I hadn't. Luckily for me, Nakamoto realized how bad things had gotten for me by the time Janeece and Maarten carried me back to the Marauder, and with the arrival of Epsilon squad, they'd raced me back to USC West and straight into surgery. Now I was the proud owner of several new synthetic arteries and was officially a casualty of war.

At least I'd be back. The doctor estimated I'd make a full recovery within a few weeks.

The bad news was that I'd be bedridden for at least the first week and a half of the recovery window. The first few days weren't so bad. I traded messages with Phoebe and Maarten, and I even sent a message to Sergeant Tyler to tell him what had happened. He responded in classic Tyler fashion with a note that read, simply, *Congrats on not dying. At least you beat Gupta.* I'm not sure what else I expected.

Pretty much everyone from our squad came to wish me well, even Mandel who had her arm in a sling. Hanson didn't drop by, but as far as I was concerned, that was a positive. I watched a lot of newsfeeds—the curated USC content included a number of local Martian channels. I'd assumed the attack on our Marauder and the subsequent venting of an entire Utopian block would've been big

news, but I had to dig back several days to find mention of it, and
even then it had only rated a two minute piece among a slew of
other similar actions. Every day brought a new wave of bombings,
demonstrations, and riots—all suppressed and contained by USC,
of course, but I got the impression they'd been going on for a while.
The reporters certainly weren't fazed by the developments. I
watched it all for a day or two before I got depressed and switched
it off entirely.

I probably would've died of boredom if not for my Net. USC
restricted the time-wasting, gaming sorts of apps available to us, but
I'd long since found a workaround to allow me to download whatever I wanted. I didn't exploit it, though. Besides the fact that I
might get in trouble, I really didn't have any interest in stacking
games and tapping simulators. Rather, I spent most of my free
hours reading books on Net design, kernel development, and
biohardware implementation. I wasn't sure I understood half of it,
but the more I read, the more I spoke the language. Between that
and tinkering on the Net worms and defense protocols I'd birthed
during my crypto classes on Luna, I mostly whiled away the hours.

The doctor let me start physical therapy after eight days of bed
rest. The exercises themselves were trivial—heel slides, quad sets,
assisted squats, and leg raises—but I was shocked at how weak my
legs were given I'd only been out of commission a week. As I found
out, the doctors had deactivated the overnight muscular activation
feature on my Net to allow for the arteries to bond to my muscle
tissue. Between that and lying motionless for a week in Martian
gravity, it was a slippery slope.

Still, by the end of the third week, I'd been cleared for a partial
return to action. I had to return to the medical building every day
for two hours of additional therapy until the doctors determined
my leg was back to full strength, but after being cooped up
between white walls for the better part of the past month, it was a
compromise I gladly accepted.

The squad welcomed me back with open arms, at least as far as they could stretch them. Mandel still had three to five weeks before she'd lose her cast. That didn't stop USC from assigning our squad plenty of work to keep us busy, though most of it was cake. Maybe they didn't want to rush us back into action after having been blown up and shot at, but rather than assigning us to patrol duty in the Utopian outskirts, we were instead assigned to guard duty at safe, USC-controlled facilities. Fusion reactors, water extraction plants, and comms stations mostly. I enjoyed the latter the most because it gave me an opportunity to pester the operators about new techniques for monitoring and intercepting Net signals. Most of the crew there found my buzzing as pleasant as that of a mosquito, but there was an elderly born and bred Martian by the name of Turnbull who took pity on me. He broke down how the Net doubled as a field antenna and showed me the apps needed to play with signal strengths. He must've liked me, because he never once reported me to Lieutenant Henson for spending more time in the comm base's offices than out in front, fingering my Badass.

Admittedly, the time spent pacing in front of USC facilities wasn't totally wasted, either. It gave me an opportunity to look, listen, and learn. As it turned out, despite the hostile environments around them, Martian city-dwellers weren't that different than those of us who'd spent our lives in the cradle of civilization. They looked a little different, to be sure. As a rule, Martians were uniformly taller than Earthers, naturally growing to a height that rivaled our hand-picked squad's average, though they didn't have anywhere near the muscle mass we did. Some of the soldiers had started calling them skinnies as a result, Maarten among them, but I steered clear of that talk. I didn't care for racial slurs.

Their height didn't fundamentally change their behavior, though. They ate, walked, talked, worked, slept, and screwed just like the rest of us—although I extrapolated the final two. I hadn't actually engaged in any voyeurism since joining the corps. What did affect their behavior, however, was our presence. Regardless of their positions toward Earthers or USC in general, locals inevitably eyed our broad jumpsuit-covered shoulders with a mixture of hesitation, disdain, or fear. Sometimes all three. Even Turnbull from communications, despite his jovial nature, always treated me with more care and distance than felt natural, as if he thought that beneath my human exterior lay the heart of a lion, one that might lash out and bite him for no reason other than it was my nature.

I tried not to take it personally, but it bothered me. That sort of behavior wasn't innate. It was learned over time.

Six weeks to the day after our arrival on Mars and just two days after Mandel had her cast removed, Lieutenant Henson gathered us in a conference room by the main USC West garage, telling us to report in our Suits and with Badasses in tow. We found Epsilon squad already assembled when we arrived.

"Zetas," he said. "Good of you to join us. Mandel. Gotta feel good to have that arm finally free, eh?"

She shrugged as she took a seat. "Meh. I rather liked having a club attached to my arm. Helped with swatting away unwanted advances."

Henson snorted, even though I know for a fact he'd been one of the rebuffed individuals in question. "And Drake. I hope that leg of yours is back to full strength." He joke hobbled a few steps toward me. "I'm sure Maarten doesn't care, but the rest of us don't want to have to lug your crap around for you anymore."

Over the weeks, I'd learned Henson didn't dislike me. He was just an asshole. "We're on Mars, Loot. Even a scrawny wet blanket like you could throw Maarten over your shoulder if you needed to."

Henson sneered and shot me a finger gun. "Alright, alright. Regardless, it's good to have you both back, and just in time, too. The rest of us have been getting bored out of our minds with the fluff assignments command's been handing us. Am I right?"

A few people shouted their agreement, notably Maarten, who slammed the table with his open palm and shouted, "Hell, yeah!"

"Well," said Henson, "luckily for us, some bureaucrat has seen fit to deliver us from our tranquil serenity." A display flashed to life behind him, showing aerial and street views of a typical silvery-gray Utopian building. Henson turned to it. "This, ladies and gentlemen, is six-oh-five west seventeenth street, and we've just received credible intel of a Red cell working out of the basement. We suspect that between the hours of ten thirty and twelve this morning, there will be at least five known Red operatives in said basement. Our mission is to bring them back alive through any means necessary. Tasers. Tranqs. Gas. Duct tape. All non-lethal options will be available. Given it's currently nine, that gives us an hour and a half to organize and make sure everyone is clear on team tasks. Any questions before I launch into the official briefing?"

No one raised their hands.

"Good," said Henson. "Now pay attention. I don't want anyone ending up in the hospital this time."

THE DOOR in front of me blasted off its hinges. The lights in the corridor went dark, and we surged forward in unison. Gas canisters hissed in the room beyond, choking the already pitch black air with smoke, but the IR sensors on my faceplate showed me what I needed to know. Badasses cracked, firing tranquilizer rounds at every hot outline that wasn't identified as a friendly on our visors.

The raid was over in less than twenty seconds. I turned the lights and ventilation systems back on via Net, having tapped into the building's maintenance panel before entering. The smoke thinned, flowing into the vents, revealing the carnage.

There wasn't much. A half-dozen lightly breathing bodies

sprawled across the basement floor between workstations, all of which held displays and servers on their surfaces. Some sort of chemistry lab stretched across the far wall, and only a few pieces of glassware had been broken in our barrage of tranq fire. A table to our right held soldering equipment, chip boards, tablets, and what looked like several kilograms of high-velocity explosives.

"Well spray me down and roll me in regolith," said Henson as he entered the room. "Looks like we snagged ourselves a genuine home-cooked bomb manufactory. This couldn't have gone any better if these Reds had gotten down on their knees and propositioned us. Good work, platoon."

I stood there, not quite believing how smoothly it had gone. Not a single return shot had been fired. Not a Red had escaped. We'd barely even damaged any of the equipment. It was a far cry from my near death experience six weeks ago.

"Well, don't just stand there," said Henson to the lot of us. "Get the prisoners back to the Marauders, bag and tag all this crap, and head back to base. If we're lucky, there might even be some extra drink tickets in this for all of us. Let's move!"

30

MAY 11, 2179

KOSTA DEMETRIOU SURVEYED the two of us, his blue eyes crisp and focused despite his age. For a moment I thought he'd tell us to get lost, but instead he flicked a couple fingers at the two guests at his table. They knew what that meant. They wiped their chins with their napkins, thanked the don for his time, shook his hand, and left, but not before shooting Mwenge and me a couple disdainful looks on the way out.

"Please, sit," said Kosta. "You'll pardon me if I don't remember your names, Detectives...?"

"Drake and Mwenge," I said. "I apologize for the intrusion. I know you weren't expecting us."

"Intrusions are a part of life," he said. "I've especially come to expect them on behalf of the city's fine defendants of truth, justice, and the rule of law. You remember my associate Mr. Kollias, of course." He gestured to the bruiser.

There was no way the juxtaposition of those two statements was in any way accidental. I glanced at Kollias, my jaw tightening despite my attempts at indifference. "I remember him quite well."

Arcenio Kollias smiled at me, his eyes crinkling with malevolent mirth. "Good to see you, Detective." He flexed his skillet-like hands as he made the statement.

Even now, I wanted to lunge at the man and plant a fist square across his jaw, not only because he was an almost certain murderer, but because he was an enormous asshole to boot. His name had chanced across my desk some four and a half months ago during Mwenge's and my investigation into the murder of a woman by the name of Isobel Newman. Newman had been strangled to death by garrote in her apartment. Her death had been clean and efficient. Pham hadn't found any bruising on her body apart from the neck, and CSU had failed to isolate any prints in Newman's apartment other than hers and a few belonging to the members of a weekly book club Newman held on Tuesday evenings. A review of Newman's financials revealed she'd been earning more than would've been expected of a junior inventory manager at a chemicals facility, however, and an audit of the chemical distributor's logs revealed a series of surprising, yet regular, disappearances from their warehouse. None of that led back to Kollias, and yet security cameras caught sight of someone who looked a whole lot like him outside Newman's apartment within fifteen minutes of Newman's time of death—which was surprising, because a pull of Kollias's Net logs showed him sound asleep at his home during the time, an alibi that was backed up by his wife of twenty-five years. Of course, I was well aware how such logs could be circumvented, but the department worked on evidence, not conjecture, and the supporting details we could muster weren't enough for our district attorney to recommend making a charge and sending the case to trial. Believe it or not, Kollias had undergone a miraculous series of near misses in his past, but again, the fact that he'd *almost* been charged with murder, assault, conspiracy, burglary, and fraud on multiple occasions didn't prove anything about his most recent infraction.

And every one of those charges had been while Kollias had

been under the employ of the man in front of me, Kosta Demetriou, one of the most powerful individuals in Elysium who wasn't employed by either the government or USC. It was hard to say how expansive his influence was, exactly, because so much of what he owned and controlled was concealed to the naked eye, but the police personnel file on him gave me an inkling. The owner of dozens of companies, many legitimate, many not. A gambler, more in the business sense than the traditional. A man unafraid of spending his hard earned coin on political influence, because he knew the value of it to his continued income. His clout was such that during our investigation into his right hand thug, never once did we seriously consider going after Demetriou himself, despite knowing Kollias wouldn't have killed a fly without Demetriou demanding it.

And for some stupid, moronic, incomprehensible reason, I'd decided to date his daughter.

I'd first run into Sophia when Mwenge and I made a trip to Kosta's estate to have a chat with Kollias in the wake of his suspicious appearance on the security vids. She'd come out of his mansion as we'd waited at the door, but instead of brushing us off, she'd relished in the opportunity to talk to us—or rather, to me. I didn't interpret is as a come on. She'd simply been upset at her father—she'd later describe their relationship as *strained*—and was willing to dish on Kollias as a means of aggravating her dear old dad. She'd even invited us into the mansion, an invitation Kosta himself later revoked, but at least it got us in the door. That probably would've been the end of things if I hadn't hatched the idea of approaching Sophia in private, sans Mwenge, in hopes of prying more details out of her regarding her father's hired gun. Though I hadn't managed to get anything of use for the case, I *had* left that meeting with a rumpled shirt, Sophia's perfume all over me, and a growing sense of disquiet over what I'd gotten myself into.

It started as nothing more than physical attraction, which made our clandestine trysts simple. She came to my place, or I to hers. But with time our relationship grew. As it turned out, Sophia was nothing like her father, or at least nothing like what I imagined him to be given my sparse set of interactions with him. She was quick-witted and occasionally severe, which matched his persona, but she was also introspective, caring, and generous, sexually as well as emotionally. Thankfully, she also didn't look anything like her old man. Though I'd never met Kosta's wife, I had a feeling I knew which side of the genetic tree Sophia had fallen from.

Honestly, things would've been simpler if our relationship had remained a purely physical one. I'd lied to Sophia the night before about not being worried regarding the implications of our relationship. I was. Though I was laser-focused in so many other facets of my life, I was lost when it came to women. Or at least I had been, until now.

Kosta spread his hands. "So, Detective. I assume you're not here to sample Kalofagás's fine cuisine, though I do recommend it. Martians we may all be, but I promise you, Greek food will always be the finest. I also assume you're not here to escort me or Arcenio to your station, otherwise you would've conducted yourself in a more *official* manner. So pray tell. What brings you to my table?"

There was no reason to beat around the bush. "Mr. Demetriou, the department is currently investigating the murder of a USC administrator by the name of Shao Wen. Are you familiar with the name?"

"How could I not be?" he said. "Her murder has been broadcast across Elysium, first by the traditional media, then by, should we say, more *underground* forces. Ones with claws."

"Did you know Administrator Wen yourself?"

"I didn't, but I might've met her," said Kosta. "I couldn't say with any certainty. I attend lots of social events with individuals in her line of work."

"*Water services?*"

"Management."

"So you wouldn't have any idea why she might've been murdered."

"I couldn't even have picked her picture from a display until I saw her story on the feeds, Detective. But why ask me? It would seem a certain segregationist has made it perfectly clear why she was murdered, and done so quite publicly."

"I'm not certain we can trust the Snow Leopard," I said.

"I'm certain you can't," Kosta said with a smile.

I glanced at Mwenge. The pressed-together lips and furrowed brow he responded with made it clear he wanted no part of the proceedings.

"Are you familiar with the Silicon Road gang, Mr. Demetriou?" I asked.

"I've heard of them."

"You should. You've done business with them recently. Specifically through one of your companies. AAA Construction."

Kosta smiled again, his teeth slightly yellowed from age. "I don't contract with mob organizations, Detective."

You don't need to when you have your own, I thought. "You wouldn't have dealt with them directly. A front of theirs, an investment corporation by the name of Red Summit Financial, purchased a number of used pieces of construction equipment from your company, according to financial records."

"And selling used equipment constitutes a crime now, Detective?"

"Murder does."

Kosta's leaned forward, his smile unwavering. "Believe it or not, Detective, I don't dislike you. Despite your chosen profession, you appear to be a man of integrity, not to mention someone who's learned how to use the slab of meat between his ears over the years—which is why I'm going to afford you a privilege I don't often give to men in your line of work. I'm going to be perfectly honest with you. I don't know a thing about Shao Wen's murder, at least not anything I imagine you haven't already uncovered in your investigation. The reason I don't know anything about it is because I wasn't involved in her death, not even tangentially. Do I make myself clear?"

"Perfectly, Mr. Demetriou," I said. "But just because you believe yourself to be uninvolved, even tangentially, doesn't make it true. Red Summit Financial, the company you've done business with, has direct ties to Ms. Wen."

Kosta's smile disappeared. "Let me see if I have this straight, then. You fancy yourself to have uncovered some grand conspiracy, one wherein my sale of construction equipment that was facilitated by an investment firm that has also done business with a dead woman somehow makes me complicit in her death?"

"Not necessarily."

Kosta leaned back in his chair. "Enlighten me then."

I took a deep breath and chewed on the inside of my lip. I didn't say anything. I had theories I was working on, whispers and ghosts of suspicions, but nothing fully formed. Mwenge had been right. It had been a mistake to come here. I'd wasted my opportunity.

Kosta read my mind. He gave his head the slightest of shakes. "You disappoint me, Detective. Not only do you interrupt my meal unnecessarily, but you prove wrong my own estimation of your intellect. Now, unless you mean to deliver me a warrant to further investigate my construction firm..." He flicked his fingers at the entrance.

It took a good deal of will not to let my anger and frustration show. Not anger and frustration directed at Kosta, surprisingly. I believed him that he hadn't ordered the murder of Ms. Wen, if not necessarily his total lack of involvement. But I hated myself for squandering an otherwise golden opportunity.

I stood. "Thanks for your time, Mr. Demetriou. Enjoy the rest of your meal."

I clapped Mwenge on the shoulder, and we wove our way back through the dining hall.

Mwenge exhaled loudly as we reached the lobby, almost as if he'd been holding his breath the whole time. "God, I hate that guy. You can smell his disdain for the law. It's impossible not to see it in everything he says and does. It makes my blood boil."

I looked back at the restaurant, feeling like the world's biggest heel. "Promise me something, Mwenge. The next time I come up with a hare-brained plan to approach a mob boss in public without intending to charge him with something or at the very least without hard evidence of his criminal activity, slap me, will you?"

"I'm not sure that would go over well if it ever got brought up before a review board."

Mwenge smiled, but I didn't return the gesture.

Mwenge clapped me on the shoulder. "Look, don't beat yourself up. You saw a connection. We tracked him here on public feeds. You took a shot at him. We didn't come away with anything, but it was worth the try."

Was it, though? I wasn't one to bluster and threaten my way into slip-ups and confessions, not that such a tactic would work with a man of Demetriou's caliber. I didn't have anything on the man other than a loose connection in a case that seemed to contain dozens. What exactly had I hoped to accomplish by confronting him? Coming here had been an exercise in futility—unless I'd chosen to come for ulterior reasons. I'd already admitted to myself my relationship with Sophia was entering uncharted territory. Perhaps I'd simply hoped to convince myself that Kosta remained blissfully unaware of our relationship, or perhaps I'd needed to get a better grasp of a man who might have a greater impact in my future than I dared to admit.

I didn't get a chance to finish my thought. A call from Reyes came in.

"Captain?" I said. "What's new?"

A sense of fatigue wormed through the digital space. "The same thing that's always new, Detective. More work for the weary."

"New developments in the Wen case?" asked Mwenge, who was included in the comm.

"If by new developments, you mean another individual dead under mysterious circumstances, then yes. Only time will tell if it's related to Wen's murder, but let me tell you, Detectives. As of now? It doesn't look good."

I cast a worried glance Bishop's way. "Send us the address, Captain. We're on our way."

AUGUST 27, 2154

I WALKED into Major Watkins office, standing at attention in front of her desk. She didn't look up as I arrived, her eyes glazed with the general detached focus of Net activity.

The Major's message to me hadn't indicated why she'd wanted to see me, and for the life of me, I couldn't guess why she would. If she'd summoned me in the immediate aftermath of our raid of the Red facilities, I might've assumed she'd want to congratulate me, but that had been three days ago, and the intervening hours had been spent on the most mundane of tasks: patrols, guard duty, cleaning, gun drills, and a decent amount of thumb twiddling.

Eventually, Watkins blinked and acknowledged me. "Private Drake. At ease. Care to take a chair?"

I relaxed, but I didn't sit. "I don't mind standing, ma'am."

"Your leg must be feeling better."

"It's at a hundred percent, as far as I can tell. I finished the last of my physical therapy two weeks ago."

Watkins nodded. "I saw that in medical reports. I wouldn't have let Lieutenant Henson drag you along on that raid if the doctors hadn't cleared you. Speaking of which, your platoon performed admirably in that. No casualties, all suspects captured unharmed, and a lot of contraband recovered. Well done."

Maybe Watkins had merely been busy for the past three days. "Thank you, Major."

"I also read in the report that you were responsible for building operation controls. I imagine it was a simple task for you to take over the lights and circulation."

"Come again, ma'am?"

"I'm speaking to your technical abilities, soldier," said Watkins. "It's not the first time you've taken the reins in that regard. On Luna, you single-handedly bested Epsilon squad in your first simulated combat encounter by delivering a visor malfunction executable via Net, am I correct?"

"Well... yes, ma'am. I suppose taking control of the building's lights and vents was fairly simple in comparison."

Watkins leaned back in her chair. "Would you like to try your hand at something a little more challenging?"

I cocked my head. "Ma'am?"

Watkins smiled. "Outbuilding B. Third floor. Find Sergeant Mishra. He'll be expecting you. Dismissed."

AN ARMED GUARD stopped me as I stepped off the elevator, but he waved me through after a facial scanner positively identified me. I walked past him, wondering what the hell was going on, but I didn't have to wonder for long. The hallway before me wasn't more than five meters long, with a single set of double doors at the end. The sign above them read 'USC Counterintelligence.'

The doors slid open as I approached. A warm hum greeted me, buzzing from racks upon racks of servers that stretched as far as I could see. There was a set of cubicles to my left, but nobody was in them. Beyond them, a hallway curved around the side of the room.

I followed the hallway, looking for signs of life. I passed two closed doors before reaching an open one.

I popped my head around the corner. Inside, a man with wavy, finger-length black hair and skin the color of sienna tapped away at a keypad. He looked up at my intrusion. "Yes?"

"Sergeant Mishra?"

"Are you asking or stating a fact?"

"More confirming it than anything. Your name is on a placard by the door." That and he looked like someone with the last name Mishra.

"You're Drake," he said.

"Another statement of fact."

"I know. I've seen your profile." He waved me in. "Give me a minute to finish this up."

I sat and waited patiently while Mishra tapped away at the keys.

"What's with the keypad?" I asked.

He didn't look away from his display. "You've never seen one?"

"Not since I launched from Titusville. All comms I've handled since have been via Net."

"You saw the sign above the front doors, right?"

"Counterintelligence. Yes."

Mishra shot me a look. "And the servers?"

"Yup."

"You think all this stuff is Net connected? That we leave those servers online?"

I swallowed back a lump of stupidity. "Right."

Mishra tapped a few more times and stood. "Sorry about that. Come with me."

"Where are we going?" I asked.

"Nowhere special." He stopped at the cluster of cubicles in the front. "Here. This'll be your workstation." He opened one of the desk drawers and pulled out a clear plastic sack full of electronics. "Look familiar?"

I looked at the tag. "It's the stuff we salvaged from the raid I was in three days ago."

"Bingo. Your first task will be to sort through these looking for intel about Red cells, targets, or movements of Red operatives. The room with all the interconnects and cables is at the back of the hall, on the right. It's a bit of a mess, so it might take some time to find what you need. Any questions?"

"A couple. So I just plug this stuff into my workstation and read it? Won't the data be encrypted?"

Mishra blinked. "Yeah."

"So how do I *decrypt* it?"

Mishra's mouth tipped into a frown. "Major Watkins said you were good at this sort of thing."

"I can code, and I've taken the cryptography course on Luna."

"You've taken the cryptography course." Mishra ran a hand through his hair. *"Okay.* So, what? You know the difference between a symmetric-key and a public-key algorithm? You've taken some basic number theory courses in college, I'm guessing? Have you ever engaged in any real cryptoanalysis?"

I tried to smile. "I'm a fast learner."

Mishra sighed. "Well, I guess I don't have anything on my schedule that can't wait a day or two. Have a seat. I'll show you the ropes."

I HADN'T LIED. I *was* a quick learner. By the end of the first day, I'd mastered the task system for sending decryption requests to the server cluster, not to mention reorganized the back room with the connector cables so it didn't look like a bomb had gone off. By the second day, I was sending batches of data to the servers to be broken down. It wasn't nearly as hard as Mishra had made it out to be. *Decryption theory* was massively complex, existing at the intersection of multiple high-level mathematical disciplines from algebraic number theory to elliptic curve cryptography, but I didn't have to fully understand those disciplines to implement them. That's what computer software was for. Ultimately, all I had to do was pick which decryption algorithm to implement, send it to the servers, wait a while, get it back, parse through the results to see if they were junk or not, and try again with a different algorithm.

Busywork though it might be, it still beat guard duty, mostly because there were highs amid the doldrums of boredom. A few days after I'd started, when I got my first successful crack on the data from one of the recovered Red servers, I nearly jumped out of my chair.

I quickly sat back down after realizing the data had not only been encrypted but encoded, but it was still exciting. Mishra helped me tackle the gobbledygook from there with limited results. Apparently USC had a database of known Red code phrases, as well as some fairly sophisticated linguistic programs that could translate the codes into a variety of potential outcomes. The problem was the Reds constantly changed their codes, remixing the phrases such that one message could mean hundreds of different things, most of them nonsensical. It all added up into a giant game of guesswork.

The downside to being assigned to fewer patrol missions was that I spent less time with my squad mates, so when Phoebe and Maarten asked me to join them for lunch at a local restaurant, I jumped at the chance.

I knew the place. Canyon Cafe, a USC friendly joint less than two blocks from the base. I ordered a tube turkey club with soy bacon and avocados. Phoebe picked the corn chowder, while Maarten plowed through the highest calorie item on the menu, a face-sized Monte Cristo stuffed with Elysian gruyere. We laughed and joked as we ate, and for a moment it almost felt like I was back in Kalamazoo, having a lazy lunch at a greasy spoon near campus at the risk of being late for class. The conversation slowed as the food disappeared. I slurped my tea, Phoebe sighed and smiled at me, and Maarten squirmed in his seat as he eyed the chemistry between us.

The big guy stood and gathered his and my plates. I tried to stop him, but he shook his head. "Someone's gotta bus these, hoss. Besides, I might stop by the counter and get another coffee. Line's looking long, though. Might take me a few minutes." He gave us a wink as he wandered off.

Phoebe shook her head. "Maarten. He's a good guy." She reached across the table and squeezed my hand. "How've you been, Ambrose?"

It was a vague question, the sort people ask when they don't expect a detailed answer, but I knew what Phoebe meant. Between my injury the day we arrived on Mars, my subsequent hospital time and physical therapy, the endless patrol work which split our squad into small groups, and my time under the supervision of Sergeant Mishra, Phoebe and I'd barely had any time to ourselves. Our carefree, sex-fueled romps aboard the *Osprey* felt years away, as if they'd taken place in another universe, one in which Ranbir was still alive and joking about his favorite shooter games.

I nodded. "I'm okay. It's been an adjustment. Taking part in real missions. Real combat. Trying to figure where we fit into this giant puzzle. I'd like to think we're making a difference, but our main purpose here seems to be making sure nobody chucks improvised explosives at USC facilities."

"Tell me about it." Phoebe squeezed my hand again. "I wish we didn't have quite so much on our plates. I've missed spending time with you. *Being* with you."

"There's a bathroom in back. I'm sure we could bang out a quick one."

That was definitely *not* the right thing to say. Phoebe recoiled, letting go of my hand. "Christ, Ambrose. I'm not just talking about sex."

"I know," I stammered. "That was a bad joke. I'm sorry. I didn't mean it that way. I like spending time with you, too."

But the damage was done. Phoebe lowered her eyes, giving her head a slight shake as she dragged her spoon through the dregs of her corn chowder.

I reached for my shovel, trying to think of a way to dig myself out of the mess I'd created, when I heard Maarten's bellow followed by a crash and a couple of angry yells.

I darted out of my seat toward the cries. I found Maarten pinning a skinny youth to the floor, his fist raised in the air above his face. A brown liquid soaked Maarten's jumpsuit at the neck and chest and had plastered his hair to his skull. Ceramic shards surrounded an upturned sandwich on the floor.

"Go on. Do it, freebreather!" the kid yelled. "Hit me! That's all your beef is good for, isn't it?"

I yanked on Maarten's arm before he could make a choice. "Maarten! What the hell are you doing?"

He stumbled to his feet, his teeth clenched, his eyes burning holes into the kid. "This little rust-fucker called me an oxygen hog and knocked my coffee all over me. *On purpose.*"

"Damn right I did, greenfingers." The kid pushed himself up to an elbow. "Get lost! Leave us alone, you Red hating bastard!"

"Why you little—"

I pulled Maarten back before he'd make a mistake we'd all regret. Phoebe had arrived, too, taking Maarten's other arm. "Guys...? We should leave."

The crowd from the queue had backed away, giving us a wide berth. Even the server at the counter looked ready to bolt.

I nodded. "Yeah. Let's get out of here."

Maarten didn't agree with our choice, but between the two of us we forced him out the door.

I WALKED BACK into the counterintelligence office, still shaking my head over Maarten's behavior. The big guy hadn't wanted to let it go, bitching about the 'fucking skinnies' all the way back to base. Phoebe had to pull rank on him to make him shut up about it. As much as I liked the guy, he was starting to get too hot-headed for my liking. I should have a talk with him. Remind him of what Major Watkins had told me, that our mission was a practical one more than an emotional one.

I tapped on my keypad, opening a secure link to the decryption servers as I loaded the latest batch of linguistic translations of the data we'd secured during our raid.

My eyes narrowed, then widened. I ran some numbers as I read. The likelihood of the code randomly aligning into the message was less than three percent.

I nearly jumped out of my seat as I tore off toward Mishra's office.

32

MAY 11, 2179

A CROWD MILLED about the office building Reyes had sent us to, staring into the Mylamene barrier and whispering to themselves. The Captain hadn't bothered to elaborate after ordering us to the scene of the crime, but the presence of firefighters as well as uniformed officers gave me some idea as to the problem.

A couple officers stood at the building's doors, keeping an eye on the crowds from behind a quickly-erected sawhorse barrier. I recognized the one on the left.

"Officer Chang," I said. "Where's Captain Reyes?"

The young woman gave us a nod. "She's on the seventh floor, Detective. I'll walk you up. The fire department froze the elevators. Just a precaution as they sweep the building for incendiary devices, but given the one that already detonated, better safe than sorry."

We headed into the building, hoofing our way through the lobby toward the stairs.

"What can you tell us about the bomb that went off?" asked Mwenge as we set foot to steps.

"Not much," said Chang. "All I know is it took out a good

chunk of an office and the cubicles outside it. Four people got rushed to Brahe Memorial Hospital. One is in critical care. Also one fatality. The individual who was in the office when the bomb went off."

"No pressure loss?"

"Thankfully, no," said Chang. "The building's fire suppression systems got the blaze under control within minutes. Could've been a lot worse."

"This is a government building, isn't it?" I asked.

Chang nodded. "That's right. Contains accounting and financial services for all sorts of city divisions. Power, water, refuse, transportation. You name it."

We reached the seventh floor landing. Chang pointed us down the hall to our right into a maze of desks and movable partitions. "Thataway, Detectives. You'll find Captain Reyes near the scorch marks."

"Thanks," I said.

Chang was right. We spotted Reyes about where the carpet started squelching under our feet. She stood outside an office, the door open and the interior windows blown into a crystalline shower that sprinkled the floor. The cubicles outside it were strewn to the sides, the partitions blackened and toppled over. Reyes stood in the middle of it all, hands on her hips and a frown on her face that might've been frozen into place by the fiercest winds of the Utopia Planitia.

"Captain," said Mwenge as we approached. "We made it as fast as we could."

Reyes glanced up from the wreckage. "No particular need for speed this time, Detective. None of this stuff is going anywhere."

"Officer Chang gave us an overview as we climbed the stairs," I said. "Care to get us all the way up to speed?"

"At this point, the abridged version *is* the full version," said

Reyes. "A bomb went off in this office at precisely one P.M. An incendiary device, not a high velocity explosive but a nasty one nonetheless. It wrecked havoc on the office, as you can see, as well as the office's occupant, who was pronounced dead on the scene when fire and paramedics arrived. A total of four others were seriously injured in the blast, most of them with burns and lacerations. The building's sprinkler systems responded appropriately, from what the fire department tells me, mitigating the damage. We haven't called in a civil engineer to examine the building envelope, but the firefighters know the ropes well enough to have given us the green light. The damage wasn't serious enough to put the building at risk of pressure loss."

I glanced to my side, into the bombed office. There was soot everywhere, over charred drywall, over the warped desk, and all over the floor, though the sprinklers had turned it into a soupy gray slurry. A white sheet, now grey at the edges from the mucked-up carpet, covered a still form. "Who was the office's occupant?"

"Deandre Jackson," said Reyes. "City comptroller, water services division."

"Water services?"

"That's right," said Reyes. "Except he was on the city side of the partnership with USC, not the corporate side."

"I can't be the only one who finds that suspicious," I said.

"You're not, and I'm just a lowly arson detective." Detective Fields walked out of the scorched office, looking as pasty and unhealthy as the last time I'd seen him. "And it's not only suspicious. I'd hazard to say it's ironic. To have two people in charge of water end up dying by fire?"

"Wen didn't die in a fire," said Mwenge. "Her throat was cut and she was stabbed repeatedly."

"There was still a fire," said Fields. "Cut me some slack, kid."

I cut him even more slack by not delivering a lesson on what irony was and wasn't. "So what can you tell us about the blast, Fields? Is this the work of the same bomber that torched Wen's bedroom?"

"At this point, I'd say it's unlikely. The incendiary devices set off in Wen's apartment were very similar in nature. Hot, quick burning devices that did a lot of damage in a short period of time. From what I can see, the device detonated here wasn't as finely tuned. I've found a couple scraps of the detonation mechanism that look homemade, and based on the soot thickness and what happened to the walls, I'm guessing the explosive itself contained a different accelerant than what was used in Wen's place. I'll have CSU run chemical traces once they get here to confirm, but to me, this job looks less precise."

"And the victim?" asked Mwenge.

"He's pretty badly burned," said Fields. "I didn't take more than a cursory glance, but I'm guessing the fire did him in pretty quick."

"Is Pham on her way?" I asked.

Reyes nodded.

I pointed to the white sheet. "Mind if I take a look?"

"Knock yourself out."

I stepped into the office, hitching my pants up a couple centimeters to get the hems off the slop. The smell of smoke hadn't totally been sucked out by the building's ventilation systems, lingering like an unwelcome party guest.

I knelt next to the body, picked the edge of the sheet, and flipped it up. Jackson was in rough shape underneath it. His hair was gone, as was most of his clothing. The skin underneath had been turned into a charred black mass, though ravines in the crust oozed and led to red pits deep within his flesh. I swallowed back a lump and lowered the sheet. I should probably check for additional wounds, but the department paid Trinh to do that, not me.

"Has anyone collected any eyewitness statements yet?" I asked.

"They're in agreement," said Reyes. "Jackson was at his desk when the bomb went off. There was no warning. Just the explosion, right at one, followed by the fire and the chaos of everyone fleeing the building."

"So no crazy knife-wielding psychopaths came through the office this morning? Nobody in a pressure suit with a blood red visor delivering the Snow Leopard's sermon?"

"Not that anyone has copped to," said Reyes. "But we don't have to take their word for it. We have security feeds."

"Of the office?"

"The hallway. It's not the best view, but you can see the office in the back. That's how we confirmed the timing of the explosion. That and the fire suppression system logs."

"You have a security feed that covers the office door, and you're only now mentioning it?"

"I know what you're thinking," said Reyes. "As soon as we got here, I asked to see the feeds myself. I only looked at the recording of the explosion, but I requested access to the building's security servers and sent the login information to Dean with instructions for him to contact me the instant he found something. He hasn't done so yet."

"Chances are the bomb would've been planted in the last twenty-four and a half hours," Mwenge said. "It wouldn't take Dean long to get through that much footage."

"Implying he's slowed considerably in middle age, or there's nothing to find," I said. "You'll recall the clean-up job someone performed on the computers in Wen's building's security cluster."

"Which would imply whoever set this charge isn't the same individual who fire-bombed Wen's apartment, but rather related to the one who murdered her," said Mwenge.

"It would make sense," I said. "I know I never really believed the idea that Wen's killer was of the serial sort. Now we have a connection that involves work, not passion. The method of murder is different, of course, but the killer could've played off reports of Wen's killing. Used media reports to craft a new way to hide his or her tracks. Fields already said the explosive appears to be different, less precise."

"Could be," said Mwenge. "Two murders of individuals in similar fields? It's a common thread. The torching of Wen's apartment isn't, though."

I sucked on my teeth, and Mwenge's brow furrowed.

Fields snorted. "You two always play off each other like this?"

"Only when we're clicking," I said. "You find any electronics in the office, Fields?"

"Parts of a display, but that's about it. From what I gather, the computing is done in the cloud."

"What else was destroyed in the fire? Hard documents? Records?"

Fields shrugged. "It's a pretty bare-bones office. Just a workspace, nothing else. I think a coffee maker bit the dust."

"Which implies Jackson himself was the target," I said.

"That seems to fit with what we know of Wen's murder, too," said Mwenge.

"I hate to break up the brainstorming session, Detectives," said Reyes, "but there's something notably different about Ms. Wen and Mr. Jackson. Public records show Mr. Jackson is married with two children. As much as I hate to force the task on anyone, someone has to notify his family of what happened here."

The wind left my sails with a sigh. "Right. The best part of the job. You want to tackle it, Mwenge?"

My partner snorted. "I'd rather go sunbathing without a pressure suit."

"You can both share in the misery," said Captain Reyes. "Let it never be said I'm not a magnanimous boss."

I gestured to the wreckage. "You've got all this under control?"

"We're not in control of anything, Drake. We just clean up the mess." Reyes gave me a nod. "Come on back when you're done. I'm sure they'll be plenty left for you two to tackle before the day's done."

33

SEPTEMBER 1, 2154

MAJOR WATKINS LOOKED up from my terminal in the counterintelligence office. "Can you confirm this information is accurate, Sergeant Mishra?"

Mishra shrugged, his arms crossed before him. "I can't corroborate the information with other sources. It could be a plant. But the information on the recovered drives was both encrypted and encoded. We also didn't hear any chatter prior to the raid indicating the Reds knew we'd be coming."

"Certainly they weren't prepared for our arrival," said Watkins, leaning back in my chair. "What about information recovered from the prisoners?"

"I haven't been able to crack the memory data recovered from their Nets yet," said Mishra. "As you know, those are harder bits to parse."

I glanced at Mishra, hoping my surprise didn't show. I knew Net signals could be intercepted and that stimuli, primarily visual, could be recorded and stored, but in all my studies and conversations, I'd never heard anyone mention the possibility of prying into someone else's memories that way. I didn't even know it was possible. How much about the Net didn't I know?

"What about more traditional knowledge extraction procedures?" asked Watkins.

I blinked. Was she talking about torture?

"There's no time for that," said Mishra. "These communications indicate the attack will come tonight. Besides, information obtained through forced measures is unreliable. Trusting what we have is our best bet."

Watkins frowned. "We have to acknowledge the possibility this *is* a plant, despite evidence to the contrary. It could be designed to draw our resources from an ulterior target. Nonetheless, I'll recommend increasing security at all USC fusion plants, not just the one referenced." Watkins turned to me. "You've patrolled the plant mentioned in this communication, right, Private?"

I nodded. "Yes, Major. I was last there about a week ago with Franks and Sun."

She tapped her fingers on my desk. "Very well. Get Zhao. Assemble your squad at the conference room in the north garage. Make sure Epsilon squad comes with you. I'll notify Lieutenant Henson and brief him on the situation. It's not quite fourteen hundred hours. This attack is scheduled for twenty-two thirty. Plenty of time to prepare."

"Yes, ma'am."

"One more thing before you go," she said. "If you're right about this missive, the enemy won't know we'll be in waiting. That doesn't mean this mission will be as clean as your last. Assume the Reds will be armed and dangerous and prepare accordingly."

I nodded and headed out, anxious but eager all the same.

I SAT IN AN UNCOMFORTABLE CHAIR, staring out the second-story window at the entrance to the fusion plant from our vantage point across the street. Lights illuminated much of the thoroughfare below, but I wore my Suit mask with the IR sensors on a half-strength overlay for good measure. I fingered my Badass as the clock ticked over to 22:30.

"You doing, okay?"

Maarten sat across from me in another crappy folding chair. The rest of the apartment was empty, unless you counted the numerous stains on the floor and the lingering smell of garlic and vinegar. I suspected the odors were the reason the landlord hadn't yet found a new tenant for the place.

"I don't like waiting," I said. "It makes me antsy. Aren't you?"

"Aren't I what? Antsy?"

"Yeah. You know. Nervous about the combat?"

"I wasn't the last time," said Maarten, peering through the window. "Why would I be this time?"

"Well, for one thing, we're missing the backup we had last time." I waved around at the empty space. "They're all guarding the other entrances, in case you forgot."

"See, I kinda like it that way," said Maarten. "Just you and me. Back to back. Hoss to hoss. Like in the movies."

"Last time I checked, neither one of us was a super spy crack shot who could kill someone with a straw as easily as with a rifle."

"Good thing we have the rifles, then." Maarten smiled and lifted his.

I checked the time again. 22:34. "They're late."

"If they're coming at all," said Maarten.

"They'd better come. I worked hard for that intel." I shook my head, keeping my eyes trained on the entrance. My foot tapped an irregular rhythm against the floor.

Maarten sneered. "I can't believe you're stressed about them *not* coming. Oh hey, don't mind me over here, stressing because I might *not* get shot tonight."

"*You* don't seem worried about the combat."

"I was born for this, hoss. That and lifting lots of weight with my big muscles, and pleasuring women with my other big attributes."

"Attributes? *Plural?* What are you packing down there?"

Maarten chuckled, then stopped suddenly, slapping me on the shoulder. "There."

A rideshare slowed to a stop before the entrance to the fusion plant. The door opened, and out popped a pair of Martians, one of them wearing a bulky backpack and the other lugging a duffel bag.

Maarten switched to the squad channel. "Zeta squad, copy. We have skinnies approaching the East entrance. Anyone seeing any other activity?"

Janeece piped in. "There's a van pulling up to the service entrance on the northwest side, too. Hold on. Yeah, they're approaching the building."

"Copy that, teams," said Phoebe. "Remember our orders. Let them enter the building before engaging. Guard the exits. Command doesn't want any of them wandering off."

"Squad leader, I'm counting five Reds here," said Janeece. "Requesting backup."

"Halabi. Mandel. Nakamoto. Move in to cover Johnson and Franks. How are you on your end, Drake?"

"Just a pair," I said. "We should be able to handle them."

"Alright," said Phoebe. "As soon as they're through the doors, move to intercept. Sun and I will sweep in to cover your position."

The two Reds reached the door. Maarten and I had a bet on whether they'd use a cutting torch or a set of jaws to get in, but the one carrying the duffel bag didn't remove it. Rather his buddy took a look around, pulled a tablet from his pocket, and tapped it. The doors popped right open.

"Crap," I said. "They've got electronic building access. Let's move, Maarten!"

We leapt from our seats and burst through the door, racing

down the steps as Phoebe cut in again. "They've disabled cameras, too, guys. I don't have eyes inside anymore."

"Wonderful," I said as we darted out the apartment's front door. "At least we know where they're heading."

Or at least we assumed to know. The captured missive had said the Reds planned to sabotage the fusion reactor with satchel charges. Counter to Franks' fears that such an explosion would lead to a massive nuclear chain reaction, the bomb would simply spray radioactive lithium around the interior of the power plant as it took out power to roughly two million residents of Utopia, but the latter result was bad enough. Subsidiary systems could probably compensate for the sudden power drop, but if they couldn't, heaters would shut down, ventilation systems would grind to a halt, and a lot of people would be left in the dark—and in fear. The weapon of choice for the Reds.

We came prepared, though. I brought up the plant's construction diagram, reminding myself of the most direct route to the reactor as we reached the front doors.

Maarten paused. "Badass hot?"

I nodded. "You take point."

I activated the door via Net and we rushed in, past the front offices and into the warehouse beyond. A quiet hum filled the air, not from the fusion reactor but from the huge, cylindrical sections of the generator in front of us. We walked quickly in a half-crouch, trying to minimize the sound of our feet despite the hum, rifles held at the ready. The lights above us glowed with a muted intensity, lowered to half power for the evening.

"Damnit, where are they?" I said to Maarten. "We didn't take that long, did we?"

"Reds entering from the northwest loading dock," said Janeece. "We're moving in behind them."

"Stay alert," said Maarten. "Maybe they didn't take the most direct route toward the reactor."

We passed the humming cylinders and turned left, crossing an elevated walkway between the coils of the electrical generator and the massive pressurized tank of the steam generator. We'd almost reached the end of the walkway when I spotted movement.

"Bogies around the corner," I said, crouching behind the back-most generator coil. "They must've crossed over at the front of the plant."

Maarten peeked over my shoulder. "They're coming this way... *oh, shit!*"

Before I could ask what the problem was, he popped out of cover, sighted along his rifle, and pulled the trigger. The air cracked as his rifle fired.

"What are you doing?" I cried. "They have explosives!"

I shot upright, Badass in hand, surveying the scene. The two Reds we'd seen sprinted down the side of the facility away from us. The one with the duffel bag jerked and fell, spasming as he went down under a barrage of fire from Maarten's rifle.

"They spotted me." Maarten jerked his rifle to the side as the other Red bobbed and weaved, heading onto another of the elevated walkways between the generator coils. "Cut him off. I'll follow. Go!"

Maarten wasn't supposed to be giving orders, but in the heat of the moment, I didn't question him. I sprinted back down the walkway at full speed. Somewhere behind me, I heard two more shots, the distinctive sounds of a Badass. Janeece cut in via Net, asking what the hell was going on, but I didn't slow. I skidded around the corner, muzzle of my rifle pointed before me.

The Red made it to the end of his walkway at the same time I made it to mine. His arm whipped my way, a gleam in his hand.

I didn't hesitate. A blast rocked my ears as I discharged my Badass.

My training worked. The Red went down, his pistol clattering against the concrete as his body hit the floor. I closed the gap between us at a run, keeping my rifle trained on his limp form. Somewhere in the distance on the other side of the reactor, I heard more shots.

Janeece cut in again. "Damnit, Maarten, you were supposed to warn us before firing."

"Everything okay in there?" asked Phoebe. "I'm thirty seconds out."

"We suppressed the Reds," said Janeece. "Got all ours, despite having to improvise."

"Drake?" said Phoebe.

I stood there, staring at the Red. A shock of messy brown hair hid half his face. His backpack hung askew, the top open and the contents spilling to the floor. A red stain spread across his chest, the blood pooling underneath him. His eyes fluttered, and he moaned softly.

I've just shot a man, I thought.

"Ambrose, you there?" asked Phoebe.

My heart hammered. My arms tingled, but I couldn't tear my eyes from the target. A day old beard covered the Red's jaw, but it was thin. Patchy. I spotted pimples. He might've been younger than me.

His breathing slowed, and his eyes rolled back.

Jesus Christ, I thought. *I've just* killed *a man.*

"He's alright. I've got eyes on him." I heard Maarten's voice in my mind, then the noise of his feet on the walkway behind me. "Good shot, hoss."

I didn't turn back to look at him. A massive weight pressed on my chest. My suit systems showed nominal Bacteria Buddy function, but I couldn't breathe. I ripped my helmet from my head, trying to fill my lungs with fresh air.

I felt Maarten's hand on my shoulder. "Ambrose. You doing okay, buddy?"

I shrugged him off, still unable to breathe as Phoebe and Nakamoto arrived. "Ambrose?"

I waved Phoebe off, trying to act like I was fine.

She looked at the body and grimaced before turning to Maarten. "Are both of your targets accounted for?"

"Yeah," said Maarten. "I wasted one on the other side of the walkway. Ambrose took care of the other."

Icy needles stabbed at my heart as he said it, but it was true. I'd killed him. Me. And I'd barely flinched.

"You *wasted* one?" said Phoebe. "Maarten, I have your Badass data. You discharged your rifle twice after your initial fire. Why?"

"The target was still moving. I had to make sure he wouldn't be a threat as I came to support Ambrose."

"So you shot a Red twice to make sure he stayed down? Maarten, our task was to secure the facility and the enemy, not to *waste* them. Why did you open fire in the first place? You should've coordinated with Johnson's team."

Maarten and Phoebe started to argue, but I barely heard them. I took a seat on the ground, feeling faint and still unable to breathe. I stared at the dead Red and all I could think of was, *I'm sorry.*

I SAT on the bench outside Major Watkins' office. She'd summoned Phoebe and me following our return to base, I assumed to chew us out over our slipshod work at the fusion plant, but Maarten hadn't been called in alongside us. I guess as squad and deputy leaders, it was our asses on the line, and we'd be responsible for discipline beyond that. Maybe we'd be stripped of our positions entirely, and Maarten would be dealt with separately. I didn't know. I didn't really care.

"Ambrose?"

I lifted my head and turned it toward Phoebe. She looked at me with concern in her eyes. "You okay? You've been abnormally quiet since the encounter."

I worked my tongue in my mouth, trying to express what I felt. The cavernous pit in my stomach. The ache in my lungs. The sorrow. The knowledge that I was responsible. That I made a choice to kill. The emotions flogged me over and over as I replayed the Red's death, him hitting the floor, his gun clattering, his blood spreading.

"I'm... fine."

Phoebe looked like she didn't believe me, but the door opened and Watkins called our names. We shuffled in and took our seats. Watkins sat there, fingers steepled before her, eyeing us with her cold blues. I sat and took her disdain, all of it, knowing I deserved it and more as I waited for the reaming.

"Zhao. Drake," she said. "Good job out there. The pair of you did some damn fine work today."

I blinked, finding my voice. "Ma'am?"

"Don't get me wrong," she said. "It was sloppier than I would've liked, but you intercepted a multi-pronged Red threat and effectively protected a valuable USC asset from damage, or possibly destruction. That's no joke. Private Zhao, you put your teams in position to succeed, which is in line with your past performance, and Private Drake? None of this would've been possible without your intel."

I still couldn't believe what I was hearing.

Phoebe responded for me. "Thank you, ma'am."

"Now," continued Watkins, "in part because of performance and in part because of necessity, I've seen it fit to promote the both of you. Zhao. You're now a sergeant, and you'll be in charge of your entire platoon. Normally, that position goes to a lieutenant, but I'm not in the habit of advancing soldiers two ranks at a time. That means you, Private Drake, are now the leader of Zeta Squad, though you'll continue to report to Zhao when she's present. Are we clear?"

Phoebe blinked, too. "Yes, ma'am. But, ah... what about Henson?"

"He's not coming with us."

"Where are we going?" I asked.

Watkins smiled, but there wasn't any mirth to it. "Apparently, we're too valuable to keep stationed at Utopia West. We've been reassigned to the field. We're shipping out in the morning. Report to the garages at oh-eight-hundred. Dismissed."

I nodded, stood, and turned toward the door. An early departure wouldn't allow much time for sleep, but I didn't care. I doubted I'd be able to catch a wink regardless.

34

MAY 11, 2179

I MET MWENGE'S EYE, my thumb hovering over the door chime. "You ready for this?"

"I'm never ready," he said. "Go ahead and ring her anyway."

I pressed the chime, and we waited in front of the door. After a few moments, I heard a shuffling and what sounded like crying. The door cracked open with a puff, pulling back to reveal a woman with red eyes and tears streaming down her face. She could barely speak amid her sobs. "Yes?"

Something told me we weren't the first ones to reach her with the news. "Excuse me. Kendra Jackson?"

Mrs. Jackson nodded, the tears dripping from her cheeks. Some of them splattered across her blouse, joining a cluster of wet droplets that had already soaked into her cloth.

"I'm Detective Ambrose Drake with the EPD. This is my partner Detective Bishop Mwenge. I'm afraid we have some news regarding your husband."

Kendra covered her mouth with a hand, and her sobbing turned into a wail. She nodded behind her sorrow as fresh tears sprung from her eyes.

"Do you mind if we come in?" I asked.

Kendra mumbled something unintelligible, but she stepped back from the door and waved us in, more or less. I took that as an invite. She stumbled to a sofa in her living room and collapsed into its cushions, her chest heaving with sobs.

I followed her in, working my way around the couch, which looked as if it couldn't have been more than a few months old. I trailed my hand along it, marveling at the softness. Lab leather, unless my senses failed me. A plush rug absorbed my footfalls, and a tall, wooden clock fashioned after the original antiques of Europe ticked softly, its long hand cycling through the seconds.

Mwenge looked distraught. "Can I get you anything, Mrs. Jackson? A glass of water, perhaps?"

Kendra did something with her head, but I wasn't sure if it was a nod or a shake. The indistinct wave of her hand didn't clarify matters.

"I'm just going to get it, then." Mwenge headed off in the direction of the kitchen before I could say anything.

I sent him a message as I sat. *Thanks a lot, jerk. Better be back with that water, soon.*

Kendra continued to sob, barely sparing me a glance. I might as well have been a holo for all the attention she paid me. Getting through to her would be difficult, but I had to try.

"Mrs. Jackson, are your children home?"

Kendra shook her head. This time she managed a recognizable response. "No."

"They're at school?"

She nodded. "They go to Westbrook Academy."

I tried not to lift an eyebrow. Regardless of where they went, they wouldn't be home for some time. "I assume you know why we're here, Mrs. Jackson. I don't mean to bring you any more pain, but I need to be forthright with you. An explosive device detonated in your husband's office this afternoon. He perished on the scene. I'm sorry."

Another sob racked Kendra's body, and her wail ascended in pitch. I stretched my jaw, thankful I wasn't a dog.

Mwenge approached around the time Kendra's moan subsided, placing a tall glass of water on the table in front of her. The glass had the thin walls and clarity of fine crystal.

"I wish I didn't have to do this, Mrs. Jackson, but as a matter of due process, I need to ask you some questions regarding your husband. Would that be okay with you?"

Kendra took a deep breath and let it out in a warble. She wiped her cheeks of tears, but that didn't stop them from coming. "I'll try."

"We have reason to believe your husband's death is a homicide. Can you think of anyone who might've wished your husband harm? Did he have any enemies?"

Kendra looked up, focusing on me for the first time through her tear-blurred eyes. *"Enemies?"*

"Yes, ma'am."

"Why would he have any enemies?"

"I don't know, ma'am. That's why I'm asking."

Kendra shook her head, bewildered. "He... no. He was a kind man. A loving man. A wonderful father. A provider. No one would ever want to hurt him."

Pointing out the obvious never helped in situations like these. "What about in his professional life? Did he complain about co-workers or business associates? Did he ever mention people who might've antagonized him or tried to coerce him?"

"Coerce him? Of course not."

"Do you know if he had any outstanding debts?"

"Not to my knowledge. He would've let me know if he did."

"Had he engaged in recent strange behavior? Anything outside the norm for him?"

Kendra's sobs subsided, replaced instead with a look of indignation. "Absolutely not. I'm telling you, Deandre was an honest man. A *good* man. I... I don't know why anyone would've wanted to hurt him." The sobs started to return. "Are you sure someone meant to kill him? Maybe it was an accident."

"It's possible," I said, though I didn't believe it. "But there's no question someone set an explosive device in his office with malicious intent."

Kendra shook her head, her eyes boring holes into the floor. "Why? Why would anyone do that?"

"I can't answer that yet, Mrs. Jackson. But you can rest assured we're doing everything we can to figure it out."

Kendra's head suddenly snapped up. "Do you... do you think this had something to do with that woman?"

I narrowed an eye. "What woman?"

"The woman on the news. What was her name? Shen, or something? Her apartment was bombed a few days ago, wasn't it? I remember hearing she worked for USC in the water services division."

"Shao Wen," I corrected. "Did your husband know her?"

"I have no idea. I suppose it's possible. But why would someone come after *him*? What do you suppose... Oh. *Oh, god.*"

"What is it?"

Kendra's sobs renewed themselves with added strength. "The video, from the Martian separatists. I didn't watch it. I didn't have the stomach for it, but I heard about it on the news. They claimed that Wen woman was involved in corruption, that she needed to be eliminated. You don't think they're the ones who came after my husband, do you?"

I sighed. For a moment, I thought I'd been on the verge of a revelation. "Again, I couldn't say, Mrs. Jackson. But we'll investigate all avenues into your husband's death, up to and including any possible terrorist motivations."

"*Terrorist?*" Kendra's eyes widened. "Wait... Do you think my family is at risk? *My children?*"

"I would imagine not, Mrs. Jackson, but if it would make you feel better, I could arrange for a police detail to watch your apartment for the next—"

Kendra sprang from her seat. "I need to check on my kids. Oh, god. If anything were to have happened to them, too. *I need to go!*"

The woman ran to her door, throwing it open before disappearing down the hall. I glanced at Mwenge as the door swung back on its hinge. "You weren't much help."

"You were doing such a fine job soothing her pain, I didn't want to interfere."

"Bullshit. You know, the only way you're going to get better at soothing widows is by practicing."

"I wouldn't go so far as to say you *soothed her*. Talked her through her thoughts, more like. Besides, I don't need to practice—unless you're planning on dying or retiring soon."

I sighed and wiped a hand across my face. "I'm not. Just would be nice to share the load sometimes."

Mwenge's joking demeanor disappeared. "Sorry. I didn't realize it weighed on you so much. If I'd known, I could've—"

"It's fine," I said. "It always hits me, talking to the family. Wouldn't be any easier if it had been you doing the talking."

We sat in silence for a moment. Mwenge picked up the untouched glass of water and took a sip. "I suppose we should probably let ourselves out."

"It's tempting to snoop around, but seeing as anything we find would be inadmissible, yeah. We should go." I stood. "On the bright side, at least we know Jackson wasn't as squeaky clean as his wife suspected."

Mwenge got up alongside me. "How do you figure that?"

"Come on. Look at this place. Leather couches. A wooden grandfather clock. Nice rugs. Big windows. I'll bet the kitchen sparkled, too. Not to mention Kendra said her kids went to Westbrook Academy. That's a private school, and not a cheap one.

Deandre was a city comptroller. As a government employee, we don't have to guess what he made. It's a matter of public record."

Mwenge focused in the way he always did when accessing his Net. He winced. "Ouch. Yeah, he shouldn't be living here."

"Exactly. And I'll bet dollars to doughnuts he was earning his extra cash in a similar way to how Shao Wen was earning hers."

35

SEPTEMBER 2, 2154

WE TRAVELLED west to Isidis by vactrain before loading onto the massive overland transports that would take us to our ultimate destination, a small mining settlement by the name of Cassini out in the Arabia Terra, some thirty-six hundred kilometers away. The terrain wasn't the best. With luck, we'd average fifteen kilometers an hour, which meant it would take us two weeks to arrive after accounting for daily exercise and charging stops.

The overland transports themselves were hulking beasts, more than twice as big in every dimension as the Marauders and as heavily armed and armored. They still weren't big enough by half. Bunks packed the second floor of each transport, head to head and butt to butt, with half meter wide passages between them for 'ease' of movement. The communal sleeping levels had been split in half, one each for the men and the women, but that one small concession was the transport's only attempt at even a modicum of privacy. The main level was massive and open, filled with seats in the middle and lined with more seats with access to the transport's defenses and computer systems on the sides. Because the powers that be were cheap assholes, the number of soldiers assigned to each transport had been maximized, which meant every seat and every bunk was filled at all times. Somehow, I was one of the lucky bastards who drew a normal daylight shift to start, but Major Watkins assured us we'd rotate as we went.

Once our entire company had loaded up, the caravan rumbled to life and hit the regolith, two of the transports in front, two in back, the hulking mobile fusion reactor that would recharge us in the middle for safety, and a handful of Marauders on the edges for support or reconnaissance, if needed. And so began the most boring stretch of my life.

I'd always assumed I'd encounter the worst travel conditions of my stint in the corps while in space, but the overland transports were tin cans compared to the spacious Mark Xs. Once space travel entered the realm where not all ships needed to be able to exit major gravity wells, the ability to construct said ships changed dramatically, allowing for weight rooms, swim tubes, dodgeball corridors, and observation decks, among other things. The transports had shoulder width paths between seats where you could hammer out low-g tricep pushups until someone told you to get out of their way or stepped on you when you didn't.

Needless to say, I retreated into my Net as much as possible. Its offerings weren't a perfect replacement for standing, moving, or having intimate contact with another human being, but the movies, books, and pointless tapping games available to us were a better alternative than staring at the heavy rivets and polished Mg-Al alloy of the transport's ceiling. I tried to be as productive as I could with my time, opting to read more books on cryptoanalysis, hacking, and neural net bioevolution whenever my brain was up for it, but even I had my limits. I found myself nodding off in my seat during shifts often, and during the times when I was assigned to a position at the edge of the Marauder, keeping tabs on transport systems, more often than not my eyes drifted to the small windows set over the displays.

The first couple days brought the most interesting features to bear. Our transport skirted the edge of the Isidia Planitia, along the edge of the ancient impact basin terraforming engineers hoped to one day refill with liquid water before beginning its several vertical kilometer-long ascent into the Syrtis Major Planum. At that point, the features become more uniform, with wide expanses of nothing interspersed with craters and the high-elevation, similarly cratered regions of the Terra Sabaea to the south. Sometimes the landscapes seemed like no more than paintings, still and cold and whisper quiet. Other times the wind would blow fiercely, whistling as it whipped over the hardened shell of the transport, choking the air with the finely ground rust red particulates of the Martian regolith, the byproduct of millions of years of sun and wind erosion, and once upon an ancient time, water.

Slowly but surely the water was coming back. Pumps at every colony siphoned it from deep underground, melting and pumping it and distributing it to the people. Some of it went outside the enclosed cities, too, enough to meet the USC quotas for rehydrating and warming the atmosphere. Swift-Tuttle would make said quotas obsolete some day. A day when there would be as much water and atmosphere as people could ever desire. A day when the sun's rays would heat the oceans and water would rain down from the sky as it did on Earth.

It felt like that day might be a million years away. For all mankind's efforts so far, they'd raised the average atmospheric pressure on Mars by a measly 1.2 kPa, mostly via added CO_2. The super greenhouse gas plants sat idle half the time, limited by low fluorine reserves in the soils. The poles froze harder than ever.

For now, the planet remained cold, red, and dead. Just like the man I'd shot.

"MAN, I HATE THESE FUCKING PATROLS." Maarten's voice rang in my head. "They're so pointless."

We walked twenty paces apart, circling the transports at a distance of a half kilometer. Long shadows stretched from the vehicles in the early morning sun. Huge cables snaked from the mobile fusion reactor to the transports, charging the batteries. Shadows hung from those, too, creating a tangled mass of dark tentacles that encircled our metal beasts in their ethereal grips. The full company of soldiers, minus us guards, bounded around the transports in a loping gait. Round and round, over and over. It wasn't the best of exercises, but it was all the cramped magnesium cans and the environment provided us, minus the nightly Net-generated muscular stimulation.

"Honestly," continued Maarten. "What do they think is going to happen? That some fucking team of super Reds is going to rise out of the dust and mow us all down? That they knew we'd stop here and spent the entire night freezing their dicks off to spring a trap on us?"

Despite the Suit's active heating elements, I shivered. At least the early morning runs warmed you up. The patrols didn't do squat. "It's procedure. Everything is just procedure. Haven't you figured that out by now?"

Maarten turned his head my way, but I couldn't see his face due to the sun's glare off his helmet. "What do you mean by that?"

I sighed and shook my head. "Don't you ever wonder why we're here, Maarten?"

"I don't have to wonder, hoss. I know exactly why we're here. To smash the crap out of some backwoods dust farmers, or at least shoot a few dozen holes in them."

We passed in front of a rocky outcropping, the shadow from it stretching down the slope from us almost to the transports. My skin prickled from the chill as soon as I crossed into the shroud. "But why, Maarten? Yes, they attacked us. I know. But why fight

back? Why not give up? Why fight for *this*? It's a barren wasteland. Beautiful at times, sure, but in a cold, detached, useless sort
of way. The beauty of emptiness. Nothing here but dust, rock,
and... *hey*. Ice."

I saw the faint patch only by the glimmer at the edge of the
shadow and sun. In the light there was nothing. In the shadow,
there was. A few specks of white, already half hidden by reddish-
brown dust. I knelt and scraped at it with my finger. It spread into
the regolith like grains of sand.

"Dry ice?" asked Maarten.

I checked my suit sensors. "Nope. Not cold enough. Water ice.
Not much. Maybe a few grams worth, but still. I'll be damned."

"What were you saying about this being a dead wasteland?"

I stood, eager to get back in the sun. "I'm not wrong."

"You lack vision," said Maarten, walking beside me. "Someday
you won't be able to tell this place from Earth except by the
gravity."

I snorted. "You can't really believe that."

"Why shouldn't I? What do you think the Earth looked like ten
thousand years ago? Not a single city, no pyramids, no great wall of
China. Not a single light in the night sky. Forests as far as the eye
could see. You think we haven't changed our planet? We put four
billion tons of carbon in the air without even trying. What do you
think's going to happen to a planet when we put our minds to it?
It's just a matter of time."

I gazed out across the vast flat expanse. Rusted soils and butterscotch sky as far as the eye could see. "I'm having a hard time envisioning it."

"You saw the ice. I'd say that's enough. Not that it matters."

"You getting all existential on me, Maarten?"

"Nope. Rather, I think I'm the one who's grounded in reality.
You're wrong, Ambrose. We're not here fighting for the planet, or
for USC, or for whatever other reason you seem to think we are.

We're here to take out as many fucking Reds as possible. At least I am. I kinda hope you're still with me on that."

I didn't know what to say, so I gave him a nod. Hopefully, the sun made my visor unreadable, too.

A FIRM HAND grabbed me and shook, rousing me out of a peaceful slumber. "Ambrose? Ambrose!"

I blinked in the low lights of the transport's sleeping quarters. A face coalesced out of the darkness in front of me, an angelic vision with dark hair and bright almond eyes. "Phoebe?"

"I'm on Net, Ambrose."

I blinked again, realizing the sound was coming from inside my head. Unless I was dreaming it, Phoebe *was* crouched beside my bunk, though, trying to rouse me. Memories of late night trysts with her flashed in the recesses of my mind, and a burning desire within me reminded me how long it had been since I'd made love to her.

I pushed those thoughts to the side with middling success. "What's going on?"

"Come with me. Get your Suit."

The Suit comment killed whatever feisty thoughts lingered within me. I rolled out of bed, removed my Suit from under my bed, and followed her between the tight bunks toward the stairs. "Phoebe, what is it?"

"I'm not at liberty to say. Come with me to the airlock."

Our feet clattered against the steps as we descended the stairs. A murmur ran through the soldiers on shift. Some of them stood at the edges, staring out the windows. That's when I realized we weren't moving. It should've been obvious when Phoebe told me to go to the airlock, but I was still waking up.

I changed into my Suit as quickly as I could, as did Phoebe. As

I was halfway through, Epsilon's Mike Murdock showed up. His Suit change was even faster than mine, though I beat him by measure of my head start.

With masks on and pressure doors closed, Phoebe initiated the cycle. "Heaters on high. It's cold out there right now."

"No kidding," I said. "It's the middle of the night. Seriously, what's going on?"

"Major Watkins told the platoon leaders to assemble the squad leaders. That's all I've know. I promise." She gave me a look that pleaded for me not to be mad.

The whirr of the pumps died as the air left the lock. The back door to the transport dropped open. Phoebe flicked on her Suit light. I did the same and followed her into the frigid, black night. We skirted the edge of the transport, up a slight slope, and approached a group standing atop the nearest ridge.

I heard Major Watkin's voice via Net. "Lights off, soldiers."

We did as commanded. The night engulfed us, swallowing us in its frigid embrace. Icy pins pricked my fingers. I tried to see if I could pump more energy into my heater, but it was already at maximum.

I waited as a few others joined our group. Their lights flicked off as they arrived, undoubtedly under the same orders from Major Watkins. I stood there as patiently as I could, looking around to see if any additional lights approached from the transports as I wondered what the hell was going on.

"Eyes to the skies, soldiers." Major Watkins again.

I looked up. My eyes still had a good fifteen minutes before they'd be fully night-adjusted, but they didn't need to be at their peak to enjoy the Martian sky. With nary an atmosphere to speak of and no light pollution as far as the horizon, the night sky sparkled, the stars bright. Specks of blue shimmered alongside ones of white amid a milky backdrop of cyan and violet, the dusty expanse of the galaxy.

I felt bad knowing most Martians never enjoyed the sky this way, their vistas blocked by metal or meters of dirt or polymer weaves that bent the light. Then again, our vistas on Earth were blocked in perpetuity by the planet itself.

An orange white flash streaked across the sky. I'd thought I'd imagined it, but then there was another. Then several more.

Someone spoke on the local channel. "A meteor shower, Major?"

She took a moment to respond. "If only, Sergeant Tallowes. Those are rockets, coming from the south. I've received word that the major cities are under attack."

I didn't know how to respond, so I didn't. Another orange trail arced through the sky.

"I've heard from Isidis and Utopia so far," she continued. "A few of the city sectors have been depressurized. The spaceports were both hit the hardest. They'll be inoperable for a few weeks, maybe months. No word on casualties. I'm sure there are many. No word from Elysium or Olympus yet, either."

"What are our orders, Major?" asked Phoebe.

Another long pause. "Same as before, Sergeant Zhao. We'll continue to Cassini. Our presence there will be more vital than ever given this attack. We can't let the Reds think they have us on our heels. There's nothing we can do in Utopia anyway."

I saw a faint glimmer from Watkin's helmet as she turned. "I simply thought you all should know. Inform your squads in the morning. Be honest. Don't hold back. This is war. This is to be expected. The fact is we were lucky to be in transit. We won't always be so lucky." She started toward the transports. "We'll start the engines in ten minutes. Don't dawdle."

I doubt any of us would've stayed in the frigid air more than that, but for a few minutes I did just stand there—watching the trails of fire in the sky.

36

MAY 11, 2179

WE INTERCEPTED Coroner Pham as she transferred Jackson's corpse on a gurney toward the government building's service elevators, which had since been cleared by the fire department as safe to use. She didn't have a whole lot to tell us that we didn't already know. Her cursory inspection of Jackson's body indicated he'd died instantly from the pressure wave associated with the incendiary bomb's detonation. The grisly burns he'd acquired were probably all postmortem, seared into his flesh while the fire suppression systems tackled the blaze. She'd failed to find any other wounds or injuries on his person, but as always, she wouldn't confirm or deny much of anything until she had time with him in her lab under the bright lights and microwave scanners. As much as I imagined it would soothe Mrs. Jackson to know her husband hadn't suffered, I didn't call her to tell her that. Better to give her time to attend to her family and grieve in her own way.

Once we'd helped Pham transfer the body into the back of the coroner van, Mwenge and I made the rounds, talking to the officers and firefighters who were still on the scene, getting witness statements secondhand and seeing if anyone had noticed useful tidbits

Fields, Mwenge, and I had missed. With that done, I found my way to the building's security office and gave Dean a call. He logged me into the feeds remotely, and before logging off, shared with me what I'd later prove to myself by looking through the feeds and log files: that as in Shao Wen's murder, the security cameras hadn't picked up anyone except Jackson and other building employees entering and exiting Jackson's office over the past five days. While I supposed it was possible one of the janitorial staff set the explosive in place, it seemed far more likely the videos had been tampered with to hide an overnight visit from someone not on the payroll, a theory supported by the same faint digital signatures I found in the security system's deleted files. When I was done convincing myself of what had happened, I called Dean back and told him to assemble public feeds of the roads and alleys surrounding the building for the past few nights. That hadn't helped us identify Wen's murderer so far, but we also hadn't known who to look for. Perhaps by identifying the people in both sets of security feeds and cross-referencing them, we'd find a common interloper in both.

When I finished up, I opened up a comm channel to Mwenge. "Hey, pal. What are you up to?"

"Not much," he said. "I'm back at the scene of the explosion overseeing CSU. I think they'd rather I not be here."

"That's a pretty normal response, to be fair."

"Funny. They're just sticklers to routine. I'm trying to stay out of the way. Find anything?"

"Only by *not* finding anything, if that makes sense. Someone wiped the servers. It's hard to prove, but the stench is all over the logs. I sicced Dean on some surveillance tasks that might bear fruit, though."

"Using two data points to narrow our suspect pool?"

"Something like that. Need any help with CSU?"

"Like I said, they'd rather not even have me here," said Bishop. "I think the Captain might need a reprieve if you're willing to offer one, though."

"What's she up to?"

"Take a look out a window."

I headed out to the hallway and looked outside. The Captain stood in front of the building, surrounded by a herd of reporters with handheld holorecorders. "Yikes. I'm not sure I can do anything about that. At least not anything the Captain would approve of. Chasing them off with my sidearm might cause a bigger media shitstorm than she's already dealing with."

"Suit yourself," said Mwenge. "You know where I am."

Mwenge logged off, and I kept staring out the window. I wasn't sure if I could make the reporters go away, but I did want to touch base with the Captain to run a few ideas past her. If nothing else, perhaps I could intimidate some of them with my well-practiced scowl.

I headed down the stairs, out the front, and found a good spot to the Captain's side, one where I could lean against the facade and get a good angle at the reporters. I frowned and crossed my arms, only superficially paying attention to the Captain's speech. It was mostly canned responses. "We're currently looking into that." "All options are under consideration." "The public isn't at risk at this time." All true statements that gave nothing away. The Captain wasn't a gambler, but she knew how to play it close to the vest.

As I stood there, a USC branded van pulled up and parked on the sidewalk. The side door opened, and a half-dozen guys hopped out, half of them in suits with briefcases in hand, the others wearing white coveralls with safety glasses in their front pockets or on their foreheads. Some of them started unloading bags. A couple of the more ambitious reporters detached from the group around the Captain and headed their way, but their efforts were quickly rebuffed. The streets might be public property, but USC wasn't beholden to truth and honesty the same way we were.

"Excuse me. Detective Ambrose Drake, Homicide Division?"

A smartly-dressed young woman with a hand recorder stood in front of me, eying me hopefully. Apparently, the USC van wasn't the only arrival that had attracted attention.

"Yes?"

"Mindy Kunal, with the Elysian Post-Gazette. You're streaming live. Do you mind answering some questions about the bombing that occurred at the Elysian Budgetary Offices this afternoon?"

I pointed to the throng with the other reporters. "Captain Reyes will be happy to answer your questions, Miss Kunal."

"Eyewitness accounts say it was the office of city comptroller Deandre Jackson that was bombed. Can you offer us any insight into why Mr. Jackson could've been targeted in this attack?"

"In case I wasn't clear, it'll be my Captain who's taking the questions, not me."

"Detective, is this bombing in any way related to the one that occurred two nights ago at the residence of USC Administrator Shao Wen?"

My frown deepened. "You don't take no for an answer, do you?"

"Detective, the Martian separatist known as the Snow Leopard took credit for the first attack on Administrator Wen. Is he a suspect in the current bombing? And is there any truth to the claims made in the video he released? How widespread is corruption in the current administration? Are the people who've been targeted profiting off the backs of Elysium taxpayers?"

A ringing in my head alerted me to a call—from Sophia of all people. I stuck a stern finger toward the reporter. "I have a call I need to take."

I turned my back and responded, thankful for the privacy of Net communication. "Sophia. What's going on?"

"Not much. Just trying to rescue you."

"Rescue me?"

"From that reporter. I'm watching you live."

"You're watching?"

"Ambrose, the whole city is. A second bombing in three days? You're a cop. You realize this isn't a war zone, right? It's abnormal."

"Trust me, I'm aware."

Sophia's tone lost its playful edge. "Are you doing okay? You seem angry in the livestream."

"I'm getting pestered by a reporter who won't take a hint. Wouldn't you be?"

"You still sound angry. Is it the case? What's going on?"

I didn't say a word.

"Still don't want to talk about it? It's fine. I'm here for you, if you want me."

I didn't want to lie to Sophia. I had to do it on a regular basis about so many other things, I didn't want to do it about this. "Sophia, I need to tell you something. I saw your father today."

"What?" Silence. *"Why?"*

"His name came up in conjunction with a financial entity connected to Shao Wen. An A is connected to B is connected to C kind of thing. I cornered him at Kalofagás and asked him a few questions."

"And?"

"And, nothing. I just wanted to let you know."

Sophia was silent for another long moment. "Ambrose, you know I don't associate with him. He's my blood, but he's barely in my life."

"I know."

"I don't love the man. I certainly don't like him. But if he's involved in this..."

"I don't think he is," I said. "I probably shouldn't have approached him. The link was tenuous at best."

"You sure?"

"Yeah."

Silence filled my head again. Eventually Sophia spoke. "I'd like to see you tonight."

I chewed on my lip. "I'd like to see you, too, but I'm not sure if I can. I have a lot on my plate on the moment."

"I understand. Call me?"

"When I can."

I ended the call and turned back toward the action to find that the Captain's time in the sun had ended—almost literally. The reporters were dispersing, and the Captain was headed my way, the sun fading behind her as it dipped below the false horizon of Elysian architecture. "Well, Detective," she said as she arrived. "How did I do?"

"Honestly, Captain? I wasn't really paying attention."

Reyes snorted. "Of course not. For all the effort I put into public relations, no one outside the media cares, and they all think I suck at it."

"The media are a bunch of leeches and buzzards. Who cares what they think?"

"The citizens of Elysium do. And you should start caring about them if you ever plan on ascending past your current post, Drake."

"Who said I had plans for that?"

Reyes smiled, but only a little. "You're too good to spend your life in homicide, Ambrose. Don't get me wrong. I love having you here. But at some point you're going to move on, hopefully to bigger and better things."

"I'd rather remain anonymous as long as I can."

"It's hard to do that in this day and age."

I snorted. "You've got that right."

Reyes cast a glance at the USC van and shook her head. "Well, it looks like the counterterrorism task force finally arrived. Good thing they're slow and we got most of our investigative work done quickly. I should make sure CSU is wrapped up before the USC folks start dragging mud onto the scene."

"Shouldn't we be working *with* them, Captain?"

"Should be, but aren't," she said. "The more bureaucracies you involve, the more red tape there is to cut. You'd know that if you were preparing yourself for a leadership role, Detective."

"Whoops. Look at that. Three new murders just showed up on the police comm channel. Gotta go."

Reyes chuckled. "Be that way. But there are benefits to occupying a leadership role."

"Such as?"

"Ordering snarky bastards like you around. Come on. Help me wrangle the last of the troops and get everything back to the station for analysis."

I TRUDGED through the subterranean tunnels, my light bobbing along the floor in front of me. I breathed in the cold air, the chill keeping me awake as much as the coffee I'd swilled before leaving my apartment. I hadn't gotten home from work until after nine—heading out early was frowned upon when your current investigation involved multiple bombings and murders that had captivated the attention of the city at large—and while an earlier arrival might've allowed me to invite Sophia over, other obligations rendered that intractable.

I checked the time as I walked. Twelve fifteen. I could've come earlier, but even in a bustling metropolis like Elysium, it was easier to move freely under cover of night. The later the better, but I still had to get to work in the morning. Early, if the Captain had any say.

I found the unmistakable marks on the rock wall at my side and followed the tunnel to the false pipe along the wall. I unscrewed the latch, turned it over, dropped the tablet into my palm, and activated it.

Though I wasn't mentioned by name, or even alluded to, the file on the tablet was a direct response to what I'd left the last time I'd delved underground. I'd expected some of what was written in the communiqué, but not the last part. That bit made my heart skip a beat.

My sources suggest the murders may be an inside job. Take all necessary precautions to protect yourself in case of unforeseen eventualities.

There wasn't an attribution on the message. There never was, but I knew who'd left it. I trusted the individual with my life. But *an inside job?* I knew what that meant, too, and it couldn't be right. Reyes. Mwenge. Dean. I trusted the people at the department implicitly. None of them would be involved in something of this nature. And yet, they all thought they knew me, too. Still, to think I'd have to protect myself against them... It chilled me. It was one thing to hide activities from your friends, and another entirely to plot against them.

I punched a response into the tablet, slipped it into the dead drop pipe, and headed back, my head swirling with unforeseen possibilities.

I didn't like any of them.

I AWOKE at just after five in the morning, not of my own volition but from a call classified as urgent.

It was Captain Reyes. "Detective. Sorry to wake you."

I blinked, my room dark as a coffin. I tried to coalesce my brain into a useable mass, thoughts and senses fuzzy after a meager four hours of sleep. "What is it, Captain?"

"It's the Snow Leopard. He's released another video."

37

SEPTEMBER 16, 2154

AS NEWS TRICKLED in over the next couple days, we learned Isidis and Utopia weren't the hardest hit by the Red rocket strikes. Phobos was. The Reds had launched roughly four dozen missiles toward the base, and while many of them had been blasted to shreds by the Phobos defenses, the base had still suffered the same fate we had aboard our Mark X. High speed shrapnel had punched holes all over the place. Not many lives had been lost, as the base's early warning system had given folks time to climb into their Suits and descend into the underground bunkers. Still, the damage was substantial. At least a half dozen fuel and oxygen tanks had been pierced in the barrage, and grapevine chatter said the base was running at thirty percent of normal. USC transports from Luna would have to be slowed. Given the Reds had also focused their fire on land-based spaceports, their goal seemed pretty clear. Keep as many Earthers off Mars for as long as possible.

I'd already been sleeping poorly in the wake of our fusion plant raid. The thought that Reds could be launching a new offensive over the next few weeks didn't ease my disquiet in the least.

Nonetheless, our transports rumbled on, leaving kilometers of dusty tracks in their wake. Red chatter died down, and no more attacks came, either on the major cities or on us. Perhaps the separatists had spent themselves, or perhaps they were lulling us into a false sense of security. I hoped it was the former, but I didn't have any recourse if it wasn't. I was riding a one way ticket into a far worse situation than the one I'd left, and hopping off mid-ride meant a quicker, more certain death than the alternative.

Our eventual arrival at Cassini wasn't preceded by any spectacle. We simply crested the edge of the Cassini Crater and slowly worked our way toward the settlement at the bottom of the basin, bordered on one side by a yawning open pit silicon mine. Even from a distance, the massive haul trucks at the edge of the mine made our transports look like children's toys.

With a population of a little more than a quarter million, the city itself wasn't impressive. Compared to the modern luxury of Utopia, it was a bleak, archaic dustbin. It spread across the crater floor, most of the buildings only three or four stories tall. Lacking any polymer weave over the streets, it didn't shimmer from afar as Utopia had. Instead, the ubiquitous Martian regolith blew through the streets, caking the sides of buildings with rust. Few people walked the roadways as our transports trundled among them, and I couldn't help but feel I'd been transported several hundred years back in time to a wild west ghost town where the folks weren't the deadliest enemies around.

The USC base sat at the edge of town, much smaller and more compact than USC Utopia West. More heavily armored, too, with thick alloy sheets plating the squat, hulking structure. Armed guards stood at mounted guns as we drove onto dusty lots adjacent to the base, the garages too small to allow entry to our transports. I spotted a lone landing pad as I exited the transport, half hidden under swirling regolith and barely big enough to accommodate a single puny Mark III—a brutal reminder of our isolation.

Our company assembled in what I assumed was the base's largest auditorium, which barely fit us as it was. Major Watkins crossed the stage, a man with crisp, evenly-parted salt and pepper hair walking by her side. She called us to attention, introduced the man as Lieutenant Colonel Cornier, commanding officer of the Cassini base, and ceded the floor to him.

"At ease soldiers," said Cornier, his voice amplified in our minds via Net. "Have a seat. Welcome to Cassini, pride of the Arabia Terra, or so the locals claim. Personally, I've seen enough mining settlements to know this one is just another pimple on the ass of Mars, but if the locals have pride in their city, who are we to quash it? I see from your travel logs you arrived without incident. That's good, but by this point you're all aware your voyage was not uneventful for the majority of other major USC positions. The Isidis, Utopia, and Elysium spaceports are all running at less than half capacity, with major repairs needed following the attacks nine days ago. Olympus somehow avoided the Red's ire, probably because it's the furthest removed from the other three by vactrain and therefore the most vulnerable to other attacks. Phobos is partially out of commission, too. Not that any of that matters much to us out here.

"In case you couldn't tell by your fortnight long journey, Cassini is what you'd call *isolated*. Your company brings us to a grand total of six hundred stationed here. Depending on your bent, that may seem like a sizable force for a town the size of Cassini's, but I guarantee you it isn't. Red sentiment is much higher here than in the big cities. There are scores of active Red cells, perhaps hundreds. Most of them are armed. All of them are hostile, though not always outwardly so. To make things worse, Cassini isn't enclosed, and our satellite imaging systems only provide accurate maps of subterranean tunnels to about eight meters. As you'll soon learn, everyone in this town makes use of those tunnels, especially the Reds, who know them better than anyone. That makes Cassini one dangerous ass pimple.

"Now, if it was up to me, I'd wave this place goodbye from the back of my Marauder and haul ass back to Isidis, but believe it or not, I don't make the rules. Because of its mining operations, USC has determined Cassini to be of strategic importance and has assigned the lot of you to secure it, and that's precisely what we're going to do. You'll be receiving your orders shortly. For now, company dismissed."

OUR SQUAD'S first assignment was to set up transponders along the outskirts of Cassini, a task the local USC troops had only recently completed in the city center. The transponders acted as routers for encrypted Net signals, which was important because the local wireless networks weren't secure. The transponders were solar-powered, nearly impossible to crack, and built to withstand whatever Mars or the Reds could throw at them. The only problem was their range sucked, which meant we needed to set up lots of them.

We'd split our squad into three teams of three to make the job go faster. In my team, Maarten worked the post auger while Mandel and I carried the transponders and jammed them into the holes. We were currently on our eighth of twenty.

The auger rumbled and whirred as Maarten ground away at the rock hiding underneath the regolith. A breeze blew, whistling as it chilled me. Not for the first time I looked over my shoulder, certain I'd heard whispers on the wind, but once again the city was playing tricks on me. The streets behind me were deserted, just as they'd been the entire time we'd been out. The wind shifted, and I heard the whistle again, this time coming from between buildings. Wind on dusty metal.

Phoebe cut in on the squad channel. "How's everyone doing out there?"

"Cold, hungry, and paranoid," I said. "The usual."

"We just hit our halfway point," said Phoebe. "You guys?"

"We're on nine," said Halabi.

"And we're stuck at eight," growled Maarten. "Damn rocks are chewing up the auger."

"Stick with it," said Phoebe. "We'll get there."

She cut out, leaving us to the wind and moan of the auger until Mandel cut back in on our team channel. "Paranoid, huh?"

"Don't tell me you're not," I said. "These empty streets freak me out. Every time I see someone darting between buildings I wonder what they're doing above ground."

"Getting ready to shoot us, no doubt," said Mandel.

"Laugh all you want. I'm keeping my Badass within reach."

"No, I'm serious," said Mandel. "I'm right there with you. Every time I see a local, I nearly break out in hives."

Clearly, I wasn't the only one with frayed nerves.

Not Maarten, though. "You know what the problem is?" he said as he jammed the auger further into the hole.

"What?"

"The Suits," he said. "They're too bulky. Can't tell who's a skinny and who's not."

Mandel cocked her head. "They're local unless they're in a USC Suit, Maarten."

"It's a joke. *Christ.*" Maarten snorted. "Seriously, though, that's the problem. We don't know who the hell we're fighting. Must've been easier in the old days, before all the migration. Shoot the brown guy. Trample the redskin with your horse. Piece of cake."

"That's a myth, you know," said Mandel. "Armies throughout history have been more diverse than most people think."

"Well, they're a hell of a lot more diverse now," said Maarten. "At least skin color gave you *something* to go on. Now all we've got is how wide a guy is in the shoulders. Hell of a thing to use to decide if you should shoot him or not."

I still didn't like that Maarten had continued to call the locals skinnies. "You realize not all Martians are Reds, right?"

"Maybe not. But every Red *is* a Martian. And even the Martians who aren't Reds don't seem to mind when Reds take pot shots at us, chuck bombs our way, or blow up our oxygen recyclers. So is it really that big of a deal if we mow down a few of them on our way to the dusty ones?" He killed the auger and pulled it from the hole. "Transponder."

I stood there, blinking. "You seriously believe that Maarten?"

He nodded to the hole. "Come on, hoss. We don't have all day."

Mandel stuck a transponder in the hole when I refused to move. I couldn't believe the nonchalance with which Maarten condemned innocent people to death, even theoretical people, but he didn't pick up on my shock. He simply turned and headed toward the next transponder site.

NOBODY ATTACKED us our first day in Cassini, nor the second, nor the third. We finished planting the transponders assigned to our squad and moved on to other equally monotonous activities, mostly of the manual labor variety. As heavily armored as the USC base was, it wasn't nearly large enough, at least not for all the activities the bigwigs in charge had planned. That meant expanding, but we couldn't use local constructors. Hell, they might be Reds eager to mine our base for secret intel. Besides, why pay good money when you have labor on hand and a corps of engineers who'd already designed suitable plans for other bases?

There was a learning curve, of course. None of us were trained builders, except for one of the members of Epsilon squad whose father had been a mason. Maarten had to learn how to operate a backhoe, and I learned how to weld. It wasn't hard. Basically soldering with a torch instead of an iron. Holes got dug and armor went up, all without incident, except when one unlucky bastard happened to be underneath a support beam that slipped its winch. She only broke her leg, thankfully.

We were assigned other duties besides construction, to be sure. Guard duty, drills, and all the other stuff we'd already been exposed to. Gun cleaning became a more regular part of our routine, though. As well built as the Badasses were, they couldn't withstand hours upon hours of exposure to the wind-blown Martian regolith. That talcum-fine crap got everywhere, including through the Suit's weave. I got to the point where I wondered why we bothered washing it off at all. Easier to be like chinchillas and embrace the dust.

Thankfully, my time wasn't fully committed to physical endeavors. Within a week of arrival, Major Watkins instructed me to report to the local counterintelligence branch in one of the camp's subbasements. My enthusiasm lasted about as long as it took me to walk down there. The server cluster was a tenth the size of the one at Utopia West, there wasn't anything that resembled a window in the entire office, and the crew consisted of skeletons and ghosts. The only other intelligence officer there was a squirrelly red-haired Sergeant by the name of McGregor. I tried to engage her in conversation, but she made it clear within the first five minutes that she preferred interactions with computers to those with people. I wondered how she'd managed to achieve Sergeant status with such a severe personality disorder, but perhaps promotions came independent of leadership skills for intelligence folks.

We didn't have any captured data to analyze right away, but at least my access to the counterintelligence office came with a side benefit—the ability to access sensitive material. In particular, my newly acquired clearance allowed me to dig deeper into the aftermath of the Red rocket strike that had taken out so many USC facilities.

Perhaps the information hadn't been made public because of how embarrassing it was. Everyone, myself included, had assumed the launch had been a kamikaze strike—that the Reds had fired as many missiles as they could in the knowledge that USC would bring the hammer down upon them within hours, obliterating every last scrap of their launch facility and whatever structures surrounded it. The problem was, the Reds hadn't initiated their launch from a facility at all. The missiles had fired from a group of artillery trucks in the middle of the Noachis Terra. How they'd gotten there was the point of embarrassment.

USC monitored Mars from a fleet of satellites, hundreds of cameras and sensors pointed to the surface searching for signs of Red activity. The Reds had taken to moving underground as a result, but missile batteries the size of those discovered in the Noachis Terra couldn't have been moved via tunnels. They'd gone overland, yet they still hadn't been spotted thanks to a combination of factors: vehicle heat dumped into sinks and buried strategically along the way, timely hacking of USC satellites to mask signals, and good old fashion rust-red camouflage. At least USC was smart enough not to glass the trucks in anger. They'd sent a team to investigate, but by that point, the Martian winds had long since blown away the vehicles' tracks, and the trucks' computers had been wiped clean. As far as USC intelligence was concerned, the Reds might've birthed them straight from the Martian core.

As it turned out, the Snow Leopard had also released a new video in the aftermath of the strikes, one that scoffed in the face of USC and urged Martian fence-sitters to join him. The video hadn't been released to our curated USC newsfeeds, which I found surprising given they'd let through everything related to the nuclear strike of Los Angeles. I guess the difference was the nuclear devastation of Los Angeles didn't make USC and all us soldiers in the company's employ look like a bunch of incompetent asshats.

The Snow Leopard's video the day after the strikes was the only one, though, which didn't sit well with me. Sergeant Mishra once told me that the closer to danger you got, the quieter things seemed, and when it came to Red chatter, all I could hear at the moment was the slow howl of the wind.

38

MAY 12, 2179

I SAT in the conference room outside the Captain's office again, the light of the rising sun only now breaching the windows. I swilled coffee as I watched the Snow Leopard's video for the second time, the first having been at home after a rudimentary web search.

The man's apparel, voice, and persona remained the same as before, but his rhetoric had been ratcheted up to a new level. The video was twice as long as the last one and not because of an excessive amount of added footage from the explosion in the government audit building. That footage had been included, of course, but it didn't add more than a few seconds to the video, and the Snow Leopard talked over it regardless, expounding on his theories of corruption and greed. He painted Jackson as another amoral opportunist, one more cog in a machine willing to oppress the citizens of Elysium and Mars as a whole for material profit, no matter the cost in lives or freedom. The Snow Leopard's claims weren't backed up with solid proof. He didn't present documents showing Jackson's corruption. He merely appealed to the emotion of his viewers, blaming the ills of society on those he'd targeted and more of their ilk, all while promising the expulsion of men like Jackson, the bought and paid for members of government, and the ultra wealthy USC overlords would bring about a new era of Martian prosperity.

It was a load of horseshit, but his emotional appeal was masterful. As good as it had been in the days of the first Martian uprising. Maybe better.

The Captain clicked the holo off. She sighed and took a seat opposite myself and Mwenge. "That video was uploaded at four twenty-three in the morning, or at least that's the first copy we were able to find. It's already been viewed as many times in the past hour and forty-five minutes as the Snow Leopard's first upload was in its first day. It seems to be having a more forceful impact than the first, too. There are protests in front of multiple city offices ongoing as we speak, most of them nonviolent, but we've had reports of missiles being launched at one of the rallies—the rudimentary kind, obviously. I'm talking rocks and bottles. We've also received a report of vandalism to the comptroller's office, or rather the front of the building. Mars First propaganda, as you might imagine. That's amid a general surge in crimes reported overnight, although some of those occurred before the release of the video and may be unrelated. The fact remains that we're dealing with a terrorist now, and the citizens of Elysium seem to be wondering if this is a fight worth choosing sides in. I'm not going to lie to you, Detectives. This case just became a whole lot more dangerous. If we don't solve it soon and bring the perpetrator to justice, things could get a lot worse before they get better. Need I remind you how the first Martian uprising began?"

"The same way every other uprising in history has begun," I said. "With people who are frustrated and desperate. We get it, Captain."

"I'm not sure you do, Detective Drake. I talked to the Chief this morning, who in turn has been in contact with the Chiefs of Police in Utopia, Isidis, and Olympus. They're all reporting incidents of unrest in their cities. They've seen the Snow Leopard's videos, too, and they're making an impact, if not as large a one as here given their separation from the violence. USC is taking note. Do you think it's a coincidence their counterterrorism squads have been so tight-lipped and standoffish? They're drawing lines in the sand. Battening down the hatches in the event a storm hits. Our partnership with USC only lasts as long as our mutual trust does, and as long as the trust of the public buoys us."

"So what do you suggest we do, Captain?" asked Mwenge.

"We solve the crime, Detective. Right now the Snow Leopard is a ghost to most, a martyr to some, and a symbol to all. But his grip on the city is centered on fear. If we stop the murders, stop the explosions, we snap the citizens out of their reverie. Either we catch the Leopard in the act, or we take out the team he's using to commit the murders. Either way, the videos stop. The murders stop. The fear is lessened. If nothing else, we get a reprieve. Time for cooler heads to prevail. Now, I know we can't magically produce results out of need. But I wanted to impress upon the both of you what we're dealing with. We need to get this done. By any means necessary."

Captain Reyes's face was tense. Tired. Drawn. It was the face of utter commitment, not one of deceit.

"We'll do everything we can, Captain," I said. "You have our word."

WHILE MWENGE HEADED out to raid the offices of Red Summit Financial, I stayed behind and worked my ass off. I reviewed witness statements collected by officers at the government offices as well as ones from Wen's apartment complex. I scanned external video Dean had collected for me, cross-referencing the facial recognition logs with our infractions database, but it didn't get me anywhere. I checked with Detective Fields regarding the results of the explosives traces, which indeed came back as distinct from those taken from Wen's apartment. I talked to Pham about Jackson. She told me to come back later, but admitted she'd failed to come up with anything unexpected from her autopsy. I wracked my brain about the obvious water-based connection between Wen and Jackson. I jumped through hoops to pull Jackson's audits from the past five years, then put in petitions with USC for every file Wen had ever touched. They balked at such a broad request, but I insisted. Despite the Captain's concerns about deteriorating relations with USC, after much back and forth with Wen's underlings, I got what I wanted—or at least I assumed I did. The amount of data they sent back might take me years to sift through.

Access to data wasn't the problem of course. Figuring out what data mattered was the hard part. The time consuming part. And time wasn't something I had a lot of.

Of course, corners could be cut. Following the rules took time, but I'd taken the Captain at her word. Solve the murder, by any means necessary, she'd said. Well, I knew Shao Wen was being paid by Red Summit Financial which in turn was owned by Silicon Road boss Giancarlo Vincenzio, or his aunt, technically. I also knew Red Summit had done business with Kosta Demetriou and his gang. Those tenuous connections wouldn't get me a warrant for Net traces on either men, but the warrant wasn't necessary for me to initiate the traces, only for me to use the data gathered in that manner in the court of law. Since I was pretty sure neither Vincenzio or Demetriou had murdered Wen or Jackson themselves, I figured I could indite whoever had using other evidence. Still, I didn't check the traces on my holo, only via Net. Despite the Captain's statement, there might be repercussions if anyone found out about my methods.

As I sat at my desk, fiddling with my computer and wishing I had a solid lead to chase, I got a call from Dean. "Got a sec, Detective?"

"Tell me something good, Dean."

"I've got financials back on Deandre Jackson. How's that?"

"It depends. Do they tell us anything?"

"Well, they tell us *something*. How useful that something is depends on your point of view. You know how you suspected Mr. Jackson of spending far more than he could earn from his government job?"

"Yes."

"Well, he's been getting regular payments from a revocable trust that was established two and a half years ago."

"A trust? So the source of the assets being paid to him isn't obvious, is that what you're telling me?"

"I'm sure we could access the trust by court order, but for now the party or parties paying Jackson are hidden behind a legal wall."

"Wonderful. You have any actual good news for me, Dean?"

An alert pinged me via Net. I glanced at it as Dean kept talking. "Actually, yes. Looks like your crack of Ms. Wen's tablet went through."

"You remember I set up an alert for that, don't you Dean?"

"Which you told me to tell you about if it went off. Besides, you didn't specify where the news had to come from. Sometimes it's better to be lucky than good."

"I'll be down in a minute."

I blanked my holo and headed to the stairs. Dean was in his usual seat when I arrived at the technical services office. He gave me a wave as I entered, but he didn't tear his eyes from his collection of holos. "Tablet's right where you left it."

"I should hope so, otherwise I'd be questioning your guard skills." I left the tablet in its dock as I checked the system analytics on the nearby workstation. I'd used a multi-pronged cracking method, one that combined a biclique attack with the Kendall and

Spearman rank correlation coefficient standards. It wasn't a particularly novel approach, but it had probably shaved a few days off the decryption time.

Satisfied that my attempt had worked, I lifted the tablet from its base and logged in using the cracked passkey. As I flicked through the files within, I frowned. I furrowed my brow, wrinkled my nose, and scrunched my lips.

As far as I could tell, there wasn't anything incriminating on the tablet whatsoever. It simply contained lots and lots of data, all of it work related. Drilling permits. Radiographic surveys. Piping diagrams. Melt rates, pump rates, use and flow rates from Elysium's central water processing facility. Time of use rates. Everything.

As I sat there skimming the numbers, I couldn't help but wonder why Shao Wen would have all the data on an encrypted tablet in her home safe. Wasn't it just as safe in the centralized USC servers? And perhaps even more importantly, why was said safe open to the touch when we first arrived in her apartment? I still didn't believe Wen accidentally left it open. Her murderer must've opened the safe using prints lifted from her body. So why leave the tablet? Had they known what was on it? Was anything else taken?

I heard another ping as I sat there, mulling the possibilities. Dean turned. He'd heard it, too.

"It's your lucky day." Dean nodded toward the second tablet, the one I'd lifted off the dust-addled narcotics peddler, Boothe.

"Any day where I'm woken up at five due to threats of terrorism and rebellion by definition does not qualify as *lucky*." I scooted over and pulled the second tablet from its dock. When I unlocked it, I found the contents more easily digestible. It contained exactly what I'd expect from a drug dealer. A massive list of contacts, most of them posted under pseudonyms like Biggy, Masher, Princess Peach, and Turtle T, all amid the more traditional tablet junk: apps, games, music, lewd pictures, some pornography, and even a wide selection of books, believe it or not. I hadn't pictured Boothe as much of a reader.

The contacts were the gold mine, though. Even though Boothe hadn't entered them under their real names, I had to assume he'd used their real contact numbers, otherwise the list would've been useless. To a police database, a number was as good as a name. I ran the contacts through our servers and received back a list of individuals, which I sent to myself under the header 'Known Associates.' I didn't recognize any of the names—Kosta and his muscle-bound crony weren't among them, thankfully—but dozens of them came back as having Silicon Road ties. It was useful information, but what could I do with it? I still didn't have a firm link between Shao Wen, Deandre Jackson, and the Silicon Road gang other than through Red Summit Financial. That reminded me to check back in with Mwenge to see how the raid had gone.

I turned to Dean. "Hey, pal. Mind doing something for me?"

"Sure, Detective. What do you need?"

I slid Wen's tablet across the counter toward him. "Make an encrypted copy of this data and place it on one of our secure servers."

"Sure thing." Dean grabbed the tablet. "Need me to analyze any of the data?"

"Not at the moment. I'll handle that myself a little later."

Dean handed the tablet back to me when he finished. I slipped it into my jacket, clapped him on the shoulder, and gave Mwenge a call as I headed back up to my desk.

He picked right up. "You beat me to it, Drake."

"How'd the raid go?"

"It went off without a hitch. The front door barely gave any resistance at all to our ram. But if you're asking what we've found, perhaps you'd better have a seat."

"That bad?"

"Maybe CSU can find drug traces somewhere, but we're at a loss. Boothe must've gotten word out to someone. Either that or he lied to us, or perhaps Silicon Road noticed he made his way to our precinct and got proactive."

"What about electronics?" I asked.

"There's none to confiscate. Which lends credence to this place being a drug front, but that doesn't help us much."

"Has anyone checked surveillance from last night?"

"Not yet," said Mwenge. "But if they did and found people moving dope in or out, that portion of the case would get passed off to Narcotics. What about you, Drake? Tell me you've had better success than me."

"Sounds like it, yeah. I cracked Wen's and Booths' tablets."

"And?"

I hesitated. "I haven't found anything incriminating—yet. But I've got a crazy idea. Why don't you join me at the Central Elysium water processing plant?"

39

OCTOBER 4, 2154

LIEUTENANT COLONEL CORNIER was no less proficient in keeping us busy than Major Watkins was. If anything, he was more adept at it. The tasks he assigned were by far more varied than those we'd received in Utopia. The circumstances demanded it. That wasn't to say they were any less boring, though.

It took me a while to learn the nuanced language of assignments. The first rule was that everything you were told by your superiors was a steaming pile of bullshit. The second was that every activity was simultaneously more dangerous and more pointless than advertised.

For example, presence patrol was billed as self-explanatory: activities intended to provide a military presence in the community, to keep the enemy off guard, to provide a sense of security to the populace, to collect intelligence, to learn about the locals, and so on and so forth. In reality a presence patrol entailed milling around, staring at a patch of dirt and hoping no Reds ran at you with sharp rocks and bombs strapped to their chests.

Overwatch positions were another task that seemed self-explanatory. Set up a *position*, generally *over* something, where you could *watch*. In reality, the only difference between it and presence patrol was that rather than moving about, you stood *still* while you watched a patch of dirt freeze, and instead of locals with bombs or guns, you had to watch for Reds planting IEDs. I asked, but no one up the chain of command was ever able to explain to me why the task couldn't be done better remotely via satellite.

Movement to contact was possibly the most asinine of our regularly assigned tasks. Someone—usually a Red, but sometimes a sympathizer—would attack one of our squads. Shoot at them, throw rocks, kick dust, whatever. Because we outgunned them and the attackers didn't generally have death wishes, they'd engage us for ten to thirty seconds before taking off in bounding runs, disappearing into the buildings and tunnel systems as quickly as possible. Leadership would then order *movement to contact,* in which a squad would attempt to reestablish contact with the enemy. What it meant in reality was you'd wander around aimlessly freezing your toes into snack size bits while you waited for the enemy to shoot you and give away their position. They rarely ever did, but we presented tempting targets nonetheless.

My favorite of the activities, and possibly the only one of the bunch that wasn't completely pointless, was cordon and knocks. There, we'd walk around underground marketplaces and through apartment buildings, knocking on doors, introducing ourselves, and generally trying to appear as non-threatening as possible. While there was always the risk of having a door opened to a muzzle in your face, most of the Cassians we met were pleasant enough. Some were cordial, others downright friendly. As I tried to hammer into Maarten whenever we had the chance, the locals were a lot like us in the ways that mattered. Most of them had families, jobs they needed to feed said families, and jobs they didn't want to die at while working, same as us. Most of the people didn't care if we flushed the Reds out or they beat us back so long as the silicon from the mines kept flowing and the fusions plants kept the air pumps and grow lights in the farms on. They just didn't care.

I couldn't fathom how I'd have reacted if Reds had shown up on the doorstep to my dorm in Kalamazoo without warning. I feel like I would've harbored resentment, but maybe I wouldn't have cared, either—at least not if they hadn't nuked a nearby city first.

MAARTEN and I stood at a pair of doors. They hissed as they slid open, despite the fact that the marketplace in front of us was sealed and pressurized, same as the underground tunnel behind us. It must've been a safety feature of the pneumatics to prevent pressure loss, as all the doors in Cassini did it.

We stepped forward into the market's bustle. Locals milled between stalls, sniffing melons and hefting bags of beets, holding synth jewelry to the LEDs overhead to judge its quality, and haggling over used rock drills. I smelled cinnamon and cloves, fresh bread, and a potent floral scent—probably potpourri, but generically-engineered roses weren't out of the question. A hum hovered over the crowd, a mixture of conversation, laughter, shouts, and the steady electrical pulse that powered the underground gathering space.

"I'm so tired of this shit," said Maarten as we worked our way into the central path.

"You mean today's assignment or just in general?" We'd been on presence patrol for the last five and a half hours, but every day brought something equally odious.

Maarten shook his head. "I don't know. Both. My feet hurt. I'm bored. I'm tired. Hungry. Thirsty. You name it." He reached for the bottle in his utility belt, hefted it as he pulled it, and swore. "Son of a bitch. Got any water left?"

I pulled mine and shook it. A few droplets rattled against the plastic. "Not much. You're welcome to it, if you want."

Maarten waved me off. "Never mind. I'll suffer. Beats me why the damn skinnies keep these tunnels so fucking dry through. Someone should break into the water recycler and crank the humidity controls, just a few percent."

I glanced around, but nobody seemed to have noticed Maarten's use of the slur—or if they had, they seemed intent on ignoring us as a survival mechanic. "Water's expensive out here. Cassini doesn't have the extraction systems the major cities do."

We passed a stall full of fresh lettuce, spinach, and assorted greens. "Doesn't matter how expensive it is, hoss. You have to hydrate one way or another. If there's less in the air, you've got to drink more to compensate."

"Someone has to pay for it," I said. "Easier to track it coming out of a tap."

"Excuse me? Gentlemen?"

I turned, trying to locate the source of the question, unsure if Maarten and I were the intended target.

Apparently we were. The man behind the stall at our backs, a burly gent with a thick brown beard and dark brown eyes, nodded as I caught sight of him. "Sorry. Couldn't help but overhear. My mother always said I had rabbit ears, and not 'cause they're big. Anyway, I might have a solution to your problem." He patted a large insulated jug on his station.

I vaguely recognized the guy, having seen him selling coffee and other hot drinks from his cart on previous patrols. "Well, ah... thanks, but I don't know. Believe it or not, we don't get paid much."

"It's on the house. It's the least I can do, given what you and your friends do for us." He snagged a couple cups from a stack and filled them with steaming liquid from the jug. "You ever tried maché? Martian specialty tea. You'll love it. Warms your insides like nothing else."

He held out the two cups, nodding to us as he did so. I took mine. Maarten was slower in accepting his.

I took a sniff of the drink, which smelled earthy and herbaceous. "Well, that's ah...very generous of you, sir. We appreciate your hospitality."

"The name's Elmarr. And don't sweat it. Go on. Enjoy."

I took a sip. The flavors exploded on my tongue, those of green tea, fennel, ginger, and bay. Something else, too.

Maarten coughed. "It tastes like grass."

"Among other things," said Elmarr. "We Martians have a great fascination with grass, you know. Perhaps one day we'll see it everywhere, just like on Earth, yes?"

"I'd rather walk on my grass, not drink it," said Maarten.

I tipped back the rest of my cup. "I don't know. It's different, but I didn't hate it."

He grunted. "Want the rest of mine, hoss?"

I was thirsty enough that I didn't say no. I tossed my empty cup and took Maarten's before tipping it toward the cart owner. "Thanks again for the drink, sir."

"Elmarr. And it was my pleasure. Safe travels, friends."

I smiled and sipped my second cup of maché as we continued our patrol. "Well that was a nice gesture, don't you think?"

Maarten grunted and cast a glance over his shoulder. "Depends on if the tea was poisoned or not."

I sighed. "Give it a break, Maarten. Stop being such an ass. Not everyone here is trying to kill us."

He sneered. "How can you say that? You *did* taste that tea, didn't you?"

He meant it as a joke, but I didn't find it particularly funny.

———

PATROLS WEREN'T all Lieutenant Colonel Cornier assigned us to. Following an attack against local sympathizers outside the silicon mines, we started being tasked with escort missions. They weren't too bad. We mostly got to perform them from the relative safety of the Marauder. Although shuttling people back and forth from work may not sound thrilling, it provided an opportunity to talk to the Cassians about their lives and activities. In that way, they reminded me a lot of the cordon and knocks. As the weeks dragged on, I found myself looking forward to our squad's early morning escort assignments, and I'd gotten to know some of the riders as well as anyone else I'd met thus far.

When attacks against sympathizers proved too difficult, local Red forces instead decided to take their frustration out on said sympathizers' facilities. The silicon refineries were bombed more than once, at different points and with different levels of success. Not that the attacks slowed down the miners much. A prerequisite for living in a remote Martian mining colony was being a whizzbang badass at repairs, apparently.

Lieutenant Colonel Cornier still sent us over to help repair equipment. I don't think he personally cared if the Reds bombed themselves, but the reason USC had us in Cassini was to keep the silicon flowing out of the mines, and if that stopped, it would be Cornier's ass in a sling. So repair we did. My welding improved on advice from actual professionals. I learned to operate an assortment of lathes, saws, and presses, and my electrical engineering expertise grew in leaps and bounds. I liked to think the experience would help me if we ever secured more Red electronics for decryption, but the guts of the machines I worked on were of the big and stupid variety rather than small and complex.

It was after returning to the base after one such extended repair session that I received instructions to meet Major Watkins by Lieutenant Colonel Cornier's office. The message was short on content and heavy on intrigue, but as I found my way to the office, I wasn't worried. I hadn't done anything but peel shavings off a metal bar all day, so I didn't imagine how I could be in trouble.

Watkins was already there when I arrived. I knocked on the door to Cornier's office, and he waved me in. "Come in, Private."

I stood at attention by the chairs and saluted. "Colonel. Major. Can I ask what this is about?"

"Soon enough, Drake," said Watkins. "In the meantime, know you're here in your capacity as a counterintelligence agent."

That piqued my interest. After a couple minutes in which the Lieutenant Colonel's eyes flicked as he manipulated his Net, Mike Murdock showed up. Watkin's assertion that I was here as a counterintelligence officer had me on edge as well as intrigued. I hoped I wasn't about to find out a foul secret about Murdock and asked to corroborate it.

Mike gave the same salute and salutation I had. "Sirs."

The door to the office puffed shut as Cornier looked up. "Good. You're all here."

"What for, exactly, Colonel?" asked Mike.

Cornier looked up. "A wise man I once knew told me the harder you work, the luckier you get. Well, our hard work seems to have paid off. A confidential informant has come forth, one of the workers from your afternoon escorts, Murdock. He claims to have sensitive information on the local Red contingent, and I'd like both of you around to help in the questioning. With a little luck and a golden tongue, we'll have the Reds on the run before they can dust the rust off their asses." He stood. "Come on. He's waiting on us. Let's not make him any more nervous than he already is."

40

MAY 12, 2179

"SO TELL me again what you want me to do?" asked Bishop.

We stood in an office on the second floor of the Elysium central water processing facility. I gazed out the windows overlooking the main floor, a space crowded with massive pumps that rumbled and roared as they forced water through underground pipes and into the particulate filtration systems and UV radiators. I couldn't have been closer than a couple hundred meters from the nearest pump, yet it sounded like I had my ear pressed to the side of a dishwasher. I suppose that's why there was a small box filled with earplugs affixed to the side of the door.

"Just try to get a good look at everyone you can and make sure you're recording it," I said. "Upload it to the cloud as we go if storage becomes an issue. Other than that, ask questions. Pay attention. See if anyone's lying to us. You know. The usual."

I glanced back out the windows. The massive pipes that exited the filters led out of the side of the building, some to holding tanks, some to retaining wells, and still others to the neighboring city sanitation facility. The fact that USC controlled water extraction while the city dealt with sanitation had always struck me as an odd compromise, but it made sense from a historical standpoint. USC had built the foundations of the major Martian cities, and as such had initially provided all the major services necessary for civilization: water, power, transportation, construction, and agriculture.

As the fledgling Martian settlements grew and expanded, the USC corporatocracy adjusted with them. Cities wanted more control, and USC didn't want to give it up. It was that tension which ultimately led to the Martian uprising twenty-five years ago. Despite the war, USC had maintained complete control over what it deemed the 'essential services': water extraction from subterranean ice, fusion power generation, and spaceport operation. Certain other city services, such as public transportation, the fire department, and the police were partnerships between individual city-states and USC, though for what it was worth, I felt like we operated independently of USC oversight. Other services were entirely run by the cities, like health and human services, education, roads, and sanitation, while agriculture and construction had long since been taken over by independent third parties. For all of USC's oversight, we still operated in a capitalist system, just one where the bulk of the tax revenue went to USC, not local governments.

The door open behind me, muffled though it was by the steady churn of the pumps. I turned to find a man entering, one with a dated, combed-over haircut, pants that were a little too loose, and a bit of sag in his jowls. "Sorry about that," he said. "The name's Jim Feathers. Leondra said you were with the police?"

Leondra had been the first able-bodied individual we'd found. When we introduced ourselves and told her we needed to speak with someone in management, she'd ushered us here and told us to wait.

"That's right. I'm Ambrose Drake. This is Bishop Mwenge. We're with the EPD, homicide division."

"You're here about Shao Wen, I'm guessing," said Jim.

Bishop smirked. "How'd you guess?"

"Well, I..." Jim stopped, probably realizing he didn't need to answer that. "Anyway, what can I do for you?"

"Did you work with Ms. Wen, Mr. Feathers?"

Jim snorted. "No. She was upper management. I'm like half a dozen rungs of management beneath that. She didn't even work in this building, as I'm sure you're aware. Administration has its own skyscraper, one with better views, fewer smells, and less noisy equipment. Women like her send down instructions to us from their ivory tower. We barely ever see them. I think I spoke to her twice in my life."

"And you're not bitter about the divide at all, I see," said Bishop.

Jim frowned and looked like he wanted to say something, but caught himself. "I'm happy with my job. It's work. That's more than a lot of people have nowadays. Are you just here to ask me about Administrator Wen?"

"Actually, I was hoping for a tour," I said.

"A tour?"

"It's where you show people around. Explain how systems work. Inflate your own importance a little."

Jim looked baffled. "Why do you want a tour?"

"It's related to Wen's murder," I said. "It's not a request."

Jim sighed. "Fine. Come with me, then. You want to start on the main floor?"

"Offices. Break rooms. You name it. Then we'll hit the pumps."

"Suit yourself," said Jim. "Might as well grab some ear protection, though."

We did as we were told, slipping earplugs into our pockets as we started the rounds. Jim tried to skip over the more mundane portions of the building, but I straightened him out. I made it clear we wanted to wander past every office, every conference room, every bathroom—though I did save him the indignity of showing us inside each of those. By the time we made it to the main floor, I could tell Jim's patience was wearing thin, but he completed the tour as asked. By that point, we'd shoved the plugs into our ear canals, turning the roar of the pumps into a dull background buzz, but our Nets allowed us to keep our communication as crisp and clear as ever.

"Well, I think that's about it," said Jim as he finished his spiel on the coagulators. "If you want to see the sanitation plant, too, I can call ahead for someone to meet you. I've got to warn you though, that place has an aroma that's hard to shake. The regulars get used to it, but you'll be smelling it for days."

I shook my head. "No thanks. We're only interested in this facility. But you haven't shown us any of the underground portions."

Jim's brow furrowed. "You want to go down in the tunnels?"

"You have personnel down there, don't you?"

"Sure. Fluid dynamics engineers. The fusion plant operators. Maintenance crews. Construction guys when there's an expansion going on. You can't honestly want to head down there, do you?"

I didn't blink. "I said I wanted a tour of the *whole* facility."

"You're killing me, man. I have work to do."

"Then delegate it, but I need to see everything."

Jim sighed. "Showing you every last scrap of tunnel down there would take days."

"Then show us the most heavily trafficked parts. We've got a few hours. Mwenge and I already stopped for lunch on our way here."

Jim wiped his face with his hand. When he pulled it back, he revealed a forced smile. "Follow me."

We hitched a ride on one of the service elevators, taking it down, down, down. Our online Net connections died not long after we'd boarded. In lieu of stories, the elevator had a depth gauge. At about the fourteen hundred meter mark, it finally stopped and emptied us into a long tunnel, one with bright lights strung at regular intervals overhead.

The second portion of the tour did indeed take over two hours, but I think Jim showed us everything of note. We passed through the underground fusion plant that powered the heaters jabbed into the subterranean ice sheet, melting it so it could be pumped to the surface for use. We saw the secondary pumps, smaller than those in the surface facility but big enough to keep the water flowing in the event of a mechanical failure. We met engineers, welders, drill operators, and wrench jockeys. Jim even showed us the cavernous room that stored the construction equipment used to hew tunnels through the ice and rock. I'd seen some big drills, but never one with a bit three times my height.

When we finally stepped out of the elevator onto the main floor of the plant, Jim didn't take any chances. He excused himself as quickly as he could and took off at a near run, leaving Mwenge and I standing amid the monstrous equipment.

"Well, I hope this was worth it," said Mwenge as we headed toward the exit. "Otherwise that's several hours we could've spent chasing more promising leads."

I didn't mention that I didn't think we *had* any more promising leads. "Trust me, pal. I'm right there with you."

———

"YOU KNOW," said Mwenge as we sat down at our desks at the precinct. "What I still don't get is why you didn't contact USC for a list of the employees who work at the water plant as opposed to trying to catch them all on camera. You know we missed some, and that's only the ones who were scheduled to be working at this hour. That place runs twenty-four and a half hours a day."

"I did ask for the official list, but there are two reasons," I said as I uploaded my Net feed to the police database for facial recognition scanning. "The most important being that there's a possibility there are people who work at the plant who wouldn't be on the list."

Bishop gave me a look. "What do you mean? Like, people who haven't been vetted by USC? People who don't have work permits?"

"Or people who USC wouldn't hire, if they uncovered records of criminal activity during their background checks."

I finished the upload and leaned back in my chair. Bishop rested his backside against the corner of my desk. "You're talking about gang members."

"Our database already has a list of known Silicon Road associates, but the tablet we got from Boothe had a contact list with many more. I'm checking the list against the identities we scraped on our walkthrough. We'll know in a moment if any of the people we ran into today have ties to the Silicon Road gang."

"I still don't understand why they'd be there if they're not employed by water services."

"I don't either," I said. "If we find any, perhaps we can ask them."

Bishop rapped his fingers against my desk. "You said there was a second reason you didn't want to go by USC's official employment roster."

"You sure you want to know?"

"Why wouldn't I?"

I took a moment, thinking of Wen's tablet. "Because I'm not entirely sure if we should trust USC to be truthful about their employees."

"I'm not following," said Mwenge.

I sighed. "You remember when we interrogated Boothe and suggested the Silicon Road gang might've murdered Wen? He claimed that made no sense because they were paying her. So why would you kill someone on your bankroll?"

"Because you don't want to have to keep paying them anymore, obviously."

I snapped my fingers. "Maybe Wen was being paid to keep quiet."

"And how does that tie into a USC conspiracy?"

I shrugged. "I don't know. I'm still working on it. I need to go through the data I found on Wen's tablet in more detail." My workstation chimed. I glanced at what had popped up. "Well, well."

Bishop leaned over to take a look. "Looks like two of the folks in the underground tunnels are on Boothe's contact list. Are they on the official employment register?"

"Give me a second. Ah... they are, actually."

"Are they on our list of known Silicon Road conspirators?"

I checked. "They're not. But that doesn't mean much. Our list is far from complete."

Bishop straightened. "So no giant conspiracy, I suppose. Although that doesn't explain why a couple of drill operators would be in a Silicon Road dope peddler's tablet."

"I guess they could be dust heads," I said. "But that seems too circumstantial."

"Are you going to pull their files?"

"I'm going to pull everything I can on them. If they once ran into Shao Wen on a darkened street corner seven years ago, I'll find out."

"I'll leave you to it, then."

I looked up from the holo. "Got something else to keep you busy?"

"I wanted to pursue the terrorism angle," said Bishop. "I think we're not paying as much attention as we should to the fact that the Snow Leopard is behind the murders, or claims to be. If we can get a bead on him and work backward, we'll find the killer."

I shook my head. "You're crazy if you think you'll find him. Trust me, Bishop, I've been down that road."

"Not him, necessarily," said Bishop with a smile. "But perhaps the people who surround him, instead."

I RUBBED my forehead and sighed. Try as I might, I couldn't establish a connection between either of the men we'd spotted at the water processing plant who were on Boothe's tablet and Shao Wen. Both of them were recent immigrants to Elysium, one of which had come from the Hellas Basin settlements, another who'd primarily worked on Luna and Phobos. Heavy machinery operators, similar to the sorts Boothe had claimed the Silicon Road gang was recruiting, but if either of them had ever heard the name Shao Wen, I couldn't prove it. They were both licensed union tradesmen, and there wasn't any evidence either of them were in Silicon Road's pocket except for their tenuous connection with Boothe. Maybe if I pulled their financial records, I'd find something, but I wasn't sure it was worth it. There was now four degrees of separation between them and Wen. Perhaps I'd gotten carried away, kept sniffing at false leads until they led me to a dead end. I'd been known to fall victim to my own laser focus before.

"Ambrose."

I looked up from my holo. Bishop stood at my side, jacket in hand. "I'm headed out. Don't stay too late. I know we're dealing with murder here, but to be fair, we always are."

"Stay too late?" I glanced at the windows. They were dark. "Oh."

Bishop smiled. "Like I said. See you tomorrow."

"Wait," I said as he turned. "You want to get a drink?"

41

NOVEMBER 20, 2154

AN ARMED GUARD stood at the door as we filed into the interrogation room. On one hand, I could understand why the Lieutenant Colonel had brought the informant there. It was a secure room, lined with sound insulation and outfitted with electronics to cancel incoming and outgoing Net communications. It was sturdily built and fitted with cameras and microphones that recorded every murmur, whisper, and raised eyebrow on encrypted drives. It also was far from inviting, with bare metal walls, a polished metal folding table, metal folding chairs, and little else inside. It had all the warmth of a gust of Martian wind.

The informant paced as we entered, a steaming cup of coffee or perhaps the locally-favored maché tea in his hands. He glanced our way at the sound of our boots on the polished floors, his eyes narrow and darting between the four of us, his knuckles white around his cup.

"Sorry to keep you waiting, Mr. Gailwick," said Cornier, pausing at the back of one of the folding chairs. "I needed to gather a few of my people. This is Major Marjory Watkins, my second in command. Private Ambrose Drake, with counterintelligence. And you're familiar with Private Murdock, I gather."

Gailwick took us all in at a glance, nodding at Mike. "Hey."

"Please, have a seat," said Cornier. "No reason to be on your feet."

"I'd rather stand if that's all right." Gailwick's voice warbled, and his cup shook.

"Not a problem." The Lieutenant Colonel nodded to Murdock, who joined him in a chair. Watkins touched me at the elbow and gestured toward the side. Apparently we were to act as flies on the wall.

Gailwick tapped his foot against the floor, beating out an irregular rhythm with his heel. He stared at his drink more than any of us, glancing our way only to make sure we weren't leaving.

"Sorry," he said. "I'm nervous."

"Take your time," said Cornier.

"They've made threats against me, you know. Against my family. The separatists, I mean. Not Franklin, but others."

"Who's Franklin?" asked Cornier.

"My cousin," said Gailwick, taking a sip of his brew. "He's one of them. A separatist. He'd never threaten my family, but some of the others? Yeah. Who knows if they'd follow through. It's hard to tell. Not really sure who's in charge. The order might not come down from the top, but that doesn't mean there aren't knuckle-heads in the ranks."

Mike leaned forward in his chair. "It's okay to speak freely here, Pyeter. We'll make sure your family is safe. Put all of you under our protection if need be."

I wasn't sure how Cornier would react to that, but he simply nodded.

Gailwick's foot stilled, and he took another sip of his drink. His hands shook so badly he needed to use both of them to keep from spilling. "Franklin and I head in to work together in the mornings. He's been trying to recruit me for a while. Never brought me along to any meetings or anything, mind you, but he hasn't had to. I keep tabs on where we stop. Where we pause for him to *drop things off.* To *leave a note.* They're cells. They have to be. I know of five. Pretty sure about all of them." He turned to Mike and the Lieutenant Colonel. "Franklin can't know. My family can't know. And I need assurances they'll be safe. Iron-clad assurances."

"We'll make it happen," said Cornier. "We can even ship you out of Cassini, if you want."

Gailwick thought it over for a moment, then the dam broke. Information gushed from his mouth as if from a firehose. He gave us addresses, directions, what he knew about the buildings involved, his estimations on how many insurgents might be in each cell, every tidbit he'd overheard from his cousin, the last date he and his cousin had stopped at each location, and anything else he could think of. Cornier nodded through all of it, letting the pressurized information come out before Gailwick thought twice about it. Eventually, when the man slowed, the Lieutenant Colonel thanked him, instructed Murdock to go through some of the points in finer detail with him, and nodded to Major Watkins and myself to follow him out.

He gathered us in the hallway. "What do you think, Major?"

"I think Mr. Gailwick just served us one hell of a meal on a platter, sir."

"And you, Private? Can you corroborate anything he's said with your intelligence?"

I blinked, wondering if the Colonel had even been down to the CI office. "Sir, we don't have much intelligence to speak of down there."

Cornier smiled and guffawed. "Well then, Private. Sounds like we'd better generate some for you. Major? Gather your squads. We're moving out first thing tomorrow."

WE RUMBLED along in the Marauder, the entirety of Zeta squad collected together for the first time in what seemed like weeks. We sat there in our Suits, helmets on and Badasses between our legs, ready for a quick exit when the time came. The portholes behind the heads on the bench opposite me were dark and dusty, only the barest glint of the early morning sunrise radiating through the panels.

"So how's everyone feeling?" said Phoebe. She sat in front of me, her face partially obstructed by the reflective coating on her visor. "Are we staying loose?"

"Loose as a goose hopped up on hydrocodone," said Maarten. "ETA is four minutes, Phoebs."

I ground my teeth at the nickname. In our intimate moments, I'd occasionally called Phoebe by some banal term of address like baby or sweetheart, but in our official capacities, I felt we owed each other more respect. Phoebe was a Sergeant now, after all. Still, if she didn't bother to correct Maarten, I certainly wouldn't be the belligerent asshole to do it for her.

"Might as well check your magazines one last time," said Phoebe. "Remember, use non-lethal rounds to start. The goal is for there to be no casualties, Red or otherwise. We won't keep the civilians on our side for long if we start spraying bullets through their windows."

We all nodded, well aware of the stakes. We'd spent the majority of the evening going over the plan of attack, memorizing the building plans, confirming our tasks. It didn't seem like it would be too difficult of a mission. We'd performed basically the same raid in Utopia when we'd infiltrated the enemy basement and recovered the drives that cued us to the attack on the fusion plant. Still, there were elements we had to deal with here that we didn't in Utopia. Less backup. Unpressurized streets. Less surveillance.

Still, I felt confident, mostly because of Phoebe's leadership. Despite not having attended the meeting with Gailwick, she'd taken charge immediately upon receiving her commands from Major Watkins, getting all of us ready for our first raid in months. It amazed me how she'd grown into her leadership role despite her earlier misgivings. She didn't hesitate anymore, didn't question herself or others, simply gave the orders and expected them to be followed. It was refreshing as a subordinate but surprising as her boyfriend, mostly because I hadn't seen the transformation first-hand. We'd spent too much time apart since reaching Cassini, even during our overland travel, despite our close proximity. It seemed as if we always had something else to do. A beat to patrol, a wall to patch, missives to read, data to decrypt.

It was my fault as much as Phoebe's. I hadn't put in the effort to keep our relationship humming, other than the effort required for a furious sexual encounter in some forgotten portion of the base every other week. I needed to do better. I needed to work on the things that had drawn us together in the first place. As I stared at Phoebe's intoxicating eyes through the gleam of her faceplate, I told myself I would.

"T-minus thirty seconds to arrival," said Maarten. "Streets look clear."

We'd been instructed to park a couple blocks away from the supposed location of the Red cell to prevent anyone from knowing we were coming. I imagined they wouldn't be peering out their windows at the crack of dawn, but the precautions had been estab-lished for a reason.

"Systems check, everyone," said Phoebe. "Get ready to move."

I checked my systems, and they all looked good. The Marauder ground to a halt, and the back ramp descended, the interior chamber having long been vented. Johnson and Mandel were out the door first, followed by Franks, Sun, Nakamoto, and Phoebe. Halabi filed past me as I grabbed the jaws from underneath our bench seat, and Maarten brought up the rear.

We jogged down the street in single file, a light breeze swirling dust at our feet, the sky growing in color at the horizon. We paused at a street corner, checking for vehicles.

"No signs of activity," said Phoebe. "Push on."

Up the street we went, bounding the last quarter kilometer to the address in question, a nondescript three-story apartment building with tinted windows that looked like portals in the early morning darkness. The outer airlock doors opened as Johnson punched on the keypad, just as we'd hoped, and we all crammed inside. The doors closed. Air whirred and rushed inside.

"Less than a minute to entry," said Phoebe. "We're doing great, folks."

Cornier had instructed the attack teams to carry out their breach maneuvers at precisely seven o'clock. If we all barged in at the same time, no one could be warned.

The airlock doors opened and Janeece crouched forward, waving the rest of us behind her. We followed in a quiet shuffle of boots and rattling utility belts. Up the stairs we went, then down the hall to the apartment we'd been directed to. Phoebe held up her hand. We waited in silence for twenty seconds before she waved me forward with the jaws.

At ten seconds till, she shot her finger at the door. "Go."

I jammed the jaws into the door and activated the pneumatics. Without an interior pressure gradient to fight against, the doors snapped open as if they'd been pushed by a stiff breeze. We swarmed into the apartment, spreading into the space with our Badasses leveled before us, past a stubby entrance hall into the living room beyond. A man with a two-day old beard wearing nothing but his underwear turned the corner from a kitchen, a bowl in hand. He barely had time to lift an eyebrow before a tranq dart took him in the neck. He collapsed in a heap, hot oatmeal spilling across the floor as Janeece, Franks, and Phoebe surged into the adjoining hallway.

I swept the kitchen with my muzzle, but other than the one

target, it was empty. Within a few moments, I heard Janeece's voice. "Clear." Then Franks. "Clear." Phoebe two seconds later. "All clear."

I walked back into the living room. There were a pair of synthetic cloth couches there, a small table between them, and a wall-mounted display. A round dining table in the corner still had dishes from the last meal strewn across it. Based upon the remains, the lone underwear model on the floor was the apartment's only occupant.

Phoebe walked back in with Johnson and Franks. She glanced around the room, a frown growing on her face. "This was apartment two-twelve, wasn't it?"

Nakamoto nodded. "Said so on the door. The building has the right address, too, at least according to GPS."

"Which means our information sucked ass," said Maarten. "God damn it. Well, we may not have bagged any Reds, but we sure as hell messed up this guy's breakfast."

"Hold on," said Phoebe. "Let me see if I can get a secure line to the other teams." She stood a moment before shaking her head. "Nothing. I'll give it five and try again. Maybe they're engaged. Which would mean the rest of the teams made contact. That would be a good thing."

"For them, maybe," said Maarten. "For us, it means we missed the only good action we've had in a month."

"You're really going to complain about not getting to shoot anyone?" I asked.

"Well, it would've made getting up two hours before dawn worthwhile, don't you think?"

Phoebe must've noticed the rising tensions. "Look, I don't know whose apartment we breached, but we're going to play this by the book. Drake, take the jaws back to the car. Stanić, accompany him and move the Marauder outside the building. Everyone else, get your evidence bags. Until I hear otherwise, we're collecting and tagging anything even slightly more interesting than the target's oatmeal bowl."

I looped my Badass over my shoulder and retreated to the entrance, picking the jaws up on the way. Maarten followed me, but he didn't engage me en route to the airlock. Air rushed out the vents between us, the outer doors slid open soundlessly, and we started our bounding trek back to the Marauder.

"You know," I said on a private channel, "it would be nice if on missions you treated me and Phoebe with the respect we deserve."

The big guy tilted his helmet toward me. "What are you talking about?"

"Calling Phoebe *Phoebs*. She's a sergeant. And as for me? You're always challenging me. Always trying to undermine me. You didn't used to be like that."

"I seriously have no idea what you're going on about, hoss."

"No? You're really going to claim you haven't treated me differently since I got promoted to squad leader? I mean, you should, but you're not doing it the right way."

"First, I shouldn't *have* to treat you differently when Phoebe's around. As platoon leader, she supersedes your authority. Second, if you have a problem with the way I'm doing things, that's an issue between me and you. If you've got something to say, say it."

I crossed the intersection, not stopping to look for traffic. I hadn't meant to have this conversation now, but it was as good a time as any. "You need to stop thinking with your gun, Maarten."

"I really hope you're not talking about what's in my pants, hoss."

"God damn it, Maarten, be serious. Ever since we got to Cassini, you've had a hard-on for shooting Reds. That's not all there is to being a soldier. Not everyone here is our enemy."

Maarten grunted. "Sorry for exhibiting some passion. Be nice if you hadn't totally lost yours."

"What's that supposed to mean?"

Maarten scoffed. "You say I can't stop fantasizing about shooting Reds. When we first met, I got the feeling you did, too. I don't know why the hell else you would've joined. That fire's lost in you, hoss. You've let the job get to you. You just go through the motions. Finish the tasks. You don't give a shit anymore. Maybe you never did."

The accusation shouldn't have hurt, but it did, like a knife twisting in my gut. Had I really become so jaded? In just six months on the job? But it *was* a job, wasn't it? That's how it felt, despite the altruistic reasons behind my enlistment.

I shook my head as we approached the Marauder. "I—"

I saw the flash before I was able to act. A rocket screamed through the sky, but luckily the hand at the helm wasn't the sharpest shot. It hit the dirt on the other side of the Marauder, spraying dust into the sky as the explosion carried through the thin Martian air. I dove to the ground, the jaws flying from my hands as the soft pings of shrapnel and gunfire ricocheted off the metal facade behind us.

"Jesus Christ!" I crawled toward the edge of our truck. "We've made enemy contact at the Marauder. Phoebe, do you hear me?"

Her voice cut in. "Say again, Ambrose?"

"Contact. Enemy contact. We're under fire."

Maarten popped his head around the edge of the Marauder and cut loose with a spray of crackling gunfire. "What was that about nobody wanting to kill us, hoss?"

"Shut up, Maarten." I looped my Badass over my head and took a position at the other edge of the vehicle.

"Ambrose, Maarten, do you copy?" said Phoebe. "What the hell is going on back there?"

"I think we found our Red cell. They must've been waiting for us to return to the Marauder." I looked around the edge of the heavy truck, trying to locate the gunfire. Muzzles flashed atop the building opposite us, and movement caught my eye at the edge of the buildings at the intersection. Two individuals in suits emerged, one of them carrying a painted red tube about the length of an extended arm. The individual dropped to a knee and leveled the tube my way. "Oh, shit!"

I sprang to my feet and took off the opposite way, grabbing Maarten by the shoulder as I passed him.

He grunted and stumbled to his feet under the force of my grip. "What the hell are you—"

An explosive force knocked me to the ground. Dirt rained down around me. Dust choked the air, turning it a thick, rusty red in color and obscuring everything more than two meters away. My ears rang, but not as much as they would've from a pressure wave in full atmosphere. I turned my head, searching for the Marauder. It was still there, thankfully, but on its side, part of its metal shell bent inward under the force of the rocket propelled grenade. Phoebe's voice cut across the din. "Ambrose? Maarten? Talk to me!"

"Send backup, now!" I shouted. Then to Maarten: "We need cover!"

He nodded, his head swiveling as he looked through the dust. The ping of bullets on metal continued to sound, the world's most frightening concerto.

Maarten hopped to his feet, scooping the discarded jaws into his arms. He pointed across the street. "I saw skinnies on the rooftops. They can't shoot us if we're underneath them."

I nodded. Maarten took off across the street at a run and I followed. I couldn't see the intersection due to the dust, couldn't know if the insurgents were hoofing it toward us, loading another rocket into their launcher or trying to pick us off with their rifles.

We skidded to a stop in the dirt. Maarten jammed the jaws into the door in front of us and flicked the power. They groaned and slammed open. Maarten picked up the implement and pushed forward into the interior airlock, hitting the power once again. The interior doors put up less of a struggle than the outer. Air rushed past us as we surged inside, a flashing red light blinking in the building's corridor and a low siren wailing beyond.

"Cover the door," said Maarten, dumping the jaws beside me. "I'll take the stairs."

"Maarten!" I swore as he took off. I hopped to the front of the exterior lock and poked my head around the corner. I pulled it back as gunfire ripped chunks from the side of the building.

"Phoebe, I've got multiple hostiles approaching from the east," I said. "Where are you?"

"Two minutes out," she said. "Can you hold on?"

"I've got no choice." I poked my Badass around the edge and took a few haphazard potshots.

A rough hand pulled me back from the edge. I almost had a heart attack until I saw it was Maarten.

"We need to get out of here," he said.

"Negative. There are hostiles approaching from outside. The rest of the squad is a few minutes out."

"Well, there are hostiles approaching from *inside,* too," said Maarten.

One of them emerged from the top of the stairwell at the far end of the corridor as he said it. I whipped my rifle up and cut loose with a few shots. The darts bounced off the far wall, and it was only then I realized I had non-lethal rounds in the magazine. I dropped the cartridge and was cramming real bullets back in when another Red peered around the stairs.

Maarten fired and swore. "Damnit!" He grabbed the jaws and slammed them into the nearest set of interior doors.

"Maarten!" I couldn't stop him before he hit the switch.

It was one thing to breach the hallway of a building without notice, but Maarten had jammed the jaws into an interior door. Without knowing who or what stood behind it.

The doors slammed open and air rushed out. Maarten darted

in, jaws in hand. The reappearance of a Red at the top of the stairs forced me behind him.

Maarten tossed the jaws to the ground. "Ambrose, doors!"

I turned to the control panel and hit the emergency switch. The doors flew back together, sealing tight, but the damage had been done. We stood in a living room, not unlike the one we'd breached with the rest of the squad, but we weren't alone. Someone lay across one of the couches, a pressure suit three-quarters of the way donned. Not just anyone, either. A young girl, maybe twelve or thirteen, with disheveled brown hair. Her body convulsed, her arms jerking in response to the sudden loss of oxygen.

"Oh, shit," I said. "Shit. *Shit.*"

A large figure clad in a suit and mask burst around a corner at the far side of the room. He darted toward us, arms spread wide, a knife in hand. I couldn't hear a thing he shouted, but the man's mouth moved as he sprinted. His face was wild, full of terror and anger and shock, but it was a familiar face. A bearded one. *Elmarr...?*

He lunged. A rifle cracked, and Elmarr went down, red spreading across the chest of his suit. Maarten stood there, his Badass following the bearded man as he fell to the floor.

"What the hell are you doing?" I cried.

"He had a knife," said Maarten. "He lunged at us."

"He was lunging for his daughter, you asshole. He was trying to save her!"

"Bullshit. You don't know that."

Someone pounded at the door, but I didn't move to cover us. I hopped forward and grabbed Maarten by the scruff of his suit. "You killed him, you bastard. The coffee shop owner. Him and his daughter, both. *You killed them.*"

"Snap out of it," said Maarten, shoving me off him. "We've got skinnies ready to pump us with lead. Save it for someone who cares."

Something inside me snapped. I jumped forward, tackling Maarten as I grabbed his gun. "Give me your weapon, soldier. You're relieved of duty."

"What the fuck are you talking about?" Maarten fought me, refusing to let go.

"You're a murderer!" I yelled. "Give me the goddamned rifle!"

"Fuck you, Ambrose! Get off me!"

Maarten pushed. I pulled. His meaty digits dug into the metal of the receiver. His fingers moved toward the trigger, but I slapped them away.

"Get OFF!"

Maarten yanked on his Badass as I switched strategies, trying to knock his hands off the weapon by slamming them against the floor. The butt of the rifle whipped down, but it didn't hit the laminate. It smashed against the side of Maarten's helmet.

I heard a crunch. Maarten and I both froze, the rifle held between us in midair, as a web of fine cracks spread across his visor.

I passed a hand over the network of cracks, feeling a whisper of air against my fingers. And then I heard a soft whine.

42

MAY 12, 2179

I LAUGHED and shook my head. "I can't say I told you so, Bishop, because I never warned you, but that's what you get for letting your kids talk you into getting a pet."

"Oh, I know," he said, swirling the dregs of his gin fizz in the bottom of his glass. "And I tried to convince them to get something everyone would like. A guinea pig, for instance. But I was outvoted three to one. So like it or not, I'm officially a cat person."

I leaned into the booth and drained the last of my lager. The bar's soft music played over the speakers, just loud enough to be audible over the steady hum of conversation. Over the past hour, I'd gone through a pair of beers while Bishop had nursed his sole cocktail, but the conversation hadn't been lacking. Anything but. And not more than five minutes of it had been devoted to work.

I smiled and gave Bishop a slight nod. "This was nice."

He nodded back. "You've got that right. I can't tell you how stressed I've been for the past two days. I don't even know why. I guess... our case feels bigger than most, you know? But I needed this. We should do this more often."

I set my bottle on the table and spread my hands. "Hey. I'm not the one with family obligations and a needy cat to feed."

Bishop straightened. "Speaking of which. Mona's calling me. Probably wondering where I am." He stood and grabbed his jacket. "I'll forward you the money for the drinks."

I waved him off. "Give me a break. You've got two kids, a wife, and a cat, and I make more than you to boot. I've got it. See you tomorrow."

Bishop waved and nodded, already bearing the focused look of someone taking a Net call.

I doubled-checked my bottle, but it held nothing but suds. I couldn't help but shake my head, our conversation still fresh. "*Christ*. Mwenge. With a cat. I should've known."

I slid my bottle to the side and stared at Bishop's empty glass. As I did so, I felt a pang in my chest, the same as I'd felt when I'd asked Bishop if he'd wanted to join me at the bar in the first place. As light and airy as our conversation had been, I hadn't been entirely truthful in my desire to talk to him. I just needed to get him to open up. Talk to me. I needed to be able to look into his eyes as he laughed, as a drink loosened his inhibitions, and make sure he was the man I'd come to know and trust and care so much about.

He was, and I'd be damned if I was wrong. I never would've doubted him if not for that blasted missive. *It could be an inside job.* Fine. Maybe it was. But Mwenge wasn't behind it, I knew that much.

I picked up the tumbler, looking at the smudges Bishop's fingerprints had left on the glass. The second part of the missive was the more disturbing part, though. *Protect yourself at all costs.* Not at Bishop's or Reyes' or Dean's expense if I could avoid it. But I would.

THE BOTTOM-MOST LEVELS of the precinct still buzzed with activity when I arrived, but the thirty-second floor was deserted. Detectives didn't have to pull night shifts except on rare occasion. I half-expected the Captain to still be in her office, but the lights within were darkened there, too.

I flicked my desk light on, fell into my chair, and activated the holo. I reached into my desk and pulled out Wen's tablet, which I'd left there after my meeting with Dean for safekeeping. After transferring the data to my workstation, I opened a terminal. Within ten minutes, I'd whipped up a quick script to trawl through the data on Wen's tablet and compare it to the treasure trove of files the USC grunts had sent my way after my insistent prodding. I set it to run, took a deep breath, and headed to the stairs.

The CSU offices were on the thirty-eighth floor. I headed past them into the laboratory on the south side of the floor. That, too, was empty, thankfully. I accessed the building's security, pulled up the camera feed for the elevators, stairwells above and below me, and for the one covering the hallway directly outside the lab, shrunk them, and placed them into the side of my vision where I could keep tabs on them. Then I got to work.

I slipped on a pair of latex gloves and walked to the 3D printer on the far counter. Using my Net, I pulled both Captain Reyes' and Bishop's personnel files, snipped the fingerprints, passed them though a three-dimensional rendering software, and uploaded the resulting file to the printer. I stuck my hands, palms up, into the demarcated zone, checked the placement, then activated the printer. The head whirred and lowered. I kept my arms frozen in place as the extrusion nozzle sprayed fine lines of polymer over my digits in quick strips, my eyes locked on the security feeds the entire time. The nozzle whirred and grunted as it lifted and started on my left hand. Bishop done, Reyes to go. A minute and a half and counting.

When the printer finished its second round, I lifted both hands and blew on my fingertips. The polymer wasn't designed to be shot onto skin. As I cooled my digits, I sent a script to the printer and activated it, wiping all traces of my ever having used the machine—and unlike the work of my murdering, fire-bombing nemesis, I did mean *all* traces. My twenty-five years of hacking and cryptography experience hadn't gone to waste.

With my eyes still on the security feeds, I stripped off the latex gloves and tucked them into the bottom of my innermost jacket pocket. As I left the CSU lab, I checked the time. I'd barely been inside for two and a half minutes. I gave myself a pat on the back as I slipped into the stairwell, no one the wiser.

My script had finished comparing the file sets when I reached my desk, so I brought up the summary document and scanned it. My jaw might've dropped if I hadn't already suspected the results.

There was a discrepancy between the numbers pulled from Wen's tablet and the official numbers provided by USC. Not a small discrepancy, either. A *big* one. Like, a city's worth of water, one roughly the size of Elysium.

I leaned back in my chair and scratched my head. Given the fact that Wen was the administrator of USC's water division and that Jackson was a comptroller for the city's water services—basically a management level auditor—I'd expected someone was fudging numbers in regards to the city's supplies, either inflows, outflows, or some other metric, but I hadn't expected *this*. The magnitude of the discrepancy was mind boggling. Wen's numbers suggested *thirty million cubic meters* of ice were missing from Elysium's underground sheet. That wasn't possible, was it? How could that much ice have been melted and lost without anyone's notice? If the ice loss were accurate, it would imply an unprecedented level of corruption and deceit on the side of USC and the city agencies that worked closely with them, not to mention a conspiracy that would involve dozens of surveyors, engineers, contractors, and more.

All of which begged an important question. Whose numbers were correct? We'd found Wen's tablet in her apartment in an unlocked, unsecured safe, *after* she'd been murdered. It was the only item left in said safe. Why? Had it been planted there? Were the numbers false, and if so, who would benefit from spreading false information?

The answer was obvious, of course. The Martian separatists. The Snow Leopard's videos had made that exceedingly plain, painting Wen and Jackson as corrupt pawns of the government. Wen's murderer could've easily planted the tablet in her safe, knowing we'd find it and crack the encryption sooner or later. They were likely banking on us releasing said data once we had our hands on it—or someone releasing it. *It could be an inside job, after all.* And once the data was out, it wouldn't matter if it was accurate or not. It would serve to advance the separatist agenda, inflaming tensions, incensing the public, and leading to a greater mistrust of government and of USC. Nothing the latter could do would ever prove otherwise to people, especially since USC was the primary data acquisition source regarding Elysium's ice reserves. Not that facts would matter in the face of emotion.

I grabbed Wen's tablet and put it in my jacket pocket, then wiped the summary files from my computer, simultaneously glad I'd asked Dean to encrypt the copy I'd had him make.

Just as I was about to leave, the alert system I'd set up for the illegal Net traces I'd put on Vincenzio and Demetriou pinged me. It was only set to notify me if either man visited a location I'd defined as suspicious, notably the site of either murder or any number of city water services locations.

The alert the program had given me wasn't because either man was in a particularly suspicious location, though. It was because they were in the *same* location.

I PEERED over a neck-height concrete wall into an estate that contained more trees and shrubs than most Elysian parks. Japanese maples, elms, white and black pines, and flowering cherries stood amid a field of lilacs, hydrangeas, and drooping wisterias. A winding path nearly disappeared among the shrubs and flowers. Tall metal poles with affixed grow lights peeked from behind the tallest of trees, half hidden from view as they held up the Mylamene barrier overhead. Most of the homes in the upscale district weren't as botanically-oriented as Giancarlo Vincenzio's home, but perhaps the mob boss desired more privacy than the typical neighborhood fat cats.

I'd stood on the sidewalk for over an hour, keeping an eye on the path to the home from a darkened spot that neither of the two nearest streetlights touched. I kept expecting a police cruiser to arrive and to have to explain to them that I was one of them, but none did. Either I was a better sneak than I gave myself credit for, or the people in Vincenzio's circle knew better than to call the police for anything.

A call pulled me from my surveillance. "Sophia. Hey."

"Hey, babe," she said, her voice warm and sensual. "How've you been?"

"Busy. Sorry I didn't get a chance to call last night."

"I understand. Work again?"

"Isn't it always?"

"Still there now?"

I kept my eyes on the home. "I'm not in the office, but yeah."

"Are you going to be finished anytime soon?"

"I hope so. Why?"

A chime sounded as I received a picture from Sophia, one of my living room. Sophia's jacket was draped across the back of my couch, and her shoes had been deposited neatly at the side. "I'm waiting."

Christ. "And I'm eager, trust me." I spotted motion on the path. "With luck, I won't be long. Gotta go."

"See ya. Soon, I hope."

The motion coalesced into two forms. I identified one of them thanks to my trace. I could infer the other based on the first.

I heard the soft whir of a rideshare approaching from down the street. As the pair reached the end of the path and stepped onto the sidewalk, I spoke. "Excuse me. Mr. Demetriou?"

Kosta's thug Arcenio spun and whipped a pistol from his pocket, pointing it at me in the darkness. I held up my hands as I stepped into the halo of the nearest streetlight.

"Put that thing away, Kollias. I'm not here to mug you."

Kosta stepped from the shadow of his muscular henchman. *"Detective Drake?* This is a surprise."

"What do you want?" said Arcenio.

"To talk. Not to you. To Mr. Demetriou."

"Where's your backup?" asked Arcenio. "Your partner leave you here alone? Doesn't seem safe."

I took a step forward as the rideshare came to a stop before us. "Since when is this man your mouthpiece, Kosta?"

Demetriou gave his thug a nod. Kollias put away the gun. "I'm a busy man, Detective, and I've recently granted you a portion of my time. What is it you need?"

"A word. In private."

Kollias snorted, but Kosta silenced him with a glance. "What is this about? The murder you accused me of being a part of?"

"I believe that you're not involved, Mr. Demetriou."

"What then?"

I nodded to Arcenio. "Not in front of him."

"And why would I acquiesce to such a request?"

"Just a hunch."

Kosta eyed me, his icy blues sharp. I thought he might've lost his tongue, but he found it, eventually. "Very well. Join me in the rideshare. Arcenio. Get another one and meet me at the manor."

His thug did a double take. "Boss?"

"I'll be fine. Detective Drake means me no harm. Detective?"

He opened the side door on the rideshare and climbed in. I hopped in, took the seat opposite him, and the car took off with a hum.

43

NOVEMBER 21, 2154

MAARTEN'S EYES widened to saucers as he stared at the cracks spreading centimeters from his nose. "Patch spray. I need patch spray!"

"Crap! *CRAP!*" I rolled off him, fumbling at my utility belt for the can. It was a temporary solution, but the aerosolized polymer would harden over the cracks, keeping the air inside his helmet until we could get Maarten to a pressurized area.

I found the can and ripped it from my belt. I'd just pressed my finger against the nozzle when Maarten's faceplate groaned and gave. The plastic shattered and sprayed against my face along with the air from Maarten's Suit as I sprayed the liquid polymer patch into the near vacuum. Maarten's eyed widened in shock before he snapped them shut. His lips pressed together tightly, trying to hold onto the air in his lungs even as his body started to shake.

"*AMBROSE!*" His frantic Net message rattled around my head like a death knell.

Phoebe cut in. "Guys, *what the hell is going on over there?* Maarten's pressure caved! Is he okay?"

"Get your ass here *now!*" I yelled back.

I sprang to my feet, hyperventilating within my helmet.

Maarten was losing consciousness rapidly. He'd be out within ten seconds, tops. His blood pressure would drop precipitously within thirty. Moisture was fleeing his body, ripped from his tissues into the void. Soon after, blood flow would stop entirely. Within seventy-five to ninety seconds, he'd be dead.

Gunfire tore the air behind me. I glanced at the door, but barring a few dents, it held. It would have to.

I jumped toward Elmarr's body—and ground to a halt.

A woman in a pressure suit stood against the far wall, her hands clenched over her heart. She stared vacantly at the bodies on the floor, those of Elmarr and his presumed daughter. Her daughter, in all likelihood.

I didn't feel the hot tears roll off my face, but I saw them splash against the interior of my mask as I knelt next to Elmarr. I fumbled with the latches at his neck, undoing his helmet even as I heard more gunfire in the hallway outside. I half-expected the man's wife to tackle me, to punch me and kick me and scream into the thin CO_2 atmosphere that I was a murderer and a heartless bastard, but the woman didn't move. She didn't leave the wall as I ripped the helmet from her husband's still body. Didn't move as I jumped to Maarten and removed what remained of his helmet from his Suit with fingers as graceful as clubs.

I wasn't sure what brand of helmet Elmarr wore, but the latch was universal. I tightened it over Maarten's neck at a minute past breach, tapping into his Suit via Net and sending a command to the Bacteria Buddy to flood his system with every scrap of oxygen held in reserve. As fantastic as the Buddy was, it wasn't the best responding to situations of uncontrolled pressure loss. Maarten's vitals showed a heartbeat, but not much else.

I turned at the sound of more gunfire. The door held, though more dents marred its face. I glanced over my shoulder at the woman, but she was gone. Vanished, as if she'd never existed.

"Ambrose, we're outside your position," said Phoebe. "What happened to Maarten?"

"He lost Suit pressure," I said. "I think I have him stabilized... I hope. How's the situation outside?"

"Generally FUBAR," said Janeece. "A few of the Reds are on the run. Some have taken up sniper positions on the roof. More are squatting outside your location. And the Marauder's looking like she got stepped on by Ares himself."

"Ambrose, are you in a secure position?" asked Phoebe.

I glanced behind me, but the mystery woman hadn't reappeared. I squatted behind the couch, training the muzzle of my Badass on the door. "I think so. Now that you're here, I think the Reds have stopped trying to breach the door."

"Hang tight," said Phoebe. "We're going to get you out of there. Just make sure Maarten doesn't die. That's an order."

I glanced at Maarten's prone figure. His vitals continued to flit along, neither improving nor worsening. From what I knew about exposure to vacuum, he should pull through—the exposure, anyway. Getting him out of our current situation might be a different story. Our Marauder was wrecked, insurgents with rifles, explosives, and the element of surprise swirled around us, and the better part of the other squads at the base were potentially embroiled in situations as thorny as ours.

I ground my teeth, put my eye to my sights, and kept my finger on the trigger.

I SAT outside the Major's office, my hands clasped between my legs and my head hanging not far over them.

We'd all survived—barely. In their attempts to free me and Maarten from the insurgents, Franks had taken two rounds to the chest, both of which had thankfully been stopped by his Suit's impact-resistant weave. Nakamoto hadn't been so lucky. A piece of shrapnel had taken her in the leg, slicing through the weave before it could dissipate its kinetic energy. She was in the hospital as I sat, having the doctors pluck the jagged piece of metal from her thigh meat and stitch her back together.

Maarten was there, too. He'd regained consciousness on the way back to base—Epsilon squad had been dispatched to pick us up in their Marauder—but he hadn't said much. He'd seemed delirious, as if he didn't remember everything that had transpired. Given his oxygen loss, it wasn't surprising he'd lost some memories, but he must've remembered enough of it, because even while catching his bearings, the guy hadn't even glanced my way.

I heard the Major's door slide open and looked up. Phoebe strode through it purposefully, her face a thin mask barely holding back a cocktail of emotions. Rage, disappointment, and frustration, among others. She looked on the verge of tears.

"Phoebe," I said, but she walked past me without sparing me a glance. She didn't even slow. Didn't acknowledge me by voice or Net, just kept walking, stomping her way down the corridor until she disappeared around a corner.

"Drake."

I stood in response to the Major's voice, entering her office through the open doors. They puffed shut behind me as I came to attention in front of her desk.

Watkins didn't ask me to take a seat, nor did she tell me to be at ease. Instead, she sniffed and nodded at me. "Private Drake. Do you recall how many cells Mr. Gailwick provided us information on?"

"Seven, ma'am, if I remember correctly."

"We sent squads after all seven. Do you want to guess how many of those seven squads suffered colossal fuckups during their missions?"

I swallowed hard. "I'm assuming just one, ma'am."

"That's right. Yours." She shot me an accusatory finger. "How do you figure that happened, Private? That all the other cells didn't know we'd be coming, yet yours managed to sniff us out? Managed to get the better of you and your entire squad."

"I can't comment without more information, ma'am."

Watkins laughed without mirth. "There will be time for self-reflection, that's for sure. Don't get me wrong, Private, I was hoping for actual insight. Because I'm as baffled as you appear to be on how you walked into a trap. But if you don't have any ideas...?"

I didn't say a word.

"Perhaps you could instead enlighten me about the turn of events between you and Private Stanić, then."

"Major?"

Watkin's voice hardened. "Don't play me for a fool, Private. I've gone over your logs. I have access to your Nets feeds, too, in case you'd forgotten. I know you got into an altercation with Private Stanić that nearly killed him. Those facts are not up for debate. I want you to explain why."

"Stanić shot an unarmed civilian, ma'am. He was out of line."

"The civilian was indeed armed, Private. Again, I saw the feed."

"He had a knife, ma'am, but he wasn't a threat. Maarten shot him in cold blood."

"And you made the determination that he wasn't a threat based on what?"

"He was a coffee and tea vendor, ma'am. He'd offered us beverages while on patrol. He wasn't a Red, ma'am, I'm sure of it."

"Because he'd offered you tea."

I didn't know what to say to that.

Watkins rapped her fingers on her desk. "While we travelled here from Luna, I spoke to you about the demands of the job, Private. Do you remember what I told you, about why you're here?"

"To protect USC assets, ma'am."

Watkins' eyes narrowed. "Spaceports are assets. Silicon mines are an asset. A Marauder is an asset. Your squad mate, Stanić, is an asset. A coffee vendor *is not a god-damned asset*. Do I make myself clear, Private?"

I nodded. "Yes, ma'am."

"Glad to hear it. Unfortunately, given your actions regarding your subordinate, your understanding in the matter isn't enough. Effective immediately, you're no longer squad leader. In addition, you've been reassigned. You're a member of Lambda squad now. Report to squad leader Montross immediately."

My heart sank, and I momentarily forgot to breathe. "What?"

The major pierced me with her eyes. "Did I stutter, Private?"

I swallowed hard, trying to fight back the rage, frustration, and hurt I felt, the same emotions I'd seen on Phoebe's face as she'd stormed out. I wanted to say something, to give the major a piece of my mind, but I knew she was right. I'd fucked up. Maarten had nearly died because of me. I'd failed my squad, and I deserved to be kicked in the ass. So instead of saying anything, I simply saluted, about-faced, and left to suffer my misery in solitude.

44

THE RIDESHARE HUMMED as it took off down the lightly-trafficked residential street. "So, Mr. Demetriou. How was your meeting with Giancarlo Vincenzio? Did you stop for dinner or just drinks?"

Kosta Demetriou sat in his seat, staring at me with his hands clasped lightly in his lap. "Detective Drake, you've got me. In private, as requested. Let's cut to the chase, shall we? I don't have a taste for idle chatter."

"Just like that?" I said. "You don't want me to turn off my Net? Prove to you I'm not recording our conversation? Make a solemn vow not to share what we discuss?"

"Why would I? We're not about to discuss anything illegal, are we? Or is that why you've arrived in secrecy on your own? If so, I *certainly* don't have anything to worry about. If you were here in an official capacity, perhaps. But I suspect you want something you don't plan to share with those you work with. Something you'd rather keep to yourself."

"Little escapes your gaze, does it, Mr. Demetriou?"

"Little under the purview of the law. On with it. What do you wish to discuss?"

I glanced out the window. Taller multi-family units had already replaced the pocketbook-wrenching mansions of Vincenzio's neighborhood. "I looked into the sale of construction equipment your company made to Red Summit Financial, Mr. Demetriou. It consisted of a variety of machines. Haulers. Diggers. Drillers. Mostly for underground work, wouldn't you agree?"

"I honestly have no idea. It would sound as if it were."

"Do you have any idea why Elysium was established where it is?"

That make Kosta blink. "I assume this is going somewhere?"

"It is."

Kosta sighed. "Elysium was founded as part of the master plan established by USC in the late two thousands, with the intent being that it, Utopia, and Isidis would all have the same elevation, one that would suit them effectively once the planet's oceans were reestablished, ideally through the introduction of water ice via asteroid Swift-Tuttle which is scheduled to arrive in, what? Three years?"

"Less than two, but that's not what I meant. Why here, specifically? Why not fifty kilometers northeast or southwest along the expected coast? Why in this specific spot?"

"Tell me, Detective."

"Because of the ice sheet sitting underneath us, Mr. Demetriou. The ice sheet we've been mining for a hundred years to provide water for the city, and to meet the city's atmospheric generation quotas set in place by USC. A sheet that according to Administrator Wen's personal notes in missing thirty million cubic meters of ice."

Kosta lifted a brow. "Thirty million?"

"It's a lot, isn't it?"

"It is, if true. What does any of this have to do with me?"

"*If true*. Funny you should say that. I've suspected Administrator Wen's data is, in fact, fabricated. But that wouldn't explain why several individuals with contacts to the Silicon Road gang are in USC's employ at Elysium's central water processing facility, or why a Silicon Road financial front purchased subterranean drilling equipment from you, or why the same Silicon Road front paid Wen substantial amounts of money on a recurring basis."

Kosta tapped the fingers of his right hand against those of the left. "You realize I don't run that gang, don't you, Detective?"

"Of course I do. But I also know you're involved with this matter in some capacity, not only via your sale of equipment but by your recent visit with Mr. Vincenzio."

"I spoke with Giancarlo at his request. He needed advice of a personal matter."

"That matter being?"

Kosta didn't reply.

"Look, Mr. Demetriou. I believe that you had nothing to do with Wen's murder. From everything I've seen, you're a man of business, and I respect that, if not necessarily all of your practices or the men you surround yourself with. And because you're a man of business, I have to imagine you wouldn't intentionally set off a chain of events that would substantially hamper your interests."

"What do you mean?"

"The murders of Ms. Wen and Comptroller Jackson? You've noticed the effect the Snow Leopard's video's have had on the public. We're balanced at a precarious point here, politically and economically speaking. There are forces pushing our society toward chaos, Mr. Demetriou, and chaos is decidedly not good for business."

Kosta wet his lips. "It can be, with the right mind at the helm, but by and large I agree with you. So this is why you think I'll help? To advance my own business interests?"

I took a deep breath. "Perhaps. Or perhaps out of regard for your own family."

Kosta eyed me for a moment. He sighed, then shifted his gaze to the window. "How long have you known?"

"*Suspected.* But only a few days."

"And Sophia. Does she know?"

"That you've been spying on her? I doubt it. I found the bit of malicious code within her Net by chance. I didn't mention anything because I didn't know what to make of it at first, but I put the pieces together."

"Well, you wouldn't expect me *not* to keep tabs on my own daughter, would you?"

"*You,* Mr. Demetriou? I wouldn't. Which is why I wasn't that surprised."

Kosta met my eyes again. "You know, Detective—it's Ambrose, isn't it?"

"You know that it is."

Kosta sniffed. "I don't hate you. I don't even dislike you, despite your profession. I told you that at the restaurant, and I meant it. You're a man of conviction, a man with a strong moral compass, a much stronger one than me, and from everything I've been able to gather, a man who's treated my daughter with the kindness and respect she deserves. I don't wish you any ill will."

"I know. Otherwise I'd be dead."

Kosta's eyes twinkled. "Wrong, for once. That would cause a great deal of chaos, and you rightly guessed that I don't care for it."

"I feel like you're about to introduce a caveat."

Kosta stretched his eyebrows and gave me the slightest of nods. "I cannot help you, Detective, even if I wanted to. In this regard, I haven't lied to you. I'm not involved in any of the murders, and my deal with Red Summit Financial was nothing more than a business transaction."

"If that's the case, why were you meeting with Giancarlo Vincenzio?"

"To try to learn what *is* going on, and to make sure the man keeps his head above water, no pun intended. While I can't reveal to you the full extent of our conversation, I can tell you this. Vincenzio and his gang didn't commit either of the murders you're investigating, or if someone in his gang did, he doesn't know about it. The man's incensed. Apparently, he was making quite a bit of money with this Wen woman."

Kosta's secondhand account matched Boothe's, but I still didn't quite believe it. "How was the money being generated? Selling what?"

"I didn't ask. I had no reason to. But if you think Administrator Wen was murdered over a gang dispute, I'd encourage you to reconsider. Someone has already taken credit for the act, someone who has confessed to doing so in video form."

"The Snow Leopard. You mentioned him at our lunch meeting."

"You've voiced your concerns for the political climate, Detective. We stand at a precipice. The Snow Leopard himself uttered those words, I think. As I said, few benefit from chaos, but there are some. Remember that revolutionaries, for all their bluster, are rarely anything more than unethical self-dealers."

I sucked on my teeth. "The revolution didn't go so well for him the last time, as I remember."

"Maybe not for his cause, but for the man? Who knows."

"And if it's not the Snow Leopard? Who then?"

Kosta shrugged. "Someone in a similar set of shoes. Someone who thinks they can move up the ladder, grab more of the pie in the event of a mass disruption. Probably someone who's too stupid or too inexperienced to see what a difficult proposition that is. Or maybe, just possibly, a genuine idealist."

I felt the rideshare slow. I glanced out the window, recognizing the neighborhood. "You know where I live?"

"I know the places my daughter frequents." The cab came to a stop. "You won't tell her that I know, will you?"

I opened the door. "I'm not in the habit of lying to my girl-friend, Mr. Demetriou." Which, of course, was a lie.

45

NOVEMBER 21, 2154

I STEPPED into the rec hall and took a look around, searching for the face I'd pulled via Net. I didn't see him by the pool table, nor by the stations with the VR goggles and the haptic gloves, but I did eventually find him sitting at a couch, talking with another soldier.

I approached the guy. Seated, it was hard to tell how tall he was, but he had a head of wavy brown hair, blue eyes, and was perhaps a bit narrower in the shoulders than I was. "Excuse me. Are you Gregory Arnold?"

He looked up, breaking off the conversation he'd been having with the hispanic-looking girl across from him. "That's right. *Oh.* You're the transfer."

I guess he'd gotten a message about me. "That's right. Ambrose Drake. Formerly of Zeta Squad."

"What'd you do to get kicked out?" asked the Latina. "Take a dump on the squad leaders' shoes?"

My cheeks felt hot, and I had a hard time unclenching my jaw. "I *was* the squad leader."

"Luciana meant that as a joke, I think," said Arnold. "We know why you got kicked out. At least I do. I'll decide when and if it's worth sharing that information with the rest of my squad."

I gave a small nod. "Thanks."

"I'm not doing it for *you*," said Arnold. "I haven't decided if you're worth the trouble yet. For your sake and the sake of everyone else in my squad, I hope you're not. I hope you just fucked up once because you suffered an aneurysm while getting shot in the ass by Reds. As far as I can tell, you've never had any interpersonal problems or chain of command issues before. You going to now?"

"No." I barely got the word past my front teeth.

"Good," said Arnold. "I've already added you to the squad's chat and shared info channels. I'm assuming someone's taken you off Zeta squad's, probably your platoon leader. Not my problem, though. You've got your new room assignment?"

Obviously, I wasn't going to be sharing a cabin with Maarten anymore. "Yes."

"Alright. You're free to leave. Don't be late to meetings, assignments, or anything else, unless you want the black mark on your forehead to cover your entire face. Got it?"

I nodded and headed for the door.

"Hey, Drake," said Luciana.

I glanced back. "Yeah?"

"The guy you're replacing was named Phong Pengphath. He died when a Red bullet took him through the side of the temple. He was a hell of a soldier."

The implication being I wouldn't be. "I'll remember his name."

———

I WOKE up that night to the crash of bombs blasting. I bolted out of bed, ripped from one nightmare into another. The pressure loss siren blared as I pulled my Suit from under my bunk and dove into it, my ears straining to catch the tell-tale whine of air bleeding though a gap over the incessant whine of the siren. Within fifteen seconds, I'd pulled it over my legs and arms. By twenty, I'd locked my helmet in place, still breathing for the time being. In the distance I heard gunshots, the ping of metal on metal in between the irregular blasts of the explosions.

Arnold's voice cut into my thoughts. "Everyone report to the basement. Lieutenant Colonel Cornier's orders. Go! Go!"

I sprinted from my quarters with my new roommate, a tight-lipped stoic type by the name of Antawaan, and headed to the nearest stairs. Soldiers streamed from all the rooms, bumping and jostling as they fought for position. The lights flickered with each of the blasts, and the ceiling rumbled, though it might've simply been me who was shaking. Down the stairs I went, past the regular basement, through the heavy pressure doors, and into the subbasement below.

"What the hell's going on?" someone asked on squad chat.

"What the hell do you think?" said Arnold. "We're under attack. Light munitions, RPGs, and grenades. No reports of air bombardments, yet."

Hopefully, there wouldn't be. Our base's bunker wasn't designed to withstand missiles screaming in from outer space at five thousand meters a second.

"You think this is in retaliation for us taking out the Red cells?" someone else asked.

"Well, they sure as shit aren't thanking us for it," said Arnold.

We piled into the basement, shoulder to shoulder and nuts to butt. The bombs continued to explode, their rumbles more distant through the layers of metal and rock and regolith. Each of the blasts shook loose a few particles of dust that floated down from the ceiling. I could almost taste its rusty flavor, despite my helmet.

I looked over my shoulder, trying to spot anyone from Zeta squad, but I could barely move let alone get a good look over the equally tall heads and shoulders around me. As the bombs continued to rattle and shake us, I couldn't help but think of

Maarten and Nakamoto, both of whom had been in the hospital the last time I saw them. Perhaps Maarten might've been released —for all the trauma his lungs and tissues had suffered, it was the sort a body could recover from quickly—but Nakamoto had been laid up with stitches in her leg. Had the bombs breached the walls? Had they managed to get their Suits on in time?

I thought about shooting Phoebe a message, asking how the squad was, but I hadn't spoken to her since before she'd entered Watkin's office. Besides, it wasn't any of my business. I wasn't in Zeta squad anymore, no matter how hard I might still want to be.

THE BOMBS DIDN'T FALL AGAIN the next night, but they didn't have to to keep me up. In retrospect, the last good night of sleep I'd had was in Utopia, the night before I'd shot the young Red in the chest during the fusion plant raid. Since then I'd suffered one nightmare after another, some of the recurring sort. The young Red's face, blood streaking down his temples like invisible claws gouging through his flesh, his eyes open, staring at me, crying out, pleading for mercy. Others were different every time, though no less horrifying. Random assignments gone wrong. Reds, pointing at me, staring, crying out with tales of their dead, their loved ones, their sons and daughters torn to shreds by USC gunfire. Reds, jumping at me with dark metal in their hands, fingers working triggers, muzzles flashing with ear-splitting force. Never before had I suffered nightmares with sound, but these had them. The cracking of gunfire. The whine of pressurized air. The moan of dying teens. Now I'd added the relentless crash and roar of bombs to the list.

At least I wasn't given much time to sleep. In the wake of the Red attacks, our squads were given twice as many assignments as we had hours to complete them. Cells had supposedly popped up in every apartment building, bodega, and flophouse. Presence patrols were doubled. Guard duty around the base was ratcheted up accordingly, but it wasn't just military assignments that pulled on our internal clocks. The Reds caused enough damage to the base that half the work on our plates involved making repairs to the roof over our head—or below us, as the case may be.

Luckily, Lambda squad was assigned more than its fair share of repair work. I spent the majority of the week following the attack below ground, working a rock drill that chewed into the earth with a hardened tungsten carbide tip some two meters in diameter. Given how unprepared we'd been following the first strike, Lieutenant Colonel Cornier had decided the subbasement levels needed to be tripled in size.

I'm not sure why Lambda squad managed to avoid combat assignments in the immediate wake of the attacks. Perhaps it was because they were a bunch of screwups, a team of incompetent nincompoops who couldn't organize a successful strike if their lives depended on it. It would've made sense given my inclusion, but it was just a guess. Not that I had any evidence to base my assertion on. No one on the squad would talk to me. I don't think they actively hated me. They would've rather had Pengphath at their sides, sure, but hate? No. They just didn't give a crap about me. In fact, I developed a thick layer of crud on my skin from all the attention they *didn't* shower me with.

Whatever the reason, I was glad to sit in the artificial white light of the drill, with plugs jammed into my ear canals and dust spraying against my Suit's faceplate. As long as it meant I didn't have to go back into the streets. Didn't have to stare down the muzzle of a rocket launcher or a rifle. Didn't have to aim my Badass and squeeze the trigger. Didn't have to watch blood spurt from a target. Maybe a fully-grown man, maybe not. Maybe a kid who'd just turned fifteen, or a father who'd do anything to save his daughter, armed only with a knife and his unyielding grief. Hell no. Give me a bore hole, a rock drill, and solitude any day over that.

Not that I got to choose what assignments I was given. I simply got lucky. The one exception was in regards to my duties as a counterintelligence officer. Despite my demotion from squad leader, I hadn't been stripped of my security clearance. The reason, I think, was two-fold. For one, most of the raids had been successful, having turned up tons of encrypted electronics in need of cracking and analysis. The other reason was that Sergeant McGregor wasn't even close to capable of sifting through the materials herself—and I was better at it than she was, to boot.

If only McGregor had been more personable, I might've spent every waking moment in the counterintelligence office, but despite the hours we spent together, she remained as inclined to talk to me as she was the humming servers or the floor under her feet. I tried not to let it bother me. Her refusal to interact was clearly a personal foible, not a statement on me—but as the days passed, my lack of interaction with anyone I could call a friend started to wear. I missed Janeece's snide comments and rolled eyes. I missed Mandel's subtle wit, Halabi's big, forced laugh. I missed Maarten's bravado, if not his racism. But mostly I missed Phoebe.

I'd tried not to send her messages at first, not knowing how she'd fared in the aftermath of her encounter with the major or how she'd taken the knowledge of what had transpired between Maarten and me, but I couldn't keep my finger off the send button forever. After a few days, I sent her a quick message, just to see how she was doing. After a couple days without a response, I tried again. Then again. Then I tried a call, which she refused to answer. If I could've talked to her in person, I would've, but our schedules kept us apart. Unlike my new squad, Zeta kept being assigned back into the field.

I'd started to fear I'd never see her again when I spotted her one day at lunch in the mess hall—eating by herself, thank god. I gathered my tray and set it down across from her as I took a seat. "Hey. Phoebe."

She looked up before quickly dropping her eyes back down. "Ambrose."

She took a bite of broccoli and chewed it slowly. I pushed some peas around on my plate with a spoon, unsure of what to say despite the dozens of messages I'd sent her way. "So... how have you been?"

"Fine." She didn't look up. I got the feeling it wasn't by accident.

I chewed my lip. "How's Maarten?"

Phoebe hesitated. "He's okay. Bounced right back following the... well, you know."

"Good." I piled my peas atop one another until they rolled off the top. "And how about you?"

Phoebe looked up, her eyes meeting mine. They weren't watery. They didn't waver, but there was sadness in them. "Ambrose... I'm sorry. I can't."

"You can't what?"

"Do this. *Us.* Major Watkins warned us. She told us not to let our emotions get in the way of our duties. She knew what she was talking about, but we didn't listen. It almost got someone killed."

"Are you talking about Maarten? Phoebe, you had nothing to do with that. It was a messed up situation that got out of hand. It was my fault. Maarten's, too, but not yours."

She glared at me, her almond eyes suddenly fierce. "You're wrong, Ambrose. I was squad leader. Platoon leader. *Whatever.* I should've noticed the tensions growing between you and Maarten. I should've talked to you about it, talked to the major about it, but I let my relationship with you get in the way. I wasn't as vigilant as I should've been. I sure as hell wasn't as strict with you as I should've been. Same with Maarten. Of all the people to send back to the Marauder, I shouldn't have sent the two of you."

"Phoebe, I'm telling you, what happened between Maarten and me wasn't your fault."

"You're right. It was *your* fault. But that doesn't make me any less responsible for it." She nodded to the side. "You should go."

My ribs pressed against my lungs, crushing them under a sudden weight. "Phoebe... If you don't want to see me anymore, or be with me, I get it. Maybe the major was right in that regard, but I'm not here for that. I just need a friend right now."

Phoebe averted her gaze. "I'm sorry, Ambrose. I can't be that for you anymore, either."

"Phoebe..."

"Are you going to leave or not?"

I chewed on my words, my saliva thick and my tongue stuck in my throat. "I can't, Phoebe. I need you."

Phoebe sighed and stood, taking her tray with her. She met my eyes, which now seemed on the verge of tears. "I'm glad Major Watkins reassigned you, Ambrose. It saved me having to ask her to do it for me."

She turned and walked away. I wanted to follow her, to race after her, grab her by the arm, spin her around, and tell her she was wrong. That I was right for her, that we were meant to be, or at the very least that we could still be friends, but I couldn't. I was rooted in place, afraid I might start crying if I even moved.

46

MAY 12, 2179

I HEARD the babble of a holo drama coming from the living room as I closed the apartment door behind me. I'd hung up my jacket and was in the process of slipping out of my shoes when I spotted Sophia draped across the nearby wall.

"There you are." She wore a crimson dress with an angled hem that started above her knee and cut across to her calf. A single strap supported the dress, one that looped over her shoulder at a similar angle to the hem. It gave her an illusion of motion, even standing still.

My shoe clattered to the floor as I straightened. "Wow."

Sophia held a lowball glass in hand, a couple fingers of brandy poured over a single ball of ice. She flicked her other hand across her hip. "Like what you see?"

"You always look unbelievable. What's the occasion?"

"Nothing too special," she said. "Dinner with a couple old friends. They wanted to go dancing afterwards, which we did, but I snuck out after an hour. Care for a drink?"

I pointed to her glass. "That for me?"

She sneered. "You wish. I'll fix you one if you like, though. The Callaghan and Sons?"

"Sure."

I followed Sophia into the kitchen, enjoying the sway of her backside as she walked. She pulled a glass from a cabinet, popped an ice sphere from one of the molds in the freezer, and measured a healthy pour over the top. I doubt she tried to make the event a sensual one, but she couldn't help it. She could probably turn spreadsheet analysis into a seductive endeavor.

She returned and handed me the glass. She held hers up, and we clinked edges. I tried to think of a dedication, but nothing came to mind. Luckily, Sophia didn't bother with one either. We each took a sip of our liquors, the bourbon warm and smoky on my tongue. As we pulled the glasses from our lips, Sophia took my hand and led me to the couch. An unfamiliar show played on the holo as I collapsed into the cushions, but I wasn't surprised. Sophia gravitated toward lighter fare than I did.

Sophia sat with her legs tucked underneath her, the hand with her drink resting in her lap, the other draped across my shoulders. She tickled the hairs at the nape of my neck and gazed at me. "Long day?"

I tried to figure out what was going on in the holo. It was a historical piece, something set in the second half of twentieth century Europe if my knowledge of fashion didn't fail me. "Aren't they all?"

"You're often home late," said Sophia. "Not past eleven, though."

"The case dictates the load. This one is worse than most."

I took another sip of my drink, and Sophia of hers.

"So what kept you?"

The actors on the holo laughed and snickered. They were the only ones who spoke.

"Still won't tell me." Sophia sighed. "It's fine. But bouncing ideas off me helps you think sometimes. Don't deny it."

"Maybe I don't want to think about the case right now."

Sophia set her glass on the coffee table. "That's fine with me, too." Her hand crept to the inside of my leg.

I sighed as I placed my hand over hers. "Sophia. I need to tell you something."

She spoke softly in my ear. "I'm listening."

"Your father knows."

Sophia pulled back, slowly. "What?"

"He knows about us. That we're in a relationship."

Sophia's hand retreated along with the rest of her. "How do you know that?"

"I asked him."

"*What?* Are you crazy? Why the hell would you do that? And why didn't you tell me this two days ago?"

"Because I didn't ask him two days ago. I asked him tonight."

Sophia stood and turned on me, her brow furrowed and her mouth open. "You saw him. *Tonight.*"

"He was meeting with Giancarlo Vincenzio, head of the Silicon Road gang, who I know for a fact was involved in Shao Wen's murder. I was trying to secure his help."

"And while you were there, you just *asked him* if he knew about us, hoping he'd help you out of displaced love for me?"

"Technically, I didn't ask. I suggested to him that I knew, and he came forward and admitted it. But no, I didn't ask on a whim. I knew he was spying on you, or at the very least I suspected it."

Sophia's face had started to flush. "Oh, really? And how did you know *that?*"

"The other night, after we made love, I spotted something in your Net. Some bit of code. I wasn't sure what it was at first, but I kept thinking about it. It was a trace. I couldn't think of anyone who might've put it there besides your father."

Sophia's voice gained in strength. "You saw it in my Net? So you were spying on me!"

"No. I wasn't spying. Someone else was. I happened across it by chance."

"It's the same thing, Ambrose!"

I stood and put my hands out as Sophia backed away. "Sophia, I promise you it wasn't on purpose. I just *saw it,* mixed with your emotions and memories. You know how it is when we're intimate and we share ourselves. It's not always a conscious choice what we see."

"You're right. But you know what *is* a conscious choice? *What you share afterwards!* Did it ever cross your mind to turn to me and say, Whoa! It looks like someone's spying on you, Sophia. Let's look into this together."

"Of course it did."

"So you thought about it, and rejected it?"

"I..." I had my reasons for staying silent. I couldn't expound on them.

Sophia's nostrils flared. "Let me guess. You thought perhaps *I* wasn't the one being spied on. You thought this was all about you. That you were being spied on *through me.* Is that it?"

"That's not true at all," I said, even though it mostly was.

"GOD! I can't believe you right now!" Sophia flew to the edge of the couch, threw her coat on, and started to pull on her shoes.

"Sophia. Please."

"You don't get it, do you Ambrose? You betrayed my trust! Not once, but multiple times. You could've told me about the trace, but you didn't. You kept it to yourself. Worse, you went to my *dad* about it! *And then you told him about us!*"

"He already knew, Sophia."

"You're missing the point! You went to him. To my father! Again. You realize I hate the man, don't you? You realize the anguish he's given me? The pain he's put me through? *I don't want anything to do with him."*

Sophia stormed toward the front door.

"Sophia. I'm sorry. I shouldn't have."

She pulled open the door and paused with her hand on the handle. "Do you have any idea why I like you, Ambrose? *Do you?*"

I stood there in silence.

"Because you're not him. You're the antithesis of him. You have a sense of right and wrong. You care about the greater good. You're willing to do things the right way, even when others aren't. Because you're a good man. Or at least I thought you were."

"Sophia..."

The door slammed shut behind her. I stood in my hallway, eyeing the bare metal. My chest hurt, feeling empty and compressed at the same time.

I felt like shit, but I deserved it. I deserved every insult Sophia had thrown at me and more, because she was right. But she'd only scratched the surface. The truth was so much worse than she could guess.

47

DECEMBER 23, 2154

I KEPT HOPING my life would suck less, but fate decided I didn't deserve any such pity. Instead, I was awarded with additional servings of suck, as much as I could shovel into my face. Most of it came in the form of assignments with my new squad. The assignments themselves sucked enough on their own—the usual assortment of escort missions, cordon and knocks, patrols, and humanitarian shit—but it was the folks with which I got to complete said assignments that really made the minutes seem like days.

A few of the Lambda squad members treated me with open hostility, though I wasn't entirely sure why. Scout Flanagan and munitions expert Kiran were among them. I often caught them talking behind my back, eyeing me with daggers whenever I approached their sphere of interaction before switching to Net communication. Supposedly, they'd been close to Pengphath before he died, but I got the impression the real reason they shunned me was because they were assholes.

Most of the members of Lambda squad didn't go out of their way to ostracize me, though. They simply did it as a matter of course. When we were on patrols, I wasn't worth talking to. When dinner rolled around, I wasn't worth sitting with. When jokes and videos and memes were passed around, I sure as hell wasn't included. Why would I be? In their eyes, I was filler. A warm body to take the place of their fallen comrade until a better one showed up or until I, too, took a bullet between the eyes. Why waste the effort getting to know someone when the old guard would suffice just as well and when the new guy's history proved him to be untrustworthy. As sad as it was, most of my squad interactions were with our leader Arnold, and even he found a way to keep directions and commands as short and sweet as possible. Perhaps he'd talked to Phoebe and learned from her mistake, intending to atone for it by being as cold, callous, and detached from me as possible.

Phoebe. Try as I might, I couldn't stop thinking about her. Her bright eyes, her long dark hair, her lean muscles and subtle curves. Every time I closed my eyes to daydream, there she was, rolling her eyes at me, smiling, or pushing herself on top of me. I'd lied to her, of course. I did still want to be with her. To push my nose against the crook of her neck and breathe in her scent, to feel the heat of her skin on my own, to push myself between her welcoming legs, to rock our bodies together in sweet, heart-pounding bliss. But I'd also told her the truth, in a way. As much as I ached to be with her physically, I missed her friendship even more. I longed to lay back on our cots as we'd done in space, to talk about school and sports and politics and science and nothing at all. I longed to send her messages when I was out on a long patrol, messages she'd respond to with biting wit and smoochie emojis. Most of all I missed having her at my side, knowing someone who'd been with me from the start, someone who'd shared my seat when I'd first woken up on the vactrain to Florida was still there with me.

Losing my relationship with Phoebe was the worst part of my expulsion from Zeta squad, but the ease with which my former squad mates discarded me was a close second. Perhaps Phoebe or

Major Watkins had instructed them to keep their distance from me, or perhaps they'd come to that conclusion on their own. Regardless of the reason, Mandel, Franks, Nakamoto, and everyone else managed to avoid me with the same seasoned ease as Phoebe and Maarten. Only Janeece made an effort to stay in contact with me and even then only via Net. Her concise messages about the success of Zeta squads' missions weren't what I'd call personal or even warm, but I did gather some meager comfort from the knowledge that the squad continued to stay safe without me. I didn't hold any ill will against them—not even Maarten, though it irked me that I might never be able to confront him about his growing resentment and racism or try to squash our disagreement via any setting more personal then a Net message.

Not that I even sent a message. After failing to get any response from Phoebe following our lunch encounter, I stopped trying to keep in contact with anyone other than Janeece, instead throwing myself as much as possible into my counterintelligence activities. Thankfully, there were plenty of those to go around. With the raids of the Red cells, we'd captured more tablets and drives than we knew what to do with, or at the very least more than we had servers and manpower to handle. The servers were the biggest bottleneck. With a fraction of the Utopia base's computer power available to us, McGregor and I couldn't decrypt near as fast as Lieutenant Colonel Cornier wanted us to. The servers hummed day and night, churning through files as fast as we could feed them in.

The server limitations left me with a lot of down time, time I refused to spend with Lambda squad if I had any choice in the matter, which meant I was forced to pitch counterintelligence ideas to Major Watkins and Lieutenant Colonel Cornier to keep me busy. The project I caught their attention with was in regards to our Net transponders. Ever since I'd helped place them around the edge of Cassini, I'd wondered how secure they actually were.

To satisfy my curiosity, I'd delved into the transponder logs to see if I could catch any trace of unwanted third parties sniffing around our data. To the Major and Colonel's relief, I hadn't. What I *had* found was a third party piggy-backing on our transponder network, sending their own batches of encrypted signals without us any the wiser. When I reported that tidbit to my superiors, not only did they pull me off my regular duties to spend more time in the counterintelligence office, but they actually increased my clearance to boot.

I *mostly* used the newly granted clearance for USC's benefit, but I couldn't force myself to work all day. When I got bored, I'd browse the extranets, perusing newsfeeds that USC didn't allow the soldiers at large to watch. There wasn't anything surprising among the content—USC wasn't as well-liked or as well established as they wanted us to believe—but I was able to come across numerous Snow Leopard propaganda videos USC refused to let us watch. In all of them, the Snow Leopard came across as calm and collected, if also unyielding. He'd beseech his Martian brothers and sisters for aid, decrying the efforts of the invaders from Earth, and always end with a call for action. As perturbing as the Leopard's blood red mask was, his videos didn't chill me the way they first had, and that bothered me. Had I become numb to his act, or had I become numb to the root cause underneath it?

I also spent the odd moment looking into tidbits about USC operations that bugged me. For one, I investigated something Sergeant Mishra had mentioned in Utopia, an offhand comment that Net data could be extracted from prisoners' minds without their consent. It irked me, not only because I'd never found anything in the literature that suggested such a thing was possible —or at the very least possible *and* safe—but also because it seemed a fundamental violation of human rights. It was somewhat comforting then that I didn't find evidence of forcible Net malfeasance in the records I unearthed regarding the prisoners taken during the Utopian basement raid. However, I also wasn't able to find *any* definitive reports about what happened to said prisoners after capture, so it wasn't exactly proof of USC's good behavior.

I also took a gander into something Major Watkins had mentioned, that she'd perused the feed of my altercation with Maarten. I'd always known our Nets could be used to track our movements, keep track of our vitals, even record sensory data, primarily visual, that we experienced in the line of duty. What I'd never seen was evidence that USC actually bothered to record that data.

Of course, once I started looking for it, it wasn't that hard to find. The server banks in the counterintelligence basement might dedicate their computing power to helping us crack Red codes, but their storage wasn't swollen with recovered separatist files. The vast majority held video recordings of the soldiers from C company. Mountains and mountains of data, primarily from the last month of activities but with selected actions going back longer. There must've been an algorithm that sorted what to keep, because even the recent feeds were chopped and sorted by priority. Perhaps suit vitals and assignment logs helped the computers decide what to keep and what to pitch.

No matter how you sliced it, it was an impressive amount of data. Data that gave me a creepy, big brother vibe—because USC *was* watching. Captain Soto had said as much when we took off from Earth toward Luna. Maybe I should've believed her.

Of course, access to the data also meant I could discover what other people were up to. I didn't abuse my power. Someone would've found me sooner or later if I had, and besides, I didn't have anyone I needed to spy on. But I wasn't entirely chaste in my handling of the records. After digging into my own Net files, I found a recording on the verge of being deleted, one in which I was intimately entangled with Phoebe before our breakup.

I'm not proud of the fact that I saved the video to my private account. I wasn't proud of the multiple *long* showers I took in the wake of saving said video, either. I didn't get rid of the video, though. The way I saw it, it was a depiction of my own experience, an enhanced memory. The video simply helped me recall it more vividly, over and over again...

Most of my time *was* spent on the transponder issue, however, in part because it wasn't an easy problem to solve. Whoever was piggybacking on our system—and I had to assume it was the Reds— was extraordinarily careful during their time there. For one, the rogue signals were intermittent. Whoever had cracked the transponders only used them when absolutely necessary or on some irregular schedule I'd yet to decipher. The spurious signals, like ours, were encrypted, but unlike ours, they seemed to be bugged, tainted by a hidden virus within the stream. No matter how hard I tried to crack them, by the time I got any of the signals through our servers I received back only unintelligible gibberish. For a while I started to wonder if the signals were just that, garbled crap whose only purpose was to annoy us, waste our time, and obfuscate more secretive counterintelligence actions, but the logical portion of me refused to accept that answer. I couldn't believe there was a Red hidden somewhere in a basement like me, someone whose encryption and cracking skills rivaled my own, who'd decided to waste their time as a purveyor of balderdash. They had to have a purpose.

I also believed my computational nemesis was up to something more nefarious because I sensed them in our system. I'd never been superstitious or touchy-feely when it came to computers. Coding was one of the most logical, process-oriented tasks you could think of, yet within a week of investigating the unidentified transponder codes, I started to *feel* another presence within our network. It wasn't anything I could put my finger on. Files looked untouched, change logs pristine, no unauthorized login attempts to speak of. Yet there was a digital funk, a lingering smell of malice that I couldn't isolate, and I couldn't help but feel there was an intruder lingering in one of the dusty corners of our cluster, looking for a crack in the mortar, searching and probing for a way to get in.

I wasted a lot of time jumping at digital shadows in the wake of my discovery, trying to figure out how I could prove the unprovable, how to find something that by all accounts wasn't there. And then it hit me. The easiest way to see if someone was at the door was to open it and invite them in.

I didn't tell Major Watkins what I was up to when I put in a request for a small amount of satellite time, simply that I was hot on the trail of the Reds responsible for the Net transponder signals and I might need a satellite to confirm a location for me when the time was right. Watkins nodded and signed off on the order, though she might not have if she'd known the extent of my plan. I then spent the better part of the next week tinkering with the firewalls on our internal network and shoring up security, the digital equivalent of bomb proofing a single room in a house. When the time was right, I took a chisel to one of the exterior walls of that bomb-proofed room and whacked it a few times with a hammer.

In reality, the vulnerability I established in our external security was more subtle than that. I hid it in a scheduled update to our computer systems, with an additional update to fix the vulnerability lingering, ready to update at a moment's notice, but I didn't propagate that one through the network. Not yet.

I didn't have to wait long. Within a day, I got a hit. Someone was trying to worm their way through the digital hole I'd left in the wall. I almost had a panic attack when I realized it was actually happening, but I worked quickly, confident the internal barriers I'd put in place would hold until I chose to ram through the patch. In the meantime, I brought up the trace software I'd worked on and got to work. Within minutes, I'd isolated the rogue signal and sent it to the USC satellite I'd reserved.

Satellites, rather. They triangulated the signal and spat back a location, a random spot at the edge of a sub-crater within the larger Cassini impact basin. I brought up a map of the area before I released the satellites. There wasn't a thing there, but I wasn't discouraged. As Lieutenant Colonel Cornier had said when we first arrived, the Red tunnel systems were *deep*.

With the location saved, I severed the intruder's connection and installed the network patch. Then I took off toward Major Watkin's office at a run.

48

MAY 13, 2179

MWENGE GAVE me a nod as I arrived at work. "Drake. You're late—for you, anyway."

I didn't take a seat in my chair, instead resting against the edge of my desk. "I had a rough night."

"You look it. Stay for a few extra cold ones after I left the bar?"

I frowned. "I'm not hungover. We need to talk."

"Sure do. There were more demonstrations overnight. None of them particularly violent or destructive, but still. The Captain gave me a briefing. I was thinking we'd—"

"That's not what I mean. Come with me."

Mwenge frowned, but he did as I asked, following me through the thirty-second floor maze of workstations to the interrogation room. I paused at the door, making sure the Net jammer was on and the room's recording systems were disengaged. Bishop gave me an odd look as I did so, but he walked in when I waved him through.

He didn't speak until I'd closed the door behind us. "What's going on, Ambrose?"

"I came in late last night," I told him, neglecting to take a seat. "You remember the tablet we took from Wen's apartment? Well, I cracked it. It was filled with data related to Elysium's water supplies and the central processing station's inflows and outflows."

"Is that why you had us go there yesterday?"

"In part. I knew the nature of the data at the time, but I hadn't compared it to the official numbers USC provided me until last night. Bishop, there's a big discrepancy. According to the data on Wen's tablet, Elysium is missing *a lot* of subterranean ice."

"How much?"

"Thirty million cubic meters, give or take."

Bishop's eyes widened. *"Holy crap."*

"Precisely."

"Have you told anyone else?"

"You're the first," I said, neglecting that I'd actually shared the news with Kosta Demetriou. That would come back to bite me if word ever got out.

"We need to inform the Captain right away."

Bishop took a step toward the door, but I stopped him with an extended hand. "Don't you think there's a reason I decided to tell you this in a secure room where no one else could hear?"

"Ambrose, I don't know why you'd want to suppress this information, but of all the people who should know, the Captain is at the top of the list. Above me, that's for sure."

"You might be right, and I won't hold it from her indefinitely, but hear me out. Wen's data differs from the official USC set, but that doesn't mean it's accurate."

Bishop frowned. "You're going to have to spell it out for me."

"We recovered Wen's tablet from her safe, which I'll remind you was unlocked when we found it. Wen's killer had already been in the apartment, and they were thorough in her murder. It stands to reason they opened Wen's safe, looked through the contents, and were content to leave the tablet, or conversely, left it there for us to find."

"The tablet was encrypted, though."

"More reason to suspect it was a plant. Wen's murderer wouldn't have left it without knowing what it contained, and if leaving it, they'd know we'd crack it sooner or later. But what really suggests to me we were supposed to find it have been the Snow Leopard's videos. A narrative is being created, one that paints Shao Wen and Deandre Jackson as corrupt pawns, as enemies of the people. The data supports that."

"Okay. Say the Snow Leopard is making everything up. What's the point of creating a false narrative? To roil people up? Won't people figure the truth out eventually?"

"Maybe. Maybe not. Even if USC hasn't done a thing wrong, there aren't a lot of nonpartisan entities who can confirm that, certainly not ones people who are already in a frothing rage will listen to."

"So your point is that we shouldn't release the knowledge that someone—USC, a gang, an unaffiliated third party—potentially stole two and a half dozen cubic kilometers of water ice because it might be an elaborate ruse? One that would, in essence, throw a match onto the pile of dry tinder that is Elysium right now?"

"Basically."

Bishop's brow furrowed. "And if the data on Wen's tablet *is* accurate? What if the Snow Leopard is telling the truth? I mean, there's clearly a connection between Wen and Silicon Road and the water distribution facility, right?"

I sighed. "I don't like to think of what happens in that scenario, because there might not be any way to keep the fire from catching. Mars isn't ready for another rebellion, Bishop. Trust me. I saw what happened the last time. I lived through it. Kickstarting the revolution again and expecting a different result this time is madness."

"You don't have to convince me, Ambrose." Bishop took a deep breath and let it out slowly. "Alright. I feel like we have to tell the Captain, regardless of the veracity of the data. It's too important not to share. But as concerning as the data is, proving whether or not it's accurate doesn't get us closer to Wen and Jackson's murderers. What I'd planned on sharing with you this morning might."

"Are you still trying to locate the Snow Leopard?" I said. "I told you last night, that's a fool's errand."

"You think the man is long dead or retired or something of the sort. I get it. But regardless of whether the same Snow Leopard of twenty-five years past is responsible, someone has taken up his flag, and finding *them* is the best angle we've got right now."

"Is it a *good* angle?"

"It's a decent one if we go about it intelligently," said Bishop. "I've been working with Dean to get what information we can from the released videos. Metadata, audio noise traces, that sort of thing—"

I shook my head.

"—and that hasn't borne fruit, but it stands to reason with two separate murders having taken place in Elysium, both of them claimed by the Snow Leopard, that whether or not the Leopard himself is in our city, there's a local arm of dissidents who are. And it's not as if our department doesn't keep track of known insurgents. If we dig into the lists, looking for elements of crossover with our case—people who've worked in water services, USC employees who were fired without cause, folks with gang ties, folks who have military backgrounds or experience with explosives, anyone with direct family or work ties to Wen or Jackson—maybe we can narrow our focus to a handful of targets."

"People with explosives backgrounds. That's a decent thought." While we'd caught the scent of the murderers, we hadn't made any progress tracking down the person who'd fire-bombed Wen's apartment. "Do you have a list already started?"

"I *was* working yesterday afternoon, you know. But it needs attention."

"I'll be honest, Bishop. This seems like a long-shot. But no point wasting time talking. Let's get to it."

———

IT TURNED out the Captain was stuck in urgent meetings, so Bishop and I worked through lunch. We split the duties between us. I would've enrolled Dean into the project too if he hadn't been busy scanning video—thinking of the mysterious fire-bomber and parachute artist from Wen's apartment made me think we hadn't exhausted our tracking options for that particular individual. But even alone, Bishop and I made good progress.

By the time we'd finished our sandwiches, we'd narrowed our list to three likely separatist sympathizers: a former metal worker by the name of Elias Merkel who'd served on Martian militias during the rebellion and had never shelved his public dislike of governments of any form, gangbanger Mort Karsten who had ties to four separate organized crime syndicates as well as to anarchist and terrorist groups, and Charlize Van Jaarsveld, a civil engineer who'd worked in both water services and sanitation who now ran underground coffee klatches where separatist propaganda was distributed.

The problem with identifying a murderer based on relationships to third parties was that it took a lot of time and resources to build a case against them, all without the use of search warrants, at least until the evidence had been jostled together. That meant tails, surveillance, analysis of public data, social media, and third-party accounts, talking to landlords, employers, and service providers. It was a lot of work, and though I didn't mind it, I wasn't sure it was the best use of our time. Then again, we'd struck out on just about every other lead we'd pursued.

As I sat there discussing our options with Mwenge and thinking perhaps I hadn't fully investigated Wen's affair with laser expert Victor Kuznyetsov or prodded into Jackson's family relation-ships, an officer stopped next to our desks. "Excuse me. Detective Drake?"

I looked up from my holo. "What it is?"

"A guy came into the station and asked for you by name. Honestly, he looks a little spooked. I put him in interview one. Figured you'd want to know."

Perhaps our Silicon Road mole had finally popped his head. "Does this guy have a name?"

"Yeah. Giancarlo Vincenzio. Ring a bell?"

It did.

49

DECEMBER 23, 2154

MAJOR WATKINS and I watched the display on her desk as we waited for the additional satellite request to come in. Eventually, the message we'd been waiting for popped up. Watkins opened the attachment and zoomed in on the composite radar image.

"Well, there's no doubt about it. We've got a tunnel system there." Watkins turned to me. "Congratulations, Drake. It looks like you've found a Red settlement in the wild."

I couldn't help but smile. "Thank you, ma'am."

"Don't let it go to your head. Discovery is only half the battle. As you well know, our satellites can only map eight meters deep with any real accuracy. Beyond this conglomerate of near-surface tunnels, there's no way for us to know what we have short of barging in."

"Which I think we could do, ma'am." I pointed to the satellite image I'd come in with. "I've suspected this from the moment I first glanced at the map. The large boulder past the lip of the impact basin seems, if not suspicious, at least out of place. And if you look at the tunnel maps from the radar..."

"There's one directly under the boulder." Major Watkins

pursed her lips. "You suspect there's an entrance to the Red lair built into the rock?"

"They've been known to use natural features to hide their movements. It would make sense."

Watkins nodded. "I need to discuss this with Lieutenant Colonel Cornier. Not a word of this to anyone in the meantime, am I understood?"

"Yes, ma'am." I stood to leave.

"Two final things, Drake."

I paused at the door. "Major?"

"Good work. If this goes well, you can expect a promotion in your future. And be ready. If we move, we'll do so quickly. The enemy has a way of slipping through our fingers like regolith during a dust storm."

AS I BOUNDED across the Martian expanse, trying to stay warm in the frigid embrace of night, shrouded as much by darkness as by the special IR-resistant Suit I wore, I couldn't help but think Major Watkins had undersold the speed with which we'd acted. I'd barely had time for a nap before I'd been summoned along with most of the other squads in C company for an emergency meeting. Watkins and Cornier had conferred and decided we needed to act on the information immediately. The possibility of a free-standing Red base within close proximity of Cassini was too tantalizing to pass up, so they'd briefed us on a brazen plan to raid the Red base within twelve hours.

It was simple, really. We'd take the city's underground tunnels as far north as we could before exiting and traveling the remaining forty kilometers on foot—a daunting distance on Earth and only a slightly less daunting one in the milder Mars gravity. Marauders and transports would follow us at dawn, hopefully returning to

Cassini full of equipment and prisoners following a successful surprise raid in the wee morning hours.

For now, all I could think of was trying to stay warm. I wasn't sure how the IR-resistant Suits they'd had us don worked. One way would've been to trap heat within the Suit to keep it from being detected. Apparently, the designers had gone the other way, figuring that if all heat exited our bodies as quickly as possible, the resulting popsicles wouldn't register on thermal scanners. I flexed my fingers as I bounded across the slope, hoping they'd all still be attached when we arrived.

Squad leader Arnold's voice cut into my misery. "Two kilometers to go, folks. Everyone hanging in there?"

I didn't have a nice reply so I didn't provide one, comforting myself with the knowledge that everyone else was in as much pain as I was, including Zeta squad. They were somewhere in the darkness around me, Janeece and Phoebe, even Maarten. I knew I'd spot them as we entered the underground facility, but I rather hoped our paths didn't cross beyond that. Seeing as we'd be diving into the base blind, there was no way to know going in. I should've been more worried about the possibility of taking heavy Red fire than the awkwardness of being forced into close quarters with my former squad mates, but perhaps the cold had addled my brain.

We took the final two kilometers at a dead sprint, or what passed for one in Martian gravity. As we crested the top of the subcrater, a black mass rose into view, visible only by the stars it blocked from view in the pre-dawn darkness. In person, the boulder I'd seen on the maps looked more like a mountain, twice as tall as one of our transports and three times again as wide. We descended upon it in silence, the six squads selected to tackle the base: Gamma, Delta, Epsilon, Zeta, Lambda, and Mu.

From somewhere in the darkness came the voice of Major Watkins. She'd refused to stay back at base and direct us remotely, claiming spearheading raids in the dark of night was one of the few perks of her rank. "Spread around the boulder. Keep helmet and Badass lights off. Search for anything that might be an entrance."

The boulder loomed over me like a giant's fist. It sat there upon the edge of the subcrater, perched at a precarious angle. It had probably hovered there, threatening to tip and fall for the last billion years.

I heard an unfamiliar voice on chat. "Major. I think I've found something. North, northwest side. Under an overhang. Looks like a tunnel, hewn via rock drill."

The spot appeared on my minimap, and I bounced my way over. A crowd was assembling in the dark. At the base of the boulder, someone switched on a helmet lamp, illuminating a dark, rough hewn tunnel leading into the rock.

I thought the Major was going to be pissed with whoever had disobeyed orders until I heard her voice. "Follow me. I'll take point. Stagger your lights. We don't need anyone blinded. Squad leaders, remember your mission parameters. Let's go."

The tunnel was only wide enough for two people to walk abreast, so I waited my turn as the soldiers in front of me filed in. A light flicked on ahead of me, and another a few individuals behind me, so I left mine off. My heart beat hard in my chest as I entered the tunnel, more from anticipation than the running that had brought me to the gargantuan monolith.

"Have carabiners handy," said Watkins. "An elevator shaft is our only means of descent. Breaching now."

I saw the metal gleam as I rounded a bend. The doors stood open, the lights above the elevator dead and dark. Someone stood to the side of the open shaft, waving people in. I stepped forward when it was my turn, attaching the carabiner on a retractable cord at my utility belt to the central cable, same as the person before me. I hopped into the darkness, using my feet to slow my descent. Helmet lights of the people below me played off the rock walls, beams of sight amid a chasm of darkness.

"No idea how deep the shaft goes, or where the elevator is, but we've got a door open," said Watkins. "We'll call it level one. Everyone through. No signs of activity yet."

As I rappelled, I spotted the light someone below me had set up at the base of the open elevator doors. As I slowed myself, unhooked from the cable, and hopped through the open doors, I couldn't help but notice the obvious. We hadn't vented any atmosphere coming through the top set of elevator doors, nor had I felt a rush of air fly past me as I'd descended the elevator shaft. Mars's thin, cold, carbon-rich embrace surrounded us, wherever we were.

I looked around as I exited the shaft. I was in a tunnel, much larger than the shoulder-width one at the surface. No lights shone, though by the gleam of the helmet lamps I could see a thick bundle of cords extending along the length of the ceiling. A single rail split the corridor underfoot, similar to the guide rail you might find under a vactrain. The tunnel was almost big enough to fit one, too.

"Where the hell are we?" someone asked on the company channel. "I thought we were raiding a base?"

I'd thought the same, but perhaps we'd stumbled across something bigger. An entrance to the Reds' system of underground tunnels. A portal into their subterranean transport system. Still, there had to be more than tunnels around. I couldn't imagine the interloper I'd tricked into hacking our computer system had done so from the cab of a speeding, underground vactrain.

"I see a split to the north," said Watkins. "Epsilon squad, take the path south, see what you can find. Zeta, take the northern tunnel. Lambda, take the northwesterly split. All other squads stay with me. I want to drill deeper, see how far this rabbit hole goes."

Arnold waved us forward, and I followed him down the tunnel. To my left, a familiar tall, feminine form bounded along behind her team. Janeece. Phoebe and Maarten must've been nearby, too, though I couldn't pick them out in the darkness. I swiveled my head toward Arnold and tried to ignore the Zetas as they split off from us in the tunnel system.

It wasn't long before Arnold waved us to the side, toward a set of pressure doors as cold and lifeless as the rest of the corridor. We assembled along the wall behind him as the rest of the squad caught up.

"Anyone bring some hand jaws?" asked Arnold.

"Don't think we need them," said Antawaan. "Those don't even look pressurized."

Sure enough, they came apart at a nudge. We activated our remaining suit lights and surged inside, past the similarly unlocked interior pressure doors.

We stood inside a room filled with displays and servers, all of them black, none of them humming. They couldn't have been out of use for long. The tables holding them were clear of dust, same as the chairs pulled underneath them. I couldn't see him, nor even sense him, but something told me my cracker nemesis lurked nearby.

Arnold swung his Badass around the room's interior, casting light over the contents. "Alright. Now we're making progress."

A trio of hallways branched off from the back of the room. Arnold gave us instructions to fan out and search for rebels, assigning me to stick with Luciana and Antawaan. We worked our way methodically down our corridor, finding bedrooms, a bathroom, a small gymnasium, and another server cluster, but no occupants. After each empty room, I found myself back in the counterintelligence office, questioning my moves. Perhaps I should've given the interloper free rein, allowed them to try to crack my strengthened intranet defenses. Maybe by forcing them out and pushing the new patch through I'd clued them to our strategy, or maybe they'd succeeded and cracked us after the fact, learning of our plans to raid the underground habitat as they came to be.

I was ready to beat my faceplate against my Badass when Luciana pressed a hand against my Suit. "Lights."

I tensed, but my training immediately kicked in. We crouched along the corridor toward the opening through which faint, flickering lights flashed. We paused at the open frame. Luciana gathered us behind her before we turned the corner, Badasses at the ready, butts pressed into our shoulders.

We stepped into an open room filled with tables and chairs. A mess hall, maybe. The lights we'd seen flashed across the hall, through an open doorway in the adjacent corridor beyond. They turned the corner, nearly blinding me as they pointed our direction. My finger tensed against the trigger, but our discipline held for the split-second it took for the identification to flicker across our visors.

"Zeta Squad, is that you?"

"Lambda?" came Phoebe's voice. "Christ, you gave us a scare."

Barely had Phoebe finished responding than someone surged from behind her, brandishing his Badass toward the right side of the room. I couldn't see his face behind his visor, but I knew it was Maarten by the way he walked. He wasn't using his Net, but I heard his voice, faintly, borne on the wings of the subterranean base's thin atmosphere as he yelled within his helmet.

I followed the light on his rifle and nearly jumped. We weren't alone.

A group of perhaps twenty people huddled against the far wall, crouched low as if to avoid the roving beam of light shining from Maarten's rifle. I caught glimpses of faces through the glare of their helmets, male and female, some of them no more than teenagers, others grizzled graybeards, all of them with eyes stretched wide, some with trembling lips.

Maarten stepped forward, gesturing at them with his rifle as he continued to yell. I caught nothing more than snippets of instructions, heated commands to get down.

I gripped my rifle tight, but I didn't point it at anyone. "Maarten, lower your weapon. These people are unarmed."

"Bullshit, they are," he said over chat, glancing at me quickly. "You think these Reds are here as prisoners? Get your head out of your ass."

"Maarten, do as he says," said Phoebe. "Lower your weapon and switch your rounds for non-lethal ones. Spread out. Keep your eyes on the civilians."

"Guys, I can't reach Arnold," said Luciana. "My long range wireless isn't working."

Someone from the wall stood, spreading their arms in the air.

Maarten jerked forward. "Get down, you Red son of a bitch. Are you stupid?"

I lifted my rifle slightly, pointing it at Maarten's feet. "Maarten, put your god-damned rifle *down!*"

"Fuck you, Ambrose." He didn't move a muscle.

"Something's wrong," said Phoebe. "I can't reach anyone via Net either. This doesn't feel right."

"It's a fucking trap!" said Maarten.

I lifted my rifle. "Maarten, *gun down now!* I will not stand by and watch you murder more innocent civilians, do you hear me?"

"Butt out, Ambrose," said Phoebe. "I'm in command of Zeta Squad. Maarten, lower your rifle!"

Someone moved along the wall, making a break for the door. Maarten turned and fired, the crack of his rifle reverberating off the walls. I swore and dove behind one of the dining tables, ejecting my cartridge and slamming a set of tranq darts in their place. By then all hell had broken loose. Civilians along the wall were diving for cover, screaming in a low, pained moan. Maarten's rifle flashed as it fired. Phoebe tackled him from behind, sending him sprawling to the floor, but Maarten's gun wasn't the only one going off. Luciana was firing behind me. As I heard a ping and a clatter, I realized we were taking fire, too. A gleam shone in the hands of one of the people along the wall.

I fired a tranq round at them as Maarten struggled to his feet. A Red moved on the wall across from him. Phoebe rose and dove for cover. Maarten fired. Someone at the wall did, too. Phoebe went down, a cloud of red erupting around her. In the darkness, I couldn't tell where she'd been hit.

"PHOEBE!" I roared and jumped up, spraying darts in Maarten's general direction.

Maarten turned and fired. So did the partisans. Luciana and Antawaan, too.

I went down in a heap, pain coursing through me with unbridled ferocity. It wasn't the pain of being shot, though perhaps I had been. It was the pain of a thousand bullets, a million pinpricks across every nerve ending in my body. I tried to scream, but my lungs wouldn't respond. My body was in shock, my brain a puddle of useless goo, overloaded with agony.

As I faded into darkness, I realized it wasn't my brain that was overloaded. It was my Net.

50

MAY 13, 2179

MWENGE and I found Vincenzio seated inside the aforementioned interview one, which was identical to the interrogation room except the seats had padding. The Silicon Road mob boss sat there, dressed in an impeccable navy pinstriped suit with a raspberry Windsor-knotted tie over his crisp white shirt and a matching raspberry handkerchief flaring playfully from his breast pocket. His hair was a couple centimeters long, peppered with grey and parted off center. He glanced at us as we entered, his arms crossed in his lap and his foot tapping a rapid, steady beat against the polished floor.

I took a seat across from him, Bishop choosing to stand by the door. "Giancarlo Vincenzio?"

The middle-aged man nodded. "That's right. You're Detective Ambrose Drake?"

They were perfunctory questions, of course. I knew exactly what Giancarlo looked like, and if he'd asked for me by name, he'd undoubtedly pulled my public file before stopping by.

"What can I do for you, Mr. Vincenzio?"

Giancarlo glanced at Mwenge before studying me a bit more. "I'm here to talk."

"I didn't expect you'd pay us a visit to mooch a free coffee. Talk about what?"

"Your investigation, of course. Into the murder of Administrator Wen."

"You have information regarding her murder?"

"I have information relating to the circumstances that *led* to her murder."

"And you're going to share that information with me? What's the catch?"

Giancarlo hesitated. "I want protection."

"I think you mean immunity."

"That would be nice, too, in the event you deem I've done something wrong, but no. I choose my words carefully, Detective. *Protection.*"

"Protection? From who? You're a mob boss. Isn't that your racket?"

"Don't insult me. I'm a businessman. And there are plenty of parties I might need protection from in the future. USC. The separatists. Mobs on the street. I don't know."

"There are no mobs on the street, Mr. Vincenzio," I said. "There have been some protests around the city. Nothing more."

"You're not as smart as I'd expected, Detective. All it takes to turn protestors into a mob is the crack of a pistol."

I glanced at Bishop. He shrugged.

"Alright," I said. "We'll arrange for your protection—the scope of which will be dependent upon the information you're willing to provide."

"No dice," said Vincenzio. "I need an ironclad guarantee. A contractual arrangement to provide for my immediate and future security."

"I can't give you that."

"*You* can't. So find me someone who will. I can wait."

I frowned. I didn't like being jerked around, but I also wanted to know what the hell had brought a man like Vincenzio into the heart of Elysium's police network.

"Okay, then. Give me a minute or thirty. I'll see what I can do."

THANKFULLY, the Captain had finally returned. Apparently, she'd been sucked into a conference call with our Chief of Police, the Chiefs of Police of the other major Martian cities, and a bunch of USC brass to discuss measures to maintain order in the event of escalating tensions. It was a meeting that should've been above the Captain's pay grade, but given the intertwined nature of Shao Wen and Deandre Jackson's deaths and the Snow Leopard's use of them for political purposes, someone deemed it necessary for her to be there. She didn't want to talk about it, instead choosing to focus on the arrival of our guest.

Within the half hour window I'd given Giancarlo, Bishop and I reentered the interview room with the Captain leading the way. Mwenge stood by the door again—out of necessity this time as the Captain and I took the two available seats.

"Mr. Vincenzio," said Reyes as she settled into her chair. "Detectives Drake and Mwenge have appraised me to your concerns and demands, and I have to say I'm intrigued. It's not every day someone of your renown walks into our offices claiming to have knowledge pertinent to an active homicide investigation. I've also been told you're more concerned about your personal well-being than about criminal indemnity. However, short of locking you in a secure location, otherwise known as a *prison*, there's not a lot I can do to protect you. I won't put a police detail on you without knowledge of a credible threat against your life. So here's what I can offer. If you can provide information leading to the capture of Shao Wen's murderer —assuming that individual isn't you and wasn't working under your orders—then I can give you a plea deal that will protect you from criminal prosecution over other lessor non-violent felony charges, specifically related to drug and property crime. What do you say?"

"I say that's a far cry from what I asked for."

Reyes shrugged. "It's what I can offer."

Giancarlo gave the Captain his poker face. "I might need witness protection."

"I can arrange that, if necessary, but first I need to know what the hell is going on."

Giancarlo didn't budge. "Do you have this in writing?"

"I can send you a document."

Giancarlo nodded, then sat there, his eyes twitching as he scanned the document the Captain had sent via Net. Eventually, he refocused on us. "Alright. I agree to the terms."

"Great," said Reyes. "Now let's hear what you're here to tell us."

"Are you familiar with the sort of work I engage in, Captain?"

"You're a drug dealer and a smuggler, Mr. Vincenzio. Does that about cover it?"

Giancarlo sniffed. "I'd say I'm in the distribution business, but I'm not here to split hairs. The fact of the matter is I have experience moving items without notice. That expertise attracted the attention of a third party some two or three years ago. I was approached by an intermediary with a business proposition—for me to excavate a series of tunnels underneath the city. The purpose of said tunnels wasn't indicated, and I didn't ask. The price was high enough that secrecy was included as part of the deal. The work took some time. In fact, it was ongoing until recently. These tunnels were large and long. At first I assumed they'd be used for human transport—"

"Human trafficking," I said.

"Whatever term you wish to use," said Vincenzio. "But it became clear to me after a while the tunnels were to be used for

water transport instead, primarily because my intermediary introduced a new measure into our business negotiation—that we begin
payments to both Ms. Wen and the recently deceased Mr. Jackson,
whose murder I believe you're also investigating, for them to look
the other way."

"Hold on," said Captain Reyes. "Are you suggesting someone is
planning on stealing the city's water reserves?"

"Captain," I said. "Evidence I uncovered late last night
suggests they already did."

"What evidence?"

"Data from the tablet we recovered from Wen's apartment. I
discussed it with Mwenge this morning. I didn't want to make it
public, primarily because I wasn't sure if the data was accurate or
not. I was going to tell you as soon as you got free of your meeting,
but then Mr. Vincenzio arrived."

"How much water?"

"A lot."

The Captain turned on Vincenzio. "So you paid Wen and
Jackson to keep quiet about this?"

"Correction," said the mob boss. "We were paid to pay them. I
never asked why. Asking questions wasn't part of the business
arrangement, but like you, I deduce things on my own on
occasion."

"So who paid you to build the tunnels?"

"I don't know," said Vincenzio. "I always worked through the
intermediary. But whoever it was had a lot of excess capital, I'll tell
you that."

"Surely you have a guess."

"I can always guess, but you people work on evidence, not
suppositions. What I *know* is that it was a financier flush with cash,
someone who could not only afford to fund the project but could
conceivably handle the arguably thornier parts of keeping the theft

quiet. And someone who would have a reason to steal the water in the first place."

"And who would that be?" asked Reyes. "A consortium of investors? A shadow government? A corporate rival of USC?"

I saw an opportunity and took my shot. "Not a rival. USC themselves."

Captain turned to stare at me. *"What?"*

"This wasn't a simple job, Captain. We're talking about the theft of billions of liters. That's hard to hide. There are dozens of people who work in the underground portions of the central water processing facility alone. Trust me. Mwenge and I were there yesterday doing the rounds. How hard do you think it would be for an outsider to suppress something of that magnitude? To keep it hidden from USC's watchful eye?"

"Why would USC pay someone to build tunnels for them and pay off their own employees?"

"Two words. Plausible deniability. By using the Silicon Road gang they could claim ignorance of this whole mess if it ever got out —as it's in the process of doing."

"But why would USC steal their own water?"

"It's not theirs," I said. "It's ours. The people's. They simply extract it, and we pay them for the service."

"It's a semantic difference."

"I beg to differ, Captain. We're the ones paying USC, and USC controls the supply. If the supply decreases, the cost increases."

"I'm familiar with supply and demand economics, Detective. If USC were to have pulled something of this magnitude off, I understand how they'd stand to gain, but how do you think they'd explain what happened to the public? Don't you think people will be a little surprised to find all that water ice has gone missing?"

"Surprised, sure, but surveys aren't perfect. Mistakes are made when you're dealing with subterranean radiography. And it's not as if there are many people to contradict whatever story they decide to sell. USC is the expert on underground ice farming. Their scientists are the leaders in the field."

Reyes rubbed her forehead. "This is coming across as crazy, Detective. USC is the largest corporation in the history of mankind. Why would they attempt such a ludicrous and potentially damaging scheme to increase the water rates on citizens of a single Martian colony? That's a drop in the bucket of their corporate profits."

I took a deep breath. This was the part where I went totally off the rails. "Because this isn't about Elysium's ice sheet. This is about the ability to sell Mars a new product."

"It is?" said Giancarlo.

Apparently, I'd left him in the dust, too. "I was up all night thinking about this. Ask Mwenge. He noted how I looked like shit when I came in. This is why. You're all familiar with Swift-Tuttle, right?"

"I'm a student of history, Detective," said Reyes.

"Then you'll know that before it was redirected toward Martian orbit, it was envisioned as a means of terraforming the planet into a livable world. A source of water for the oceans and nitrogen for the atmosphere. The problem is subsequent testing aboard the body shows a whole hell of a lot more water ice than ammonia. There's not enough nitrogen on Swift-Tuttle to even get close to providing a breathable atmosphere for Mars. It can provide other things, of course. Tidal heating, for one. But mostly water. It's just hard to sell people on that when they already have it."

Reyes sat there, staring at me. I thought I might've broken her. "You're suggesting this isn't the only place USC has done this."

"For it to make sense, they would've had to enact similar measures in all the major Martian colonies. It's the only way it would be profitable."

"But what would USC have done with all that ice?"

"I have no idea, but if it was me in charge, I would've boiled it and vented it to the atmosphere. That would be the most effective way to keep it out of the hands of Martian citizens and force people to pay for new ice from Swift-Tuttle. If I'm right, the partial pressure of water in the Martian atmosphere should've risen over the past two years, but even that much ice wouldn't move the needle much."

The expression Reyes affixed me with wasn't a familiar one. Her brow was furrowed, but her eyes held concern, not anger. "I expect this sort of conjecture from one of the Snow Leopard's videos, not from you, Detective."

"Conjecture it may be, Captain, but unlike the Leopard I'm doing my damndest to make sure Mars *isn't* split by another revolutionary war."

"And if you're right? What do we do with the knowledge?"

I shook my head. "I wish I'd gotten that far."

Reyes turned to Vincenzio, who sat there open-mouthed. "Well, you've just been exposed to the most far-fetched conspiracy theory I've ever heard. What do you have to add?"

The mob boss blinked. "I'll be honest, I'd guessed the first part, but the rest beats the hell out of me."

Reyes leaned back in her chair and sighed. "I can't believe I'm going to say this, but even if this is correct, I'm not sure what we can do with any of it. It would explain why Wen and Jackson were murdered, to be fair. To shed light on the conspiracy, just as the Snow Leopard said. But it doesn't get us any closer to finding Wen and Jackson's murderers, which is the only aspect of this case we're legally charged with investigating."

The police scanner app in my Net blinked, and I checked it reflexively, same as Reyes and Mwenge must've.

Reyes waved it off. "Possible homicide uptown. I'll assign another team to it."

"Uh, Captain?" said Mwenge. "Maybe not. We might need to check this one out."

"Why's that?"

I stared at the name of the victim on the app. *Charlize Van Jaarsveld.* That was why.

51

DECEMBER 25, 2154

I BLINKED, my head a bundle of raw, screaming nerves. I couldn't think, could barely process what I was seeing. Blinking lights. Slow ones. Perhaps not blinking, after all. One would appear, a streaking flash, only to disappear into the darkness. A period of time later, another one. I wasn't sure if it was seconds or minutes later. Time escaped me. Somewhere in the middle perhaps. Then another. And another. They blurred as they passed me, their light reflected off something. The face plate of my helmet. I was still in my Suit. And the lights *were* passing me. Flashing by me. Which meant I was moving. Somewhere. Somehow, I wasn't sure.

I tried to turn my head to get a better look, but my body refused to cooperate. I couldn't move. Couldn't even twist my neck to the side. I focused on my eyes. My mind screaming in protest, but they rolled up. When the next light flashed by me, I noticed a little more. Bundled cables on either side of it. I'd seen those before. In the tunnels. Was I on a vactrain? Or a rideshare of some sort?

I pushed my eyes further to the side. There was something there. An indistinct white blur. Was it moving, or was that me? I focused on it, waiting for the next burst of light. The blur shifted in the darkness. It was moving. A white form.

The corridor brightened. The flash came, and I saw the outline before me. Someone in a white pressure suit, perched at the side of a cart. Their head tilted in my direction, but I couldn't see their eyes. The light was there and gone too fast. It rippled off me, bouncing off my retinas, white light tinged red as it reflected off a bloody visor.

I tried to speak, to move to do anything, but the shock was too great. Consciousness slipped through my fingers as I spiraled back into darkness.

FEELING FLOODED BACK to me as I opened my eyes, this time without the anguish of before. I blinked, staring at a bare ceiling above me. The lights hanging from the center weren't moving, nor apparently was I.

I shifted, expecting my brain to shatter into a thousand aches and pains, but it didn't. I felt a minor strain behind my eyes, as if I'd been staring at a display for too many hours, but other than that I felt fine. Well, almost. My stomach grumbled, and I felt parched.

I reached up, realizing I wasn't wearing my helmet. In fact, I wasn't wearing my Suit at all. I wore a simple white long sleeve shirt and pants. Socks, too, also white. I wiggled my toes. They responded, neither frostbitten nor cut off from my neural chain of command.

I sat up in my cot. There wasn't much furniture in the room to go along with it, just a folding table and accompanying chair. The room didn't contain any windows, though there was a lone door on the far wall. Was it a cell, then? At least the cot had some padding.

I brought up my Net, thinking to use it to establish where I was, but it wasn't in the state I'd last left it. Not only could I not find a wireless signal, the majority of my applications had been locked. 'Access denied' flashed across my vision as I tried to open my messaging app, chat app, and newsfeed app. I'd been locked out... *somehow.*

As I failed to log into my terminal, I heard the door open. A woman entered, tall and lithe with olive skin and dark, shoulder length hair. She wore one of the white pressure suits, same as the one I'd seen on the Snow Leopard in his vids and—if my memory didn't fail me—in real life, but she didn't wear a helmet. She closed the door behind her, pulled the chair from the table, and sat down in it. She didn't speak at first, as if she expected me to break the ice, but eventually she relented. "Welcome. My name is Marina Vieira Coehlo."

I worked my tongue against dry lips. "Ambrose Drake."

She nodded. "I know."

I eyed her white pressure suit. "You're a Red."

"Some people call us by that name."

"*Some?*"

Marina crossed one leg over the other. "Let me guess. Someone at USC—a superior, a trainer, perhaps a fellow enlistee—told you that's what we call ourselves. That we preferred that designation over others, and you, of course, assumed they were right."

"So what do you call yourselves?"

Marina shrugged. "Nothing in particular. The separatist movement. The resistance. Most of the time, we call each other by name. I can't imagine you go about proclaiming yourself an Earth colonialist or that you *are* USC."

"Fair enough." I glanced around the room. "Where am I?"

"In a secure location."

"Underground?"

Marina smiled. "It's secure."

"I don't know. You seemed to walk through that door pretty easily."

Marina waved toward it. "Want to try to leave?"

"Maybe. Who'd stop me? *You?*" I probably outweighed Marina by thirty-five kilos.

I'm not sure if Marina reacted to my disparaging tone of voice or my look, but she uncrossed her legs and leaned forward. "I wouldn't make threats if I were you. In your position, they only make you seem smaller, weaker. Besides, we stripped you of anything you might be able to use to fight back."

I glanced at Marina's belt. I didn't see a holster. "I don't think I'd need a gun to overpower you."

"That's not the most powerful weapon we deprived you of."

Marina smiled, and my vision went fuzzy. It swirled and spun, making my stomach heave. A thousand icicles lanced through my mind, sending a chill down my spine, but as soon as they flew through me they were gone, leaving behind nothing more than the faintest of traces. A shadow of their presence. The barest hint of a familiar digital funk. My chat popped up, and an anonymous message appeared. "Hi, there."

I blinked as my vision coalesced back to normal, but I couldn't take my eyes of the message. "How'd you do that?"

"Practice. Apps. Long hours spent in front of a terminal."

A sudden thought slammed into me like a runaway vactrain. "Wait... The hacker in our transponder network. That was you, wasn't it?"

Marina's smile widened. "It was me."

I wet my tongue again. "So I didn't kick you out with my patch, did I? You knew about the attack."

"Not everything. To your credit, you worked quickly. I had a hard time getting my people out."

"That's why you left some behind. You couldn't evacuate everyone in time."

"In part," said Marina. "I also thought one good trap deserved another."

I took a deep breath. We'd failed then. Been tricked into launching an attack against a Red base that was prepared to fight back. "I'm a prisoner, then."

Marina nodded.

It didn't hit me as hard as it should've. Then again, I'd already figured it out. "And? Why are you here? To gloat? To frighten me? To get me to talk?"

"For now? To ask you a simple question."

"Go on."

Marina leaned forward a little. "During the gunfight, before we incapacitated you with a Net blast, you opened fire on one of your own men, one Maarten Stanić. Why?"

"Because he's an asshole, and I wasn't about to let him murder innocents, even Reds. Not again."

"Again?"

"He'd done it before. There was an... incident."

"So as a general rule you oppose senseless slaughter? Even of Martians?"

I laughed, though there wasn't any mirth in it. "Yes. Believe it or not, unlike you, I oppose the murder of innocents."

Marina's eyes narrowed. "What do you mean, unlike me?"

"Give me a break," I said, my voice getting hot. "If you're the hacker you claim to be, you're far from stupid. Why do you think I'm here? Why do you think any of us are here? I was perfectly happy, playing basketball and working on my computer science and engineering degree until you and your bloodthirsty asshole friends decided to wipe thirty million souls of the face of Earth with a single pre-dawn blast."

Marina pointed a finger at herself. *"I* did that?"

"You. The Reds. The separatists. Whatever the hell you want to call yourselves. Oh, I know. *Murderers.* That's a good non-partisan term that fits the bill."

The woman eyed me coolly. "I wouldn't throw around accusations if I were you. You don't know anything about me. As a matter of fact, you don't seem to know anything about *us.*"

My cheeks grew warm. "I know that regardless of what you call yourselves, you're cold blooded killers. Reds or not, you're a bunch of filthy murderers."

"But not filthy enough for you to murder us back, apparently. You changed your rifle rounds to non-lethal darts before you opened fire on us, and you tried to stop your friend, Stanić, from killing us as well."

"Maarten isn't my friend."

Marina cocked her head. "I suppose not." She stood and started toward the door.

I blinked, struggling to understand what had just transpired. "Wait."

Marina turned. "Yes?"

"What happens now?"

Marina shrugged. "That's still to be determined."

I gulped, my heart suddenly in my throat. "Do you mean...? Are you going to turn me over to... *him?* The Snow Leopard. I know he's here. I saw him while you transported me." I couldn't admit that it might've been a hallucination.

"The Snow Leopard will be introduced to you if and when the time is right. Any other questions?"

"Yes. What happened to the others?"

"You mean your *not friend* Stanić? Believe it or not, he escaped. I'm still not entirely sure how. He's a tough son of a bitch. That and your supporting squads didn't make our retreat easy."

"No. Not Maarten. I meant... Phoebe. Phoebe Zhao. She was there, in the room with the rest of us when you attacked. Before you knocked me out, I saw her... I saw..." I couldn't bring myself to say what exactly I'd seen.

Marina's face fell, if only slightly. "Mars isn't kind to those who take bullets in vacuum. I'm sorry."

Marina left, and despite my dehydration, I found I still had enough liquid inside me for tears.

52

MAY 13, 2179

THE SKYSCRAPERS HID the sun from view as Mwenge and I walked down the alley toward the scene of the crime. Somehow, the day had gotten late without me even realizing it. Captain Reyes had remained at the precinct, trying to figure out how to deal with Giancarlo Vincenzio. He hadn't exactly provided us with much, only enough to give credence to the theories I'd spent the last night cooking up, but those theories might be turning into reality before my very eyes.

A crowd of a dozen milled about on the near side of a strip of caution tape some officers had set up between yellow sawhorses. I stepped over the tape as the officers waved us forward, around the edge of the nearest structure into a hidden space between buildings. It wasn't a plaza, exactly, but there were a few benches oriented in a rough square, some stunted trees in planters that needed sunlight, and even a tattered basketball hoop on the far end of the space, with only a half court for dribbling.

Not far from the benches, a woman in a canvas jacket and slacks lay in a pool of her own blood. An officer stood over her. He looked relieved when he saw us.

"Detectives." He nodded. "Good to see you. I'm feeling out of my element, here."

"Nobody ever feels in their element around the dead, officer," I said. "Even we never entirely get used to it. Give us the rundown."

"Facial recognition identifies the deceased as Charlize Van Jaarsveld, twenty-nine years of age. As you can see, it looks like she was gunned down in cold blood."

I eyed the body. She lay face down on the ground. Her jacket was soaked in blood. Amid the red morass, I spotted a pair of bullet holes. The two in the back of her head were harder to miss, however, given they'd made a mess of her skull and splattered the asphalt with bits of gray matter.

"No paramedics on the scene," I said. "I'm guessing she's not Net enabled."

"Nope," said the officer. "I already checked in with Brahe Memorial."

"So who called in the murder?"

The officer pointed to the furthest bench, where a young man hung his head, staring at the ground. An officer stood nearby, more as a matter of rote than as a safety precaution. "That guy right there. Felix Goya. He was waiting for Miss Van Jaarsveld to show up for a get together. Coffee, he said. When she didn't show, he tried to call her, but she didn't answer. Eventually, he came up to vape and found her here."

"Mwenge, do we know who this Goya tom is?"

"I'm doing a search now," said Mwenge with glazed eyes. "If anything, he's a bit player."

"*A bit player?*" said the officer.

"Don't worry about it." I pointed to a shoulder bag on the ground a meter from the victim. "I'm assuming that was here when you arrived?"

"Yes, sir."

"You didn't touch it?"

"No, sir. I can't guarantee Goya didn't, though."

Given the haphazard way it lay on the concrete, flap side down, I didn't suspect anyone had messed with it. I flipped it over and opened it. There wasn't a ton inside: a bottle of water, a sack lunch, the contents of which had mostly been eaten, a nondescript tablet, and several dozen pamphlets espousing the virtues of a free Mars. Leave it to budding separatists to resort to the tried and true method of distributing actual paper. It was harder to track than Net messages, that was for sure.

I held up one of the pamphlets. "Hey, Mwenge. Check this out. And go see what you can squeeze from that Goya youngster, okay?"

"You got it." Mwenge grabbed the folded paper and headed toward the bench.

I grabbed the tablet from the messenger bag, but it was locked. Miss Jaarsveld was right next to me on the pavement, however. After pressing the tablet's scanner against her thumb, I flipped through the calendar and notes apps, but nothing struck me as out of the ordinary. Van Jaarsveld had several more meetings planned, and her notes were mostly keeping track of current events and demonstrations around the city. I checked the contact list, as well, but none of the names jumped at me.

I pocketed the tablet as I stood. "Officer... what was it?"

"Mason."

"Right. This meeting Goya said Miss Van Jaarsveld was coming to. I'm assuming it was to take place close by?"

"In the basement of that building over there." Mason pointed it out.

"Did Goya hear a gunshot?"

"I didn't specifically ask. Just took his statement of how he found the vic."

"Anyone else?"

"I haven't conducted interviews. Goya was the only one on the scene when I arrived."

I ran my tongue across my teeth, not liking what I was hearing. "Okay. Thanks."

I called Dean.

He responded right away. "Detective. I heard you got summoned to another homicide."

"I'm there as we speak, Dean. Outdoors, in a communal gathering space. Can you pull public security cam footage of anything in my general vicinity for the past few hours?"

"Sure. You want me to send it over when I have it?"

"I can stay on the line. I'm curious what the feeds are going to show, to be honest."

"You got it, Detective. I'll work quick. Let's see, here. Pulling a trace on your location. You're off Wadley Avenue, between Fifty-Third and Fifty-Fourth?"

"That's right. Please tell me we've got coverage on this spot."

"It looks like you do. Nothing in the alley, but there should be a camera on the southeast corner covering most of the outdoor space you're standing in. I've got two more on the street, one with partial views of the alley entrance."

I turned and looked up, trying to locate the camera Dean had alerted me to. I found it, pointed roughly in the direction of Van Jaarsveld's body, just underneath the protective Mylamene barrier. Something about it looked off, though.

I pulled my own tablet and opened the camera app. "Got those feeds yet, Dean?"

"Downloading them, Detective. Give me a sec."

I zoomed on the camera and looked at it through my display. *"Son of a bitch."*

"What is it?" asked Dean.

"Looks like someone shot the security cam."

"With a gun?"

"Right through the lens," I said. "Maybe another through the side. Pretty god-damned risky considering how close that thing is to the Mylamene."

"Give me a moment on the feeds. I'm looking through the one on that camera now. And... yup. *Shit*. The feed cuts out about an hour ago. Nothing but static since."

"City services must've noticed."

"Probably," said Dean. "But they wouldn't have any reason to think it wasn't a standard malfunction."

I sighed. "Well, I wasn't expecting any security camera footage, though I'd expected a more technologically advanced approach, not mechanical sabotage. Run through the alley entrance feeds, Dean, at least for the past few hours, and get back to me with a list of anyone who came in and out."

"Will do."

I cut out as Mwenge approached. "What did you get from the witness?"

"Not a whole lot that the officer didn't, I'm afraid." Bishop glanced back at him. "He's pretty shook. The victim appears to have been a good friend of his. He might've even been keen on her being *more* than a friend."

"And he didn't hear a gunshot?"

Mwenge shook his head. "No dice."

I blew air from between my lips. "Crap, Bishop. I don't like this. Not one bit."

"What's to like about murder?"

"That's not what I mean. Tell me it's a coincidence that Miss Van Jaarsveld, a Martian separatist who we'd started to investigate as a person of interest in regards to the murders of Shao Wen and Deandre Jackson, suddenly shows up dead."

"It's not," said Bishop.

"Exactly. But she wasn't stabbed. She wasn't bombed. She was shot. Twice in the chest. Twice in the back of the head. You looked at the entrance wounds. How did the spacing on those sets of shots look to you?"

Bishop frowned. "Tight. Like she was shot by someone who knew how to use a pistol."

"Exactly. Someone who knew not to take any chances, and who was enough of a deadeye to nail the camera overlooking this place with another couple well placed shots." I pointed it out. "A pro took her out, and no one heard a gunshot. Guns are loud, and this Goya character was in the building on the corner down one story in the basement. I'd wager whoever murdered her used a silencer. You know how hard those are to come by."

Bishop nodded, his frown deepening.

I stepped closer and lowered my voice. "Bishop, this was a professional hit. And she's obviously not part of the conspiracy involving Wen and Jackson. Hell, she might've been part of the group who took them out. It looks like someone came to that conclusion before we did."

"But who?"

"Someone who didn't want Wen and Jackson's actions having any more light shed on them. Someone who wanted the Snow Leopard videos to come to a stop."

"Are you suggesting USC personnel murdered her?"

"Possibly. But if so, they've shot themselves in the foot in a *major* way. Who found Van Jaarsveld?"

"Goya."

"Right. A member of her Free Mars group. Even if we keep Van Jaarsveld's identity under wraps, there's no way he will. This murder is going to be all over the web within a matter of hours."

"Christ." Bishop's face was drawn. "You're right. We need to get in front of this, like, yesterday."

"That's what I'm saying. I don't know if there's any way for us to do that, short of solving this murder and the ones from the past few days before the shit hits the fan."

My police scanner app chimed, and I opened it. I shook my head as I read. "And the hits just keep coming. Shots fired at Musk College of Science and Engineering. Possible active shooter situation."

"That's not far from here," said Mwenge.

"It says all officers are instructed to respond." I glanced toward the mouth of the alley. "I've got a bad feeling about this, Bishop. A very bad feeling."

53

DECEMBER 25, 2154

I'M NOT sure how long I sat in my cot, grieving Phoebe's loss. What I know is that when the tears finally dried and the ache in my heart subsided to a steady, dull throbbing, the body parts I'd thus far ignored refused to be mistreated any longer. My stomach rumbled, shaking my belly, and my bladder pushed on my pelvic wall, reminding me it had needs, too.

I rose and crossed to the door, pounding on it with my fist. "Hello? Anyone there? I'm starving in here, and I really need to pee."

I gave it a few moments, but no one responded, so I tried again, louder this time. "Seriously? How long are you going to keep me in here? I have rights, you know."

Still nothing. Out of frustration, I pounded my open palm against the door, rattling it in its frame. When that failed to draw any attention, I tested the handle.

Surprisingly, it gave.

I opened the door and peeked into the hallway beyond. It looked empty. "Uh... hello? Anyone there?"

I stepped out, looking back and forth along the hallway. Lights lit it at regular intervals, but there weren't any windows set in the walls. I didn't even spot other doors.

"Well, this is damned strange." I looked to the ceiling, trying to find security cameras. Failing to spot any, I spoke to no one in particular, like an idiot. "I'm going to try and find a bathroom. Just have to pee is all."

I picked a direction. I did find another door soon. I hadn't seen it due to the shadow of the hallway lights. I tested the handle, but it was locked, so I kept going.

I froze as I spotted someone headed down the hall in my direction. The interloper came into focus: a guy, probably in his early thirties, with short light brown hair and a curly, golden brown beard. He wore a jacket and jeans, but no pressure suit. He gave me an odd look as he approached. "Nice getup there, buddy. Forget your shoes in your quarters?"

I glanced down at my socks. "Uh. No. That is—"

The guy's mouth opened and he leaned his head back. "Hold on. You must be the prisoner." He didn't seem angry to find me in the hall, though, nor threatened, either.

"That's right. I'm the prisoner... I guess. My room's down the hall." I felt like an idiot pointing in its direction.

The guy followed my finger. "Alright. So what are you doing out here?"

"I'm hungry and I need to pee."

"Oh." The guy stretched his eyebrows. "Well, I can help with that I suppose. The name's Jorge. I can show you to the bathrooms."

"I'm Ambrose." We shook hands, as odd as that was. "By the way, why wasn't my room locked?"

Jorge shrugged as he set off down the hall. "Marina said we didn't need to keep you confined."

I blinked, struggling to grasp what was going on. "You're not worried that I'd try to break free and kill everyone?"

Jorge shot me a confused glance. "You'd do that? What are you, some kind of psychopath?"

"No. I wouldn't do that at all."

"Well, there you go. No need to worry about it then."

"But aren't you worried about me escaping? Seriously, I just walked out of my room."

Jorge chuckled. "I think you'd find breaking free of this place entirely would be a bit more difficult than you're envisioning."

I considered the fact that I had no idea where I was, all I had to my name was a pair of pants, a shirt, and some socks, and my Net was almost entirely nonfunctional. "Maybe you're right."

"I know I'm right." Jorge paused in front of a door with the universal bathroom sign attached to it. "Here you go. I'll wait outside. When you're done, I'll find you something to eat. Well? Go on."

I had more questions, but my bladder insisted I ask them later.

I SAT in a modest dining hall, shoveling food into my face from a bowl filled with julienned cucumbers, zucchini, garlic-sauteed mushrooms, wilted spinach, sprouts, rice, and fried egg protein. I tried not to moan or slurp as I ate. I only barely succeeded. "This is delicious. What did you call it again?"

"Bibimbap," said Jorge, enjoying a bowl himself. "It's originally Korean cuisine, but it's been appropriated several times over the centuries."

"Well, it's really good."

"Fresh ingredients make for tasty meals." Jorge nodded to a couple as they pulled up seats and sat down with their own bowls. "Lauren. Cal. How's it going?"

The woman, tall and thin with long blonde hair, nodded back. "Afternoon, Jorge. Merry Christmas."

"Right back at you," he said.

I looked up from my bowl. "It's Christmas?"

Lauren nodded. "Sure is. Seasons' greetings and all that. You going to introduce us, Jorge?"

The bearded one hesitated. "Right. This is, ah... Ambrose Drake."

Lauren nodded curtly. *"Oh.* I see."

She and Cal both seemed to understand who I was. They made smalltalk with Jorge as I ate, keeping the conversation light and airy. When I finished, I set my empty bowl in front of me, waiting for everyone else to clear their plates. It didn't take long. The bowls weren't enormous, and the food within them delicious.

The conversation died, as it always does when it's forced into pleasant banalities rather than real discussions. Jorge eyed my bowl and gave me a nod. "Well. I should get back to work."

"I understand," I said. "If you could just show me back to my quarters."

Jorge glanced at our table guests. "I could. Or not. Have you ever worked a farm?"

I furrowed my brow. "Uh... *what?*"

"You know? A farm. Like where you grow the food we just ate."

"I've tended a garden. Why?"

Jorge shot another glance at Lauren and Cal. When they didn't say anything, he gave me a nod. "Well, we're always short a few hands in the grow rooms. No point in having you sit around if you're willing to pitch in, maybe learn a few things."

I blinked. "You want me to help tend your lettuce?"

"We actually don't grow much lettuce," said Lauren. "Spinach has more vitamins and a better yield."

The confused look I responded with must've been evident. Jorge shrugged. "Or you can go back to your quarters. It's up to you. Me, I'd rather do something to keep the boredom at bay."

"I'm a prisoner, right?"

"Right."

I chewed on that for a moment. "Okay. Sure. Show me the farm."

CASTLETON FOX STOOD next to me. About sixty years old, with a neatly trimmed graying beard and a thick crop of hair that had just the right balance of salt and pepper, he looked like he'd spent his life modeling expensive watches, tuxedoes, and starring in ads for high end tequila, but he claimed to know nothing else but gardening. I don't know if that was true, but he certainly did know it.

"What you want to do is trim back the vines above the guide wires," he said, pointing to the rows of grapes that lined our current aisle. "We use the two bud method. Trim the dead growth past the second bud of each shoot. Prioritize vines that are pointing up toward the lights. If any are headed down, chop them off at the base. We'd rather lose a few shoots and encourage growth on the ones that are more likely to produce fruit. Any questions?"

"I think I've got it."

Fox handed me a pair of pruning shears. "Show me."

He watched as I trimmed a plant, nodding and grunting his encouragement as I went. When I finished, he gave me a congratulatory nod. There was a little more motion in it than his normal version. "Nice job. I'll be a couple rows over tending the beets. Let me know if you need anything."

"Sure." I hesitated briefly. "Actually, if I could ask you something."

The old man turned and nodded again, the regular version this time. "Yeah?"

"Why are you being so nice to me?"

"Would you rather I treated you like dirt? Actually, that wouldn't be much of a difference. I treat dirt pretty nice." The guy laughed at his own joke.

"No, I don't *want* to be yelled at or mistreated or tortured. I just don't get it. Do you treat all prisoners like this?"

"To be honest? We don't have a lot of prisoners."

"That doesn't answer my question."

Castleton furrowed his thorny brow. "Look, if you want answers to something other than gardening questions, ask Marina. My expertise is in green things that grow. Now are you going to prune those grapes or not?"

"Yeah, I'll prune them," I said. Then quieter, as Fox left: "I'm not sure *why* I'm doing it, but sure. Let's prune some grapes. Why the hell not?"

THE DOOR to Marina's room was open when I arrived, but I knocked on the frame regardless. Marina sat at a desk, staring at a display as she tapped away at a keypad. She looked up at the sound of my knuckles.

"Excuse me? Ms. Coehlo? I need to talk to you."

"You can call me Marina, Mr. Drake. Everyone else does. Come in."

I stepped into her room, barely bigger than my cell and not much more lavishly furnished. "Alright. But only if you call me Ambrose. No one's called me Mr. Drake in my life."

"I suppose they haven't yet." She gestured toward a chair. "Have a seat."

"I'd rather stand if that's okay."

She shrugged. "Suit yourself. So what brings you here?"

I swallowed hard. "Who shot Phoebe Zhao?"

Marina lifted an eyebrow. "Really? You wander into my chambers unsupervised, and *that's* the question you want to ask?"

"It's one of them."

Marina took a deep breath. "You're sure you want the answer?"

I hesitated. "Yes."

"Very well. It was your erstwhile friend Maarten Stanić. I have a surveillance video of the altercation to prove it, though I'd suggest you only watch it if you're certain I'm lying. Given the affection you seem to exhibit for Ms. Zhao, seeing it again could be... painful."

I looked at my feet. "I don't need to see the video."

"From what I've gathered from watching it, it appears to have been an accident," said Marina. "Tensions rise quickly when shots are fired. Unintended targets get caught in the crossfire."

"I'm well aware of that." I hadn't meant to growl the response, but I did.

Marina gave me a moment. "You said you had more than one question for me?"

I looked up. "Yes. The more important one I guess. What the hell are you up to?"

"What do you mean by that?"

I sighed, exasperated. "I wasn't locked in my room. I'm free to move around. Your Red associates have let me use the restroom. Fed me. They asked me to work your vertical farming operation. Hell, they've been nice to me. *Why?*"

Marina's lip curled with a hint of a smile. "Because I'm trying to prove to you that I'm not your enemy."

"It's pretty clear that you are. You captured me in a combat engagement."

"That doesn't prove my animosity."

"I disagree, but that skirts the root of my question. Why don't you want me as your enemy?"

"Why would anyone desire more enemies?" said Marina. "But that's also not the answer you're after. Really, I think it would be obvious, Ambrose. Because I need your help."

54

MAY 13, 2179

I TRANSMITTED our police override to the rideshare that picked us up. It screamed off down the streets, barreling toward the Musk College of Science and Engineering at a hundred and thirty kilometers an hour. More reports poured in as we tore across the asphalt, the cabs in front of us automatically pulling to the side as they received our emergency signal. The shots had taken place in the Geology and Mars Sciences building near the Shotwell Aerospace Museum on the north side of campus. It was unclear how many injured there were, but witnesses in the building had heard well over a dozen shots fired.

The architecture morphed around us as we sped into the main campus, the buildings adopting a more classical feel with rust red brick layered over the interior Mg-Al walls that maintained building pressure. My clock said it was just after six. Students walked along the tree-lined esplanades and across the wide malls between buildings. Some of them had started to run, no doubt having received the public safety alert that had just been distributed.

Our car screeched to a halt outside the Mars Sciences building. Bishop and I jumped out and ran to the front doors, where a pair of officers crouched with guns drawn. I pulled my piece and crouched behind the one on the left, Mwenge taking position across from us on the other side. The guys looked like campus security.

"Officers," I said as another cab pulled up behind our rideshare. "Detective Drake, homicide. What's the status?"

"We arrived less than ninety seconds ago," said the guy in front of me. "No shots fired in that time that we could hear. Building system pressure appears nominal. Numerous calls have been coming into dispatch from within the building. The remaining professors and staff are locked inside their rooms as per active shooter protocols."

"Any students inside?" I asked.

"Not many. A few grads, maybe a study group. Last class in the building ended an hour ago."

"Any idea of the state of affairs inside, Officer...?"

"Herrman. And no, sir. I tried to pull security feeds, but they're on the fritz. One of the calls reported seeing a body on the third floor, though."

Of course the security feeds were out of commission. I yelled to the cops who were approaching from the rideshare behind us. "Officers, two of you stay here. The rest loop around to the back. Cover the exits." I turned to the campus cop. "You know the building?"

"Yeah."

"Good. I'm going to need you to escort Detective Mwenge and me to the third floor. You have any experience under fire?"

"Uh... no, sir."

"Then bring up the rear and tell us where to go. Bishop? Let's move."

The doors slid open as we entered. We moved quickly, efficiently, pistols gripped in the isosceles stance. We swept across the building lobby, past plaques and paintings of deans of yesteryear and past the administrative offices on the first floor. The door looked secure, so we headed up the stairs, pausing at the second floor landing. We checked the hall, and being clear, continued to the third floor.

It was there I spotted the first signs of trouble. A cubicle partition had been knocked into the hallway. I nodded to Mwenge. "Eyes peeled. Weapon ready."

We crept along the hall, checking the doors as we went. All of them were closed, with lights off. I didn't hear a sound. If any professors remained in their offices, they were quiet as mice.

The hall opened into a common workspace with movable partitions and desks for students. Several had been knocked over. Others had bullet holes in them, as did the walls. The window of a nearby office was shattered. The door to said office was open, too. I spotted blood within.

I popped inside and swept the room while Mwenge stood guard at the door. A woman lay on the floor, face up with glassy eyes. Blood soaked her blouse, a pair of gunshot wounds clustered tightly over her right breast. Two more holes pierced her forehead, leading to a near perfectly round pool of blood behind her head.

"Clear." I motioned Mwenge out. "Officer Herrman. Get me an ID on that woman."

Bishop and I crept back into the hallway alcove with the partitions. Mwenge went left. I went right. As I walked, I spotted a trail of blood heading toward another stairwell on the far side of the hall.

"Drake," said Mwenge. "*Holy shit...* Come over here."

"Can't. Secure the area. I'll be right back."

I followed the blood trail. It grew as I approached the door. A bloody smear glistened on the stairwell door. I pushed it open, and there, leaning against the wall on the topmost stair was a middle aged man with light brown hair and a curly golden beard. He held a pistol in one hand, and a bloody tablet with a cracked screen in the other. Blood soaked the back of his jacket, and he wasn't moving.

I hadn't seen the guy in ages—unless you counted when I'd spotted him tailing Boothe on the security feeds outside Red Summit Financial.

I knelt and checked his pockets. Empty. Then I slipped the tablet out of his hand and hit the activation button. It winked on, no passkey needed. The video app blinked from behind the cracked screen, but I ignored it and checked a few other apps. Calendar. Contacts. Web. They'd all been wiped.

Mwenge's voice carried. "Seriously, Ambrose, get your ass over here. This shit is concerning."

I slipped the tablet back into the man's hand, then rushed back to the windows where my partner had stopped. He stared at another victim who lay on the ground. He wasn't breathing, probably due to the gunshots he'd taken to the ribs, leg, and abdomen. I didn't know his name, but he sure as hell looked familiar.

"Who is this?" I said.

"I just scanned him," said Mwenge. "It's that new arson detective we met at the graduation ceremony. Name's Milovich."

"What the hell is he doing here?"

"Detectives," called the officer from the nearby office. "The victim is Juliette Lemagne, associate professor of hydrology."

"Great," I said. "Call the rest of the officers. Tell them to get their asses up here. Clear the building. I want every remaining civilian evacuated."

"You're certain there aren't any remaining threats?" asked Mwenge.

I holstered my weapon. "I'm certain. Back to this guy. What the hell is he doing here?"

"The idealist in me wants to say he was the closest to the scene and responded faster than we did. Except..."

Mwenge flicked a finger at Milovich's hand. I'd noticed it, too. The pistol he gripped had a silencer attached to the end.

"God damn it," I said. "Did I not say I had a bad feeling about this?"

"Tell me you found the other shooter," said Bishop. "Give me some hope."

"I found him, and his pistol wasn't silenced. But hope is a bunch of crap. What we need is ballistics reports."

"Show me."

I took Mwenge to the stairwell and pushed open the door. "I found him here. Looks like he took a couple GSWs to the chest. Maybe one to the back. Hard to know what's an entrance wound and what's an exit wound."

"Any idea who this is?"

I lied. "Nope. Haven't run facial recognition on him yet. I was about to check on this when you called me."

I pulled the tablet from his hand and activated it. The video app was still blinking.

Mwenge looked over my shoulder. "Go on. Don't look a gift horse in the mouth."

I hit play on the most recent video. It was a first person feed, presumably a recording the dead man took, routed through his visual cortex to his Net and saved on the tablet. As the video played, the *presumably* became *certainly*. The recording showed a view from the hall, the communal office in the alcove already empty. Two pairs of soft pops sounded, and the arson detective, Milovich, exited the office. That's when he spotted Jorge, and the gunfight ensued. Each man fired a good dozen rounds. We already knew how it ended.

"Jesus," said Mwenge. "It was really him, then. Milovich shot that professor, and Miss Van Jaarsveld unless something crazy is going on. And then this guy? Who is he? And what the hell is he doing here?"

"Presumably he was trying to stop Milovich from murdering anyone," I said. "The motives are unclear at this point. There are too many moving pieces. Too many factions."

Mwenge shook his head and started to pace in the narrow stairwell. "Ambrose, I don't know about you, but this is kind of freaking me out. Homicides I can handle, but this? I don't even know what the hell is going on. We've got Martian rebels murdering folks. Mystery people in pressure suits fire-bombing apartments and offices. USC's stealing the city water. Our own man just murdered a professor, and now we've got some sort of vigilante taking him out and leaving a video behind as proof? The whole city's on edge, and it feels like someone's trying to start a war. *Christ.*"

Something Kosta had told me in the rideshare came back to me, suddenly and forcefully. "Only someone too inexperienced to know better would try to start a rebellion, Bishop. Speaking of which, we need to get eyes on the rest of the detectives."

My partner frowned. "What detectives?"

"All the recent graduates," I told him. "The ones we met at the gala."

"Why?"

"Because they must've come to know Milovich in training. And because they've been on leave since the ceremony until next week when they're to officially start."

———

I BURST INTO THE APARTMENT, my pistol out. Mwenge was right behind me. We moved quickly, and the apartment wasn't big. Within twenty seconds, we'd swept the kitchen, living room, bedroom, and bath. I reunited with Bishop near the front.

I had a comm channel open with Reyes, who'd remained at the precinct, overseeing the distribution of several dozen cops to the residences of the recently graduated detectives. "He's not here, Captain."

"What do you mean Watters isn't there, Drake?" said Reyes. "His Net trace says he's there. Check the closets. Check under the couch."

I zoomed in on the map with his trace on it. The GPS was accurate to less than a meter, and sure enough, there it was, blinking under my feet. Almost anyway. I followed the dot into the kitchen.

"Detective Drake? Tell me something."

I'd lined my dot up with Watters' trace as best I could, but I still wasn't precisely over it. In fact, I *couldn't* get exactly over it.

I opened the fridge, looked on the shelves, then found what I was looking for in the vegetable crisper. I reached in and pulled out a transponder.

"Captain," I said. "Trust me. He's not here."

55

DECEMBER 25, 2154

I REPEATED Marina's words slowly, to make sure I'd heard them right. "You... want my help."

The olive-skinned woman nodded. "I do."

"But... why? For what?"

Marina leaned back in her chair. "Well, the why is easy. Perhaps you have a deflated sense of your own self worth, Ambrose, but in case you weren't aware, you're a valuable asset, and I don't base that assessment upon your ability to run fast, jump high, or shoot a rifle accurately—no offense if you can indeed do any of those things well. Rather, I'm interested in your mind. You're not the only one working in intelligence, you know. Part of my job is to keep track of who USC puts in positions of relative importance. You caught my eye when you were assigned to counterintelligence. They don't usually assign people of your experience level into those positions. Perhaps you were forced into it based on need. That's possible. But it's why I wanted to get a closer look at what you could do myself."

"Are you saying you've been spying on me?"

"I've stolen your records from USC's database, so in that

respect, yes. But more than that I've been testing you. Seeing what you're capable of."

"You're talking about the transponder signals."

"That, and everything that succeeded you finding them."

"So the messages on the transponders weren't of any importance. It was all a game to see how I'd respond?"

"You, or someone else, but you're the one who found them. You're the one who tried to decrypt them. You're the one who tried to keep us out afterwards, and the one who lured us into your system in hopes of finding us—which you did, I might add."

"So?"

"*So?* Ambrose, it means you have talent. You can code. You can crack. You can think outside the box. And of notable importance, you worked in USC counterintelligence. What you know could be useful to us, both in terms of your current knowledge and what you might be able to gather if you were to crack back into USC's systems."

"Alright. That's coming across. What *isn't* is your reasoning. You seem to think I'm going to betray my friends, my superiors, my homeland, my *entire planet,* all to help you, a ragtag band of underground vault dwellers, murderers of tens of millions, and aggressors of interplanetary war. And why? Because you fed me, let me wander around without shackles, and because you're *nice* to me?"

"We're not being nice to you in the expectation that our generosity will turn you," said Marina. "It's simply the humane thing to do."

"A strategy you'll pursue until you realize I'm not a turncoat," I said. "At which point I have to assume you'll turn to torture. Maybe physical. Maybe mental. Or perhaps you'll skip that altogether and pry the knowledge from my cold, unwilling neurons. I'm aware memories can be pulled from a Net."

"Not reliably," said Marina. "To my knowledge, that particular technology is in its infancy. I'm not very familiar with it. I find the idea of violating someone's mind in search of information chilling. I'm not a fan of advanced interrogation techniques, either. They're not particularly useful, believe it or not. When someone's afraid or in pain, they'll do anything to make their tormentor stop. They'll lie as much as it takes."

I blinked. "You're going to have to spell this out for me then, because I'm not getting it. You want my help, but you honestly seem to believe that I'm just going to *give it to you*. Of my own free will."

"That would be ideal, yes."

"Why would I do that?"

Marina shrugged. "You're the one in counterintelligence. Maybe that's something you should figure out."

I SAT IN MY QUARTERS, twiddling my thumbs. Marina had partially reinstated my Net, to the point where I could access some of the features on the local intranet but little else. My terminal was still locked, as were the more advanced apps and utilities. Try as I might to find a way past the barriers that had been put in place, I failed. Marina claimed I might be an expert hacker, but lacking access to even the most basic of tools made me feel like a caveman at the moment.

So I'd ignored my Net and decided to work with my hands instead. I joined Fox in the farm for a few days, where I tilled soil, distributed fertilizer, trimmed dead growth from bushes, and picked everything from green beans to raspberries, the latter of which turned out to be thorny little bastards. I'd never given a thought to why raspberries were so expensive, but after a full day of picking the fruit, I figured out why.

The manual labor gave me a chance to clear my mind. At first, I'd assumed Marina was lying and that she did expect me to warm to her and her Red associates over time, like a Stockholm Syndrome situation. While that was certainly possible, I couldn't help but shake the feeling that Marina had been telling the truth. That she did expect me to help her sooner or later, of my own free will, for some reason she thought I'd discover on my own. It drove me crazy, mostly because I had *no idea* what that reason could be.

What could possibly make Marina think I might turn my back on my friends, on my commitments, on everything I held dear? She'd stolen my records from USC. It must be something she'd discovered in them that led to her smug self-assurance. But what? My incident with Maarten? Sure, it had led to my demotion, not to mention irreparably severed my relationship with the man, who I now knew to be a violent, racist asshole rather than the jovial, bear-shaped Iowa boy I'd first met, but that incident alone wasn't going to change my opinion on the Reds. Yes, Maarten murdered an innocent civilian. I tried to stop him in the wake of said murder, just as I'd tried to stop him from murdering more civilians before Marina and her crew captured me, but there was a big difference between my refusal to murder non-combatants and a subversive desire to help the enemy.

So what then? Was it something to do with Phoebe's death? Marina had told me Maarten was the one who shot her—perhaps inadvertently—but she hadn't shown me the video. She claimed she'd show me if I desired it. Should I call her bluff? I wasn't sure I could bear to watch Phoebe go down amid a spray of her own blood again, and even if I could confirm it was Maarten who shot her, what then? Would I be supposed to believe Maarten was a secret agent and Phoebe had been shot as part of a larger conspiracy to anger and demoralize me? That was totally insane.

So I asked myself again, what then? Should I search within myself to scrutinize the actions and motivations of everyone who had trained and commanded me, from Sergeant Tyler to Major Watkins and Lieutenant Colonel Cornier? It wasn't as if I was blind to how they saw the Martian separatists and warfare in general. Tyler viewed it all as a no-win existential fight to the death. Watkins viewed everyone and everything on Mars as little more than assets. And Cornier? I got the impression he wanted nothing more than to make it home to a green patch of land and die of natural causes.

I wracked my brain, but no matter which of my compatriots I considered, no matter which of my experiences as a soldier I recalled, I couldn't think of any that would warrant me wanting to abandon my mission, a mission I'd volunteered for. So I came to the conclusion it must be something outside my sphere of influence that Marina thought would bring me to her side. But what?

My newsfeed access had been restored, so I tuned into those to see what I could learn. The feeds weren't curated as they had been at USC. They included standard Martian feeds, the USC ones I was familiar with, as well as an additional feed, one apparently distributed only through resistance channels. It didn't feature the Snow Leopard, as I thought it might've, but instead a rotating supply of anchors, giving reports on the lesser Martian colonies, USC troop movements, weather reports, and notifications of supply shortages, among other things. It was interesting to hear about the conditions on the ground straight from the mouths of the rebels, but it didn't change my perception of the war. As a counter-intelligence officer, I'd already had access to the non-USC feeds. I knew people across Mars were tired, hungry, and scared. I knew people were dying every day, not just from bullets and shrapnel and spontaneous venting accidents but from malnutrition and thirst and lack of access to medical care. The war had disrupted supply lines, hamstrung businesses, and sunk the entire planet into a miasma of despair.

As much as USC wanted us to believe we were winning the fight, we weren't. The separatists weren't either. Everyone was suffering. Everyone was sustaining casualties. Yet both sides refused to submit to the other.

I didn't know if either ever would.

———

I WALKED into Marina's quarters, choosing not to knock this time. I glared at her as she looked up from her display. "So, I get it, alright? War sucks. People die on both sides. People *suffer* on both sides. No one every truly wins, except maybe the folks at the top who profit off weapons and never dip their toes in the dust. I didn't understand that when I enlisted, but I'm not as naive as I once was. But just because war is awful and we'd all be better off having never got involved in this mess doesn't mean your side is any better than my side. It doesn't mean I should help you stop USC any more than I should help USC stop you."

Marina blinked, trying to get a grasp on my sudden outburst. "Well... you're probably right about that."

"What part?"

"All of it. War *is* terrible. Combatants are scarred by it for life. Both sides usually end up worse off for it, especially the side on whose patch of dirt the war is fought."

"Your side, in this case. Mars."

Marina nodded. "Despite the nuclear strike against Los Angeles, Mars is undoubtedly worse off in this war than Earth is. You'd agree with that?"

"Maybe. It doesn't make me feel sorry for you, though. It doesn't make me want to help you."

"I didn't think it would."

I wanted to scream. "Then what *do* you think is going to make me reconsider your offer? That I'll discover my parents are secretly Martian emigrants? That I have regolith flowing through my veins?

Or perhaps you think I'll fall in love with the lifeless beauty of the Martian expanse and think it worth saving from terraforming?"

"I don't think any of those things, Ambrose."

"Then WHAT?"

"Perhaps you should look closer to home for answers."

Marina gestured toward the door. Despite my anger and confusion, or perhaps because of them, I took her offer and left.

56

MAY 13, 2179

CAPTAIN REYES PACED BACK and forth in her office. "Three cops, Detectives. *Three.* Milovich from arson is dead after murdering at least one civilian in cold blood, and two more, Watters from homicide and Keller from cyber crimes, are gone. Vanished. Where the hell are they?"

I stood behind the guest chairs with Mwenge, feeling as on edge as the Captain looked. Reyes' question was a rhetorical one, but I answered anyway. "There's no way to know for sure, Captain, unless they reactivate their Nets, but if they're smart—and they are —they won't. Nonetheless, they won't get far. They've been flagged in the public security system. If a camera spots them, no matter how remote the street corner, we'll know."

Reyes rubbed her forehead as she paced. "God, this is a night-mare. How could this happen? *Martian separatists infiltrating the police?* Am I supposed to believe our vetting procedures can keep people with violent disorders and superiority complexes out, but we can't identify revolutionaries and insurgents?"

To be fair, we weren't sure yet if Milovich, Watters, and Keller were in fact separatists, but it was the theory that made the most sense. With the help of established Red cells, or perhaps in conjunction with elements of the Silicon Road gang, they must've discovered USC's conspiracy to steal Elysium's water—a conspiracy I was now convinced was real—and chosen to expose it through the murders of Shao Wen and Deandre Jackson. Keller was a cyber crimes expert. She would've been able to hack the security databases and hijack the feeds to make it look as if nobody had been at Wen's apartment or at the comptroller's offices. Milovich, the department's lone incoming arson detective, would've known how to craft an incendiary device that would've immolated Jackson instantly. And Watters had been late to the graduation ceremony, giving him the opportunity to have been at Wen's apartment during the time of her death.

But the trio hadn't stopped at a pair of murders. They'd gone one crucial and exceedingly dangerous step further. They'd murdered Charlize Van Jaarsveld and Professor Juliette Lemagne. We could only speculate as to why, but I had a pretty good idea. Van Jaarsveld was a former water services employee and well-known separatist sympathizer, and Lemagne was the city's premier academic hydrologist, perhaps the person best suited to validate or refute the theory of USC's water theft. By killing both in targeted hits, made to look as if they were performed by professionals, they could plausibly lay the blame at USC's feet, making it seem as if the corporate behemoth had silenced the major players who could expose them. At least, they could've laid the blame at USC's feet if Milovich hadn't died in a firefight. Then again, perhaps they still could. People eager for revolution would be only too eager to believe a rogue cop was also a paid USC assassin.

"Don't blame yourself, Captain," I said. "Moles can infiltrate any organization. I learned that during my time in the corps. As a unit, we'll learn and grow. That's all there is to it. It's a moot point now, though. We know who we're after, and we have to stop them."

The door opened, and an officer stuck his head in. "Captain?"

She turned on him. "Yes?"

The poor man gulped. "We've received reports of rioting near the scene of Miss Van Jaarsveld's murder. Troops with gas and body armor have been dispatched to deal with the crowds. Thought you should know."

Reyes nodded, and the man disappeared, closing the door behind him.

"Christ. Riots already," said Reyes. "And the Snow Leopard hasn't even released a video yet. How long until he hits the web, blaming USC for this? Blaming *us* for this? You know what happens then, Detectives?"

"The proverbial crap storm, Captain," said Mwenge. "We know."

"What happens then is more people die. Innocents. People who have absolutely nothing to do with this mess, and that's in the best case scenario. In the worst? Well..."

Reyes trailed off. She didn't have to finish the thought. The worst case scenario was history books listing Elysium as the place where the second Martian rebellion began, and I'd be damned if I'd let that happen. Freedom I supported wholeheartedly, but not at the cost it demanded. The cost of senseless bloodshed.

Reyes gripped her chair and eyed us fiercely. "Detectives. Find me Watters and Keller. We need them, not just to stop the violence, but to prove to the public we're on their side. To show them there's no need for a war between Mars and USC."

"We will, Captain," I said.

"Quickly, I hope," she replied. "For all our sakes."

"I DON'T GET IT," said Mwenge. "How the hell isn't this guy in any of the databases?"

We sat at our desks. The windows were dark, the last vestiges of day having disappeared during the Captain's frustrated tirade.

The police scanner kept flashing intermittently, reporting incidents in all corners of the city, most non-violent but at the edge of trending the other way. If we were beat cops, we'd be in line for a long night. Of course, we were in line for a long night regardless unless we figured out where Watters and Keller were hiding.

"Drake? Are you even listening?"

"What?" I tore my eyes from the window. "Yeah. Who are we talking about again?"

"The mystery guy we found at the Mars sciences building. His facial scan didn't match any police or government database. It's like the guy's a ghost. How does somebody manage that in this day and age? How did the guy work or make bank transactions or pay his taxes? Was he an off-planet counter terrorist agent?"

Part of the reason I was so distracted was because of Jorge. I'd held it together remarkably well at the scene of the professor's murder, but now? I couldn't stop seeing the man's face. Different than I remembered it, of course. There had been a lot more gray in his beard, and the lines in his forehead had been deep and weathered. I still couldn't fully explain his involvement, though I had my suspicions.

"Do you think he's the guy who fire-bombed Wen's apartment?" said Mwenge. "I know Dean thought that individual was female based upon his analysis of the feeds he'd tracked her through, but it would seem to make sense, right? That the vigilante who tried to wipe Wen's death off the map would also try to stop Milovich from murdering more people? I mean, both are acts of suppression. This guy must've been trying to stop the separatists from executing their plan."

I shook my head. "Mwenge, you're barking up the wrong tree. Whoever this mystery man is, he's dead. His past is unimportant right now. What matters is we find Watters and Keller. That's the goal. That's what we need to focus on."

"I'm with you," said Mwenge. "But their Nets are disconnected. We can't track them directly, and we've already got their faces flagged through the public security network. If they show up anywhere, we'll know. The only options left for tracking them are manpower intensive. I mean, we could start knocking on doors, talking to friends, family. That's a time consuming route, and all the help we could normally muster is currently deployed around the city making sure riots don't break out. The other thing we could do is get warrants for surveillance taps on places where they might be hiding, and even that's not a sure help, not if they've already hunkered down inside someone's basement."

I paused and stared at Mwenge. "Private surveillance."

"Public surveillance can't see everything. Besides, we've used it before. We might not even need warrants. If we can talk to the landlords directly, most of them are pretty accommodating, certainly when we're talking about murderers on the loose."

"You're a genius, pal."

Bishop squinted at me. "Thanks?" But I was already calling someone from the Musk College of Science and Technology security office. He answered straight away.

"Officer Herrman? Detective Ambrose Drake. Are you still on campus?"

"Yes, sir," he said. "Who knows how long it'll be before I see the underside of my bedspread."

"When we arrived and found you at the scene, you said the surveillance system from the Mars Sciences building was on the fritz? What did you mean by that?"

"Exactly what I said, sir. As soon as we got the reports of shots fired, I tried to access it remotely to see what was going on. I couldn't get through. Just got a system error that the feeds weren't accessible."

"Are they now?"

"Uh... Hold on." The was a moment of silence. "No. They're still off-line. I don't know what the hell's going on."

My heart skipped a beat. "Officer, I'm going to need a remote passkey to your security system. I need to get in there."

"Well, I suppose I can pass that along, but why—"

"Don't ask. Just get me connected."

Herrman didn't argue. Within a half minute, I was connected, parsing through the MCSE security servers remotely on my holo. Mwenge stood by my desk. "What are you up to?"

"Give me a minute."

I found the security feeds for Mars Sciences and tried to access them. Sure enough, I couldn't. The system claimed a file modification was underway, but security systems saved continuously. If a modification was underway, it was because someone was actively modifying it, but I had a hard time believing someone had been actively modifying the files for the past two hours.

"Hot damn," I said.

"Seriously, Ambrose, are you going to tell me what you're doing?"

"The security feeds weren't wiped from the university's servers," I said. "Or at least I don't think they were. I can't access them because someone's placed a shell over one of the servers to hide their tracks. It's the same thing whoever hacked the servers at Wen's apartment and at the comptroller's office did."

"So? We don't need the security feeds. We know what happened thanks to the mystery man's video."

"I don't care about the security feeds. I care about the fact that someone put a shell over the server. And that they haven't deleted it."

"Why? Can you crack it somehow?"

"I don't want to crack it. As you already said, we don't need the security feeds."

Mwenge looked confused. "I don't get it."

"Bishop, the shells used to disguise the hacker's tracks had been deleted from Wen's apartment servers. The deleted file containing the shell was the only way I knew a hack had taken place. This shell is still in place."

"And?"

"The shells were put in place remotely. This one is still active. While it's active, I can trace it."

57

DECEMBER 31, 2154

CLOSER TO HOME? What did Marina mean I should look closer to home for answers? It was an incredibly stupid piece of advice, but the Red pseudo-leader didn't strike me as a stupid individual, so there must've been a meaning behind her suggestion. So I did as she asked, putting in requests for newsfeeds from back in Jackson to see if anything strange had transpired in my hometown since I last left. The feeds were slow to arrive, more by the speed at which Marina or one of her lackeys approved my access request as by the time it took for communications to travel between Earth and Mars.

They arrived eventually, though, bearing all the exciting news I could've hoped for: stories about a local bar being forced to shut down by new zoning ordinances, a decision by the city council to establish January as Great Lakes month, and a number of fluff pieces on elementary school kids, firefighters, and an old woman who'd befriended a squirrel at the local park. I checked the feeds from Kalamazoo, too, thinking perhaps Marina had meant my transplanted home, but those were equally uneventful. So I kept expanding my search. I checked the Detroit newsfeeds, then the ones from Cleveland, Pittsburg, Toronto, and Chicago. I expanded my search to include national US feeds. None of them gave me any indications as to Marina's clue. In fact, news across the United States was blissfully uneventful. It seemed as if not much of note had occurred since the nuking of Los Angeles. Rather, the ongoing recovery and rebuilding efforts, even eight months later, dominated a portion of every news program.

As I thought about it, Marina's reaction to the nuke bothered me. I'd clearly offended her when I'd accused her of murdering tens of millions of my fellow Americans, as if the blood of those innocents hadn't been on her hands alongside those of the Reds beside her. Maybe in the grandest sense it wasn't. She certainly wasn't in charge of the separatist movement, no more than Major Watkins or Lieutenant Colonel Cornier were in charge of USC. But even if she'd been no less influential in the separatist camp than I'd been in the corps, she'd still bear some of the blame for the dead. She'd joined the movement knowing what they intended, hadn't she?

As I sat there, thinking about the attack, I recalled a conversation I'd had with Ranbir aboard our transport to Luna. That no one had discovered how the nuke had made it past the country's missile defense system. Speculation at the time had been that the explosion had instead been detonated at ground level. I looked into the matter and found that scientific analyses had since confirmed what we'd suspected at the time. Los Angeles hadn't been destroyed by a nuclear missile, rather a bomb placed in the city center by separatists. Not that it made any difference. It simply proved there were Red cells at home, as well.

Was that what Marina meant when she'd told me to look closer to home? That the Reds were there, too? Given the details of the nuclear explosion, it seemed likely, but knowing the war had spread to Earth didn't change anything. It didn't change the fact that Reds had detonated a bomb that killed tens of millions. It didn't change the fact that millions more would die before the conflict was over. Even with Red cells in the states, most of those casualties would happen here on Mars, just as Marina had admitted.

Which, if I thought about it, made the nuclear attack of Los Angeles kind of a bad idea. Surely the Reds realized that USC, the United States, hell, *the whole of Earth* wouldn't roll over and show their belly to Mars in the wake of an unprovoked nuclear attack. Sure, the strike helped instill fear, but it hadn't stopped the war. Far from it. It had ratcheted tensions to a new high and brought a fresh wave of soldiers and weapons to the Martian doorstep.

How had the Reds made such a grave miscalculation when they'd decided to attack Los Angeles? They wouldn't have decided to vaporize the city unless they'd thought it would help their cause. The attack must've triggered *something* that aided the Reds, either directly or indirectly. With that in mind, I started mining the Martian newsfeeds, looking at every report of Red activity I could find since the nuclear attack.

Try as I might, I failed to find anything that might be seen as positive. In the months after the nuclear strike, unrest upon Mars had *grown*. Food shortages were more common. Looting was more prevalent in the major cities. Violence of all kinds had spiked, from murders to assaults to sexual crimes. And, of course, there were the additional problems brought on by the influx of USC resources in the wake of the attack. Troop deployments were up. The air strikes against the spaceports had slowed things, but even accounting for those, more ships were landing. More soldiers were patrolling. More military actions were taking place.

In fact, USC seemed to be the only entity who had benefitted in the wake of the nuclear strike. Enlistments were way up. Even now, they remained higher than they'd been prior to the nuclear blast, but it wasn't just the influx of troops that had buoyed the company's military efforts. The stock price had soared. They'd sold billions in war bonds. A cynical man might've said *they* were the ones profiting off the war with Mars, but then again, their head-quarters had been in Los Angeles, the modern home of commercial spaceflight...

I frowned and tapped my fingers against my leg. As I sat in my room in thought, I opened my Net browser and headed to the main USC site. I clicked over to the About Us section and scrolled until I found the relevant passage. 'Headquartered in sunny Oxnard, California, the United Space Corporation is...' I disregarded the rest, opening my maps app. I knew Oxnard was a suburb of Los Angeles, but where exactly was it? I searched, finding it to be up the coast from LA proper, to the northwest of the city center. But how far away, precisely? I checked. About a hundred kilometers. And the blast radius from the nuke? Thirty-five to forty. Damage was negligible at fifty kilometers.

Sweat beaded at my brow, and my heartbeat quickened. I pulled up the weather from the day of the blast. Winds were out of the west at fifteen to twenty miles per hour, as they often were coming in from the ocean. Not only had the nuclear blast not taken out any of USC's facilities, they hadn't even been threatened by the fallout.

With my head spinning, I jumped from my cot and darted into the hallway. I took off down the corridor at a run, sprinting up the stairs and back down again in search of Marina's quarters. She was at her desk as she always was when I burst inside. I worked air in and out of my lungs forcefully, and my cheeks felt flushed despite the short distance between my cabin and hers.

She eyed me with concern. "Ambrose... are you feeling alright?"

I gripped the edge of her desk in an attempt to keep the room from spinning. "Answer me one question, and answer honestly Marina. *Who nuked Los Angeles?*"

58

MAY 13, 2179

OUR POLICE VAN skidded to a halt outside a ten story multipurpose building, one with a grocery on the main floor, real estate and tech offices on the next three floors, and residential units on the top six. Mwenge and I hopped out of the van as another one pulled up behind us. SWAT units poured out, clad in black body armor, bulletproof face shields, with police-grade Badasses gripped tight and an assortment of tranq rounds, gas grenades, flash grenades, and taser bolts strapped onto bandoliers.

They headed toward the building at a trot, with Mwenge and I behind them. They'd been briefed on the way. They were to infiltrate the building, splitting into smaller teams, each taking one floor where they'd sweep every nook and cranny in search of Watters and Keller. Unfortunately, we didn't know exactly where they'd be. The shell they'd placed over the servers at Musk College had been done through a hard line, not a Net interface. That meant we couldn't track it to a point, only to the building from which the signal had originated. I just hoped Watters and Keller hadn't abandoned their computer systems and already gone into deep cover.

Bishop and I stood outside the building's front doors as the SWAT officers filed in. Given the nature of the case and the state of the city, a judge had granted us broad search powers for the entire building, protocol be damned, and the officers each carried copies of the warrants on their tablets in case any of the tenants weren't Net enabled and wanted to give us a hard time.

The minutes felt like hours as I waited for the officers to check in with their progress updates. "Floor one clear. Moving to the fourth."

With the strain on the department from the riots and demonstrations, we'd only been able to muster a dozen SWAT members, enough for three teams of four. The sergeant in charge wouldn't split them any more than that, and they'd tackle the floors in order.

The seconds ticked away. "Second floor clear. On to the fifth."

Another minute, maybe two. "Third clear. Moving on to the sixth."

Eventually, the crew in charge of the fourth cleared their way through the last of the offices, putting all three teams in the residential units. The wait became an eternity as the teams moved their way methodically through each and every apartment.

I shook my head as updates failed to come in. "I don't like this, Bishop. I've still got a bad feeling."

"The SWAT teams can handle themselves. They'll be fine, Ambrose."

"That's not what I mean. I have a sneaking suspicion Watters and Keller aren't here."

"You mean that they left the shell on as a distraction? To trick us?"

"Maybe. I don't know." I called Dean. "Dean, are you still at your workstation?"

"I'm not going anywhere until this is over, Detective. What do you need?"

"Can you confirm we're in the right spot with the trace?"

"Your signals are just about on top of it, yeah."

"Just about?"

"Sure. A couple meters to the north, but close enough."

I checked my Net map. The building itself was to our north. The street was to the south.

"You sure about that Dean?"

"It's what the trace shows."

I glanced at the darkened Mylamene barrier overhead, rippling with the reflected light of the streetlamps. If there wasn't anything overhead...

"Dean, is there anything below our location?"

"It's Elysium, Detective. The question isn't if, it's what."

"Now, Dean."

"Sorry. Pulling city blueprints. Uh... you've got sewers. Some tunnels—the quantity and quality unknown. And a city pumping relay, one of the little ones that maintains even water pressure far from the central facility."

How poetic... "Dean, I need directions on how to get down there. Tell me there's a hatch close by."

There was. Dean directed us to a nearby manhole. I shot off a quick message to the SWAT leader to let him know what we were up to before plunging down the hole.

I pulled my tablet and activated the flashlight as I put hands to rungs. Mwenge did the same above me. Dean directed as we descended.

"From the plans I've found, you're going to want to head to the bottom of the ladder. Head left down the maintenance tunnel. Within ten meters you should find a stairwell to your left. Take that down and it should spit you out near the front of the pumping station."

I dropped to the tunnel floor and hooked a left, hearing a faint rumble in the distance. The stairwell was where Dean said it would be. Lights glowed faintly from the bottom of the stairs. I pocketed my tablet and pulled my sidearm.

"Dean," I said as I descended the steps. "Looks like we found it... Dean?"

I glanced at Mwenge. "I've lost online Net access. You?"

"Same," he said as he unholstered his weapon. "You want me to head up to send an update to SWAT?"

"They know where we are, and they'll know we've lost contact. They'll send a team down in a minute. In the meantime, stick together. Keep your eyes peeled. Local Net communications only." I held a finger to my lips for emphasis.

We snuck down the rest of the steps, the lights bringing the stairwell into view, dim as they were. The rumbling intensified, the same dull roar of the pumps from the central processing facility, just muted to a manageable level.

"Mwenge." I stopped at a corner as the stairwell spit into the station. To my right, I spotted three banks of pumps, each a little taller than me. Shop lights had been strung from makeshift scaffolding overhead, but only a pair of them were lit, giving the place an eerie glow as shadows from the pumps stretched into corners. At the wall before us, a desk had been shoved up against a switching station built into the concrete. An outdated display stood on the desk. A cord snaked from it to a portable server, and another to the electrical panel on the wall. A folding chair had been pushed underneath the desk, and a lone sleeping bag lay on the ground beside it.

"Looks like you were right. Don't you ever get tired of that?"

"Not the time, Bishop." I nodded toward the far side of the pumps. "You take left? I'll take right."

"Think they're still here?"

"There's a sleeping bag and the shell's still in place. I'd wager at least one of them is."

"Okay. Let's coordinate movements as we go."

I nodded. "Ready?"

"Let's do it."

We hopped out. I hugged the wall to my right as Mwenge moved to the left side of the room at a brisk pace.

The crack of a pistol cut over the hum of the pumps.

I spun and crouched, discharging my sidearm in the direction of the noise. Mwenge jerked and fired. I spotted movement and fired again, three times in quick succession. Mwenge fired two, but more shots than that filled the air. The shadowed figure at the far side of the room went down, as did Mwenge.

"Bishop? *Bishop?*" I rushed to my partner's side, my pistol still trained on the shooter. It was a woman—I could tell at closer range. Keller, the cyber crimes detective, I assumed, but I didn't close in to check.

I broke my rule about no verbal communication as I shook Mwenge by the shoulder. "Bishop? Talk to me, buddy."

He moaned, and I could see blood spreading across his chest from two different gunshots, one in the area of his lung, another in his abdomen.

"Shit. *Shit shit shit.*" With pistol still in hand, I looped Mwenge's arm over my shoulder and dragged him toward the desk, my eyes and gun trained on the corridors at the sides of the pumps. As I reached the corner leading to the stairwell, the shop lights went out.

I blinked in the darkness, laying Mwenge upon the floor as gently as I could. A voice rang through the underground tomb, audible but muffled by the rumbling pumps.

"Don't be a stranger. Who's there? Come on, don't be shy."

I recognized the voice, not only because I'd met him, however briefly, but because I'd watched his interviews from detective training to familiarize myself with the man. John Watters, would-be homicide detective and traitor to his brothers in arms.

"It's Drake and Mwenge," I called out. "We've got you, Watters. Turn yourself in."

"*The* Ambrose Drake? Good to know I warranted the best. But

I think you meant to say it's just you. Detective Keller doesn't miss often, and I don't hear your partner making threats."

I crept around the corner and back into the pump room, my pistol gripped tight. "You think your punk partner could kill Mwenge? He's tough as nails, and the only targets you and Keller have ever shot at stay still and are held up with tacks. Now turn the lights on and walk out backwards with your hands up."

"I don't think so, Detective." Watters' voice echoed around the room, making it hard to pinpoint where he was. What I wouldn't give for a pair of IR goggles. "If I know police protocol, you've got a team on the surface, but without a wireless signal, they don't know you're in trouble yet. I'm planning on keeping it that way."

I thought on my feet, taking an audio sample of the pumps as I took cover against them. I subtracting the sample from my hearing after routing it through my Net, reducing the roar by a good twenty decibels. "So that's your plan? To murder more cops and hope it gives you another few hours on the run? How the hell did a worm like you make it through basic training let alone detective school? Where's your sense of duty? Of honor?"

"That's rich coming from an Earther who failed to murder as many Reds as he wanted and didn't have the balls to go back to Earth when he was done."

Even with the reduced pump noise, I couldn't get a sense of the man's position. "Sticks and stones, Watters."

"Did I touch a nerve? Don't tell me. The reason you became a homicide cop was to absolve yourself of the guilt of all the Martians you killed while in the army. Am I close? So don't talk to me about duty when your whole reason for catching criminals is to make yourself feel like less of a piece of shit."

Was that a footstep? Christ, I couldn't hear, and I sure as hell couldn't see shit. I wanted to activate my tablet's light, but Watters would likely mow me down the instant it sprang to life. "You don't know what the hell you're talking about."

"I know you're full of shit when you talk about duty. You came to Mars from Earth, part of a multinational corporation whose sole purpose is to squeeze every last drop of blood from Mars's native sons, as if the dust wasn't red enough already. You had nothing to lose coming here. Us Martians have everything to lose, but some of us are willing to die to set Mars on a path to finally being free. I'm willing to die for that future. That's duty. That's honor. Are you willing to die for what you pretend to believe in?"

Watters voice sounded closer. He was closing in on me. "You're making a mistake, Watters. You think another rebellion will bring Mars its freedom? It's only going to bring more bloodshed and pain."

"Mars is stronger this time. We've learned from fighting USC before. The people are ready to finally be free of Earth's yoke."

I pulled my tablet and set it on a chest-high pipe behind me, turning the volume up as high as I could. I spoke via Net, routing my voice into the tablet so it projected through the speaker. "You're wrong. Another rebellion, fought the same way as the last one, will only make things worse. USC will tighten the noose. They'll take preemptive strikes against anyone who speaks up. They'll turn Mars into a prison state, or at best a dictatorship. The way to a free Mars, a Mars that will grow and prosper and won't attract the ire of Earth, isn't that simple to achieve. It's a long game. An economic one. A political one. A fight that's fought through legal channels, from the inside, with information and laws and journalism and bold new ideas. You had a piece of that—USC's theft of our water. You could've used it against them the right way, and instead you've squandered it."

I slipped along the wall, using my hand to guide me. I ducked behind another pump when I found one.

"Proper channels? Mars is being bled to death, and you suggest we kindly ask our tormentors to obey the law? No thank you. I'll

use what works. *Fear* and *violence*. Look around you. The city is primed to explode, and all it took was a few murders."

"I'll forgive you for being young, Watters, but not for being an idiot. Everyone involved in the Martian rebellion came to regret using fear tactics. All they did was lead to a harsher response. Even your beloved Snow Leopard learned that."

Watters voice sounded close now. "Bullshit."

"It's true. He told me himself, in a way."

"He told you? That's the biggest fucking lie I've ever heard."

"How do you figure that?"

"Because *he's not even real,* that's why."

A pistol ripped through the air, firing ten shots, a full magazine. I heard the bullets ping as they ricocheted off the pump at my back.

I moaned in what I hoped was a believable fashion, the sound coming from my tablet perched a few meters down the aisle.

Watters' voice strengthened as it approached my tablet. "You stupid Earther. You think you can come to my planet, *my home,* and lecture me? How the hell would you know the first god damn thing about the Snow Leopard?"

"Because I am the Snow Leopard."

I swung around the edge of the pump and opened fire.

59

DECEMBER 31, 2154

I SWAYED, the room titling precipitously around me as I gripped the edge of Marina's desk for support. She stood and walked toward me, her arms held before her. "Ambrose, you're not looking so good. Perhaps you should take a seat."

"Yeah. Sure. Sure." Marina pushed the chair underneath me as I lowered myself into it. My breath came in quick gasps, my heart beating like a drum.

Marina activated something, and the door slid shut behind me. She took her seat and clasped her hands over her desk. "To answer your question, Ambrose, I don't know who nuked Los Angeles. None of us do."

"You *don't know*," I said.

"Not definitively, no. We don't have enough evidence to *prove* who ordered or performed the deed. But we have our suspicions. Who do you think nuked Los Angeles?"

"Why do you want me to say it?" I said, my vision still fuzzy.

"Because I don't want to influence your judgement in the matter. Conclusions you arrive at yourself are more powerful than ones pushed upon you by others."

I swallowed, the spit in my mouth feeling thick. "It seems to me the only party who's benefited from the bombing is... USC."

Marina gave a minuscule shrug, mostly with her eyebrows. "That's the conclusion most of us have come to as well. Again, we can't prove it. We don't have knowledge of illicit transfers of fissionable material on Earth, never mind the access to the networks that would move and exchange them. But it's a logical hypothesis, for many reasons, not least of which is that none of the Martian factions have nukes, nor do they have the means to smuggle them to Earth."

"Factions?"

"You like to call us all Reds, but as I told you earlier, we don't call ourselves that. At least, not all of us do. We're not as consolidated a group as you might think."

I blinked, the room starting to settle. "What do you mean by that?"

"We're separatists, Ambrose. Partisans. Guerrillas. We collect in small groups. We often act independently of one another. Mars isn't like Earth. It's not encircled by billions of kilometers of cables. Communication occurs primarily via satellite, and those are controlled by USC. Naturally, there are multiple factions who are all working toward Martian independence in their own way. But I can say with a high degree of confidence that none of them could've pulled off the nuclear strike on Los Angeles."

I leaned forward, pressing my face into my hands. "So it's true. Everything I've been led to believe is a lie. The woman I fell in love with is *dead* because of a lie. Tens of millions are. A city was destroyed, turned into glass for no other reason than because a larger, more valuable *asset* needed to be protected. *Christ.*"

Marina was silent for a moment. "I'm sorry, Ambrose. Again, I can't prove it..."

"You don't have to prove something for it to make sense. More sense than any of the alternatives. Except..." I lifted my head from my hands. "The Snow Leopard. He took credit for it. For you. For the Reds."

Marina nodded. "The video that was released did show that."

"That's a strange way to phrase it. What are you saying? That the Snow Leopard is a USC stooge? That he was captured? That the video was faked?"

"Pull your chair around, Ambrose. There's something I'd like to show you on my display."

My breath had slowed, as had the pounding of my heart, instead replaced with a deep ache in my chest, the same ache I'd felt after the death of Ranbir and more recently of Phoebe. I hadn't lost anyone, but I'd suffered a death, in a way. The death of honesty. Of morality. Of ideals.

I nodded. "Okay. Sure."

I stood and grabbed my chair, bringing it around so I could face the screen. Marina minimized what she was working on and opened a new app, something called Visual Architect.

I recognized the interface as it popped up. "This is video editing software."

"Close," said Marina. "It's video *generation* software."

She clicked over to an existing file. A window opened, showing the familiar backdrop from the Snow Leopard's videos. Marina worked a few sliders, and the Snow Leopard came into view, white pressure suit, blood red mask, and all. Marina typed some text into a side window, and the Leopard spoke in the same modulated voice as before. "Welcome. Have a look around. Like the place?"

"Hold on," I said. "Are you saying the Snow Leopard isn't even a real person? He's a computer simulation?"

Marina nodded. "We're not entirely sure when USC realized it. We suspect it was after a raid in which we lost one of our counterintelligence officers and all of her equipment. USC officials must've found the software. Instead of trying to expose the Snow Leopard as a fake, they decided to use him to their advantage."

"By faking a video taking credit for the nuke."

"It's speculation, but yes."

"So why don't you come forward? Admit that the Snow Leopard doesn't exist? You could prove to people you didn't launch the assault on Los Angeles. This whole war could've been prevented!"

"The war has been going on for years, Ambrose. The strike on LA didn't start it. It merely accelerated it, got it to burn at a hotter temperature. Besides, as I've told you, we don't have any hard evidence to support our suspicions that USC detonated the weapon. To make our case, we'd need bills of sale. Shipping manifests. Message chains. Audio recordings. Video. We have none of that. Not to mention that no one would believe us even if we did come forward with said evidence. Think about it. Now you're willing to consider the possibility, but when you enlisted, would anything have convinced you that us Martians, a theoretical, distant, by all accounts violent and savage people, didn't attack you? That it was Earth's own titan of commercial spaceflight who did it instead?"

I chewed on my lip. "Probably not."

"Besides," said Marina. "Admitting to that would mean we'd have to announce the Snow Leopard isn't real."

"Why is that a problem?"

"Ambrose, the Snow Leopard may not be a real individual, but that doesn't mean he's without power. He's an institution. A symbol. We can use him to influence decisions, to spread information and misinformation, to instill fear. Presumably, some individuals at USC know he's not real, but soldiers like you don't. He has power over them. And even if he didn't, he's important to us. He's our mascot, in a way. We aspire to be what he represents."

"And when you say *we*, you mean the separatists?"

"I mean us, specifically. Myself. Jorge. Lauren. Cal. Castleton. Everyone you've met."

I took a slow breath, still staring at the screen. "You know, ever since I woke up in my cot a week ago, I've assumed you were Reds, or some manifestation of that term. This is probably a question I should've asked before now, but better late than never. Who, *exactly,* are you?"

Marina smiled. "We're the Martian counterintelligence, Ambrose. Collectively, we *are* the Snow Leopard. So in a way, he does exist. We are all him."

"So when you said I'd be introduced to him when the time was right—"

"I said he'd be introduced to you. And now he has been. *We* have been. So?"

I turned to Marina. "So, what?"

Marina eyed me in silence for a brief moment. "I'm sorry you've come to the same conclusion the rest of us did regarding the bombing of Los Angeles. It's true what they say. Ignorance is bliss. But you don't have to suffer your anger, frustration, and sorrow in vain. You can act to make things right. My offer still stands, Ambrose. The Martian counterintelligence could use someone like you. Together, with enough hard work, enough time spent, and a little luck, we might be able to turn the tide against USC. And some day, perhaps we *will* be able to expose them for their crimes. So what do you say? Knowing what you now know, will you help me? Will you help *us?*"

I thought I might have to chew on the offer for a few days, or at least over a night of sleep, but the answer was obvious. Maarten was my enemy. Phoebe was dead. Ranbir, too. USC had lied to me, used me, treated me like a pawn in a grand game without regard for my life, my desires, or my intellect. Why in the world would I go back to that when I had another option?

"Yes." It came out as a whisper, so I tried again. "Yes, I'll help you. I may not care about Martian independence, but I care about right and wrong. It's time I make amends."

Marina clapped me on the shoulder. "I'm glad to hear it, Ambrose. Welcome to the Snow Leopards."

60

MAY 13, 2179

THE EAGER HANDS of medics were waiting at the top of the manhole, reaching for Bishop's body as SWAT Officer Tiancheng and I hoisted him up the ladder. In a flurry of motion, they'd strapped him to a stretcher, placed an oxygen mask over his mouth and nose, and fed a bag of synthetic blood into him intravenously. They rushed him into a waiting ambulance at a run, the medics barely slamming shut the back doors before the van sped down the street, weaving through parked police cruisers. The flashing red and blue lights washed over me like a cold rain.

Mwenge was still breathing when I'd stumbled my way back to the stairwell after neutralizing Watters. Still breathing when I'd met the SWAT officers and rushed back down with them to grab him. I'd assumed he was still breathing as I'd passed him to the medics. If anyone would pull through, it was Bishop. He was a jokester at heart, but that son of a bitch was as tough as they came. He'd be fine. I hoped.

Noise and lights surrounded me. The screech of tires. Slammed doors. Shouts. Orders. All I could do was watch the taillights of the ambulance disappear as the van turned a corner several blocks down.

Christ. Mwenge. My partner. He hadn't taken a bullet for me, but he'd taken one with me, which was as good as the same. My partner, who'd been with me for close to a decade, through thick and thin. My partner, whose prints I had on a glove inside my jacket pocket in the event that I needed to incriminate him to keep my own name clean. Thank god I hadn't needed to use it.

And Watters thought I didn't understand the meaning of duty.

"Detective Drake."

I turned. Captain Reyes stood behind me, eyeing me with a look of concern. "Talk to me, Detective. Are you okay? You've been in and out of Net contact for the past ten minutes. The SWAT team passed along a message saying Mwenge had been shot. What the hell happened?"

I swallowed, trying to find my tongue. "We got them, Captain. Watters and Keller both."

"You captured them?"

I shook my head. "Keller opened fire. Mwenge and I responded. He took two shots, one to the chest and another to the stomach. I wasn't hit. Keller was. Not sure if it was me or Mwenge who got her. She bled out on the scene."

Reyes muttered a curse. "And Watters?"

"He more or less confessed. Tried to murder me. I flipped the script on him and neutralized him. He's dead, Captain."

"Shit. You realize this isn't ideal, Detective?"

"I don't take lethal force lightly, Captain. They almost killed Mwenge and tried to do the same to me. I did what had to be done."

Two vans emblazoned with the credentials of a pair of Elysian news stations slowed to a stop past the temporary barrier of police cruisers. The doors opened and crews poured out, rushing toward the scene. SWAT officers moved to intercept them.

"Oh, for crying out loud," said Captain Reyes. "There's never a moment of rest with those bloodsuckers."

"Perhaps it's a blessing this time," I said. "You said we needed to prove to the people that we're on their side. Well, we caught the murderers. That may not appease the rioters, but it's got to count for something."

"Something, yes, but not all. I'm still not sure how to present this to the media, what with USC's potential, or rather almost certain, involvement. Did you get Watters' confession recorded?"

I cleared my throat. "He killed the lights, Captain. I shot him in pitch darkness. And the pumps down there drowned out most of our voices."

"Perfect. We'll comb over it tomorrow, then. See what we can isolate."

I nodded. "Sure. We'll figure something out, Captain."

The reporters were shouting over the outstretched arms of the SWAT team, calling questions out to Captain Reyes. She sighed. "Might as well bite the bullet now, right Detective? As you said, anything to soothe tensions."

"You'll figure it out as you go along, Captain. You always do."

Reyes looked toward the journalists, hesitating. She met my eyes, then reached up and grabbed me by the shoulder. "Good work, Ambrose. That's the first thing I should've said to you. I'm sorry I didn't."

"I don't need you getting sappy. Go on. Mop this up."

She snorted and started walking.

"This is why I don't want your job, by the way," I called.

She flipped me the bird behind her back.

I turned back to the manhole, which had become an anthill of activity. SWAT officers came up holding bagged evidence only for others to follow them right back down. Another cruiser pulled up. This one disgorged a group of crime scene investigators already dressed in white coveralls. I wondered how long it would take for Coroner Pham to arrive, and if I'd be placed on administrative leave in the morning. That was the standard operating procedure for any officer who killed a suspect pending further investigation, but given the circumstances, perhaps I'd have my paid vacation waived.

As I stared at the scene, I received a call. "Sophia."

"Oh, thank god, Ambrose. I saw the news and I... well, never mind."

"I'm already on the news?" I glanced at the group of journalists and cameramen, which had grown into a mob.

"Well, yes. I mean, I saw you in the background. But I've been worried for the past ten minutes. I've been glued to the coverage of the riots and disturbances all over town, and then the anchor-woman came on with reports of a SWAT raid downtown. People were calling in and posting on social media that their apartments were being broken into. That the officers were looking for the murderers you'd been searching for. I tried to call you a couple times to check in, but your Net was out of service."

"I was underground, that's all. I'm fine."

"Oh. Okay. Good."

I took a deep breath. "Sophia, I'm sorry. I violated your trust. I never should've talked to your father without coming to you first, and I definitely shouldn't have kept what I saw in your Net to myself. That was wrong, and I apologize."

She was silent for a moment. "Thanks, Ambrose. I appreciate you saying that."

"I mean it. I don't want there to be any secrets between us. I don't want to lose you because of mistrust."

"I don't want to lose you either, Ambrose."

"I'd like to come see you. To talk to you. Can I do that?"

"Don't you have to stay, to wrap things up or something?"

"The important threads here are irrevocably tied. The officers on the scene can take care of the rest."

"Okay. I'm at my apartment. See you soon?"

"As soon as I can get a ride."

I disconnected and sent the Captain a message. *Gotta go. Need to go tell someone that I'm okay.*

She responded with a simple, *Do what you have to do. And again, good work.*

THE DOOR OPENED. Sophia stood in its wake, wearing tights and a sweatshirt and with her hair pulled back. "Ambrose. Come on in."

I stepped into the familiar condo, so much roomier than mine, with high ceilings, polished magnesite floors, and a faintly floral scent pumped in through the air circulator—gardenias, I'd long since come to learn. Sophia's favorite. I stopped at the edge of the kitchen, my hand resting on the giant island in the center.

Sophia gave my arm a squeeze. "Have you eaten?"

"No. Never got around to it."

"Can I get you anything? I probably have something I could warm up."

"Not right now, but thank you."

Sophia looked me in the eyes. "The newsfeeds say you caught them. The men who murdered Administrator Wen and Comptroller Jackson."

"Men and women. And I'm not sure if caught is the right term. I killed them, Sophia. One of them at least. Bishop might've gotten the other."

Her eyes were soft pools. "Did they deserve it?"

"They murdered four people, and were willing to throw the city into chaos as a result. I'd say so."

"Then why do you look so conflicted?"

"I've never killed anyone I didn't regret in some way. Sophia, I need to talk to you."

"I'm right here."

"Maybe you should take a seat."

"I'm comfortable where I am."

"You won't mind if I do, though." I pulled out one of the tall chairs at the island and sat. My back welcomed the respite. "As much as I simply wanted to see you, there's a bigger reason I'm here. I said I didn't want any secrets between us. I meant it."

Sophia's face tightened. "Uh-oh."

"Uh-oh doesn't even begin to convey the sentiment, but I doubt you have any idea what I'm about to tell you. If you do, then I've spent the last nineteen years of my life in failure. But before I tell you I need you to disable your Net."

"What? Why?"

"Trust me. Just do it. I'll help you if you don't know how."

And then I told her. *Everything*. How I hadn't spent six years as a POW in the hands of the Reds. How I'd joined them after learning that USC had nuked Los Angeles as a way to increase revenues and enlistments in their space corps. That I'd fought USC during that time, all while keeping my identity a secret, and then, when it seemed as if the fight for Martian freedom could no longer be sustained, that I'd made the ultimate sacrifice. That I'd agreed to go undercover and try to effect change on Mars for the better, but through subterfuge and legal means rather than traditional violent ones. I told her how I'd spent the last nineteen years working toward that goal, often in complete isolation from everyone I'd met during my years working with the separatists, fueled only by the knowledge that by staying the course, I'd someday put myself in a position to help free Mars from under USC's thumb. And I told Sophia about the case. About USC's theft of ice from the subterranean Elysian sheet. About Milovich, Watters, and Keller. And about the Snow Leopard, how the figure people knew from the videos wasn't real, merely a computer generation that could be accessed by anyone with the right software, including a group of angry young detectives intent on starting a revolution. But the Snow Leopards as a group did exist, and I was one of them. One of the last remaining, so far as I knew.

Sophia stared at me through the whole speech, eyes open, brow slightly furrowed, lips pursed. She didn't gasp. Didn't nod. Didn't say a word. Just took it all in. When I was done, she waited a little longer, as if to make sure I'd said all I meant to say, then finally spoke. "So... you're a separatist. You have been almost as long as you've been on Mars."

"That's right. Same as Jorge, who must've been wise to the USC ice scam, too, otherwise he wouldn't have been following the detective recruits. Same as whoever fire-bombed Wen's apartment, though I still have no idea who that might've been. Would've been nice if my contacts let me know about either of them, but that's the problem with deep cover agents. You have to keep them secret, even from each other."

Sophia stepped over to me, snaked a hand across the back of my neck, and leaned in for a gentle kiss.

I blinked at her, confused, as she pulled back. "What was that for?"

The look she replied with was one of complete satisfaction. "That's for being the man I always knew you were, but a thousand times more."

"You're not angry with me for keeping everything from you?"

"We've only known each other for four months. What's that against twenty years? Besides, in the ways that matter, you hadn't lied to me. You're the man you always presented. Courageous. Loyal. A champion of justice. A man whose concern is for the people. I always thought that concern was exhibited through your profession. Turns out its so much more than that."

"Still, I'm sorry for not being honest with you. For not *being able* to be honest with you."

"I understand. Really, I do. And I finally understand how a catch like you has stayed unmarried all these years."

I had to smile. "It's rather hard to maintain a relationship and your duties as a secret insurgent at the same time. This goes without saying, but I hope you won't tell anyone."

Sophia smiled. "Or you'll have to kill me?"

"I told you I've regretted taking every life I have. I'd regret yours the most."

It was a joke. Thankfully Sophia seemed to take it as one. "There's one thing I don't understand."

"Only one?"

Sophia snickered and shook her head. "Why tell me now? You've kept this to yourself for so long. What changed?"

"Two things," I said. "The first being that the time for subterfuge may be coming to an end. Look around us, Sophia. Elysium is on edge. Utopia, Isidis, and Olympus are, too. I may have stopped a few young revolutionaries from plunging us into war again, but how long will that last? The Snow Leopard videos didn't create this. They only convinced people to make their anger public. Maybe we can keep the people of Mars under control for a few more months or years—for all our sakes, I hope we can. But Martians won't stand not being free forever, and USC will never change. They'll always put profits over people, no matter the non-monetary costs. I'm going to have to act, soon, Sophia. I don't know how, exactly. I just know I'm going to have to lead the people of Mars along a different path than they tried the last time."

Sophia crossed to her window, looking out upon the city below us. "And the second reason?"

I sighed. "Because I think I'm falling in love with you."

ABOUT THE AUTHOR

Hi. I'm Alex P. Berg, author of *Magnesium and Ice*. If you made it this far, then you know this isn't the ending of Ambrose Drake's journey. In fact, it's just the beginning. Be on the lookout for the sequel to this novel, *Lead and Snow*, in which more of Drake's past comes to light and where he puts everything on the line to try and free Mars from the shackles of USC.

Can't wait for the next Tyrants of Mars novel? Why not try my Daggers & Steele series? It features paranormal homicide detectives Jake Daggers and Shay Steele solving crimes in the fictional metropolis of New Welwic, a city filled with mystery, strange creatures, and more than its fair share of magic. The complete ten book series is available now, so what are you waiting for! Read it today! You can even buy the complete series in a single low-priced omnibus volume.

Word of mouth is **critical** to my success. If you enjoyed this novel, please consider leaving a positive review on Amazon. Even if it's only a line or two, it would be a *huge* help. Thanks!

Want to connect? Visit me at www.alexpberg.com or contact me on social media.

For a complete list of my books, please visit: www.alexpberg.com/books/.